RIVALS FOR LOVE

Praise for Ali Vali

Writer's Block

"Absolutely great! A totally unexpected story filled with a touch of erotica, a hidden gem, and a scenario so brilliant I had no idea what would happen or how the story would turn out. I was so excited to read this, then when I started I couldn't believe how addictive it was, nor how clever it was all going to be. A fantastic story that I couldn't put down and cannot recommend enough!"—*Lesbireviewed*

One More Chance

"This was an amazing book by Vali…complex and multi-layered (both characters and plot)."—*Danielle Kimerer, Librarian (Nevins Memorial Library, Massachusetts)*

Face the Music

"This is a typical Ali Vali romance with strong characters, a beautiful setting (Nashville, Tennessee), and an enemies-to-lovers style tale. The two main characters are beautiful, strong-willed, and easy to fall in love with. The romance between them is steamy, and so are the sex scenes."—*Rainbow Reflections*

The Inheritance

"I love a good story that makes me laugh and cry, and this one did that a lot for me. I would step back into this world any time."—*Kat Adams, Bookseller (QBD Books, Australia)*

Double-Crossed

"[T]here aren't too many lesfic books like *Double-Crossed* and it is refreshing to see an author like Vali continue to churn out books like these. Excellent crime thriller."—*Colleen Corgel, Librarian, Queens Borough Public Library*

Stormy Seas

Stormy Seas "is one book that adventure lovers must read."—*Rainbow Reflections*

Answering the Call

Answering the Call "is a brilliant cop-and-killer story…The crime story is tight and the love story is fantastic."—*Best Lesbian Erotica*

Lammy Finalist *Calling the Dead*

"So many writers set stories in New Orleans, but Ali Vali's mystery novels have the authenticity that only a real Big Easy resident could bring. Set six months after Hurricane Katrina has devastated the city, a lesbian detective is still battling demons when a body turns up behind one of the city's famous eateries. What follows makes for a classic lesbian murder yarn."—*Curve Magazine*

Beauty and the Boss

"The story gripped me from the first page…Vali's writing style is lovely—it's clean, sharp, no wasted words, and it flows beautifully as a result. Highly recommended!"—*Rainbow Book Reviews*

Balance of Forces: Toujours Ici

"A stunning addition to the vampire legend, *Balance of Forces: Toujours Ici* is one that stands apart from the rest."—*Bibliophilic Book Blog*

Beneath the Waves

"The premise…was brilliantly constructed…skillfully written and the imagination that went into it was fantastic…A wonderful passionate love story with a great mystery."—*Inked Rainbow Reads*

Second Season

"The issues are realistic and center around the universal factors of love, jealousy, betrayal, and doing the right thing and are constantly woven into the fabric of the story. We rated this well written social commentary through the use of fiction our max five hearts."—*Heartland Reviews*

Carly's Sound

"*Carly's Sound* is a great romance, with some wonderfully hot sex, but it is more than that. It is also the tale of a woman rising from the ashes of grief and finding new love and a new life. Vali has surrounded Julia and Poppy with a cast of great supporting characters, making this an extremely satisfying read."—*Just About Write*

Praise for the Cain Casey Saga

The Devil's Due

"A Night Owl Reviews Top Pick: Cain Casey is the kind of person you aspire to be even though some consider her a criminal. She's loyal, very protective of those she loves, honorable, big on preserving her family legacy and loves her family greatly. *The Devil's Due* is a book I highly recommend and well worth the wait we all suffered through. I cannot wait for the next book in the series to come out." —*Night Owl Reviews*

The Devil Be Damned

"Ali Vali excels at creating strong, romantic characters along with her fast-paced, sophisticated plots. Her setting, New Orleans, provides just the right blend of immigrants from Mexico, South America, and Cuba, along with a city steeped in traditions."—*Just About Write*

Deal with the Devil

"Ali Vali has given her fans another thick, rich thriller…*Deal With the Devil* has wonderful love stories, great sex, and an ample supply of humor. It is an exciting, page-turning read that leaves her readers eagerly awaiting the next book in the series."—*Just About Write*

The Devil Unleashed

"Fast-paced action scenes, intriguing character revelations, and a refreshing approach to the romance thriller genre all make for an enjoyable reading experience in the Big Easy…*The Devil Unleashed* is an engrossing reading experience."—*Midwest Book Review*

The Devil Inside

"*The Devil Inside* is the first of what promises to be a very exciting series…While telling an exciting story that grips the reader, Vali has also fully fleshed out her heroes and villains. *The Devil Inside* is that rarity: a fascinating crime novel which includes a tender love story and leaves the reader with a cliffhanger ending."—*MegaScene*

By the Author

Carly's Sound

Second Season

Love Match

The Dragon Tree Legacy

The Romance Vote

Hell Fire Club
in Girls with Guns

Beauty and the Boss

Blue Skies

Stormy Seas

The Inheritance

Face the Music

On the Rocks
in Still Not Over You

A Woman to Treasure

Calumet

Writer's Block

One More Chance

A Good Chance

Never Kiss a Cowgirl

Rivals for Love

The Cain Casey Saga

The Devil Inside

The Devil Unleashed

Deal with the Devil

The Devil Be Damned

The Devil's Orchard

The Devil's Due

Heart of the Devil

The Devil Incarnate

Call Series

Calling the Dead

Answering the Call

Waves Series

Beneath the Waves

Turbulent Waves

Forces Series

Balance of Forces: Toujours Ici

Battle of Forces: Sera Toujours

Force of Fire: Toujours a Vous

Vegas Nights

Double-Crossed

Visit us at www.boldstrokesbooks.com

RIVALS FOR LOVE

by
Ali Vali

2023

RIVALS FOR LOVE
© 2023 By Ali Vali. All Rights Reserved.

ISBN 13: 978-1-63679-384-9

This Trade Paperback Original Is Published By
Bold Strokes Books, Inc.
P.O. Box 249
Valley Falls, NY 12185

First Edition: November 2023

Credits
Editors: Ruth Sternglantz and Stacia Seaman
Production Design: Stacia Seaman
Cover Design by Tammy Seidick

Acknowledgments

Thank you, Radclyffe, for your friendship and support—I treasure both. Thank you, Sandy, for all you do to keep me on track. To my BSB family, know that I value the family and friendship you have given me. It's a gift to have such rock-solid support. After a few years, it was nice to see some of you again.

Thank you to my editor, Ruth Sternglantz. Ruth, it's nice to learn from each other with each project. I'd also like to thank Tammy Seidick for the great cover. You did a great job with one of my photos of the swamp that inspired me for this book.

Thank you to you the reader. I appreciate all the posts on social media, the reviews you write, and the feedback you send. It was wonderful to reconnect with some of you recently, and to meet some of you who have written to me through the years. I appreciate you all.

The planes are flying again and we've taken our passports out of hibernation, so I'm ready for new adventures with my navigator in all things, C. Verdad!

For C
Always

CHAPTER ONE

The damn numbers. It always came down to the damn numbers, and Fallon Goodwin had done everything but write them upside down dancing the tango, but they still wouldn't stretch as far as she needed them to go. Her plan had been to expand into luxury yachts—only without a business loan, all they could afford was to expand into toy sailboats to maneuver in the bathtub, but not by much.

Her idea had been percolating over the last couple of years. If the pandemic highlighted anything in the boat business, put a spotlight on it really, it was that people had taken to the water in record numbers. A few of their friends had spent months anchored off the islands in the Caribbean fishing, sunbathing, and homeschooling their kids. The water had been the perfect place to escape the misery of being stuck inside or assholes trying to skirt the mask mandates. The market was right there waiting for her to take advantage of it.

There was one glaring problem with that. The roadblock she was butting her head against was one she was related to and was like trying to put Mount Rushmore in her trunk and drive away. Her father was a real hardass when he wanted to be, and on this topic he'd look at her like she was not worthy of running the company.

"You think Dad will go for the fifty million price tag?" Franklin asked. "From my projections, that initial investment will be paid back in less than eleven months." Her brother had worked as long as she had on this project, so the amount they needed was accurate.

Goodwin Boats concentrated on river tugs, service vessels for offshore, and large commercial fishing boats. Her father Alfred had been the one who'd diversified into tugs and had almost cornered the market on new construction. He'd done that, as he liked to remind her, without a loan of any kind.

Just one time she'd like to remind him that he'd been able to do that because her grandfather had saved the first and every dollar he'd ever made. Her father hadn't needed a loan because he was sitting on a boatload of cash. There was business genius, and then there was a massive inheritance when he was the only beneficiary. Now they were profitable, but not enough to start building the kind of vessels she wanted to build.

"Alfred Goodwin would rather lop his ears off than let us borrow money." Fallon glared at the financials again, hoping something would jump up and chew on her leg. She was supposed to be the rainmaker in this generation, but when it came to new avenues of business, she'd run into drought after drought.

"You can ask, Fallon—all he can say is no." Franklin always sounded so reasonable, and also like he'd never met their father. He was like a puppy who made his way through life with a cute face and his earnestness.

Fallon was the oldest of four, and she and Franklin as well as her sisters Eliza and Beatrice worked for their father. There was a certain dynamic to the family business that was like a spiderweb. She was stuck at times like she was now, and her only option was to wait for the big spider to come and suck the life out of her. Or at least that's how it would play out if she explained they needed to go to the bank and borrow money. All her plans would be dry husks once her father quashed them.

She'd sat through that lecture enough times to be able to recite it line for line. It started once a upon a time at the knee of her great-great-great-grandfather, Baskin Goodwin, who started the business making pirogues. The small Louisiana wooden boats for no more than two people were easy to get into the marshy areas during duck hunting season. Baskin taught his sons, who then taught their sons, and so forth until they were building boats priced in the millions.

Her father was the fourth generation of Goodwins who had worked hard, was successful, and was devoted to his family, all the traits he'd taught her and her siblings as they built the business. Not one of those lessons had to do with trips to the bank. To Fallon it was an antiquated way of going about things, so she figured he had his savings in mason jars buried in the yard.

"If you're interested in running the business, just admit it. You don't have to throw me to the big bad wolf so he'll devour me, making room for you." She straightened her papers and placed them in a file.

They'd go back in the drawer waiting for her father's entry to the nursing home because he couldn't remember where he'd buried even one mason jar. "I'll be happy to give up the headaches and gift you the chair."

"It's not my fault you can't find the cash, so don't take it out on me. I'm not interested in your job since I already have one I get shit about. There's no way I'd ever put myself in Alfred's crosshairs daily." Franklin shook his hands so much she thought he was refusing her job with jazz hands. "Just don't give up. We have a full lineup this month, so let's revisit this after we get through some of these projects."

"Thanks, Frankie." She leaned back and closed her eyes for a short mental break. It made her wonder how much a stress ball cost. She could use one to throw at people who stressed her. The bruises could be handled by HR.

"Well?" Beatrice asked in as close to a yell as she could get without actually yelling. Their youngest sister had a way of starting conversations giving no one else a clue about what she was talking about. Beatrice marched to her own drummer, and they had no idea who that percussionist was, but he or she was slightly offbeat.

"Yes?" She gazed over her shoulder as their other sister Eliza waved.

"Let's see it." Beatrice held her hand up as she pointed to her bare left ring finger. It made Fallon jealous.

The diamond ring on her *own* finger felt like it didn't belong there, and would take some getting used to. It was invading her space as well as her peace of mind, and she wanted to throw it in the nearest body of water, like in all romance movies. Every time Fallon touched it with her thumb, it gave her a sense of surprise to find it there, sort of like walking up in Vegas and discovering not only had you gotten married while in a drunken stupor, you'd also tattooed a gigantic T-Rex on your face.

Saying yes to Curtis Boseman's proposal was not a well thought out plan, which had quickly blown up in her face. Curtis had been someone who'd pulled her out of her routine and forced her to face her loneliness. He'd been sweet, attentive, and he'd been in her life for so long she could see herself talking to him about whatever came to mind for years to come.

Maybe that'd be enough, because the grand love affair everyone talked about hadn't materialized. It made her question if anyone was really ecstatically happy. Life wasn't about over the top romance, but a business arrangement. You worked hard at it and tried your best to make it a success.

Her mother had listened to all her concerns, and after Curtis shared the news she'd gone into a planning frenzy that included a lot of talk about ice sculptures and dress designs. Clothes and large parties weren't Fallon's thing, though, so she'd left that to her mother to agonize over. Some of her reservations came from the way Curtis had gone about the whole thing since she really didn't have a problem with him. It was the production aspect, starting with the proposal.

She'd never really sat and fantasized about how she'd like someone to propose to her, and once it happened, she'd thought about how she'd not wanted it to go. Curtis had gotten everything wrong. He'd dropped to one knee in the middle of Blanchard's on a Saturday night, and it had gotten her goddamn manners in a twist. Saying no would've embarrassed him, and somewhere in the logical part of her brain she knew that. Saying yes to someone you hadn't considered marrying to save their ego was on par with that face tattoo. Mergers should be quiet and dignified.

Some people, she was sure, dreamed of the big display. They would look back on the proposal part of it all, because of course there'd have been a professional photographer hiding behind a potted plant, but for her it was the wrong choice on so many levels. She'd come to care for Curtis, was grateful to him for showing her she could have a life outside work, but did they have to share all that with a restaurant full of people all saying *aww* like they'd coordinated it?

It had, though, been a lesson on breaking up with someone or proposing in a crowded restaurant. Going with that option upped your chances of getting what you wanted. No one in their right or rational mind said no or made a scene. Either of those options made you the bad guy or the hysterical, irrational woman.

The problem was that her stomach had knotted up at the word *yes* coming out of her mouth, and it hadn't relaxed since. Losing sleep over *The Big Mistake*, as her mind referred to it—in large flashing pink neon letters—wasn't something most future brides did, she guessed. She, though, sat up nights wondering how this was her life.

She'd known Curtis from birth, loved him even, but she was pretty sure she was supposed to be *in* love with her fiancé. Wasn't that the rule of a long and happy relationship at this point? She had no fucking clue. *Pat, can I buy a clue along with a vowel?* she thought, wanting to laugh at the absurdity of it all.

How she loved Curtis was more in line with how she loved Frankie. Sure they were from the South, but marrying your brother was taboo even south of the Mason-Dixon Line. It simply wasn't done. Like an idiot, though, she'd agreed to do just that even though she wasn't ready. She was a planner, and Curtis had thrown her off her game.

Her mother had assured her all her feelings were normal, and all that mattered was that she was comfortable with Curtis. Loving him would come later like in the old Victorian romance novels. She was comfortable with him, and she had to face that epic romances didn't exist outside those books. That reality fit her more no-nonsense view of life, so this relationship was perfect.

Once she'd embraced that, she agreed to the event her mother wanted, and they were getting married in the spring. It'd give her mother and Miss Scarlett the time to plan the social event of the year. The only upside was her mother-in-law's name was Miss Scarlett... because of course it was. It was in eight months, but Fallon thought she might miss the wedding because of the ulcer forming from worrying about having yet another crowd of people witness something else she didn't necessarily want to share.

Fallon raised her hand, and Beatrice whistled. It was a beautiful ring, and she'd have been impressed too had she seen it coming. "He said it belonged to his maternal grandmother."

"The old woman had good taste," Eliza said. That Eliza had limited her comments to that made Fallon sure there was plenty left to say. *Are you fucking crazy?* she was sure was playing like a chant in her sister's mind, and only wiring her jaw shut would keep it inside.

"She sure did," Beatrice said. "But, ah, are we just going to continue to ignore the giant rainbow elephant in the room?" Bea made a circular motion with her finger.

"What?" Franklin asked, clueless as usual. It was a good thing their brother had become an accountant and was their CFO. The man had a talent for numbers but very little going for him in people skills. "I think it's nice."

"It is, doofus," Bea said shaking her head. "Nice is not in question. What is the current million-dollar query is why the hell she said yes."

"I have no idea." Fallon covered her face with her hands and finally told the truth. There was no good explanation except that she was done dating. Curtis wasn't the love of her life, but he was kind and was a good listener. Passion and love would come later, her mother had assured her. That logic wasn't convincing the little voice in her head.

Not even close. This relationship needed more time to percolate like a fine espresso.

"Don't cry, whatever you do," Eliza said. "You make other people cry, so together we should come up with a plan."

"My plan is to think about it. I feel as if we're rushing it, but I care for him. I owe it to him to take the time to see if this is the right move. If it's not, I'll give him this ring back and break it to Mom there's going to be no wedding. Right after that, I'm going to have to change my name and move to some obscure island to get away from her disappointment if that's my decision."

Her sisters stared at her as if she'd lost her mind. "Fallon, it's either right or isn't. Do you think another year is going to wrap this up in a pretty bow that'll make sense?" Eliza asked.

"I'm not taking a year, and I don't want to break up with him per se. He's been good to me, and I like spending time with him."

"That sounds like a roaring endorsement," Bea said.

"Drop it, all of you." She needed to think, and this wasn't helping. At this point bourbon was the only thing that'd help, but it was too early for that.

❖

In a world full of vices, the Cohiba Behike 52 Brooks Boseman rolled between her fingers was in her top five. There were a few things that vied for the top spot—like money, beautiful women, and a good gumbo—but New York never could deliver on that last one.

People, no matter what culinary accolades they had, had to wrap their heads around the very plain truth—gumbo should never, not ever, be red. That was a sin to her heritage, so she always had to wait for her mother's shrimp and okra heaven when she visited home.

"Is there a problem, Ms. Boseman?" The little weasel the Bank of China sent as their representative squirmed in the prevailing silence after his spiel. This fucker was no Mr. Yang, and his nasal delivery was getting on her nerves.

"I think there is, but I'm interested in knowing what you think." She took the snips out of her breast pocket and cut the tip of her smoke before putting it back in her mouth.

"There's a no smoking policy in this building." His voice got squeakier, and it was like an ice pick to the brain.

Brooks squinted at him, and he crossed his legs for some reason.

His response made her partner Bria Lilly Giordano cover her mouth to hide her laugh. "Do I look like a fool to you? Do I appear to be an unreasonable person who wouldn't be aware of that?"

"No, but if you'd paid better attention, we could be finished and be on the sidewalk lighting that." Weasel boy smoothed down his lapels and narrowed his eyes at her. It was like he was practicing his intimidation techniques, and they were falling way short of the mark. He'd made an effort to lower his voice, so Brooks figured the drop in octave was his attempt at manliness. "This is a lot of money, so I wouldn't want you to miss anything. Mr. Yang wants you to understand the parameters of this deal. It's the only offer we're going to make."

Sarcasm only worked if the person delivering it was a bit more confident and way smarter than this. Yang's lapdog was lacking, and his Bronx accent was starting to slip through as his composure cracked like an egg under heavy boots. Brooks thought everyone should be proud of where they came from and not hide under some preppy school bullshit.

She lifted her cigar to her nose and came close to lighting it to see what he'd do, but she placed it back in her mouth. The slight tingling burn on her lip reminded her of her old man. Maxwell Boseman smoked a different brand, but he didn't suffer fools well either. Those two things were some of the very limited traits they had in common.

"Son, you need to stop shoveling before we all choke on the stink." She pointed her cigar at him when she saw him rise slightly out of his chair. "Please don't make it worse. If Mr. Yang did tell you all that, then he's made quite a few changes he decided not to share with us from our last meeting. Now, if you took some liberties with what he said, thinking it was going to get you out of a cubicle, you can explain that to him because Bria and I are going. We're leaving before you insult my intelligence any more than you have already."

"How about lunch?" Bria asked as Brooks helped her on with her raincoat.

Brooks had met Bria Giordano in her last year of college and was drawn to her because of her analytical mind and charming personality. It wasn't until they were accepted into the business school at Harvard for their MBAs that Bria brought up the possibility of forming their own firm. The only thing Brooks had planned was joining one of the large banks or brokerage houses that were courting her with lucrative offers. Their own firm was enticing, but there was one little hiccup.

Bria Giordano was the only daughter of Angelo Giordano. You had to live under a rock for the name not to raise major red flags. Angelo was the head of the mob on the East Coast, the top guy. His reach was long, and punishment for infractions never involved lawsuits. They were more of a hospital stay in nature. To each his own, but after years of school and work, she wasn't planning to spend the rest of her life in a federal penitentiary for cleaning the mob's money.

It had taken a weekend trip to the Giordano family's estate on Long Island to persuade her there wasn't any jail time in her future if she said yes. Her grandfather Boseman would've found it hilarious that she was the go-to for all the families when it came to investing their legal money. He'd always found the mob a fascinating organization.

When it came to that hard rule, a warning from Angelo was like having the law chiseled in stone. Her and Bria's firm was completely legit, and Angelo gave his word to keep it that way. Anyone fucking with her or Bria wouldn't be cognizant enough to make financial decisions or eat solid food once Angelo paid them a visit.

For the first five years, that had been the majority of their business. Then their results drew enough new business that their firm now handled billions. The BoseLilly Hedge Fund was as solid as they came, and she and Bria worked to keep it that way. Lilly was Bria's mother's maiden name, but using it didn't keep the IRS and other interested federal agencies from watching them closely. Brooks found it humorous that her FBI file was probably thicker than Al Capone's.

"Lunch sounds good if there's alcohol involved." She offered Bria her arm and escorted her to the car. "I need to wash off the bad taste the meeting left with me. Could Yang have found anyone more pathetic?"

"I already texted Yang and told him to forget it. Let the Goldman Sachs boys take it." Bria placed her Chanel bag on the floor of the car as she reapplied her lipstick. "Papa invited us out this weekend. He'd like to talk to you."

"Is he unhappy about something?"

"Sometimes he just wants to see you because he likes you. There's nothing wrong, but I think he knows you have a better business mind than I do." Bria smacked her lips in her direction and laughed. "Either that, or he wants you to make an honest woman out of me."

"I'd have asked already, but you said we had no spark." Brooks smiled when Bria slapped her arm.

"You're like my sister," Bria said, slapping her again. "Not that I don't find you attractive, but there's no reason to think it would work the second time around. Papa doesn't want to hear it, but it's the truth.

He's never going to accept it, so I'll have to live the rest of my romantic life with him comparing everyone to you."

They'd dated for a month, and they were compatible but missing that *it* that made you passionate about the other person. She loved Bria, though, and was always her date when the Giordano family hosted some function. The family had taken her in when Bria had first brought her home, and that had surprised her. Angelo was not that trusting, which made sense when you considered what he did, but he'd always been open with her because of her closeness with Bria.

Every so often Angelo would invite her personally to spend time at the Long Island estate to talk over a variety of topics. At first it intimidated her, but Angelo was like every other guy who loved his family and was loyal to his friends. It was easy to almost forget exactly who Angelo was when she sat on his patio and shared a drink and cigar with him. In the years she and Bria had worked together, spending time with her and her family alleviated the pain of missing her own.

It had been months since she'd been home, but it was hard to consider Louisiana that any longer, considering everything that'd happened. Her relationship with her father was strained to the point of breaking, and it wasn't fair to keep making her mother stand in the middle, playing referee.

Her mom always said it was because she and her dad were too much alike. No one besides her father, though, was that unbending and judgmental, so Brooks had always thought of that as an insult. She'd been born a girl and wasn't at all what her father wanted in an heir, and she'd come to one conclusion after that realization. It was what it was—and neither she nor her father was ever going to stoop to make the first move toward reconciliation.

"I'll be happy to if you try and talk your mother into making lasagna."

"Honey, talking my mother into making lasagna is like trying to talk a bored housewife into her third martini." Bria kissed the tip of her nose. "Want to skip lunch and head out early? Papa's taking a few days off, so I'm sure his invitation has everything to do with having you watch some games with him while you run the win ratios. He'll be doing that while praying a novena that you'll eventually become the son-in-law he's always dreamed of."

"Angelo would make an awesome family member, especially if you're having an *issue*." They both laughed and she told the driver their change in plans. "How about I drop you off so you can pack, and I'll be back in an hour? We can head to the helipad to save ourselves the drive. I promise to bring snacks."

Bria's phone rang and she turned it so Brooks could see it was Yang. "How about we put him on ice until we get back?"

Brooks nodded and hopped out to open Bria's door when they reached her apartment building. "Call the office and let them know we'll be heading out, and I'll run over the trades we have slated for today. They're set, but it doesn't hurt to be sure."

"See why my father loves you?"

The helicopter Brooks had ordered landed on the side yard of the Giordano mansion, and the guards scattered on the property seemed to be standing at attention as if making sure it was a friendly visit and not something that would require their intervention. Angelo was right on the edge of the large patio that overlooked the water, and he hugged them both and kissed their cheeks.

"My girl," he said to Bria as he held her against this chest. "It's good to see you."

"You saw me last week, Papa," Bria teased him.

"True, but that doesn't mean I can't miss you. Come inside, Brooks. You can help me with the spread on some of these games. I swear if I have to pay out like I did last week, I'm not going to be a happy man."

They talked inside as they had drinks, and Bria caught her mother up on every aspect of her life. It was a great way to spend time until dinner was served and the famous lasagna came out to Brooks's applause.

Dinner wasn't rushed as they kept up their light conversation with plenty of laughs from the jokes Angelo had heard that week. She kissed Bria's parents good night and went up to her room to clear the deal that'd wasted their morning. She wanted it off their books so as not to have to think about it before the markets opened overseas. There were a few things she was following in preparation of the opening bell on Wall Street in the morning.

Her phone rang at a quarter to eleven, and she smiled when her mom's picture popped up. She didn't need psychic powers to know there was a lecture in her future. "Mom, hey."

"Did you lose my number?" Scarlett Boseman enjoyed being

ignored as much as her namesake in *Gone With the Wind*, and she wasn't shy about telling you. "Five months is a lifetime, Brooks, and if your excuse is work, keep your mouth shut."

"Be mad at me after you tell me how you are. The flowers every Friday should get me some points." She put her feet on the desk and stared out the window to the floodlights illuminating the yard.

"I love the flowers, but I love hearing from you even more." Her mom paused and Brooks waited. There was something wrong, and pushing Scarlett would only clam her up. "Why is it of the four children I had, you're the only one who understands me completely?"

The question might've been rhetorical, but Brooks took a chance. "Because we're complete opposites, but I see you, and I appreciate the sight."

"No wonder you're loaded." Her mom shared her laugh before she paused again. "Have you called your father lately?"

That was a bit of a loaded question. If she lost her mind and called her father and not her mom, it upset her mother, but not calling either one landed her in the same shit. "I know you hate the answer, but it's been a while. I tried for you, but he was pissed out of the gate, and I'm still trying to figure out why before I try again—*if* I try again."

"You need to come home, Brooks, and not for your usual five-minute visit." Her mom's voice broke, and Brooks dropped her feet to floor as if they were weighted.

"Why? What happened?" Her visits weren't frequent, but she moved through life like someone who knew she had a soft spot to land no matter how far she fell. "Mom? Please don't punish me because I'm not there. Tell me."

"I'm not punishing you, my love, but he needs to see you. He wants to talk to you, and he wanted me to call. And don't punish him because it's me who's calling." Her mother was crying, she could hear it in her voice, but she'd never completely break, not on the phone anyway.

She stood and stared at the sliver of water she could see from this spot. How was it possible she was surrounded by such peacefulness, and she was in turmoil? "Is he sick?"

"Don't dig a hole for yourself, boo-boo, and don't take too long. I need to see you soon as well, so please, just this once, do what I'm asking."

Her mom hung up, and it pissed her off. If there was something wrong, she deserved to know. The view blurred, and it was only then that she realized she was crying. That was way off her norm, but a chasm had opened in her chest at the thought of something happening to her father. The man was like no other in the way he lived, and she'd tried to emulate the best parts of him so he'd be proud of her. It was doubtful she'd ever succeed, but it didn't keep her from trying. In a way she hated herself for even trying, considering all the shit he'd dumped on her for the entirety of her life.

"Bria," she said through the connecting door, "I need to go." She did her best to explain the cryptic call from her mother, and she didn't want to take the chance her mom wasn't bluffing. The need to go home was swamping her, but if her father was gone, would that part of herself that bled because of him ever heal?

"Honey, please sit." Bria picked up the phone on the desk and called someone who sounded like Angelo over the line. "Don't worry, we'll take care of it."

"I just need to find a flight." She wiped her face, trying to control her emotions.

"You don't think I can do a little better than that?" Bria moved closer and put her arms around her neck. "Go on and get dressed and let me do this for you."

"I love you, you know that, right?" Brooks closed her eyes when Bria's only answer was kissing her forehead. Whatever she was facing would be easier with Bria and everyone she'd chosen to be her family, but she wasn't selfish enough to ask.

CHAPTER TWO

The first engagement party is coming up, so make some time to go shopping." Fallon's mother Eleanor had her planner open like it was a Bible that had to be followed like the word of the Lord. "That means a cocktail dress. Your sisters are joining us, so don't try to get out of it. Do that and plan on wearing something with plenty of ruffles in pink taffeta."

"When and where?" Fallon had resigned herself to the runaway freight train her life had become, and only a heart to heart with Curtis was going to change it. The problem with that brilliant plan was that Curtis was suddenly unavailable to come to the phone. She wasn't sure what the problem was, but there was a problem. Had he come to the same conclusion she had, that they needed more time, and hadn't found a way to tell her? Whatever it was, his radio silence did not bode well for a happy marriage.

"Tomorrow at lunch. We'll meet at Galatoire's, then hit the boutiques. Scarlett, Charlie, and Prudence will try their best to make it." Just like that the planner slammed shut, and her mom was out the door.

"Fuck me," she said softly. One thing on her mind aside from her huge saying yes mistake was that there were going to be a lot of disappointed people when she gave Curtis the ring back. Hopefully, the only thing everyone would be out of was a cocktail dress and a few cases of booze.

"Did you recently start taking drugs?" Eliza asked. Their offices connected, and Fallon had thought her sister was at a meeting. "Or perhaps you ordered a complete personality change from Amazon and didn't consult me before you installed it."

"What are you talking about?" she said, knowing full well what she was talking about.

"Curtis Boseman, seriously?" Eliza rolled her eyes, and Fallon thought of how dizzy that would make her. "You can't marry this guy. So tell me why in the world you'd say yes."

"You know we've been spending time together." There were excuses that would get her an F if they were graded, but she was starting to lean to it not being a mistake. She'd been alone for a long time, and she wanted something different for herself. Having someone to come home to sounded nice.

"You spend time with Clarence your hairstylist, and I don't see you running off with him. Actually, you should—I like him better than I do Curtis." When Eliza threw her hands up, she figured it'd be a long afternoon. "What the hell, Fallon? I go on vacation, and you completely lose your mind. I thought Bea was kidding until she convinced me—in her sledgehammer to the face kind of way—she was not kidding."

"Let me finish." Fallon pointed to a chair in front of her desk, hoping it'd stop the pacing. "I told you about how I hadn't seen Curtis in forever, and after a few dinners it was easy to talk to him. That's all it was. It'd been so long that I spent time with someone who wasn't after a deal or money—I found it refreshing. We have a lot in common."

"And that's your threshold for marriage? If that's true, you've been hit in the head and didn't mention that either." It was hard to disagree with Eliza's logic. She was as good at reading her as she was with numbers.

"No to the hitting my head or the Amazon option. Six months of platonic dates makes me think he and I will be a good fit. I just didn't expect to turn into all this." She covered her eyes with her hands and wondered if perhaps it was time to finally plan a two-year visit to Antarctica. If she lived among the penguins, no one would expect her to spend her weekend shopping for a cocktail dress.

"And?" Eliza's voice stopped her fantasy cold. "That can't be the whole story."

"I wasn't thinking marriage, but he surprised me in a crowded restaurant surrounded by a million of our business contacts." The next words would take courage considering Eliza's temper. "I didn't want to embarrass him, so I said yes."

"Uh-huh," Eliza said, closing her eyes. The silence that followed was disconcerting.

"My plan was to follow that up with a private conversation about me wanting to think about it." The more words came out of her mouth, the more unhinged she sounded. She was sane enough to figure that out. "My problem is that hasn't happened, and I'm not sure that'll happen now that Mom has gotten involved. All hell's going to drop like shit on me if I give the ring back."

"You're sticking to that even if you're in love with someone else?" Eliza had a talent for lifting her eyebrow high enough that you'd think it'd pop off and beat you to death. "Please tell me that you're kidding."

"I'm not *in* love with anyone, thank you very much. Curtis and I fit. Am I madly in love? No, but I don't think he is either. Comfortable and easy isn't a bad thing." She'd started to question Curtis's true feelings after about three months, but Curtis was a perfect gentleman. A perfect gentleman with no sex drive, but she guessed those type of guys existed, sort of like Bigfoot and mermaids. It also should've been a big clue as to the validity of their relationship.

"Let's review that, shall we?" Eliza's inquisition was starting to grate on her like a block of Parmesan cheese in a grinder. "You're not interested in sleeping with him because you're gay. Did Mom send you to some fundamentalist conversion camp where they pray the gay away? If she did, tell me so I can leave town before she ships me off to the same place. Considering how well it worked on you, I'm sure she's going for a group rate."

"Having three gay daughters I'm sure wasn't in her plans. She's always said it didn't bother her." Her coming out wasn't the nightmare it had been for some of their friends with devout Catholic parents, and she'd thanked her family for being so understanding. By the time Bea had broken the news, her mother's reaction was limited to the twitch in her left eyebrow. Fallon at times figured it was from the state of shock that hadn't cleared all these years later.

"Of course she said that, but her over the top reaction to your big news might make her slightly full of shit." Eliza finally laughed with her. "Now that we've agreed that you've completely lost it, tell me why you're really doing this?"

"If I knew that, I'd be in Vegas right now instead of stuck in this conversation." Fallon lowered her head to her desk and knocked her forehead into it a few times. "I want to be happy and have someone. Curtis is going to be that someone, so you all will have to accept it."

"You'll never have to worry about us not supporting you if you really want this. Have you considered one small wrinkle?"

She turned her head and sighed before falling for Eliza's comment. "What?"

"Your good news is going to lure the person you're not *not* in love with to town. Her brother is, after all, getting married." Eliza sounded way too gleeful, and Fallon wanted to throw her stapler at her. "I forgot, though, you're not in love with anyone because you're buying matching pajamas with Curtis so you'll both be comfortable when you braid each other's hair."

The sarcasm was not appreciated, so Fallon sat up. "First off, the someone you're talking about left me with no remorse, so she's not worth mentioning. Secondly, that was done years ago, and I'm over it. Number three, I don't want to talk about it anymore."

In her junior year of high school, Brooks Boseman had flipped a switch in her that had changed her life as quickly as she'd fallen in love. That didn't surprise her because Brooks had made it easy. The freedom LSU had given them had been blissful, and they'd spent every night together making plans for their lives together down to how many kids they'd have. Brooks had proven the all-encompassing love affair not only existed, it was mind blowing.

LSU, ten years prior

"Have a good day, people, and remember that finals are coming up," Fallon's professor said as her last class of the day ended. She walked out to Brooks sitting on a bench under the big oak tree she loved.

Brooks had a notebook open and a pencil in her hand, which meant she was doing complicated math problems for fun. They had plenty in common, but that was not something that made the list. "Hey, beautiful," Brooks said when she noticed her.

"Are you done for the day?" She'd been thinking of Brooks from the moment they'd had to part that morning.

"I am, and I've been sitting out here thinking about you." Brooks stood and put all her stuff away so she could take Fallon's hand. "How about we go home and talk about what we're ordering later while we're naked."

"You have the best ideas," she said and laughed. They'd been together for years now, but they still couldn't keep their hands off each other.

The apartment they'd rented was right off campus, and it wasn't in one of the large complexes most students gravitated to. This place was owned by an older woman who used the rental over her garage as her retirement plan. The nice thing about it was how much privacy it gave them, since Brooks teased her about how loud she could get. That couldn't be helped.

She stripped her shirt off as soon as Brooks closed the door, and jumped, fully expecting Brooks to catch her. Brooks did and held her up against the wall. "You drive me wild," Brooks said as she put her hand between her legs and sucked on the side of her neck. The jeans had to come off, but she didn't want to move now that Brooks was touching her.

Brooks put her down just long enough to get her pants off, and she wanted to scream when Brooks entered her without much buildup. It wasn't needed. She was wet and ready, having anticipated the pleasure Brooks was capable of since the beginning of that management class.

"Yes, baby," she said, pulling Brooks's hair and tightening her legs around her. The wall at her back gave her enough leverage to buck her hips against Brooks's thumb. She wanted this time around to be fast and hard. The desire had built all day until she needed Brooks to take care of it before it drove her to distraction. "Fuck," she yelled when Brooks pressed down on her clit like she was trying to take her pulse.

"You ready, sweetheart?" Brooks never lost that stroke that drove her need.

"Please, don't stop. I want..." Brooks slammed her fingers in. "I want you to make me come." Brooks grunting in her ear with her fingers inside her was enough to make it impossible to hold her orgasm back. If she had her way, it wouldn't be the only time today that would happen. "Ah...ah, shit," she said as she came hard.

"I always want to be the one who makes you feel good." Brooks carried her into their bedroom and laid her down like she'd break if she wasn't gentle. "I love you more than you'll ever know."

"We only have a year left, my love, then you're going to marry me, and we can start on those kids we both want," she said as she lifted Brooks's shirt off.

Brooks kissed her, and she could feel the permanence in the act. No matter what came, Brooks was hers, and they belonged together. Nothing was ever going to break them apart. "I'm going to give you that and more. Whatever you want," Brooks said as she worked on her pants next.

"All I want is you, so I'm happy. The rest is lagniappe," she said, using the French word for something extra.

Present day

Fallon thought she'd found the perfect person for her until Brooks had gotten an offer to spend a year in England. A year she knew nothing about until Brooks was gone. She'd tried to make it work long distance, but Brooks never took her calls, and instead of coming home after graduation, she'd picked Harvard over her. Brooks seemed to be done with her and made the split as painful as she could.

Fallon had given up after that and stopped thinking of what they'd had and tried to accept the reality of what she'd lost. The experience had left her wary of letting her defenses down again, and time hadn't made it better. She still didn't have a clear idea of why they'd broken up, and it was doubtful she ever would. And if Brooks came back now, finding out Fallon was engaged to Curtis was going to not go over well with the woman she still dreamed about. That was something she'd never admit to anyone.

"I'm not lecturing, sis," Eliza said, "but I'd like to see you happy. To me that's not something I see you having with Curtis. Even if you were straight, the guy's a bit of a dick. I love you, and if you want my help to get out of this, you have it."

"I love you too, and I'll let you know. If anything, you'll get a new cocktail dress out of it." They laughed together and she stood to hug her sister. All this had made her forget her business woes, which were more worrisome than this. "How about you? Any love drama to report?"

"Compared to you I'm like *Little House on the Prairie*. You're more like *The Kardashians* and *Maury Povich* all rolled into one." Eliza winked as she let her go.

"There'll be no big reveal as to who the father is, you ass."

Eliza laughed hard enough to cry as she pointed up. "The day you get pregnant, I'm sure a big star will appear announcing divine intervention. We'll all make the news when men on camels bearing gifts show up at the hospital."

"Get back to work, comedian." When she was alone again, she couldn't help herself and thought of Brooks. She'd kept up with Brooks's career through the financial news, knowing she had the golden touch when it came to making money. What was never reported was who Brooks shared her life with.

One night after a few drinks she'd broken a promise to herself and asked Curtis. He either didn't know or wasn't willing to tell her. All he hinted at was there'd been some trouble between Brooks and their father. It explained a part of why Brooks had been gone so long, but there had to be more than that.

"Jesus, my life really has turned into a reality show."

The plane Brooks accepted from Angelo landed at Lakefront Airport after four in the morning. She didn't ask who the plane belonged to or whose radar it put her on by accepting, caring only about the need to see her parents. That'd always been a complicated relationship, enough that it had driven her to escape Louisiana. Her father had been someone who never got tired of pushing all his kids to the level he thought they should achieve.

His expectations meant she went through her childhood carrying boulders and bags of wet sand tied to her feet. It'd been way too much, but hell if she hadn't tried. She still kept up with the family business to an extent, but she doubted he had any idea the state they were in. Or if he did, something catastrophic must've happened.

Max had wanted Curtis to run the business, and she'd kept quiet knowing it was a battle she'd never win. The Boseman company always had been and always would be run by a male member of the family. Curtis had been the anointed one in this generation, and he loved to brag at the family get-togethers how well things were going.

Her brother was either touched in the head or treading water as fast as he could to keep them afloat. She leaned heavily on the insane option. Either that or he had no idea how to do books. If something had happened to her father and Curtis was free to do as he pleased, the company wouldn't last another six months.

"Ms. Boseman"—the driver Bria must have ordered opened the door and took her bag—"Ms. Giordano secured you a room at the Piquant. I'll be available whenever you're ready tomorrow, unless you'd like to go somewhere before then."

"Thank you, and the Piquant will be fine." She wanted to work a bit before going to bed. It wasn't that she was heartless; numbers were the way she wrangled her emotions under tight control—but her concentration was shot. The suite was nice, but all she was interested in was the big bed, so she stripped, crawled in, and tried to shut off her brain. She was a good enough forecaster to know that was an impossible task.

It didn't seem like she'd been asleep long when the phone woke her. Since it was the room phone it had to be Bria, and it took her a moment to clear her head and place the voice. "Monroe, hey."

The oldest daughter of her uncle Bryce was two months younger, so they'd grown up together. They were closer than some of her siblings, and Monroe visited often. Her uncle and aunt were a little different than her parents, but it was a good different, and she had good memories of them.

"You want me to come up, or do you want to come down and have breakfast?" Monroe sounded as if those were the only two options she was willing to accept. "It's a nice morning, so how about the latter?"

"Give me thirty minutes to shower and wake up. It'll give you time to work up to being in a talkative mood if you're not." If Monroe knew she was here, her mother couldn't be too far behind.

"Stop overthinking," Monroe said. "I called Bria, and she told me where you were. I'm here to talk to you before you go home and get waylaid."

Brooks put on a pair of a khakis and a golf shirt, not having the energy for a suit. Getting waylaid probably meant this was all about money. It had taken plenty to prop Curtis up in the time he'd been at the helm of the family business. If that's what all this was about, her mother had scared her for nothing, and if that was true, it'd be a while before she came here again.

"It's good to see you." Monroe hugged her and kissed her cheek. They actually looked more alike than Brooks and her siblings did in height and coloring, with their dark hair and green eyes. "Bria told me Aunt Scarlett called you."

Monroe was in charge of the processing plant on Bayou Lafourche. Local shrimpers were able to dock and unload their catch to be peeled, washed, and packaged for resale. Their other cousins did the same with their crab, squid, fish, and oyster plants. Boseman Seafood Company sold nationwide and was being run by the sixth generation of the Boseman family. As with all things in life, even good things had to come to an end.

"Funny thing is, neither she nor you have a lot to say about what's going on." They sat outside, and the heat seemed to be the most welcoming thing so far. The high temps were the proof she was home. Others found the humidity and heat oppressive, but they were a reminder of summers spent learning what made their business work. The only time she thought of it now was when she ordered seafood.

"That's your mama's story to tell, but she did try her best to keep it under wraps as long as she could. You coming home isn't anything you planned on, I'm sure, but I'm glad you're here."

The team of waiters took their order, and they spent time gossiping while they waited for their food. Nothing had changed much from what she could tell listening to Monroe's stories. Fishbowls could learn a few things from this place. It's why she loved her life. Her family thought she was boring because she worked so much, but work didn't breed this much drama. That, she avoided like an IRS audit. Their problem was, while her uncle and his children worked for the company, it was owned outright by her father.

Families were strange living entities, in her opinion. Strangers at times turned vicious when it came to money, but that paled when it came to family fortunes. In her family, the oldest inherited outright but had to pay their siblings their share of the fair market value the day they took the helm. After that the profit belonged solely to the heir.

This had worked for six generations. It didn't take much time for the oldest to make up the big payoff since the business was so successful. The process assured the company didn't get split into so many little pieces that it was run by committee and not by the anointed one—perfectly understandable back then when families had fourteen kids and whoever was chosen knew their ass from a buffalo, but that rationale had flown into the abyss in their generation.

From the reports she'd gotten from the family complainers, Curtis didn't have a complete grasp of what it was they did. The business goals, bonuses, and reputation were now nonexistent. Monroe had answers but seemed more afraid of the gatekeeper than of losing her livelihood. The sentinel on duty was not her father but her mother. Crossing Scarlett was not forgiven easily, if at all.

"So, you're not going to give me at least a hint?" She signed for breakfast, wishing someone in New York knew how to make biscuits like the three she'd just eaten. "If this is only about my mother making me jump through fiery hoops, I'm not going to find it funny. I'm also going to include you in my displeasure for keeping me in the dark."

"Like I said, it's her story to tell, Brooks. Just hear her out and know that things would be better with you around." Monroe seemed pensive, but that wasn't a clue either since she wasn't exactly effusive by nature. "You've never really told me the real reason why you left, but that was the start of the business not doing as well. Not your fault and no one's ever said, but I figure you're our silent investor when things got really tight."

"You know what Max was like when we were growing up. He had some very specific round holes he wanted to jam us into, but I was born more of a square peg. When I rebelled, he tightened the leash and said I'd never make it without him." She rubbed her face and took a deep breath. "The threats were baseless, but the intent helped me grow wings. I didn't want to keep beating my square head against those round holes for the rest of my life."

Monroe nodded and sighed. "I'm sure that was the cleaned-up version. Your old man is tough, but whatever the true version is, I think he regrets it."

"I doubt that, and he got what he wanted in the end. With me out of the way, he didn't need to pretend there was a chance in hell he'd let me have a say in the company. Curtis was always his boy, and that's the way it's always been." She believed they should've named the company Boseman and Sons since that's why it existed—men who worked so their sons could take over for them. "He got what he wanted, but that old saying of being careful what you wish for came back to bite him in the ass."

"No matter what, I'm glad you're here. It'll be good to catch up."

She reached across the table and covered Monroe's hand with hers. "Thanks, and you can't know how hard it was to give up some of the things I miss about this place. The people I love and grew up with are at the top of that list."

"You're missed by plenty, and don't forget that we love you too. No one's expecting you to uproot your life, but it's time to remember all that stuff that's important."

"What an interesting thing to say. Now I'm a little off-balance."

"Go home, Brooks."

The family home, the place she spent almost every weekend and summer as a kid, was outside Grand Caillou Bayou. It was close to a hundred and thirty years old, but her grandparents had purchased a large home in the Garden District in New Orleans. After that, most of that generation moved to the city, where the main offices of the business were located. Her father had been too attached to both homes, so he'd bought out his siblings when they'd voted to tear the Grand Caillou home down because of the extensive repairs it needed. He sank a fortune into it and still enjoyed spending time there, from what she could tell.

It was close to the processing plants and some of the boats in their fleet. Brooks had plenty of memories of playing in that yard with Caillou Bayou along the back. The oak and mimosa trees had been their jungle gyms, and the bayou was used more than the pool. She was the only one of her siblings who loved that house as much as her father. To her it was steeped in the history of who they were, and the painting behind her desk in New York was from an old picture she'd taken with her.

"Which home?" The place to the south wasn't somewhere her mother thought of as home.

"They're in Grand Caillou, and I had one of the guys drop off a company truck." Monroe handed over a valet ticket and patted her shoulder as she left.

"Who knew my family could be this cryptic." She went up and took her bag with her laptop and work files. If this turned out to be bullshit, she'd be on the way home by tonight.

CHAPTER THREE

Fallon stared at the contract their sales department had put together and blinked a few times, thinking her eyesight was telling her brain the wrong thing. The paperwork for the two tugboats for the offshore service company was all in order—it wasn't chump change, though not what she needed for her dream expansion—but the other contract under it had her confused. Twenty-five shrimp boats with rigging would boost their profit margin to the point her father couldn't ignore.

That was the problem. It was too good to be true, and she saw it as a big pile of shit waiting for her to step on it and blow her world to hell. Falling for this would bankrupt them when the company wanting to hire them couldn't pay.

The contract was like a carrot that'd choke her if something went wrong, and her gut said there was plenty to go wrong. The order was from Boseman Seafood, and she figured this had to be Curtis's idea. That meant her fiancé was probably looking for a deep discount and thought it was going to be hard turning him down. No matter what he was expecting, turning him down was what was going to happen.

"Did you get the contracts?" Franklin asked. He came in and sat across from her desk, appearing a bit pale. "If someone from our company put that together, it should be sufficient cause to fire them."

If she needed proof that Curtis's marriage proposal wasn't all about a deep love for her, this might be it. "I was getting ready to call Stacey in sales and ask."

Bea joined them and dropped into the other seat. "Eliza is five minutes out. She was called out to the yard."

"Do you know who wrote this up?" Fallon handed over the paperwork, which was thankfully not signed.

"Curtis has been taking Stacey to lunch, and this is what they hammered out." Eliza came in wearing jeans, work boots, and company T-shirt. "It's total bullshit, but Stacey told me he had your backing."

"Let's get through everything else. I need to talk to Stacey, and then I have to run by the Boseman place." God, she hated getting played, and she detested letting that happen in front of her family. "Do you have anything else?"

"No, Bea and I'll meet with the supply company and get started with their project," Eliza said. She stood and squeezed her hand when she came around the big desk. "Call us if you need help kicking ass."

"This time I think I can handle it."

The quiet that followed helped her gather her thoughts. In a way her anger was soothed by the clarity it gave her. The time for thinking was over, and Curtis couldn't come up with a good enough story to get his ass out of this crack. If he tried, there was no going back even as friends.

Her mother brought that peace to an abrupt end. All the papers on the desk ruffled when her mom dropped a large book at the center. "The invitations have gone out, and the house will be ready. I'll pick you up tomorrow at nine." Eleanor had a way of laying down the law that gave you limited options of escape.

"I'm meeting Curtis today, so there's a possibility there's not going to be a wedding. The invitations are a blip, but I'm sure there's time to send a retraction. It's just a party to announce something that might not happen." It was her turn to set down some rules. "I told you I was thinking about it and not to make any plans. You did anyway, so that's on you."

"Listen to yourself. Did Curtis coerce you? And you want a family." Her mother talked over her, and Fallon shook her head.

"There's more than one way to have a family, and I'm not sure about all this. I don't know how else to put it."

"Agree to the party and you'll see I'm right. I'll pick you up to go shopping so we can spend some time together, and I'll be happy to talk to you about whatever you want. You and Curtis can work it out whatever's bothering you. I just don't want you to throw away this chance." Her mom picked up her book and shoved it back in her big purse. "We invited everyone important to both sides, and I don't want to be the main gossip for the rest of the year."

"Are you serious?" It boggled her mind the ideas her mother

had about social standing. If she'd been smart, she would've picked somewhere else to live and work, like Brooks had done.

"An engagement party is our expense and will be a few hours of your life. It's no time to act like a five-year-old. Considering the guest list, you're going to be happy about it. It's a group we do business with, so smile and deal with it." The sigh her mom aimed her way was like a hint she should know all this. "My goal in life is to see my children happy. If marrying Curtis Boseman isn't going to make you happy, then give the ring back. Can I ask why you want to do that?"

"We all have our weak moments, Mom. I'm not saying I don't want to marry him, but I want to be sure. This isn't like buying a dress for this party. Marriage is something I don't want to fail at."

Her mom cocked her head as if thinking of what best to say. "I'm sure there's more to it, but you don't have to share if you don't want to. I was surprised, not by the family, but by the member of the family you picked. There was a Boseman you loved, and it wasn't Curtis."

"Ancient history, and that's not why I'm backing out." She glanced at her watch and grimaced.

"Go ahead. I'm sure you have stuff to do." She smiled at the kisses her mom pressed to her cheeks and she walked her out. It was too easy and her mom had given in too fast for her to trust the turnaround.

The business district was close to the interstate, so it didn't take her long to be out of the city. Curtis wasn't a guy who spent a lot of time in the office. On most days he was at the docks where they kept their fishing boats. That didn't mean he was working, since it was where he kept the cruiser he maintained to support his addiction to tuna and swordfish hunting.

Maxwell had made all his kids work on boats, so they knew where the money came from. All those lessons seemed to have been lost on Curtis, but it wasn't her business. All she remembered about the Boseman patriarch was he was a tough man who'd scared the hell out of her when she was a kid.

Unlike her father, though, Max had completely stepped back when he retired, so she hadn't seen him in a while. She could about imagine what he'd have to say if she rejected his son. That's exactly what was going to happen, and she doubted there'd be much downside to that. Max hadn't appeared happy when Curtis had brought her to Sunday lunch. Maxwell had glared at her down his nose and acted like she was a parasite set on killing his family tree.

It took over an hour to arrive in Grand Caillou, and the guard at the gate of the seafood company waved her in. The smell of this place took some getting used to, making her take a deep breath before she stepped out of the car. She saw Curtis eating an oyster close to one of his boats. He nodded as he threw the shell into the water.

She waved when the fisherman pointed in her direction, and he gave her that big smile that made him nothing but handsome. "Hey."

"Hey, babe, you're a good surprise." Curtis hugged her like he meant it and pressed his lips to hers. His five o'clock shadow scratched her face, so she leaned back to bring his greeting to a stop. "Needed a break?"

"Something like that. I need to talk to you." She took a step to the side and smiled at the fisherman.

"Sure, but try this first." Curtis pointed to the pile, and the man shucked another oyster and handed it to her. Raw oysters weren't her thing, but she ate it. "Isn't the salt content amazing?"

"Delicious, but isn't it too warm for oysters?" The thought of food poisoning or worse made her nauseous.

"We pasteurize them, ma'am, and there's always a market for them." The fisherman took the shell back and signaled his guys to start unloading the burlap sacks full of their catch. "The new favorite dish around town is charbroiled, so it doesn't matter the month we catch them."

"I remember my grandmother's rule," she said, waving off another one. "Don't eat these suckers in months without an *R* in them."

"My granny lived by the same rule, but we all have to make a living."

"Fallon, I'd like you to meet Dellow Hayes," Curtis said, waving his hand toward the fisherman with a bit of an attitude. "Dellow and his family have fished these waters for as long as there's been people here."

"Don't forget what we talked about," Dellow said to Curtis after slightly nodding in her direction.

"I got it under control." Curtis held his hand out to her and started for the office he kept here. "I'm sure you're not here for a lecture on oysters, or meeting our local guys, so what's on your mind? If it's about the engagement party, I've had my fill of that." He made a slashing motion under his neck.

"I'm here about the meetings you've had with Stacey." She pulled her hand out of his and fought the urge to wipe it on her pants.

Curtis's hand was clammy and sweaty. "Your order has put me in an uncomfortable position."

"We need to update our fleet, and I thought I'd keep it in the family." Curtis closed his door as if needing this conversation to be private. "Do you not want our business?"

"Do you want me to have this conversation with you?" That was going to be the only offer to save his ego she was willing to give him. "Withdraw the contract before we sign in good faith and do our due diligence."

"Coy isn't you, and I'm going to be your husband. Marriage is a partnership in all things, Fallon." Curtis glanced up at her as if daring her to disagree. He was delusional if he thought that was going to work. "You might not feel that now, but we have time."

"Curtis." She prayed for the patience it took not to strip naked and run out the door, howling at the moon made of Roquefort cheese. "Listen—" The explosion from outside knocked her across the desk. He ran out, not seeming to care whatever it was she had to say. The boat they'd been standing by was now in flames, and Fallon hoped the workers were clear of it. Dellow, the guy she'd just met, was motoring away from the dock as if trying to put some distance between his boat and the fire.

She watched everyone in action and wondered if the Keystone Kops had written their emergency plan. It had to be the only explanation for the way Curtis and his employees were running around while the boat burned. The sound of sirens in the distance was a relief, and she was impressed with their response time. It was probably shitty to drive away, but there wasn't anything she could do to help.

Curtis had to be the luckiest man alive. She doubted he blew up a boat to cut their talk short, but she couldn't dodge the thought that that's exactly what'd happened. Her first thought was there was something hinky about this, but it wasn't her problem. The Boseman Company was going through some issues, but none of them were hers, and she wanted to keep it that way.

It was chaos outside, and the guy not dressed to fight the fire headed right for her. "Do you know what happened, ma'am?"

Her explanation was short since she wanted no part of this in case it was exactly what she thought it was. Curtis and the business could no more afford twenty-five new boats than they could sail them to Mars. That he had the balls to want to sign a contract was a major clue as to why he'd proposed the way he did—his obvious idea of partnership was her and her family taking on his debt and him getting a new fleet out of it.

"So, you were standing next to the boat minutes before it exploded?" The tone the guy used was sharp and accusatory. She couldn't blame him.

"I was here about a possible contract and tried one of the oysters they were unloading. There's really nothing more I can add." She was pissed, but she didn't want to take it out on this guy.

"Was the engine running?"

She closed her eyes and thought. "No, they were docked and unloading, or getting ready to. In my opinion that might mean a gas leak, but I'm not the fire marshal." She shrugged, and the short chubby guy with the impressive comb-over stopped writing.

"In your opinion? Do you have experience with boat explosions?"

"I have experience in building safe, reliable vessels. Because of that experience, I know there's very few things that can cause that." She pointed to the boat that was partially submerged and then crossed her arms over her chest.

"Do you have any idea if it was deliberate?" He now sounded as if they were a team in a quest to uncover dastardly and nefarious doings.

"Of course she doesn't think that," Curtis said, louder than necessary. "It was an accident, and Fallon's my fiancée. She can vouch for me and my company. Can't you, honey?"

"You two are engaged?" The Sherlock of fire appeared not to believe Curtis, and Fallon wanted to kiss him. He might not find arson, but he'd figured out she and Curtis didn't belong together.

"Yes," Curtis said when her silence appeared to make him uncomfortable.

"Fallon? Are you Alfred Goodwin's kid?"

"Yes, sir, so you know how to find me if you have any questions. Am I free to go?" The best move she could make was to put miles between her and whatever this fucked-up situation was. "The only thing I did want to ask was about the workers. Did they all get clear?"

"Everyone's been accounted for," Curtis said.

"Miss Fallon, are you sure it'd be okay to call you? You and your people might be able to help when we examine the vessel, once everything's cooled off."

"Sure." She walked to her car and handed him a card.

"Don't you want to stay?" Curtis asked.

"We have plenty to talk about, but it can wait. I'd think you have enough to do here." She slammed her door before Curtis could feed her any other lines.

Everything she'd told her sister was true. Curtis had been an amazing listener, and she'd shared an embarrassingly lot with him, but that's not what had drawn her in. No, that had been his face and those damn dimples. Curtis bore a strong resemblance to his sister in some ways, and the defenses around her heart had crumbled at his kindness.

Now she knew better. The defenses were there because of the bitch who'd thrown her away and forgotten her. It hadn't been real love back then, and it wasn't with Curtis. Her only goal now was to put the Boseman family in her rearview and leave them there.

"Maybe today was like a bomb to implode our future. If Mom has puppies, we'll all offer to adopt one, but I'm not getting forced into this. It's not like we're going to be run out of town."

❖

"Fucker!" Brooks screamed at the driver who'd come out of the processing plant like someone had taken a mob hit out on them. Considering everything Bria had told her about those, whoever this asshole was probably deserved it, since she'd almost ended up in the ditch.

A few police cars pulled out right after, but they went in the opposite direction in a much calmer rate of speed. She pulled back on the road and followed, not surprised when they pulled into Long Willows. Her father was someone the police chief liked to be friendly with and keep happy, so these guys most likely had something to report. She turned in and drove to the parking spots out back.

The kitchen smelled like her childhood, and the memories came like a Southern May flood when the rains fell for days. She stared at the older woman stirring something at the stove, and a wave of melancholy swept over her. Sarah Jones had been cooking here for forty-five years, and Brooks loved her like family. Sarah had been widowed early and never seemed interested in remarrying. Instead, she'd spent a lot of time taking care of her and her siblings with the kind of devotion she would have shown her own children.

Brooks had sat here plenty of afternoons, confessing her life to Sarah as if she'd put truth serum in the food. It didn't matter which one of her siblings it was, Sarah always listened without judgment. They could all count on that, and that her food was always good. Her beautiful blond hair had more white streaked in it than the last time Brooks had been home, but Sarah didn't seem ready to retire.

"I hope that's shrimp stew," she said, and Sarah screamed.

"Jesus." Sarah put her hand to her chest, laughing. "You trying to give me a heart attack, you big ox? Your mama told me you were coming, so would it be anything else?" Getting a hug from Sarah always made her warm even if the older woman only came up to her midchest. "Welcome home, Brooks. You should be ashamed that it took you so long."

"I know Mom hates the work excuse, but that's all I seem to be doing lately." She kissed the top of Sarah's head and let her go. "Do you want to tell me what's going on?"

"All I have to report is that today one of the fleet boats blew up." Sarah pointed to the chair and got a small bowl out. It was an hour before lunch, but not too early for a snack in Sarah's world. Loving them and feeding them was her life's mission. "The police are talking to your mother before they start their investigation."

"Interesting, but not what I want to know. Why am I here?" The bowl full of brown gravy, shrimp, and rice triggered all the pleasure sensors in her brain, momentarily halting all her questions.

"Wait for Scarlett since I'm too old to get fired and thrown in the street." Her father had built Sarah her own little house on the property when a local restaurant had tried to lure her away years before. Sarah's house had come with a raise and a vehicle, though one of the guys usually drove her whenever she needed to make a supply run.

"Okay"—she took a bite and closed her eyes at how good it was— "what are the police investigating, then? The company doing so bad we've resorted to insurance fraud?"

Silence almost always told a complete story. When you had tests at the hospital and asked your doctor if you were going to make it, silence meant no, you would not. Silence in a church or at a funeral was a sign of respect. And silence after a question of insurance fraud was as good as admitting guilt. It was the opposite of a doctor's silence in that the answer was yes—yes, it was exactly that.

"Tell me the cops and fire department aren't suspicious." The stew in her bowl lost its appeal. "Is this why I'm here?" Just fucking great. There were enough federal agencies interested in her life. She didn't need to invite them in as a way to get to Angelo.

"Brooks, leave Sarah alone." Brooks was convinced Scarlett Boseman's voice could cut diamonds, and her mom face could stop a charging bull. Her mother had the stern expression down to that level of perfection. "Kiss me, and let's go talk in the office."

Brooks had to laugh as she embraced her mom and kissed her cheek. A lot of people could learn plenty from Scarlett when it came to getting things done.

The office was her father's domain. Getting summoned into the teak-lined room that smelled of leather and cigars was the equivalent of a trip to the woodshed when they were kids. Blowing up a boat deserved at least the old man coming out and saying hello if he wanted her help getting Curtis's balls out of the fire. She'd only been in the house ten minutes, and she was ready to go. She found this place and everything it stood for oppressive.

"What the hell, Mom?" She stopped them in the hall, not anxious to face the man who'd never given her a bit of credit. All that crap he'd said to her had thickened her hide, as her grandmother was fond of saying, but it still ached. The memory of the words cut just as deep as when he'd uttered them. She stared at all the old framed photos in the hall, and in an instant she decided it wasn't worth it. Trying to reach an unattainable finish line wasn't worth another moment of her life.

"Brooks, we don't deserve it—your understanding, I mean—but I'm asking for it. Once we talk, you have the right to leave if that's what you choose to do."

This was a new approach. "Let's go, then. We wouldn't want to keep him waiting."

"Your wit and sarcasm I'm sure have gotten you far, but I'd appreciate it if you turned it down just a notch. All you need to know is I asked you here because *I* need you here." Her mom opened the door to an empty room.

The sight of it was like cool fingers caressing up her spine, and not in a good way. It was ridiculous to hate a room, but this place was like a cursed empty pit that held nothing good. At least for her. "Tell me. All this buildup is giving me a headache."

They sat in the chairs by the window that overlooked the bayou. The ashtray on the table between them was empty, and it was a harbinger of something being very wrong. Maxwell Boseman was the original creature of habit, so the absence of all his visible vices meant he was either dead or close to it, and her mother was covering it all up for some reason.

"A year ago, your father suffered a small stroke." Her mother's hands went up when Brooks's back came off her chair. It was true she didn't live close, but a stroke was something someone should've told her about. "Please, Brooks, let me get to the end."

"A stroke? Why didn't you call me?" Jesus Christ on a walker, because a stroke called for more than a crutch. "You know full well why I don't come here a lot, but I'm still a part of this family unless I missed a memo. If you wanted to make me think I've been completely cut out, congratulations, I get it. Did he tell you not to call me?"

"You're my firstborn and will always be family, but you aren't like your brothers and sisters, and we didn't tell them either." Her mother wiped her eyes and took a deep breath. "You were first, and it wasn't perhaps fair, but we put a lot of expectations on you, more than the others. When I say *we*, I know you believe it was all your father."

"Today isn't about me, Mom." The effort not to be harsh was exhausting, so she tried to keep quiet.

"In a way it is, honey. You're the only one who wasn't afraid to fly from here and build a life that's your own. You're also levelheaded, and we need that right now more than ever."

"You've got a talent for rewriting history." She laughed at the speech and where it was headed. "*Do* you know what made me leave? You never asked me, so I doubt you do."

"Your father is a product of his upbringing—not that that's an excuse. Max had a set of beliefs that were instilled in him by generations of chauvinist assholes, and it's cost him. That price was something I've paid too, even if I didn't agree with him. I've lost so many years with you, Brooks, and I want that to end." That was something Brooks believed but had never heard her mom say. "And you're right. I never asked."

"It was Christmas of my junior year." She was impressed by her mom's words, but the river of resentment was vast and deep. Forgiveness would take time if it came at all. "Max told me I'd take whatever job he saw fit to give me, and my part of the equation was to be grateful for his generosity. In his opinion, I wasn't equipped to run the company, let alone a household, because of my deviant behavior. I wasn't the child he expected, much less wanted."

"Oh, Brooks." Her mom's tears started to fall as if she was in real pain. Ignorance or avoidance wasn't acceptable any longer, though, so she listened to what Brooks had to say.

"I couldn't stay here, but I had a problem. I was in love, and I knew she would've followed me if I'd asked, but I'd never make her give up so much. It hurt like hell to leave her, and to ensure that she didn't follow me, I made sure she hated me. She most likely feels exactly that, and I don't blame her for what she thinks of me."

"You should've come to me, sweetheart."

"For what? Back then you rarely disagreed with him, and I wouldn't do to her what Dad had done to me. No one should feel shame for who they love, and I'd never subject her to Max and all his delightful opinions. His belief was always that women had their place, and it wasn't running anything, except maybe children to school. You don't do that to someone you love, so I let her go because she loved me enough to put up with me if I hadn't." If she had a regret, Fallon Goodwin was the one most important person on her list.

They'd made so many plans in an apartment in Baton Rouge, and she'd made promises. She'd broken every single one when she got on a plane for England before the new year. She paid her way with what her grandmother had given her, and she'd never come back. Fallon hadn't understood, and Brooks had been too embarrassed to admit the truth of why she ran, what it would've cost Fallon and her entire family had she stayed and defied Max.

Fallon's family were devoted to each other, and it would've killed her slowly to live apart from them. That she knew, without Fallon having to explain it to her. Love shouldn't require so much sacrifice, at least not on Fallon's part. Brooks hadn't had the courage to face her and tell her she was leaving, so like a coward she'd left a note after that last conversation with her father, and she'd felt like shit for it ever since.

Brooks's junior year at LSU

"Don't make any plans this summer," Maxwell Boseman said, pointing to the chair across from his desk with the unlit cigar in his hand. He bought the biggest ones he could find as if compensating for something else. "I'm sending you out with one of the crews to prove to you this is a man's job."

She stared at him, trying to decipher if he was kidding. In the silence he clipped his smoke and put the torch to it, filling the space over his head with the bluish smoke that smelled like burnt tires. Sometimes size just meant big and not good. "That's what I've done for the last three summers. Is this some special boat where the guys will try and teach me what real men can do?"

"Once I'm finished paying for school, I'll find something for you, but Curtis will take over." He ignored her question and her reminder that she did indeed know the business from the grunt work up.

"I know what our business is better than you. The markets we sell to could care less what gender I am, and if you'd like to expand, get your mind out of the twelfth century. The places that have the highest profit margins won't put up with that kind of bullshit thinking." Two more weeks of this and she'd lose what was left of her shit.

These meetings weren't a voluntary exercise, though. They were Max's command performances, and her part was to sit quietly and listen. That's what he expected out of every female except her mother, who'd kill him in his sleep if he told her to shut up. This one had a definite tone to it, and she hoped he'd get to the point.

"Do you want to see how fucking funny you are after peeling shrimp all day?" His voice was gruff and loud, but he looked hilarious with the cigar bobbing up and down like a metronome with every word. He was angry, but she wasn't a kid any longer. Intimidation wasn't something he could pull off like he had when she was twelve.

"Why don't you stop, old man?" The words came out without any thought, and she could see they landed like a nuclear bomb in the middle of his forehead. His face was so red she thought he'd pop something vital. "No one, especially me, has said I'd work for you, so keep the tough man act for Curtis. You'll need to up your fear game to keep him from fucking up the company."

"You little bitch."

"Why am I a bitch? Because I'm not going to scrape and kiss your ass like Curtis? Guess what, that's never going to happen. I have plenty of opportunities that have nothing to do with the business. And considering who you intend to leave it to, I doubt it'll be around for another ten years." She was panting as hard as he was when she was done, but this macho act was wearing on her evolved mind.

"Oh yeah? You think Alfred Goodwin's going to welcome you with open arms? You think that's going to happen when he finds out about you? Don't deny it, I know all about that girl and what you've been doing. She's probably the reason you have all these ideas and where you learned your disrespect." He used the cigar to point at her, getting ashes all over the desk. "It's disgusting, so don't act like I'm the one who's wrong."

"Keep the company, Dad, and leave us the hell alone. If I have to peel shrimp all day, like you said, that's what I'll do to get away from you."

"You're not right in the head." He was getting louder, and it was sucking all the air out of the room. "No, I'm going to call Alfred and tell him his kid is as sick as mine, and I'm sure we can come up with some plan to fix this."

"Try it, and you won't like the results." She stood and leaned over the desk. When he pulled back it gave her a sense of satisfaction to know he could spew this crap, but he couldn't take it. "As for the girl, stay away from her, or you won't like my reaction to that either."

"If you have some illusion of coming back here, think again. No kid of mine is going to flaunt that kind of perversion where my family lives."

She wondered if he understood what he'd said. His family and his home. That didn't include her. "What's wrong with you?"

"What's wrong with me?" Her father stood and thrust the cigar at her again as if to make his point, and he ended up burning her chin. "There ain't shit wrong with me. Had I known you were defective, I'd have given you away. Get out and do me the favor of changing your name. Unless you fall in line, you're on your own."

"Consider it done, old man. You'll have to beg me to come home."

"Leave, but this isn't over. You stay around here with that slut, and I'm going to make your life a living hell. I'm starting with calling in the loan Alfred came here begging for. They're going to lose everything, and that little bitch and all the Goodwins will know it was because of you." He pointed the cigar at her again, and she'd had enough. She slapped it out of his hand and watched it roll against the wall. If he didn't want it to burn the house down, he'd have to go over there and pick it up.

Her chin hurt, but there was no way she'd give him the satisfaction of showing pain. "Remember what I said—leave her alone. You want me gone, I'm gone, and I won't ever come back. This is her home, though, and I won't deprive her of it." She crumpled the new cigar he'd pulled out and threw it at her feet. "You, though, are going to have to live with what you did. If Alfred really did come to you for a loan, trust me that I won't contact Fallon again. The only one who'll lose anything in all this is you."

"You'll be back in a week, begging me to take you in. You need me."

"I'll starve before I ask you for a fucking thing. Remember this, though, because if you ever need *me*, it'll be you who'll have to beg."

Present day

The slamming door was something she heard in her dreams sometimes. It was the literal moment she'd shut out her past and started on the life she had now. She'd been shaking when she drove to Fallon's to tell her what had happened and how they could start over somewhere else. Max's threats about the loan and what Fallon's family could lose stopped her.

It had taken that one glimpse through the front window of Fallon with her siblings laughing at something with their father to know she couldn't do that. This was where Fallon belonged, and she wouldn't be the reason they'd fall victim to Max's vindictiveness.

She tried to bury her feelings for Fallon from that moment on, and she'd worked hard to make a living. There was enough money in her bank account for her to disappear completely and eat pie all day if that's what she wanted. The drive she had to keep at it, though, she owed to her father, so she'd stay with Bria until she either got bored or there was no challenge in it any longer. No matter what she decided, she'd have to find someplace other than here to do her pie eating.

Bria had recommended talking to someone, and she wasn't opposed, but she liked who she was and the life she'd built. There was only one thing missing. It had been a while since she'd googled Fallon, but not because she wasn't interested. All that daydreaming of what could have been was her definition of an exercise in futility.

Leaving Fallon where she was had been her parting gift. This was where Fallon was the happiest, and she was working to build on her family's success. The Goodwins had been there to support her through the worst, of that Brooks had no doubt, and at times she was jealous of the way they loved each other. She was successful, but forever an outsider.

"What is it you want from me?" If it was to make amends, she was talking to the wrong parent.

"Your father wants to talk to you, and he's smart enough to know you'd never come if it was him asking. There's that, and I want to talk to you before you make your decision." Her mom grabbed her hand as if she was afraid she'd run. "If you don't feel you can, no one's going to force you, but think about it."

"You still haven't said what all this is about. I'm not that fragile, Mom, just tell me." Her phone buzzed in her pocket and she ignored it. Bria wasn't her lover, but she'd become her family, and she liked checking in. That protective streak doubled when Brooks got morbid, as Bria liked to call it.

"I don't agree with your father on a lot of things, but I promised him I'd make the call." Her mom let her hand go, and it was like being set adrift. "I needed you here more than he does. All this is getting to me, and I need your strength, Brooks."

In the years she'd lived in New York, her mom had come to visit often. She'd come alone a few times and with one of her sisters and Etienne when they said missing her drove them to want to see her. She'd introduced them to a couple of her dates, and they hadn't disappointed her when it came to acceptance. Not that any of those women were permanent, but what she wanted was acceptance of who she truly was. It was time to return the favor, no matter what her mother wanted.

"Where is he?" She didn't need to think about it. If Max wanted to see her, she'd meet with him because carrying the weight of Fallon was enough—she didn't need any other burdens. "I see bravery isn't one of his strong character traits if he has you doing his dirty work."

"The other thing I don't have a right to ask is for mercy, but I'm going to anyway. At least please consider it." Her mom was still crying and staring at her as if begging for her to give in to what she was asking.

"For you I'll try, Mom, but I don't know if I can say for sure." She'd never admitted every single hurtful thing her father had said, not in its entirety to anyone, not even her mother. There was no denying Max was a product of his upbringing, but that was no excuse to treat your child like shit.

His feelings toward her not only were painful to hear, but they also embarrassed her. When someone who was supposed to love her instead tried to convince her to feel shame for something she had no more control over than the color of her hair, it was wrong. It also made her question how the world saw her, and it had made her withdraw until she'd met Bria.

Bria had taught her to see things another way until it sank into her thick head, as she loved to say. She hadn't chosen to be born, that she knew with certainty, just like she knew she had no control over what family she was born into. What had confused her for years was why have children at all if you couldn't be accepting? In Max's case the answer was simple enough, she guessed. He wanted heirs not only to carry on the business but to carry on all those beliefs he held dear.

"It's a lot to expect of you, but you're the best of us." Her mom stood and hugged her. "The truth is, it's us who failed you, not the other way around. To me, in my eyes, you are perfect just the way you are, my love. I'm sorry you were told otherwise."

"Thanks," she said, holding her mom. "We've got a long way to go, but we'll get there."

CHAPTER FOUR

Fallon was still shaking after almost hitting the truck right outside Boseman's. There was no way she could blame it on the guy in the truck—she'd been angry, and her control had slipped to the point of recklessness. She'd find them and apologize, but the cursing she was sure the other driver sent her way was enough to make her want to skip that. All she had to do now was get a hold of her father before he worked himself into a tizzy if he'd seen the contract.

"Then Mom can go ahead and print those retractions because there's no way in hell I'm going to an engagement party with someone I don't even want to be in a room with." She drove the ten miles to her parents' place not wanting to call ahead. Her dad had mentioned a fishing trip in the morning, and the big house down here was the easiest place to launch from.

She laid her head back for a moment and tried to figure out for the millionth time the moment her life had run this far not only off the rails but off the stratosphere. It all came back to fucking Brooks. Their life had been planned out down to the fourth kid before Brooks ran as fast as her big feet could carry her. The shithead ran all the way to England, so having a conversation in person had been impossible.

She'd been more in the mood to clobber Brooks, even though she wasn't a violent person. "Goddammit, stop feeling sorry for yourself. She's the fucking asshole, not you." Thank God she had the car and the steering wheel to take her frustrations out on. It saved a pile of money for a therapist who'd tell her it was all on Brooks. That's what she got from the one and only therapist she'd actually seen. Once she'd heard that, she'd felt vindicated for her murderous thoughts toward Brooks the shithead.

The slamming door brought her back out of her head to glance in the rearview mirror. "Ah man, fuck me." Seeing Curtis walking toward her wasn't something she was in the mood for.

He got in on the passenger side, and plenty came into focus. Her life went to shit the moment she'd decided to move on and had picked Brooks's brother. He'd been what she'd needed when they'd met, but she should've seen the landmines her feelings for him would cause.

Curtis was his own man, but he was still Brooks's brother. They were nothing alike, especially when it came for their feelings for her. Brooks had run away from her, and Curtis had done nothing but run toward her. That should've been enough—he wanted her and it should've been enough. The big problem, though, was she'd never felt the same level of warmth with him that she had when Brooks held her.

"Hey, I had to chase you down." He smiled, and she wasn't immune. Curtis was handsome, somewhat charming, and his face was so like the one she'd fallen for. The stubble of his five o'clock shadow ruined the effect, though. Her blond hair next to Brooks's dark made a good contrast in her mind. But it was those dark green eyes that had made her wish their children inherited that from Brooks. The eye color had skipped Curtis. "Why'd you run off so fast?"

"I didn't want any part of whatever the hell that was." She got out and leaned against her car and crossed her arms so he'd get the hint she didn't want to be touched. "I also didn't appreciate your tone before your boat blew up. If you think you're going to roll over me, think again. I'm your friend, not your banker."

"Fallon, come on." He moved closer and leaned against the car next to her. "I've been under a lot of pressure, so I'm sorry. I was wrong, and to prove it, go ahead and rip up that contract if you want. We need new boats, but there's other options that won't make you feel like I'm trying to get one over on you."

"What was that today? We both know boats don't blow up for no reason." She tried not to grimace when he pressed against her. He was sweaty and smelled like smoke. "We don't have time right now to talk about your ideas of what you think our relationship is supposed to be. But maybe it's time to—"

"I know you want to talk, so let's make the time," he said, cutting her off. "We'll have dinner and go over everything. We can also finalize things for the engagement party. Your mom has called a few times, and it's like in a week."

"Let's finish the talk we really need to have before we finalize anything." He reacted like she'd just zapped him with a cattle prod. "I told you I needed time to think, but you and everyone else including my mother is anxious to rush me to an altar. It isn't going to happen unless I'm ready for what comes after that. I don't know how else to explain it."

"I'm not trying to rush you into anything. We'd be good together, and it's the only reason I asked. Get back to me and we'll do that dinner, but I've got to get back." He left before she could say anything else, and she couldn't figure all this out. Instead of clearing her mind, talking to Curtis had confused her more.

She watched him go and wondered if he'd started self-medicating or perhaps was drinking heavily and she hadn't noticed. That wasn't important or worth thinking about as the front door opened and her father waved her over. Her mother might not have understood her, but her dad did and hadn't taken her news of marriage to Curtis well at all.

"Hey, Dad." There wasn't much she could count on staying consistent in her life, but Alfred Goodwin never disappointed her on that score. Her father wasn't a big guy, but he loved each of them, told them that all the time, and was always ready to stand up for any of them.

"Is your dog sick or did it run away?" Her dad kissed her forehead and swayed them side to side as he hugged her.

"I don't have a dog."

"Could've fooled me, kiddo. Come in and tell me what's bothering you without me having to smack you with limp noodles." He led her to the back of the house and the line of rockers on the porch. "What's wrong?"

"Plenty, and I have no clue where to start."

"The beginning is always good." Her father stuffed tobacco into his pipe but didn't light it. "One of your problems is there's excited blushing brides, and then there's you. Do you want to start there?"

She shook her head, not ready to admit how unsure and skittish she'd become. "No, right now let's talk about business. I'm sure someone told you about the contract with Boseman."

He nodded, but she couldn't tell if it was in agreement or him simply listening. "That's enough to get you into those fancy boats you're dying to start up."

"Give me more credit than that, Dad. Curtis could no more pay for all those boats than I could swim across the Atlantic. My plans aren't dependent on this, and Curtis pulled the contract." None of this was her fault, but she was still responsible for the amateur misstep. "Who gave me up?"

"Your brother and sisters didn't say a word, so stop frowning. It wasn't anyone in the company either, but I have my sources. All you need to know is I have faith in *you*, so I wasn't worried."

"What do you mean?" She was confident in the job he'd trusted her with, but at times she still craved his approval.

"I don't care what Curtis did with the contract. There's no way in hell you would've gone through with that. That I'm sure about, but why you're with Curtis is still a complete mystery."

That made her laugh. "He showed up at the right time. I needed a friend and he was that, but then he wanted more."

He smiled at her in that way that should've been followed by a *bless your heart*. That was in no way a compliment or comfort. "Let me tell you something, kiddo. You went off to college and were happier than me in the middle of a school of tuna on opening day. That Boseman kid looked at you like you were the sun she was orbiting around. Then she disappeared, and you haven't smiled the same since."

"That was over a long time ago, Dad." Leave it to her father to figure out what her mom refused to see.

"Got that too, so let me finish. Something happened, and I think you still haven't figured that one out, but when you were together, your mama wanted different for you. Not that she would've tried to change your mind, but your life would've been easier had you picked different. Your mom figures someone like Curtis is just that." He reached over and held her hand. "I only want you to be happy, that's it."

"Thanks, Dad."

"No need for thanks, it's just the truth. The day you came home with Curtis, though, your mama perhaps pushed until you were cornered. You came home with the right model in her eyes even if she'd said otherwise forever, and the next thing that happened, invitations were printed, and you thought you were stuck." They nodded together. "The thing to remember is it's just paper, darlin'. Don't get bullied into contracts of any kind."

"Thanks, and I'd appreciate if you had this talk with Mom."

"Do you want to go fishing to escape your mother?"

"That would be great, but I love you too much to put you in the crosshairs." She kissed his cheek when he stood as his friends headed up from the water. They were going to the camp her dad had in the marsh. "Have fun."

"Remember to speak up or your frown's going to be permanent, and that I love you."

She sat back down and stared out as her father and his friends took off. Her phone buzzed with a message, and she sighed at Curtis's name. It was an invitation to dinner the next night, and he added a rose emoji. Those were something she didn't understand, so she responded with just *yes*. There was no reason to elaborate with cute little pictures.

The trip back to the city gave her time to think about all the work they had coming up and how she really wished Curtis could afford the contract Stacey in sales had written up. To her, stagnation came from not taking chances, and that wasn't in her nature. It wasn't like she wanted to bet the whole company on black at the roulette table. A loan could expand their business in ways that would lead to better things, but her father was allergic to going to the bank unless it was to make a deposit.

"Where are you?" Eliza asked when she answered her phone.

"On my way home. I went down the bayou to see Curtis and Daddy. Everything okay?" She reached the on-ramp of the interstate and pressed down on the accelerator. All she wanted now was to open a bottle of wine and sit in the tub until her skin pruned. Maybe if she stared at a candle long enough, she'd hypnotize herself into the new personality Eliza had mentioned. "Please tell me I don't have to go back to the office."

"*No*," Eliza said, elongating the word. It was her sister's tell. Had they been playing poker, she'd have the advantage.

"Go ahead and spit it out. I can't possibly be in a worse mood, so now's the time if you have bad news." She let up a bit on her speed when she noticed she'd passed ninety-five.

"Oh, I don't know about that," Eliza mumbled but was still understandable.

"Focus, will you," she said to reel Eliza back in.

"I had lunch with Monroe today."

Monroe Boseman and her sister had danced around each other since junior high, but neither of them made a move to commit. It was for the best, since committing to any Boseman was risky business. Everyone should stay the hell away from all those pesky feelings. Sex was the best level to keep any relationship on. That she'd testify to in court, considering how often Brooks could make her eyes roll back in her head. She'd barely kissed Curtis, and she planned to keep it that way. She in no way wanted to have sex with him, and she was sure that wasn't how it was supposed to go. Freud would have a field day with her.

"And you had to save her from choking on a hush puppy?" What pleasure did people get from dragging stuff out to the point you wanted to hold them at gunpoint to get them to start talking?

"*No*," Eliza said, making the word longer than necessary again. "She had breakfast with Brooks."

She slammed her hands on the steering wheel but otherwise stayed quiet. Of course she knew Brooks came to town every so often to visit her parents, but she'd never reached out. At least she'd kept her distance and not tried to give her some weak excuse for treating her like dirt. The trips Brooks had made seemed to last only a few days, and she was never around long enough for them to run into each other.

Curtis had invited her as a friend for Christmas last year, and she'd started working on her ulcer way in advance in preparation for seeing Brooks again. She'd arrived to a home full of Bosemans except for the one who mattered. It had been Scarlett who'd told her Brooks had come for the day on the twenty-third and left a few hours later. When Brooks had cut ties, it seemed it was with more than just Fallon.

Brooks hadn't even spent the night, and the family—except for Curtis—seemed subdued without their older sister not being there not only for the holiday, but ever. The most sullen of the group had been Max. Brooks's absence had quieted his usual opinion-filled commentary, and while Fallon enjoyed the peace, it was unnatural. At least, she'd guessed it was his eldest not sitting at his table that had prompted his silence.

She caught him staring at her a few times not only as if it was her fault that his missing kid was gone, but also that there was no world peace because of her sorry existence. Scarlett was the one she felt the most for, but she'd tried to smile throughout the day. The only times Scarlett's smile slipped was when she glanced at the family photos. Scarlett stared at them as if her table was a jigsaw puzzle missing the most important piece that completed the picture.

The pain was something she couldn't ever figure out. Brooks had abandoned them all without thought, and the hurt her family must have felt only made her hate Brooks more. It was like Brooks's soul had died one day, and no one mattered anymore. That was not at all the person she'd fallen in love with, and still missed, though she was loath to admit that.

"When did Monroe become such a jet-setter?" She had to force the words out, and it woke her anger at herself. Brooks shouldn't matter when it came to anything, and asking was a personal defeat.

"It's shrimp season, sis. Monroe would no more leave for New York than she would shave her head and tattoo a crab on the top. No, Monroe had breakfast with Brooks at the Piquant." Eliza paused and sighed. "The prodigal prize of the litter has returned."

"Why are you telling me this?" She didn't care what the hell Brooks did or who she had breakfast with. "And she's not the prodigal anything. Brooks is an asshole, but she never cared about the family's money or possessions. That's what prodigal means."

"Good Lord, would you focus. I'll meet you at home so we can prepare."

"*No,*" she said, proving she too could make the word last an hour and a half. "Just finish up at the office, but take your time. You can still come over—I just need time to think."

"Curtis hasn't mentioned anything happening that has to do with his father, has he?" The question was like someone coming out of nowhere and tackling you to the ground. Totally unwarranted and unexpected.

She hadn't seen Max since Christmas, but she hadn't given him much thought. The old guy wasn't one of her favorite people, and she was glad Curtis's view of life in general was a world apart from his father's. Now that Eliza started this conversation, she was surprised not to have seen him today. Max, from what Curtis had said repeatedly, hadn't wanted to let go of the reins.

"Curtis only complains at his lack of freedom to do what he wants. He rarely talks about his family except to complain. What does that have to do with anything?"

"Monroe didn't tell me everything. I picked up on that, but she's a hardhead when she wants to be."

"Are you losing your touch?" She couldn't help but laugh. The need to question how much worse her life could get was something she really needed to overcome. "I would've been willing to gamble a month's salary you'd have all the facts by now even if it took tying Monroe to a chair and dripping shrimp juice on her head."

"You're hilarious, and I didn't push Monroe because she seemed sad and anxious. There's something up with the old man Max, though, and no one's talking. All Monroe said was she hoped Brooks stayed. Scarlett summoned her, so that means it's serious, don't you think?" Eliza was being tactful, or as tactful as her sister ever got.

"This is all news to me, so I'm not sure why you're telling me all this." She did know, but she needed to collect her emotions before they scattered like confetti. Seeing Brooks again was something she needed to work on until she was sure she'd give nothing away. "There isn't anything I can do about it."

"You have an engagement party in a week," Eliza said as if she was trying to talk her off a high ledge. "Are you ready to face Brooks with Curtis standing next to you?"

"What part of the fact that Brooks left me do you all not understand? It won't matter who I'm standing next to."

Eliza laughed as if she had just told a good joke, and Fallon was sure the universe was laughing with her. "Go home and drink something and I'll come over later."

"I'm not going to worry about that now, and I want to talk to Curtis tomorrow before I commit to anything." She slapped her steering wheel again and bit back a groan. "Today was not a good day, and it clouded my view of our future."

"Are you calling it off?"

The questions made her want to say yes, but something made her hesitate. "Would it be bad if I say yes?"

"His dad might be dying. You're not that cruel. You can make it through one night with a big smile on your face. You also need to find the sexiest dress in the city." Eliza sounded as if she was making a list Fallon was expected to follow to a T.

"Did you not understand the part where I'm not sure? The last thing I want to do is appear like I'm hunkering down for a long and happy marriage." Pretty soon she was going to start researching caves she could run away to. There had to be something on Vrbo or Airbnb that came with animal skins she could wear while hiding from the world.

"Believe me, you do not want to look like you live in the swamp. Do you want Brooks to think you've been pining?" There was a span of silence that was uncomfortable. "Uh, the correct answer here is no to the pining or living in a swamp. You need to project someone in charge who thinks of her as something under your shoe that needs to be scraped off."

"On second thought, don't come over. I want to be alone." She glanced around the car in search of the hidden cameras. "I'll see you tomorrow for our shopping trip." She said that with the enthusiasm of someone waiting for an enema.

"Try not to overthink, and whatever you do, don't spiral."

"Got it. No overthinking or spiraling." She ended the call before Eliza added anything to her list.

Of course she was going home to do both those things with a large dose of panic. "Can you tell me what I did?" she asked the roof of the car, so whatever Supreme Being would hear her. "Just so I don't do it again." As usual, there was no answer, and she was on her own.

Brooks stood outside the main bedroom, trying to figure out what the hell she was feeling. Her father had never been one of her favorite people, yet she hurt for him. A stroke hadn't been the end for him, so there had to be something else. Par for the screwed-up course her mother didn't bother to lay out for her.

She opened the door to save him from talking. He was sitting up on the bed with a pile of pillows behind him. The blue pajamas, like the pillows, didn't seem right, and he stared at her as if he was having trouble coming up with her name. Hell, she'd been gone a long time, but she hadn't aged to the point of being unrecognizable.

"Brooks." He said her name with his hand out toward her. It dropped just as quickly, and he started crying.

In truth, that freaked her out more than the market ever could. Maxwell, male extraordinaire, never shed a tear even when they seemed appropriate. Her grandfather dying, the loss of one of his dearest friends, throwing his kid out with disgust were all tear-worthy, but Max hadn't managed one then. Facing a sobbing control freak now had her itching to escape.

"Max, take a breath." After that night she'd never been able to call him *Dad* again. He'd lost that right, and he seemed to flinch whenever she said his name. When she visited, he kept his distance after a quick hello. He acted as if he couldn't deal with the sight of her, so this was strange and an out of character response. "You wanted to talk to me?"

"Brooks, thank you." He wiped his face and followed her advice and took some deep breaths. "Thank you…for coming." His speech pattern was stilted and breathy, making her come closer so he could save his strength.

"How are you?" Damn, she'd had a better rapport with the little shit Yang had sent as his representative for the meeting with Bria. It was all her frozen brain could come up with, though.

"Not great." His chuckle was strained. "I've had a month of sitting here with daytime television."

"That'll rot your brain." She mentally slapped herself. They didn't have the best relationship, but there was no reason to be insensitive.

His laugh was more genuine this time. "That's why the damn thing is off. I didn't need an exceler—" He seemed confused all of a sudden and couldn't finish the word. "I didn't need to speed things up. All the quiet gave me time to inventory my life, and I keep coming to one conclusion."

"What's that? That your life has been great except for throwing your kid away because of all the damn deviance?" There was feeling sorry for someone and then there was reality. Max made it hard to ignore the truth of what he'd done, no matter how feeble he appeared.

"You're never going to believe me, kid, but I was wrong. I can't make it up to you, but I am sorry. I don't have that much time, so I hope you know that I mean that."

"No need to get dramatic, Max. Mom said the stroke wasn't that serious." They needed to get to the business of whatever this was. She had a life to get back to. "I'm sure if you follow the doctor's advice, you'll be fine in no time."

"I need you to accept my apology." The tears were back, and he acted desperate. Again, this was so out of character for him. Max would fall on his sword before he showed any weakness, but he sounded contrite and genuine. "What I did, all that stuff I told you…it shames me. There was no excuse for my behavior, and I don't expect you to believe me right off, but I need you to hear me." He sped up his words as if he was afraid she'd run out on him before he finished.

"What's this about?" She studied him, and he seemed okay aside from being a little pale. "Is there something more than the stroke?"

"The doctor diagnosed your father with early onset Alzheimer's," her mom said from the door. Brooks closed her eyes tight at the news. "The doctor has some ideas for some drug trials, so we're going to stay optimistic." Her mom came in and sat next to her dad, taking his hand and kissing the back of it.

"I still have my mind, so don't think this is about me trying to clear my slate before I work my way to becoming a stalk of celery." Her father held her mom's hand in both of his. "I don't have that much time before I lose the world I know. The doctors keep telling me I might be here, but I'm not going to be. Understand?"

"I don't know what to say."

"Don't say anything. I'm not afraid to die, Brooks. It happens to all of us no matter the life we've led. What I don't want is to fade away with you not knowing how sorry I am. Like I said, at least I think about it. You might not believe me, but I need to know that you heard me say the words. I hope you come to believe them."

"Don't make it sound like it's happening tomorrow," her mom said. The way they were both staring at her was disconcerting.

It was a lot to absorb. Actually, it was like playing dodgeball when it was one against five thousand. She was getting pummeled, and there was no escape. "Did you get a second opinion?"

"More than a couple," her father said. He seemed to tighten his hold on her mom's hand. "I started noticing a while back, before the stroke. It was hard to focus, and the day-to-day stuff was like trying to grab smoke and hold on to it."

"So you put Curtis in charge full-time?" That had to be true if her mom was here taking care of him. Curtis had finally gotten what he'd been promised all his life, and her brother and sisters were most likely in the same state of mind as Monroe. They all worked for the company, and having Curtis at the helm was bad news for their job prospects.

"You can go ahead and say it." Her dad smiled in a way she hadn't seen in years. It was as if he'd found his sense of humor again. "Any one of you would be better than Curtis, but the best choice, the only choice I should've made, was to pick you. If you were at the helm, I could die in peace, knowing everyone won't be homeless in a week."

"Just explain that to Curtis, Etienne, Pru, and Charlie. If they work together, everything should be fine." There was no way she was coming back here to fight Curtis and her siblings for control of the company she had no connection to any longer. With acceptance came peace, she'd read somewhere, and she'd accepted that their family business belonged to the rest of the Bosemans, not her.

"Could you come back?" her father asked. He went from a laughing figure to what seemed like an empty balloon. He was completely drained.

"I'm not going anywhere, so rest." She stood and hesitated before leaving. "We'll talk some more, but I did hear you. Thank you for apologizing. What's done is done, but there's no reason for us to not—" There was no way to finish that without sounding like an ass, so she stopped.

"I know, Brooks. It only counts if you believe me, and I'm not so gone yet to know you don't. That you're not so easily swayed makes me proud that we raised someone who can not only survive without us, but thrive because I gave you no other choice. You weren't wrong in thinking your old man's an asshole." He nodded and covered his mouth as he yawned. "Just don't take it out on your mom."

"Take a nap, old man, and I'll be here when you wake up." After a day of stress, she finally laughed. "Everything will be okay, and we have to have faith that the drugs will work."

She waited in the office until her mother came back down. The weight of a Mack truck fell on her shoulders, and it was too much to think about. She'd never damned her father for being such a mean bastard, but if she had, she would've never picked this. Alzheimer's was something she'd researched for some drug stock they'd invested in, and it was the cruelest of ways for someone to go. It robbed not only the patient but their families of the time they had left.

"The strain of trying to function wears him down." Her mom wiped her face of the tears she probably cried every day and sat next to her after pouring herself a drink. "I thought he was remarkable when I met him, but now I find him extraordinary."

"I'm so sorry, Mom. Why didn't you call me sooner?"

"There was no way to know all this would come of one small stroke." Her mom laughed, and it sounded bitter. "Whatever the hell that means, but the doctors kept repeating it. Your father took it in stride and told everyone he was taking some time off but refused to let everyone know what'd happened. The stroke sped up his decline, yet he wills himself to keep going until he can leave us all in a good place."

"If you think that place is me at the head of the business, that's not going to happen. I can't come back here, and I won't leave Bria." She needed to get out for a bit and breathe.

Her mom finished the small amount of bourbon and shook her head. "Brooks, I'm not clueless. The last thing I want is for you to uproot your life. What I want is for you to help us right the ship without you having to pour money into the business. That's not why I called you."

"Can you simply tell me what you want? I feel like I've been stuck in a mystery novel since I arrived."

"Easy." Her mom smiled at her, and it made her smile in return. "Stay, look at the books, and step in for your father. Once you figure out what the best course is, you need to make the decision as to who is best equipped to take over."

"Is that all? Hell, why didn't you say?" In her parents' opinion, this was probably the best solution since she was already an outsider. If her siblings hated her, she'd be getting on a plane once all the decisions were made, and they could heap the blame on her.

"We both know that the best thing—actually the simplest and best thing—we could do is sell. That's the smartest play, but I can't do that while he's still alive. Even if he doesn't recognize any of us, I don't want him living knowing he was the one who failed." Her mother would've been good at closing deals. She used guilt more effectively than anyone she'd ever met.

"When will he wake up?"

"He's better in the mornings. Today he waited for you, hoping you'd come." Her mom hugged her, and it eased the intense feelings warring inside her. "I know you're probably going to be more comfortable in town, but I'll get your room ready if you're willing to come and stay with us."

"I'm not leaving you, but what happened today?" Considering who her business partner's father was, she was familiar with the police and their involvement at times. The authorities, though, didn't make a habit of coming to your house to announce an investigation. "And let's promise to be honest with each other. If, and I mean if, I stay to help you, nothing will be gained by lying to each other. We may not always like what the other has to say, but it cuts through the bullshit."

"Is that your secret to success?" Her mom seemed to enjoy holding her hand.

"My secret is hard work and commitment, and those traits I learned from my parents. The thing you should believe above all else is you might've disappointed me, but I've never hated you. I love you both."

"You're a gift, Brooks," her mom said, tears falling again.

"One you might want to take back once you tell me what happened and I give you my opinion."

She listened to her mother's explanation and what she knew about the explosion from what the police had told her. The expert who happened to be on-site when it happened suspected arson, and the local guys were chasing that theory down. If their boats were in as bad a shape as she suspected, arson as a way of updating the fleet wouldn't be hard to prove. All they had to do now was wait on filing an insurance claim.

"This should be fun." Reeling Curtis in from the abyss of bankruptcy alone would be torturous. If he was trying to commit insurance fraud as a business plan, Boseman's was in more trouble than she thought.

Hell, it shouldn't be this hard. They sold seafood, and unless you were allergic or had religious reasons not to eat it, everyone mostly loved shrimp, fish, and oysters. It was like selling chocolate. Even McDonald's sold seafood. It might be a square piece of fish that she at times questioned came out of the water, but it was still seafood, for the love of Poseidon.

"I know. Your brother has tried hard to run the company the way your father did, but with all that's been going on, I haven't had a chance to check up on him. The police coming by today was a surprise." Her mom sounded like a woman who didn't need another thing put on her plate of problems. "We've had some issues lately, but he's working hard. No one's told me otherwise yet."

"I'm not saying Curtis blew up a boat for the insurance payout, but if he did and he's caught, he might forfeit more than the business. That kind of fraud carries some serious jail time." There was also the fact that Curtis was one of the most obnoxious people on the planet. He wouldn't last a week in jail before someone shanked him. "If you want, I'll stay a couple of weeks and look at the books. Once I do that, I'll lay out a plan to move forward. I can't force anyone to follow my advice, and if they can't handle brutal honesty, I'll leave it with you."

"Can you do that in two weeks?" her mom asked.

"We'll see, but the business doesn't have that many facets. You catch, cull, clean, and sell different types of seafood. It's not like a company with a thousand divisions." She thought of the deal she was trying to make with Yang. Five different countries, with seventy-five divisions. Boseman wasn't anywhere close to that. "Don't worry, I won't leave you hanging." That's what a small part of her wanted to do, but she was slightly more mature than the average bear.

The business according to her father hadn't been a place for her, so she shouldn't give a shit now. Her problem was she did. She needed to know that the business that had spanned so many generations would continue to do so for her siblings and their families. It was her turn to make a mark even if she'd never have another thing to do with it.

CHAPTER FIVE

The small water stain on Fallon's ceiling was still the same as the day before. She'd purchased the Acadian style three-bedroom in the Garden District two years ago and poured her time into the renovation. She didn't literally do the reno, but she was involved in every aspect. The moment the contractor handed over the keys and she'd moved in, it'd rained on her head the first night. She hadn't painted the ceiling yet to remind herself that even when you got everything you wanted, it still wasn't perfect.

She'd set an alarm but couldn't motivate herself to get out of bed. Shopping for a dress for a party she didn't want to go to was the equivalent of a root canal by a pack of angry gorillas. Her phone rang and she reached for it, smiling when Bea said hello.

"Are you dressed yet?"

"I'm staring at the stain on my ceiling. I keep waiting for it to open a portal into an alternate universe, but no such luck."

"We thought the sooner we get through this, the faster we can get to lunch, which will mostly consist of liquids poured out of fancy liquor bottles." There was someone else talking on Bea's end, and Fallon strained to listen. "Frankie's in, so go take a shower."

"Frankie needs a new dress too?" She laughed before taking a deep breath to get going.

"He said he's going with linen, but he'll be happy to offer vetoes if necessary." Bea offered to pick her up in forty minutes, then hung up.

Fallon was ready in thirty and had finished her coffee when Franklin blew his horn. No matter what came next, she could count on these guys to get her through.

Their mother was waiting at Saks, and with any luck it'd be the only stop they'd have to make. The third floor housed most of the eveningwear, but she sent everyone up ahead, wanting to find a pair of shoes first. If her feet hurt, she'd leave before she finished her first drink, and she didn't need an etiquette book to know that was bad form.

The clerk was pulling some selections, so she sat and chewed on the hangnail on her thumb like it was her job. Was it wrong to wish she had an identical twin so they could trade places until all this wedding hoopla was over? One day they could make a movie out of that—if only that twin materialized before Saturday.

There was something to be said for ripping things off your body with your teeth. If she'd been clearing her email from her phone as was her habit, she'd have missed her. All the years since the last time she had seen Brooks in person had done nothing to dull her body's initial reaction. In all the pictures she'd found of Brooks when she was pretending not to stalk her, Brooks was in a suit with a severe expression on her face. It made her think Brooks had forgotten how to be happy.

This, though, was her Brooks. The dark jeans and the untucked white shirt made it easy to see how tall Brooks was. She loved this relaxed version, who'd done things like dancing with her in the rain or serenading her in the car. She was shocked when her vision blurred because her eyes filled with tears. God, this was so stupid. Brooks was on the escalator moving away from her, which was what she did. She was never moving toward her, so going to the engagement party was going to be extra special now.

"All we need is dramatic music and the right lighting, and we'll have our own soap opera." She took two pairs of shoes and headed to the elevator. Meeting Brooks again was a given, but not today. Nope, today was for drinks with her family and crying in the shower when she got home.

"Did you get lost or pick shoes that needed to be cobbled together by elves?" Eliza asked. She stopped her teasing when she noticed her face. Obviously it wasn't easy to hide tears.

"Not now, okay? Where's Mom?" She accepted a mimosa from Franklin and sat down to quash the urge to run.

"They have this one in all our sizes," her mom said. The dress she was holding against her body would've made a disco ball proud.

"We are not wearing matching outfits," Bea said, "unless Franklin gets one, and silver lamé is so not his color."

"Okay," their mother huffed. "I thought it would be fun, but what do I know? Everyone has a few selections in their dressing rooms, so get in there. If we can't find it here, we'll head to the boutiques on Royal next."

Everyone headed into the dressing room area, and they all ended up in Fallon's, including Franklin. "Frankie, I love you, but I'm not getting naked in front of you." They laughed, and Eliza stood in front of her as she undressed. She went for the black dress, thinking it was a perfect fit for her mood.

"Hurry before Hilda the Hun comes back with something more hideous than that silver dress from hell," Bea said. "What's going on with you? You usually don't get so weepy over shoes."

"I saw Brooks on the escalator." Just saying her name out loud made her tear up.

Was it foolish to think about—dream about, really—someone who wasn't worth the effort? The problem was Brooks had been perfect for her, so not thinking about her was impossible. She'd fit in a way that no one else had come close to, and one day that connection was severed. It was done and she'd had no say. The pain it had caused scarred her, and that scar had thickened with resentment.

Franklin raised his hand and snapped his fingers. "I freaking knew it. The only question is why in the world are you wasting your time with Curtis?" All her siblings said Curtis's name like they'd sucked a bad lemon.

"Because she can't appear like she's tossing everything down a hole because the marathon runner of relationships has come back." Bea sounded so wise, but nothing about Brooks was worthy of her time. "Your job is to find a dress that'll scream *You're a fucking loser, Brooks Boseman.* You need to show her not only that you're fine, but what a mistake she made."

"You think it's going to be that easy? I saw her, like, a mile away and I'm a total mess. If she talks to me, you're going to have to shoot me with a tranquilizer." She wiped her face again. "Why in the hell is she even here?"

"Haven't you heard?" Eliza said. She'd been quiet up to then, and her sudden announcement was something she probably didn't want to hear. "Her brother's getting married." She was right—Fallon didn't want to hear it.

"That's debatable, and Curtis hasn't mentioned her visit." She put the dress on and reached back for the zipper. "Believe me, we had some short conversations about Brooks in the beginning."

Bea finished the job of zipping her up. "You never told us that," Bea said.

"It's not his favorite subject, and it's a major understatement to say it's not mine either."

Their father had given her the chance to take over from him. He'd done that by stepping away while overseeing what they were doing. She was happy that he never second-guessed her, and he wasn't breathing down her neck constantly. Some things she and the family had had to learn on the job, but their father had given them the opportunity to do so.

Curtis wasn't forthcoming about his family's dynamic when it came to their business, much less anything else. His father *was* forever looking over his shoulder and berating him when he didn't get it right. Curtis never talked about it much, but the one thing he did confess in his own way with a lot of cursing was his dislike of his older sister. Curtis talked about Brooks as if he'd never live up to her, and Fallon doubted he realized that's how it was coming across. To her it sounded like pure jealousy. "He and Brooks don't get along, but I doubt Brooks knows anything about it. Curtis has built her up as the bogeyman in the closet who's waiting to take the company away from him."

"In the closet," Franklin said. "Interesting choice of words." They all laughed.

"You think she came back for you?" Eliza asked. The question made Franklin and Bea smile for some reason.

"None of you get any funny ideas," she said, and they all nodded. "Promise me you're not going to push Brooks on me."

"We promise," they all said together, holding up their hands.

"She forgot about me a long time ago, so maybe she is back for the engagement party. If she is, what a shitty thing to do." Unless Brooks had become a total asshole, she had to know what her attendance would do to her. That would be true even if she was madly in love with Curtis.

"Babe, you need to calm down. Monroe didn't quite say why Brooks is back, but I have a feeling the last thing in the world Brooks is aware of is you marrying Curtis." Eliza grabbed her by the shoulders and shook her gently. "You're going to be okay, and we promise we'll run interference. Brooks Boseman won't get within ten feet of you. If you do talk to her, it'll be because that's what you choose to do."

"It's only this party," she said, taking a deep breath. "I'm not going through with anything like this again."

"The only other thing wedding related you'll have to do is the honeymoon," Bea said.

"Again, let's not get ahead of ourselves. I'm not sure about Curtis, and everything else is just as confusing lately. I hate it."

"Nah, it's not for you and Curtis since we thought you'd never go through with this. We brought the honeymoon," Franklin, said twirling his finger to include all of them. "We're all planning to go with you, like in *Sex and the City*."

"Where are we going?" She had to laugh at her very metrosexual brother.

"We thought Paris, but Eliza thought that was too clichéd, so we picked Curaçao," Bea said. "It's less touristy than Aruba, but they have just as many drinks with umbrellas in them."

"Sounds as great as you guys." They all went to their dressing rooms after that and picked clothes so they could leave.

Their mother wanted to continue the shopping trip, but everyone refused and headed to the top floor of the shopping center for lunch. It gave her the rest of the afternoon for the bath she'd promised herself the night before. She texted Curtis and told him she'd meet him in the Quarter for dinner, not wanting to have him drive her home. For once she wanted to be selfish and take care of herself. That meant going home alone.

He readily agreed, making her think again that Curtis wasn't your average of the male species. She'd never dated men and had figured, incorrectly it seemed, they'd be more aggressive when it came to getting her into bed. That was something to be grateful for, she guessed.

She put on a sleeveless blouse and dark slacks that were just dressy enough for the restaurant they'd decided on. Curtis might not have pushed for sex, but the guy did love his meat. Mackie Blanchard's place was a favorite spot of his, so they'd gone often. The hostess let her down the stairs to the main dining room, and she'd beaten Curtis there, which was unusual, considering there was prime ribeye to be had.

She finished half a glass of wine before Curtis showed up, appearing agitated. "Hey, sorry I'm late."

Their waiter didn't even bother putting down a menu since Curtis always ordered the same thing, and nothing the color green appeared on his side of the table. "Everything okay?" With any luck someone would come in and arrest Curtis before the appetizers arrived. If that happened, she could go home and watch television in her pajamas and have chocolate-chocolate chip ice cream for dinner. That boat explosion had been on her mind.

"My sister's in town," he said, spitting the words out like a bad piece of cheese. "My mother called an hour ago to tell me and said we're having a family meeting in the morning."

Nonchalant. She repeated the word in her head ten times until she calmed down. "Why is she here?" She didn't have to say the name because in no way could it be Prudence or Charlotte he was this upset over.

"Hell if I know." The waiter dropped off a large glass of bourbon with a small ice garnish, and Curtis stared at it like he wanted to marry it instead of her. "Maybe my old man finally decided to cut her off for good and wants to do it in person for the entertainment value."

There could be no fucking way in this universe Max was still financially supporting Brooks. If anything, Brooks could buy and sell anyone in the family. Not that Fallon was a stalker, she just read the financial papers. "You don't think that, do you? You never did tell me what happened, but when Brooks left, I figured she didn't want any part of the business."

"I didn't think she did, but she might need the money. Who the fuck knows? Families are strange, and they can get nasty when it comes to their piece," he said, then took a long drink. It was enough bourbon to induce a coughing fit.

"But why did she leave? There had to be some reason she gave all of you."

"My father told her something before Christmas that year, and she couldn't handle the truth. I mean, did she really think she was going to run the company?" He laughed, and that answer made her even angrier.

The thought that Brooks had left her and everyone else behind because she hadn't gotten her way made Fallon want to hunt Brooks down with her car. If that was true, Brooks hadn't given a crap about her, and letting go hadn't required any thought. What a juvenile thing to do. "Is that what Maxwell told you?"

Curtis stared at her as if just noticing she was talking through clenched teeth. "You think Max talks to any of us about anything?" He laughed again. "He'll run things the way he wants with the people he wants until he's dead. What he wanted was the company to go to me and Etienne. My sisters will always have a job, but I'll be making the decisions." He took another long drink and pointed a finger at her with the glass still in his hand. "I'm the one equipped to handle it."

"Are you being serious right now?" This was a side of Curtis he'd kept well hidden. "I'm going to take over for my father—have already, if you ask him. Our future is going to be made with my sisters and brother working with me."

"Not all businesses are the same, Fallon, so they can't all be run the same. Anyway, none of this will matter once we're married."

"Please don't tell me it's because you want me to stay home and raise a family because I'm equipped for it." What she needed to get through this meal was the bottle of wine and a straw. It would save her the time of pouring it. "If it is, we need to end this right now. I'm not equipped to put up with that, especially from someone who's supposed to be my partner."

"God no. That's not what I'm saying. It's just that we'll be business partners in more than marriage. I'll have a say in what you do, and you have a say in mine. That's how it works since we're practically in the same business."

The really amazing thing about people was they didn't know how deep a hole to dig. They voluntarily picked up the shovel and didn't have the sense to glance up and notice how far down they were, how deep the hole was getting with each ridiculous thing that came out of their mouth. Curtis was a prime example of why it was important to stay quiet. He would be more aware of the people around him and what a fool they thought he was if he actually just paid attention and dropped the shovel.

"Look," she said with both hands up. If she needed to think about this, that was over. "I don't know about you, but I seriously rushed into this, and I'm having second thoughts."

"What? You can't be serious." Curtis could pull off earnest when he wanted to as he took one of her hands. "What can I do to reassure you?"

Curtis could also be a brick. "Let me rephrase. You took me by surprise, and while flattering, I have no interest in marriage right now. I said yes but said I needed time. I've taken time, and this isn't what I want." So much for a smooth and polite ending to spare his feelings. "You've been a good friend, and I've enjoyed our time together, but there's no way this is going to work out."

"Wow," Curtis said, his shoulders drooping. "You waited until less than a week before the damn party to tell me? Who does that?"

"In fairness, I've *been* trying to tell you. You've ghosted me because I think you knew this was coming, and you did it anyway. I had to track you down, and right when we were going to talk about it, a boat blew up." She almost laughed when his earnestness changed to victimhood in an instant. "Come on, don't act surprised." His scowl did make her laugh. "Tell me you're madly in love with me, and I'll apologize. I'm still not marrying you, but I will apologize."

He took more deep breaths than she thought necessary but shocked her when he answered truthfully. "I'm not madly in love, but this is a good move for both of us." He put his hands flat on the table when she cocked her eyebrow. "Okay, it's a good move for me."

"How so?" Her eyebrow wasn't coming down, and Curtis seemed to get more nervous. "And it's time for a complete honesty. You bullshit me and you'll need to find a stand-in for this party."

"I need to prove that I am settled to cement the job." He'd do an auctioneer proud, the words came out so fast.

She nodded in a slow cadence. "Your father told you that?" His family was more screwed up than she first thought. That made her brain zero in on Brooks and what the real story was because what Curtis had just said was total crap. There was a mystery she had no interest in unraveling, but it might have something to do with this. "If he did, Max does realize what year it is, right?"

"No, but the—" He stopped as if he didn't want to say another word.

Her brain filled in the rest with wild scenarios, which proved she watched too much true crime at night. The body in the yard no one was supposed to talk about might finally be discovered was her first thought. All the answers lay with Maxwell and his backward-thinking ways.

"Curtis"—she twirled the ring on her finger—"since you can't tell the truth, then tell me what you want."

"I've only wanted one thing my whole life." Curtis spoke in a tone that screamed defeat. "It's probably something you'll think is silly."

"There's no way I can promise anything unless you tell me, so start talking."

The waiter dropped off another glass of wine, and she listened. She had to give it to Curtis. He knew what he wanted, and he'd figured out how to get it. That he was planning on stepping over everyone to achieve his goals should've bothered her, but Brooks deserved some pain. He'd have to make some concessions when it came to Pru, Charlie, and Etienne, but that wouldn't be hard since Curtis would have to buy them out.

"Once Dad sees how well I'm doing and that I'm marrying someone he thinks is a good fit, he'll feel better about stepping back," Curtis finished, and the whole thing sounded beyond ridiculous, but she had to consider who he was trying to convince.

The Boseman family had more than few screws loose if this was the kind of children they'd raised. They all thought the world was going to believe the crap they were saying because they were the ones saying it. But who was she to judge? Perhaps Brooks had done her a favor before they'd brought any more little Bosemans into the world.

"We're friends, Fallon, and you probably don't think I care about you, but I do. If you do want to marry me, I promise to make you happy."

"We are friends, but I wish you'd been honest. Your dad had never thought I was worth the time of day, so I understand where you're coming from." She also understood they both now knew what they wanted from each other. "All you need to understand is, once you get what you want, we'll part ways. I can't stress that enough, and we end this way before anyone books a church. Understand?"

"Yes, I do," Curtis said, holding his hand out. "So, we have a deal?"

"We do, up to a point. I'll help you, but don't ask me to lie to the insurance company or anyone else about that boat." She was wondering what her father would say. He was proud of her for a lot of things, but she doubted this would make the list.

"That's on me, and I'll take care of it."

"Then I'll see you next weekend."

❖

It was dark by the time Brooks made it back to the Piquant. This was as close to an emotional overload as she'd ever gotten, and that did not improve when Etienne, Prudence, and Charlotte were all waiting in the lobby when she got out of the elevator from the garage. She pointed to the bar, sensing she'd need alcohol if the next hour was going to be all about assuring everyone they weren't going to lose their jobs.

They each took a turn hugging her before they sat at a table away from the live music. "We can tell you've talked to Mom," Charlie said as a conversation starter. "How fucked are we?"

"Let me start by saying I'm not here to take over or take anything from you." She nodded her thanks to the waitress for her old-fashioned. "I came because Mom called."

Pru leaned in and placed her elbows on the table. "What if we want you to take over while there's still something to take over?"

"Being the head of the company is more than trying to get as many pretty girls as you can talk into sleeping with you and buying boats to impress your friends." Etienne was the one sibling who resembled her in the most in both looks and temperament. He was a man who didn't mind being alone and working hard. That's what they'd need going forward. "Do you want to tell us what's going on? Dad has all but disappeared, leaving Curtis making all the decisions at work. When we have Sunday lunches, he only comes down to eat and barely says anything. That's not like him, and Mom won't say a thing."

Her mom had given her the key to their dad's office in the city as well as the one on the bayou. She'd also asked Brooks to break the news she hadn't been able to. It wasn't a job Brooks wanted, but they all deserved to know. She doubted Max would ever be able to go back to work, so it was up to them to band together and save what they not only loved, but counted on.

Bria always told her she was too nice, and she was beginning to think she was right. This shouldn't be her responsibility, but her mother was like an invading horde holding a sword to her neck to get her to do the dirty work. The sword in this case was guilt invented and perfected by the Catholics. That's the one thing Scarlett kept from the religion they were baptized into.

"Recently Dad had a stroke." She waited for the reaction of shock to pass. "He survived it, obviously."

"That explains so much," Pru said, seeming lost in thought. "Did you see him?"

"I spoke to him for a little while this afternoon. He tires easily, so I didn't want to exhaust him, but I listened to what he wanted." They all stared at her with expressions of both dread and anticipation, which in this case might be the same thing.

"And that is…?" Charlie made a rolling motion to get her talking.

"He wants to have a family meeting Sunday before lunch." In the morning she'd glance over the books and give Max an update. If he wanted to make decisions, they needed to be made with all the information he could get. Her mom needed to be there so no one could say she'd manipulated him into anything.

"He's been off, like way off," Charlie said. "There has to be more."

She took a deep breath and thought the direct approach now would be best. "He's also been diagnosed with early onset Alzheimer's." Saying it choked her up, and she was questioning her feelings. "You're right in that he's off, but he's trying his best to stay positive. The stroke sped things along, so without talking to his doctors, I get the impression this is going to be a fast decline."

"Oh, Brooks," Pru said, sounding like she was in pain. "I know how you feel about him, but my God, this can't be happening."

She offered her hand to Pru, and Charlie and Etienne took their free hands. "I'd never wish this on him or anyone, and I'll do what I can to help. Mom's had a hard time coming up with how to break this to all of you. I'm sorry to throw it all at you at once like this."

"When she told us she called you, we knew it had to be something." Etienne's voice was soft, and she could see the tears in his eyes. He was the most soulful of them all. He'd never wanted to run anything except maybe a trawl net. He was the happiest when he was on the water, but she doubted he'd ever be happy with Curtis as his boss. "What are you planning?"

"The company belongs to the four of you if something happens. I doubt Mom wants to run the day-to-day, so you'll need to decide before tomorrow what the future is going to be." That wasn't going to be easy since Curtis hadn't joined them. Partnerships were never in her brother's vocabulary when it came to the business.

"The company belongs to all of us," Pru said and Charlie nodded. "Until Dad dies, and then we all know what comes next."

"Think about it, though," she said. "Curtis has to pay you fair market value, which right now isn't going to let you walk away with enough to retire. I've been keeping up with what you've sent me, so I can tell you that he's set it up to get what he wants for the least amount he can get away with."

"We know that better than anyone. We needed you all this time, and you left us," Etienne said with a little heat. "You did that, and we never knew why. We waited and hoped you'd come back, but you didn't. Asking Mom was a dead end since she tells us all the time she doesn't know."

"She didn't, not until this afternoon. That's a story for another time. We have other things to worry about." She finished her drink and sighed.

"You don't have to tell us if you don't want," Charlie said. "But don't disappear on us again. I doubt you're going to give up your life, but we need you."

"I told Mom I'd stay for a couple of weeks to see where you are. If it takes longer, then I'll stay longer." The relief on all their faces came close to making her nervous about all this. She could close huge deals, but she was never emotionally connected to the outcome. Here, with this, they'd all expect miracles.

"Have you talked to Curtis?" Pru asked.

"Not yet. Something happened at the docks today, so I assumed he was dealing with that. Any of you have any insight on what happened?" The expressions of relief changed to what she remembered when they'd smashed her car into a tree on the property when she was in college. "Okay," she said and glanced at her watch, "I'll be at lunch tomorrow and at the office on Monday. Try to keep a positive attitude for both Max's and Mom's sake."

"You think you'll have something by tomorrow?" Etienne asked.

"I'm going to start looking at the books tonight, but don't hold me to anything yet. I'll get to the house early to visit with Mom and Max before lunch. There was some stuff he wanted to tell me, but like I said, I didn't want to exhaust him." Her phone buzzed, and she didn't want to put Bria off again. "I have to take this, but why don't you all come an hour earlier than you usually do. We can set up a schedule to help Mom out going forward."

They all nodded and left. She took a moment before calling Bria back. For some reason Fallon popped into her head, so maybe it was time to reach out. She'd moved on, as she was sure Fallon had, but what had happened between them was undone. She wasn't someone who left anything undone.

"Are you trying to avoid me?" As always, Bria sounded like she was ready to conquer the world. Whatever had gotten Angelo to the top ranks ran strong in his two children. Bria worked with her, and her brother was the heir apparent to the throne Angelo owned. "Just remember, I know where you are. Don't make me hunt you down."

She laughed and the pressure on her shoulders released. "I figured you'd had one of those locator pellets you put in Duke when you had him fixed installed in my ass."

"The doctor wasn't supposed to tell you that." The sirens on Bria's end meant she was in the city. "You'll be happy to know Yang closed today with better terms than we wanted. He learned his lesson about trying to fuck with us."

"That's the good news part of the equation." Her story kept Bria quiet until she was done. She made it up to her room before she was finished, and all she wanted was to sleep for a week when she lay down. "Can you fucking believe it?"

"I'm so sorry, Brooks. You don't really talk about your father, but I've always gotten the impression you were waiting for something to make peace with him and the whole family."

"I don't have a problem with my whole family."

Bria tsked to get her to take the sarcasm down a bit. "You know what I mean. My family loves you, and it's because you're a good person. Give your family the chance to see that."

"Some people seek the new because it's in their nature to crave adventure."

Business drove her—it had from the beginning out of necessity. Brooks had been on her own from the moment she'd walked out of Max's office, and if she failed, there was nothing to fall back on. Max had cut her safety net as effectively as he'd cut her heart out.

She'd found comfort in Bria, the Giordano family, and in the little escapes she had a fondness for. Most Sundays she visited different museums, and she liked to sit in the Rose Reading Room at the library. She read romance novels in her downtime and hadn't shared that with anyone since some people thought them cheesy. Fallon, though, had taught her what a great escape they could be.

She tried never to compare her life to the ease with which a lot of those characters breezed through everything after finding their match. There was fantasy, and then there was her reality. She'd never find that. It was punishment for what she'd done to Fallon, even though her choices had been made out of love. As she'd gotten older, she wasn't so sure any longer. Fortune at times favored the selfish.

"True, but what does adventure-seeking have to do with you?" Bria was somewhere quiet, and Brooks hoped it was because she'd made it home.

"Some of us get thrown out of the nest to the curb and told to cope. I was in the evicted portion of that equation. I had no choice but to seek adventure in some sort of twisted game of survival of the fittest."

"That doesn't matter, Brooks, not anymore. Try to settle things because once he's gone, you can't. Death is final. There are no second chances, and in this case your window might not be death. Alzheimer's is a terrible thing that to me is worse than dying." Bria said out loud what Fallon had been thinking since she'd seen her father. He already seemed like there was something missing that was an important part to what made him the man she knew.

"Can you hang on for a couple of weeks?" She kicked her shoes off and placed her feet on the bed. "I need to get an idea what's happening and where things are. If Curtis is really blowing shit up as a business plan, I might not be able to fix this."

"Not necessarily a bad plan, depending on your insurance coverage and how good you are at blowing shit up," Bria said and laughed. "I'm kidding, if any feds are listening in on this call! We never condone violence of any kind, and we pay our taxes faithfully."

"You're a riot, but back to the boat, now at the bottom of the bayou. Losing insurance coverage is a killer to any business, so that'll have to be the first thing I deal with. If the crackerjack team of cops down here figured that on day one, we'll have a problem."

"You know persuasion goes a long way." Bria laughed again, and it lightened Brooks's mood. "You're a brilliant businesswoman, darling, but you're also a charmer. Think of all the clients who trust you with your money. I mean *really* trust you," Bria said, and she could almost see the wink that followed.

If a financial magazine that centered on mobsters and what they did with their clean money existed, she and Bria would be on the cover every month. Those guys had trusted them from the beginning because she and Bria were good at what they did. She could've done the same with her family's money, but she'd never offered. Being disowned was something she wanted to experience only once.

"Do what you do, but also try what you didn't."

Brooks sat up and exhaled a long-measured breath. "What's that, and did you start writing fortune cookies in your spare time?"

"Unleash the personal. You've only ever done that with Angelo, and see how that turned out? He's my father and he loves me, but it's you he listens to." That was true, but not for the reasons Bria most likely thought.

"You think he trusts me more when it comes to business?"

"No, he talks to you because he likes you. You're not an underling, and you don't hold back. Fear isn't the basis of your relationship. My father likes to talk to you about me, and it's because he loves me— worries about me. He expects you to watch over me, but at the center of all that, he respects you."

"He does love you, but he mostly asks me to run statistics on the games people are betting on," she said, and Bria cracked up. "He also warned me that he'd break my legs if anything happened to you, so there's that."

"He did not."

"Don't believe me if you want, but you know your dad." She wished Bria was closer, but the hug she craved would have to wait. "Are you going to be okay?"

"I miss you, but remember—charm, Brooks. Don't forget to use it, and I'll call with anything that'll require both of us." Bria blew a kiss in the phone and Brooks smiled.

"Remember to be careful. I want you in the same condition I left you in." They might not have been involved in Angelo's more nefarious business, but Bria was still a target because of her last name.

"I will. Daddy sent over some friends, so don't worry. Did you bring enough clothes?"

"I'll run by the mall tomorrow." Leave it to Bria the fashionista to think of that. "I don't want to spend two weeks in jeans. I might break out in hives."

"I'll call Steve tonight so all you have to do is pick up. You hate shopping, and I'm not going to force it on you now."

"And that's why I love you."

"It's mutual, my friend. Call me if you need reinforcements or someone to knock folks around. I know people." Bria laughed again and made more kissing noises before hanging up.

Sleep was elusive, so Brooks googled Boseman Seafood to see what came up. These kinds of searches always led her down wormholes that made her restless, so she was disoriented the next morning. She followed the directions Bria had texted and asked for the personal shopper in Bria's text message after she assured her Saks and Brooks Brothers were her only stops.

Brooks Brothers had been a joke between them. Bria said Brooks's mom had most likely had a premonition the day she was born, and named her after the store because of her love of suits and crisp white starched shirts. According to Bria, navy-blue pinstripes were her favorite color.

She'd gotten a chill on the escalator in Saks but chalked it up to her crazy night. After she paid, she headed toward her parents' place. It was time to start whatever this was so she could finish and go back to her life.

CHAPTER SIX

It's all there," Scarlett said when Brooks arrived. The boxes by the door had last year's financials and contracts, and her first clue there was a problem was how few boxes there were. "That's what the accountant put together, and the people at the office can fill in whatever you need. I called a staff meeting for Monday."

"Thanks." She placed the stuff on the front seat of the truck and went back inside. "Do you need me to sit with him to give you a break?"

"Go on out back. He's been waiting for you." Her mom pointed to the yard. "The water relaxes him and quiets his mind. That makes him concentrate better."

Her mom didn't join her, and she walked out to the chairs on the deck over the bayou. He was sitting with his eyes closed and a cane leaning against his legs. Max appeared weak—feeble, really—and she had to center herself before she announced her arrival. There was another folder full of papers next to him on the table. Whatever it was, she'd wait him out.

"You can look if you want," he said, not opening his eyes.

"How are you feeling?" Bria's words echoed in her head. This was her chance to make peace with him, but she couldn't force herself to make the first move.

"I'm scared," he admitted. "You ever feel like you can't hang on to the important things because you've wasted so much time on trivial bullshit?" She shook her head, not sure of what the right answer here was. "Maybe that's just me, then. Can we have a frank conversation?" He stared at her, and his green eyes were clear and familiar. She'd inherited those and his dark hair.

"You can say whatever you want." If they'd made any progress, she thought he was about to unravel it. Frank conversations were usually reserved for things you needed to say to someone who didn't want to hear it.

"What I did was wrong. You left because of me, and I thought you'd come back to give me a chance to make it up to you." It was as if he couldn't keep eye contact, so he concentrated on the slow-moving brown current. "You didn't, and your mother and mine have never forgiven me for it. I know they both love me in their own way, but I'm a disappointment to both of them."

"You, if I'm honest, made me who I am," Brooks said. When he'd gutted her, she made only one promise to herself, and she'd sworn to keep it. She'd survive no matter what. If that took being a ditchdigger, that's what she would've done rather than asking him for anything. For a long time, knowing that she hadn't given him the satisfaction of needing him for anything had been enough. Seeing him now, she realized it wasn't. She needed more.

"I built a business and a life away from here because you gave me no viable choice. But like I told Mom, I never hated you for it—I couldn't. If you've worried about me, stop. I've been okay."

"I took your family away from you." His tears were as foreign to her as a three-headed fish. "That's unforgivable. All these years you've been alone, and it's brought me nothing but misery."

"I forgave you a long time ago, Max, so don't think about that anymore. I'm sorry all this is happening to you, but getting upset over things that can't be changed isn't good." She placed her hand over his and smiled. Maybe forgiveness was a stretch, but she didn't want to be cruel.

He wiped his face and placed his other hand over the folder. "Thank you, and you're a good kid—kind, when I've been anything but. This thing I have hasn't stolen my reasoning yet, and I'll try to hang on as long as I can." She nodded at that. Her father could will himself into pretty much any state of mind. "What I want, I put into motion before the stroke, and Dan will explain it to you." Her dad waved in the direction behind her. "You remember Dan, right?"

"Mr. Collins." She took his hand. His hair had gone completely white since the last time she'd seen him, but he still dressed like he was presenting a case to the Supreme Court.

"Brooks, please, it's Dan." He sat closer to her and handed her a folder that seemed to have the same information in it.

"What is all this?" She opened it to the first page.

"Max wanted to make plans for the inevitable. Power of attorney, do not resuscitate wishes, and the updated will." Dan read off a list on his phone. "The will and all the other documents were drawn up a year before the stroke."

"Did you think something was going to happen to you?" she asked her father.

"You were right about a lot of things, kid. The business hasn't thrived by doing it the way we've always done it. I'm an asshole for not coming to you sooner, but there was an ocean between us, and I was afraid we'd never bridge it." Max sounded as if there was nothing wrong with him, like the monster ready to take his memories and everything else wasn't biting at his ass. "I've made so many mistakes, Brooks, but the biggest one was not accepting you for who you are."

"I promised Mom I'd help you, so you don't have to say all that to get me to stay." She wanted to believe him, but it was hard to believe what he was saying. He'd imploded the life she thought she'd have, and there was no apology that was going to erase all that. "I'm sorry," she said, embarrassed by her outburst. Her father wasn't that bully who'd thrown down his ultimatums in his study years before. He was a man trying to grasp at the time he had left, and beating him down was beneath her.

"You have nothing to be sorry for, Brooks. Let Dan finish, and we'll go in and talk alone."

Dan glanced at her and smiled as if acknowledging her kindness. "Because of all the diagnoses, you'll see we've included the doctors' affidavits as to Max's state of mind when he drew these up. I've done my due diligence to avoid a court battle with anyone who wants to contest your dad's wishes. There's not a court that'll undo any of this, even if he's mentally incapacitated at death."

That was a hell of a thing to say, but she was only halfway listening after studying the first page. Her father had given her power of attorney not only for the business but to make medical decisions for him. "You might want to change this to Mom." She pointed to her name. "I'd think she's the one who's best qualified to do this for you."

"Brooks, this isn't to punish you, but I need the most competent person in the family making the right choices from here on out." Her father appeared anxious, and she wanted to minimize his stress. Upsetting him into having another stroke wasn't something she'd ever forgive herself for. "Your mother doesn't know, but we're in trouble. I'm not in the office every day, but Pierre's been keeping me updated."

Pierre Falgout was her dad's foreman over the entire fleet they owned and dealt with the independents they purchased from.

"You're supposed to be resting." He might've been apologetic, but some things would never change. Max was a worse workaholic than she was, and that wasn't an easy thing to accomplish.

"He's waiting on your call. He'll give you everything you need, and he won't sugarcoat it. I don't want to lose my head and leave your mom in a bad situation." Max held on to the handle of his cane like it would keep him tethered to reality. "I had no choice but to put some of our money back into the company."

She pinched the bridge of her nose hard enough to hurt, trying to convince herself this wasn't a bad dream. "How much?" The answer was obvious in how he couldn't look at her.

"All of our capital." The words hit and ricocheted in her head, tearing through her entire peace of mind. "The people who make up who we are have worked for us for years, most of them second- and third-generation employees. I couldn't face anyone in this community if I'd had to let them go."

The hard facts were that he'd sunk all their money and assets into the business. It was like trying to bail the *Titanic* with a teacup and expecting it to stay afloat. Money, though, was the easy part. A capital infusion would be the crutch to get them back on their feet. She had loads of experience with that when it was a project she cared about.

What worried her was the explosion. If there was an investigation, it wouldn't be easy to quash it without raising suspicion, and suspicion was like determined termites. It spread and ate away at the reputation you'd built in the business community, and by the time you stopped it, the damage was at times irreversible. If no one worked for them or sold them whatever seafood was in season, the only thing left would be empty facilities and crappy boats. Not exactly the nest egg you wanted to retire on.

This situation called for a different kind of experience—the kind she'd learned from Angelo. It was naive to ignore exactly who Angelo was and what he did, but he'd lived his whole life under the FBI's microscope. Some would find it stifling, but he'd learned to thrive under the pressure. He'd often told her that's how diamonds were made.

If the investigation was serious and she couldn't kill it, the best course of action would be throwing their doors open and inviting the investigators in. She'd let them crawl up her ass if that's what it took, but it would come with a warning, one that she'd be glad to follow up on. If they wanted to go that route, they'd better find something, or there'd be hell to pay. Those payments would come in the form of lawsuits for questioning their integrity.

She opened her eyes after she'd calmed down and smiled to put Max and Dan at ease. "Don't worry, I'll take care of it."

"All I want is for you to take care of your mama. I've already taken too much from her." He struggled to his feet, and she helped him back to the house. That's when she noticed his left hand was clenched in a fist that wasn't relaxing. It seemed to have more to do with the stroke than his business problems.

"Stop thinking about it." She got him upstairs and into bed for a nap. "You're going to be okay, and so will the business."

"I'm sorry, Brooks, so sorry." He repeated that a few times as more tears tracked down his face. It was almost like he'd forgotten he'd apologized plenty already, and it worried her. "I messed up, and I have to tell you about it, but I'm so tired."

"Sleep now, and we'll talk when you wake up. Everything is fixable, I promise."

Her mom was waiting downstairs with a drink, but Brooks didn't want anything. It was confusing how he could be so coherent in the moment, only to drift away as fast as a stiff wind. It made her appreciate Bria's words more. There wasn't much time at all, and it wouldn't be death that would rob them of the chance to make things right.

"Are you sorry I called you?" Her mom poured her a cup of coffee with steamed milk and pointed to a chair in the kitchen. The next thing her mom got out was a small bowl that she filled with gumbo.

"No, I thrive on family drama. I especially love it when it's my family about to crash into the rocks." The gumbo was delicious, and even better when she tasted the potato salad her mom had added.

"That bad, huh?" Her mom sat across from her and winked. "You want to tell me what this morning was about? He usually doesn't need Dan to back him up."

She froze with the spoon in her mouth. It gave her time to think of something both her mother and father would be happy with. "I have to work through some things before we talk about it."

"Don't worry, let him have his secrets. Your father did his best, even when that meant screwing the pooch."

Brooks didn't know about that. Her father was a caveman when it came to business. His plan consisted of letting his son take over for him because that's the way it had always been. If that was true, who was he to change tradition? "I don't want to keep anything from you, Mom, but I have to work through some stuff before we have a frank conversation. There's no reason for all of us to be concerned, and I'll do my best to be thorough but fast."

"Honey, we could lose everything tomorrow and it wouldn't matter that much to me. I was poor before marrying your father, so it won't be anything new." The way her mom shook her head made Brooks want to tell her every detail of their meeting, but she held back. "That might come as a shock to your brothers and sisters, but poor isn't death, is it?"

"No, and no one is going to be poor and homeless. I promise you that just like I promised him," she said, pointing up.

"Can I ask you something?" Her mom placed her spoon on the table and gazed at her with an indecipherable expression.

"I think you know everything about me." She picked up a piece of French bread and slathered it with butter. This was so out of her comfort zone. She wasn't used to having to lay herself bare, not anymore.

"Not everything," her mom said, letting her go. "Your father told me last night, but I can't rely on everything he says."

"What do you want to know?" It wasn't a good thing, for her at least, to be surprised.

"The girl you left, sacrificed so much for"—her mother spoke as if trying not to scare her off—"why didn't you come back for her?"

"Because some things are unforgivable. You should know that." She put her spoon down as well and pushed the bowl away. "I wouldn't take her family away, and ruin them, so I took her choices away."

"What's that mean?"

"That I made sure she picked her family. The consequence of that means she won't forgive me, and I can live with that."

Her mom let it go as if she didn't want to hear anything else, and Brooks went back outside. She was drawn to the cottage at the edge of the property. One of the people she missed the most was her grandmother, the one person who'd outlive them all, and the one who visited her the most often. Heddie Boseman was a freethinker, and she taught all of them to never stay quiet. She always said their voices were their greatest gift, and they should use them to accomplish great things.

"Hey, Brooks," one of the gardeners said. "Are you looking for Miss Heddie?"

"Is she not in?"

"She's in town for her class reunion," the man said, holding his hat. "She'll be back in a few days and said she'll tan your behind if you leave before she gets here."

The threat made her laugh. "Let me get back to the fun, then."

She sat in the office and went through her emails. The satisfaction of getting through the list helped her find the kind of centeredness she hadn't found since arriving. It didn't take long before she heard multiple voices coming from the front of the house. With any luck they'd be as amicable as the night before.

They all went into the dining room with her mother, and again, Curtis was missing. If it bothered her father when he made it downstairs, he hid it well. The nap had done its job since he didn't appear lost and exhausted. Max had his cane and the folder from earlier, and Dan followed him in.

"Sit, everyone." Max tapped the cane to the floor as if it was a gavel. "Your mom tells me she had Brooks talk to you about what's going on with me."

"Are you feeling okay now?" Charlie asked. All three of her siblings appeared afraid and pale. There was something bad coming, and none of them knew how to handle it.

"The stroke could've been worse"—he smiled, and Brooks could tell it was to put them at ease—"but it's the other thing that there's no coming back from." She couldn't help but stare at the tight fist his left hand was still clenched in. It wasn't from anger, emotion, or not accepting what was happening to him. The best way she could explain it was that his body was betraying him one small bit at a time.

All her memories of Max, the good and the bad, revolved around his physical presence. He was a big guy, both in height and bulk. When she was a kid, he'd made her feel safe. It's why that day he turned on her stayed in her head like a weight. He took away his security, so she'd found her way, and her sense of safety came from within now. Her father's anger had made her strong, and it was surreal that now he looked to her for the comfort he'd given her until the day he'd stopped.

"I'll let Dan explain the rest, but I hope none of you will give Brooks a hard time. I asked for her help, and she's agreed to give it. You're all family, and that's why the business has always worked. I've done a piss-poor job, but family should stick together, work side by side, and do what they can to love each other."

They all watched Max leave, and Brooks noticed how her siblings stared. She couldn't blame them—she'd done the same when the news sank in. "Dan, could you give us a minute, please?"

"How did we not figure this out?" Pru asked.

"Because Max has always been bigger than life. It's hard to see him vulnerable." It was the simplest explanation. "We need to promise to give back something that means everything to him. He can't slip away knowing he's the one who lost the company."

"We're glad you're here, Brooks." Etienne stood and hugged her.

"We all are, in case you were wondering." Charlie got up and fell against her as if asking for comfort. "Why's all this happening?"

"I don't know, and I'm sorry it's come to this, but I'll do my best to fix it." She held Charlie and lifted her free arm to hold Pru. "We'll start tomorrow."

❖

It had been a long week, and Fallon wanted to spend Saturday alone. She wasted an hour staring at her bedroom ceiling, trying to find her courage. In less than eight hours she had to face most of the people she knew and try to convince them she was madly in love with Curtis, the man she was supposed to spend the rest of her life with. She took a cleansing breath and got up.

"All you have to do is get through four hours, tops. Then you get back to your life." She finished her makeup and stared at the dress before putting it on. The black designer outfit wasn't like anything in her closet, and she ran her fingers along the hem. She'd splurged on the Louboutin heels and almost regretted they were for this. The red soles were like flags warning her that this was a mistake from beginning to end, and she should use the expensive heels to walk away.

She'd slipped into the shoes when her doorbell rang, and she opened the door to Curtis in a tuxedo. It was easy to see what most women found attractive in men. Curtis was classically handsome in almost every way. The exception was his eyes, and she'd never noticed until the night they worked out this godforsaken pact that he was the only one in his family who had inherited Scarlett's gray eye color. But Curtis's didn't reflect the same warmth.

"You look beautiful." He held her hands as his eyes moved up and down her body. "I might want to change our plan and keep you."

She laughed and shook her head. "There's no renegotiating now,

Curtis, and I'm not a puppy. It's time to get back to reality. If you need a clearer picture, we go back to being friends and only friends."

Curtis wasn't in a rush to leave, so he held up the bottle of wine he'd brought. "Let's have a glass before we have to be social for the rest of the night."

There was something off, and he was acting like he'd rather do anything to skip what was coming. "Everything okay?" She got two glasses down and sat at her kitchen island.

"Just a long week. I've been trying to get some of our contracts back on track, and it's been frustrating—it's going so slow." He slid her glass over and drained his like he was in a frat drinking game. "Some of our fleet guys took the week off, saying they were traumatized by the explosion, which left us short. When people are expecting orders and they get squat, they get pissed and go elsewhere."

"I thought Pru and Etienne are in charge of that part of the business." The fact that Curtis was as forthcoming about work as he was about Brooks, which was not at all, made her anxious to finish this. Whatever Curtis was up to, she didn't want to be linked to it.

"They've been wrapped up in this overview my father ordered, and it's starting to piss me off. It's shrimp season, and they're wasting time on that. Trying to fix things that aren't broken is costing us, which is the definition of stupidity. If you think about it, it's downright hilarious. They're reviewing to make things better, and that's making us go up in flames."

"Is Brooks still here?" She knew the answer since Monroe and Eliza were still dancing around each other sharing their family gossip. According to her sister, Brooks had been at the Boseman offices doing a deep dive into the books. A large part of her hoped Brooks wouldn't make it tonight. She wasn't ready to see her and deal with what it'd do to her to actually see her.

"Yes, and that's who Dad picked to lead this farce." He drummed his fingers loudly on her granite countertop and stopped himself before he was truly shouting. "The real person to blame here is my mother. I know that's who called Brooks, and I'm sure she's begging her to stay. Whoever said parents didn't have favorites never met Scarlett."

"Have you found out what's wrong with your father? It's not like him not to change a million things on the contract we agreed on." She'd said yes to one boat—the replacement of the one that blew up, and that was it. The only one present for the whole process was Curtis, which raised her worry flag. Max wasn't someone who spent three million dollars without having a say.

"There was a family meeting on Sunday," he said and laughed. "I skipped it so I didn't have to bow and kiss the ring of the mighty business god."

"Curtis, if you want the company, maybe petty isn't the way to go." Great, just great. This was hard enough without adding a family feud to it.

"There's no wanting in this equation. The company is mine, and nothing's going to change that." He pointed at her like he wanted to get that point across. "Brooks can research all she wants, but that is the hard fact she's not going to be able to work around."

She nodded, not needing to rile him up anymore. They finished their wine, and she stopped short when she saw the car in her driveway. She wasn't a car expert, but this looked sleek and expensive—an attention getter. Boseman's books were closed to her, but she had a feeling their bottom line wasn't this rosy.

"Isn't it beautiful?" Curtis sounded like he was talking about his child. "The Aston Martin Valhalla, zero to sixty in two seconds, and the only one on the road in Louisiana. An early wedding present to myself. I was shocked when I opened it since it was exactly what I wanted," he said, laughing like a simpleton.

"Good for you," she said, hoping it'd end this conversation. There had to be an airhead he could leave her for who shared Curtis's narcissistic tendencies. She could pretend to be devastated for a moment of her life, then bring a Le Creuset Dutch oven to *their* wedding.

"Let's get going. We need to get down the bayou." He closed her door and appeared giddy when he slid behind the wheel. Lots of money obviously didn't translate into comfort, at least she thought so as she moved around in her seat. She wasn't about to say that to Curtis, who was touching the steering wheel like it was his mistress. "Why my mother picked the house down there for this party is a mystery."

"It's where she and your father had their engagement party. She thought it'd be like a family tradition for you and your siblings." If Curtis didn't share Brooks's last name, she'd swear he was adopted. It was like Max had raised him to be this macho caricature who was totally enraptured with himself. The world revolved around only him and his wants. If only he'd shown this side of himself before she accepted the second dinner invitation, she could've saved herself a lot of grief.

He'd fooled her this long because she hadn't been paying attention, and she blamed herself. Her theory was that he caught her when she was feeling lonely and he was on a mission. It was the perfect storm that'd resulted in tonight. In a way she couldn't wrap her head around the notion that Max would think someone a better leader, or a better person, for that matter, because of a marriage.

Had she really been that clueless because she detached herself from a personal life? She could analyze herself later. Right now she just had to get through the night. Despite his many faults, Curtis had brought her an iota of something missing, so she'd try and help him as best she could unless it was illegal. Then she was out.

Curtis drove like he was James Bond and an international bad guy was after them. The ride that usually took forty minutes, Curtis made in twenty-five, and her fingers hurt from clutching the seat. When he turned into the driveway, the house was lit up, and there were a few people getting out and handling their keys off to the valets Scarlett had hired. It was one of the small things that would add up to a big guilt trip later. Putting people out wasn't something she'd easily get over.

"Ready?" Curtis asked. He parked out front and locked his new toy. The valets wouldn't get a chance to move it anywhere.

The urge to yell *no* was hard to fight. "Let's go, and later on I'll catch a ride with my sister, so don't worry about driving me home."

He chuckled, and it was starting to sound condescending. "We haven't started and you're already trying to get away from me?"

"Curtis, I told you I'd help you because we're friends and I care about you. I'll stay as long as is appropriate since your mom went through a lot of trouble tonight and it's making me feel bad that I allowed her to do that. Remember, it's all make-believe." She didn't wait for Curtis as she started walking. "Come on before I change my mind."

They stopped outside to talk to some of their parents' mutual friends and business acquaintances and thank them for coming. From the din of the conversation in the house, very few people had passed on the invitation. They made it inside where both their moms were waiting to introduce them to the crowd. Scarlett gazed at her with an indecipherable expression. Fallon couldn't be sure, but if she was forced to describe it, she would've gone with pity, but that wasn't it exactly.

"Did you invite Dellow Hayes like I asked?" Curtis asked his mother.

"I did, but he never responded to my invitation. Has he become a good friend or something?" Scarlett stared at Curtis as if trying to read his mind. Fallon recognized the name as the fisherman who'd been there the day the boat blew up and couldn't figure out why Curtis would want him there.

"You look so good together." Her mother spoke with her hands pressed together as if thanking God Fallon had come to her senses the minute she'd agree to marry Curtis. "Are you ready?"

"Ready?" The one-word question came out of her mouth, and it was a bit like shoving a stick up a bear's ass. If you wanted the big animal to devour you whole while ripping pieces off you, that'd be the way to go. Whatever her mom's answer was going to be, she figured they'd have about the same outcome.

"We thought we'd announce you. Sort of like what'll happen at the wedding." Her mother hopped a little after that and she wanted to gag.

Scarlett appeared to not be excited by this plan, but she stayed composed. "If you want, just mingle—this is for you and Curtis, after all."

"Thank you for this." Fallon accepted Scarlett's hand and kissed her cheek. Scarlett was one of the only people she'd miss not seeing often. "The house looks amazing."

Scarlett opened her mouth to reply when Fallon's mother placed her hands on Fallon's and Curtis's biceps and pulled them into the main room. Their arrival stopped all conversation. Her breathing became shallow, and all she could hear was the blood rushing in her ears. She'd never had an anxiety attack, and after this she didn't want any more experience falling down this pit that made it hard to function.

"Ladies and gentlemen," her mother said, projecting her voice, "let's raise our glasses to Curtis and Fallon. We can't wait to welcome Curtis into our family."

"To Curtis and Fallon," the crowd said, their glasses lifted high.

They were all holding the toast position except for one. Brooks looked as if someone had clocked her in the face with a frying pan. The sight of her was hard to explain to Fallon's brain, and she wanted to shake out of her mother's hold and escape those beautiful eyes that reflected pain. If her plan in all this was revenge, she'd succeeded, but it was like kicking a puppy because you could. No one in their right mind did that.

"Shit."

CHAPTER SEVEN

Brooks was barely paying attention to the older man who was giving a detailed explanation of the new oyster cleaning process they'd deployed. Talking about oysters was as boring as having one as a pet. Then Monroe stepped up with drinks and handed one over.

"You need to come by the plant and take a look. Once you understand the process, the easier it'll be to leave our department whole." The guy smiled, but it did nothing to hide his fear of loss.

"You have my word—you and your staff will be okay. The review isn't about cutting for the sake of cutting, but to make things better so you can expand."

There'd been torturous parties in her past, but at least she had Bria in her ear giving commentary on everything from what people had decided to wear to what was wrong with the food. Tonight had been something her mother had harped about her coming to for a week, so the tux she'd insisted on didn't fit like the one in her closet back home. At least Saks had one in stock they'd rushed through alterations, so she didn't have to wear jeans.

She'd endure the baggy crotch to see who Curtis had convinced to marry him. Her brother was known more for his taste in escorts than anyone their mother would want to spend time with at the holidays. She was expecting a pole dancer with a heart of gold.

"Thanks for this." She held her glass up to Monroe as Charlie joined them. "It'll help with all the socializing, but since the mother of the bride invited everyone we've all met collectively, I won't be missed when I head out."

"Let Mom catch you doing that, and you're going to get grounded," Pru said, holding a wineglass. Both her sisters looked great in their tuxedos, including pants that fit like they should, making her jealous. "Actually, Mom wanted more subdued than this, which I now know was because of Dad, but she was outvoted."

"It does scream Curtis, doesn't it?" Charlie asked and laughed. "Has he called you yet?"

"His assistant told me he was busy with the accident," she said, taking a sip of the perfect old-fashioned. The biscuits, gumbo, and libations were perfect since coming home, but tonight she wasn't in the mood for good booze or food. "He can't run forever. Who's he marrying? No one has mentioned—"

She was cut off when her mother and Eleanor Goodwin led the happy couple in. Eleanor said, "Ladies and gentlemen—"

Brooks's hearing shut off after that, and she was suddenly standing in a tunnel with Fallon Goodwin beaming on Curtis's arm at the other end. She was still beautiful and still had the same effect on her, as she held her breath and her drink too tightly. If karma was a woman, she was a mean spiteful bitch who had a sword sharper than anything she'd felt as it sliced into her heart. To think Fallon hadn't moved on never crossed her mind, but marrying Curtis required more imagination than she possessed.

"We're sorry, Brooks," Charlie said, taking her hand.

"We didn't know how to tell you," Pru added.

The toasts were over and the buzz of conversation started again. She needed to get out of there, but her feet were nailed to the floor. She noticed the noise level dipped again, and the crowd parted for a newcomer. There weren't too many women she knew who could carry off couture quite like Bria. Seeing her gave her something to hang on to as she regained her balance.

Bria put her hands flat on Brooks's chest and smiled up at her. "Kiss me hello, handsome, then show me the yard."

Brooks did as she was told, and the world righted itself when Bria took her hand. "Not that I don't owe the universe a huge favor, but what are you doing here?"

"Charlie and Pru called me since they knew what was coming. Your mom insisted you be here for your dad, but your siblings wanted me here for you. And don't blame Scarlett. She didn't know how to tell you either." The back doors were open, so Bria led her outside and away from the crowd. "I knew there had to be a girl you left behind, but this is rather Shakespearean, don't you think? Or would Jerry Springer be a better fit?"

She laughed, loving Bria's humor. "At this point I'm not sure. It's a toss-up."

"It should make for some interesting holidays if you ever come back here." They sat at one of the small tables scattered in the yard, and Bria flagged down a waiter.

"How do you figure, aside from the obvious?"

"Someone can start the Thanksgiving conversations by asking for everyone who's seen the bride naked to raise their hand. That'd be a great icebreaker, don't you think?"

"I'm sure that'd make me popular. What I don't understand is why no one told me. Hell, they called you." She finished her drink and was ready to go.

"It's because they love you that they couldn't tell you. Charlie gave me that long explanation, and I believed her. Who in their right mind wants to hurt someone they love?" Bria thanked the young man who set down a glass of champagne. "So…do you want to talk about it?"

"No more than your father wants to talk to the feds." She chuckled when Bria slapped her arm. "I promise I'll tell you, but give me a day. You're staying at least that long, right?"

"I'm staying as long as you need me, but right now you need to take me somewhere that isn't here." Bria finished her champagne and stood. "First let me tell your mother and her other offspring hello. You need to get out of here, but there's no reason to be rude."

She stayed out back, not regretting her bit of cowardice, and stared at the floating candles in the pool. Hands landing on her shoulder startled her into flinching, but she didn't turn around. "Hello, Brooks."

She didn't say anything as Eliza sat across from her and smiled. "Hi," she said, sounding like a dunce. Fallon and her sisters were all beautiful, but Eliza was different in personality. She was edgier—or maybe sharper was the right term. "How are you?"

"God, Brooks, really?" Eliza popped up with her hands on her hips. No one needed to be an expert on women to understand that move. "We haven't seen you in forever and you show up *here*. Are you fucking serious?"

"It's my family's home." She held up a finger, not anxious for the onslaught of Eliza's rage. "And my mother told me to put the suit on and be here at six. I was surprised my brother decided to get married, but the who totally blew me away when I saw them walk in." A second finger went up.

"You expect me to believe you didn't know?" Eliza's fists tightened on her hips.

"I don't expect anything from you," she said, standing and buttoning her jacket. "You might think I'm an asshole, but I'm not a liar. Now that I know I'm not welcome even if I live here, I'll leave."

"Brooks, wait."

"Look." She slid her hands into her pockets and rubbed the coins in the right one to try to distract herself from everything in her head. "I'm here because my mother asked for my help with something, so don't worry. You can put your bulldog routine away since I'm not going to mess up anyone's festivities. I'm sure the happy couple will have a beautiful wedding, even more so without me there."

Eliza called after her again, but she kept right on walking. She texted Bria that she was checking on her father one last time so they could head back into town. The back staircase allowed her to avoid everyone at the party, so she knocked on her dad's door without running into a soul. He was sitting in one of the wingbacks close to the fireplace with a book, appearing peaceful. His pajamas and robe meant he wouldn't be making an appearance downstairs, and she envied him that. Had anyone bothered to tell her who the guests of honor were, she'd be in her pj's somewhere too.

"You look good in formal wear," he said, snapping the book closed.

"I'd rather join you in a good book in my pajamas." She'd never known her father to read for fun, but it might help keep his mind working, so she was glad. "Add a good cigar and I'd be in heaven."

"I haven't had one of those since I can't remember when." He seemed to stop and think after that and laughed. "Considering my brain is screwed up, I guess that's normal."

She laughed with him, glad he could find humor in the completely unfunny diagnosis. "Did the doctor limit you on those?" The leather case in her inside pocket had two Romeo y Julieta cigars from Cuba. They were some of the perks to knowing the head of the East Coast mob. "Let's sit outside so we don't get in trouble with the boss," she said of her mother.

The ritual of preparing them to smoke was comforting. She'd seen Max do it for years, and she wondered if it's what had started her own habit. Max put the cigar under his nose and inhaled. These were worlds away from the crap he used to smoke when she was a kid. Her philosophy now was that life was too short to drink bad coffee and bourbon, and way too short to smoke bad cigars.

The torch got him to move it to his mouth, and he appeared blissful when he inhaled. "This is wonderful." He blew smoke over his head. The quiet of the yard was broken when the music started. "What'd you think of the party?"

"It was nice," was all she could think to say. "Mom hasn't lost her touch, though I think Eleanor Goodwin might've taken over on this one."

"The girl," he said puffing again. "She's *the* girl, isn't she?"

"For Curtis? Yes." This wasn't a conversation she was having with him. She intended to make amends, but not about Fallon. That road was permanently torn up and closed. He had, after all, been responsible for dynamiting it.

"No, for you. I ruined it for you." He sounded so agitated, and she moved to take his fisted hand when he hit himself in the head. The way he gazed at her made her think he was trying to put some pieces together, but there were missing swatches of memory. "Your mother called you because we're in trouble. That's right, isn't it?"

She shook her head and tightened her hold on his hand. "You need to concentrate on resting, and I'll help you with the everything else. I'll take care if it, I promise. The past is no place to dwell—it's only the future we need to concentrate on."

"No, I don't deserve it." He sounded upset, and it was escalating. She shook her head again and moved closer to him. "I did so much wrong, and I ruined your life. You're alone and it's my fault."

"I have a good life, Max." She held his hand tightly since he was fighting her to hit himself again and spoke as soothingly as she could. "You need to hear that, and that I forgive you."

"Do you love someone? Enough to have a family. You did once and I stole it from you. I did that."

"Listen to me." She moved and crouched in front of him. "What happened is done, and the blame lies with me. I should've handled it differently, and I should've asked her. I should've talked to her father and asked him too. Maybe she would've turned me down and maybe she'd have left with me. And maybe her father would've understood." He started sobbing again, and she felt something crack inside her. The man she'd known all her life was gone, and what was left was this broken soul she wrapped in a hug. "It was my mistake, okay?"

"Brooks, I'm so sorry. You're my child and I failed you so badly."

He fell against her and hung on as he cried. "We should be celebrating for you tonight, not anyone else."

"Dad"—the title made him cry harder—"we're going to be fine— *I'm* going to be fine. The rest worked out like it was supposed to, I guess. She and Curtis will be happy, and I'll do whatever it takes to make sure everyone else is good."

She held him until he calmed, and she got him inside and into bed. He held her hand until he fell asleep, and she watched his face relax. All those feelings she had when it came to him seem trivial as she watched him smile in his sleep. There was no choice now but to stay for as long as she had him and he'd understand what she was trying to tell him. What would it be like to have him stare right through her with no recognition? It would be a slap in the face for all the time they'd lost.

"You're a good kid," her mom said, and she embraced her from behind. "You're also stronger than I could ever be."

"I'm not that strong. Making money and existing doesn't take much effort." She let go of her father and turned to hold her mom. "God, why is this happening now?"

"If you ask your grandmother, she'd explain life's grand plan that leads us all to the grave. There's no escaping it. To me, though, it's nature's way of giving us a chance at peace. You know, having all those conversations everyone wants before it's too late." Her mom made sure her dad's blanket was perfect before moving to the chairs.

"What's that line…*Man makes plans, and God laughs*." She sighed and closed her eyes. "He must be having a great laugh now."

"This didn't happen to punish anyone, my love. Don't waste the time we have trying to find a reason. Both of you needed to find forgiveness, and it was good of you to offer it."

"Do you think he believes me?"

"I do." Mom smiled. "Now tell me how the girl you love ended up engaged to Curtis."

She laughed as she relit her cigar. "If there's such a thing as a million-dollar question, that'd be it."

❖

Fallon wanted to shove a stuffed shrimp in her mom's mouth to stop her big introduction and toast. If seeing Brooks at Saks the other day had affected her, now the shocked expression frozen on Brooks's face kicked her heart into overdrive. Her heart rate and rapid breathing were making it hard to stand there acting as if she was the happiest woman in Louisiana.

Curtis seemed to notice and tightened his hold on her by placing his hand on her hip and pulling her closer. She closed her eyes for an instant, but it was long enough for Brooks to disappear. That made her want to escape because becoming hysterical in the middle of a party with so many people wasn't a good idea.

People surrounded them, but she heard nothing as her attention went back to where Brooks had been standing surrounded by her siblings. This time she couldn't blame her for leaving, and Curtis's laugh was like an ice pick to the eye. He seemed to be glancing in the same direction, and she guessed it was the source of his amusement. He took her hand and led her to the dining room, where the caterers had filled the table and side buffets with enough food to feed three times more people than were there.

"That was hilarious. Fuck, that was the best," Curtis said as he grabbed a plate. "She couldn't take it and ran out of here like a chickenshit."

"What?" Her lungs were heaving like she'd run here from the city.

"High and mighty Brooks. Guess there are things in life where it doesn't matter how hard you work or how much money you have." He was gloating, and she didn't understand. "She's a loser, and she's way too late."

"Jesus." She walked away, but not before she noticed the woman who'd come in and greeted Brooks like she was the only one in the room. The woman was sitting at one of the cabaret rounds outside, but no Brooks. Curtis kept laughing, and she found it repulsive. Gloating was something she'd never found attractive in anyone.

The backyard was hot, but it was quiet except for a couple of people who were sitting and enjoying the food. The mystery woman was staring at her phone, and Fallon zeroed in on the empty glass across from her. She was about to head over and introduce herself when she heard talking from above. The deep voice that she still heard in her dreams drifted down, paralyzing her in the shadows.

The way Max cried and Brooks's responses made her sure they were talking about her. And when Brooks mentioned Curtis, it proved it. All she cared about was Brooks's response to Max's great confessions. Their relationship ended and she'd never known why, and it was the reason she was still angry about it.

When she'd been happy, that's all she concentrated on. There weren't any catastrophes in her future that would snatch it all away. She had everything she wanted, and she'd spend a lifetime building on the foundation she and Brooks had laid. Sure, they might face some unpleasant people once they went home after graduation, but she'd never expected the separation to come from Brooks.

It ended in a way that gutted her. Nothing had filled that hole, and it'd stayed empty. She couldn't stop the tears when she listened to the regret in Brooks's voice, but it wouldn't be that easy to forgive her. She'd carried all these emotions for too long to let go of them now with a simple I'm sorry.

"There you are," Bea said softly. "Are you okay?"

That question was getting tedious. She wasn't that much of a weakling. "I've been better, but I'll be okay. That'll be especially true once this is over."

"Don't be mad, but Eliza confronted Brooks."

It was amazing—when someone told you not to get mad, the complete opposite happened. Her sisters and Frankie loved her, and she loved them for looking out for her, but sometimes she wanted to fight her own battles. "Okay," she said, holding up her hand. "I don't want to know."

"We love you, and we're here. Don't forget that."

"I love you guys, and I need you to get me home."

"These people are here to celebrate you and Curtis, so you're not going anywhere." Her mother had been wrapped up in this wedding planning to a point where Fallon thought she'd lost touch with reality. "Get back in there and talk to people. If you think of leaving, I swear I'll hog-tie you to a chair in the front room."

"Mom, I love you, but you need to chill. I've done everything you wanted, but this isn't a game. I need you to back off."

Eliza showed up and held her hand out to her. "Are you ready?"

"Fallon, just take a breath." Her mother had both her hands up, and that's how Curtis found them.

"What's going on?" He took her hand and walked her away from everyone. "I know you aren't thrilled with all this, but it's only the night." He spoke in a harsh whisper, and she pushed him away by putting both her hands on his chest.

She was about to say something else to her mother when she noticed Scarlett step outside. They didn't know each other well, but it was obvious Scarlett was upset. "Everyone calm down, I'm not going anywhere. Just give me a minute to get some air."

Scarlett didn't look at her when she joined her on the deck out back. She didn't hear the whole story when Brooks was on the balcony, but it wasn't good. "Thank you for all this. I haven't been very helpful, and it sounds like you have your hands full."

"I'm surprised Curtis noticed," Scarlett said and laughed. "Can you tell me where he's been? We've all needed to talk to him, and he's disappeared until tonight."

"I don't have a good answer for that." It was as if they were both learning from each other how to navigate the landscape they were living in. The landmines were plentiful. "He said he was dealing with the accident, so he's been scarce."

"He's been avoiding family meetings." Scarlett finally faced her, her mouth in a tight line. "Monday, we'll begin the changes both Max and I want, and he's going to have to abide by those. You're going to be a part of this family, so it might be time to include you in all this."

"Scarlett, whatever you're facing—I'll be happy to help you. Curtis doesn't talk about your family much, and his mind has been on the boat you lost." Damn her decision to come out here. There hadn't been that many years since Brooks for her to forget how perceptive Scarlett was. "You can trust me to keep whatever's happening to myself if you need someone to talk to."

"Curtis likes to think he's Rockefeller when it comes to business, but his ideas don't always make much sense. Trying to get a contract for an entire new fleet is a good example of that." Scarlett laughed when she flinched. "Curtis can't get much past me, but I haven't been paying much attention. We're broken, and I don't care about anything but Max right now."

"Is there anything I can do?" Admitting to overhearing Brooks and Max didn't sound like a good idea.

"The world doesn't make a whole lot of sense, and it's only going to get more confusing." Scarlett pressed her palm to her cheek and stared up at the sky. "If this…" Scarlett pointed behind her and seemed to study her as if something important depended on her answer. "If this is what you truly want, then don't let go and love our boy. Life's too short to compromise on happiness and love. Remember that as you move forward with plenty of people pushing you in a direction you might not want."

What she'd wanted was long gone and unrecognizable. Brooks had moved on and had come back with her complete opposite on her arm. The outfit she'd gotten for this farce wasn't her normal style, but it didn't come close to Brooks's girlfriend. Hell, anyone would feel frumpy next to the beautiful brunette.

"Forget about the contract and everything else. I promise whatever you need from me, I'll do it."

"Remember, honey, life's also too short not to forgive. All these secrets have torn us all to shreds, and we've all lost out on so much." Scarlett hugged her and walked away.

That left her conflicted. She wanted to go, but this was where she belonged at the moment. All she could promise herself was to talk to Brooks if she saw her, but she knew she was gone, and she wasn't chasing after her. The rest of the night was long, and it was a relief when Eliza drove her home. She changed and sat on her sofa for an hour before she couldn't resist the need to move.

The drive to the end of Canal Street next to the aquarium didn't take long, and she parked on the street. The spot was perfect for watching boat traffic and the lit-up bridges that traversed the river. She and Brooks had ended plenty of their dates here, and they'd shared plenty of those secrets Scarlett had talked about at this spot.

That Brooks was sitting on the bench at the end wasn't completely unexpected, but still surreal. If she could turn back time, it wasn't hard to imagine Brooks waiting for her. When they both had enough of their families, Brooks would go for a run and she'd pick her up here. They'd enjoy the view unique to the city—the one that gave New Orleans its nickname. The crescent was at its most pronounced and a navigational nightmare, but she loved it. This spot was theirs and where you could really see the power of the river.

"Why are you back?" Her question maybe wasn't a place to start, but she deserved answers.

"Hello, Fallon." Brooks didn't turn around or stand. "There's not anything I can say that'll make a difference, but—"

"That's where you're wrong." She stopped when she saw Brooks's tears. "All I've ever wanted was to know why. Why the hell did you leave me here alone and cut me out of your life?"

"I lost out too." Brooks wiped her face and turned away from her. "I left so you could have a chance at a happy life. You were the most precious thing to me, and your family was important to you. I can't take it back, but I did my best in the choices I had to make. In my very limited choices."

"That's total bullshit. If you wanted more than I could give you, admit it. I'm a big girl, and it would've saved us all this." She wanted to scream as a way of releasing all her frustrations but didn't want to alert the police.

"Believe what you want, and congratulations. You've moved on, so none of this should matter."

Fallon shook her head and pressed her hands to Brooks's chest to push her away even if she wasn't moving toward her. "No…you don't get to play the victim."

"You're engaged to Curtis," Brooks said like someone had fed her cow manure. The words seemed to taste bad in her mouth. "Congratulations. I'm not here to mess that up, so you can tell your sisters to stand down. If I'd known it was an engagement party for you and Curtis, believe me, I would've skipped it not to upset you."

"Why are you here, then?" God, she sounded so self-absorbed.

"My father's been diagnosed with Alzheimer's, and he made some bad business decisions that've put them in a bind. He and my mother need help, and I'm here for the cleanup that has to happen. That's all. The last thing I'm going to do is screw up your plans." Brooks sounded like she hurt. It was the type of ache that reached your soul. "Curtis has missed all the meetings Max has arranged, so go ahead and tell him."

Brooks was leaving, and Fallon felt small and more than petty. Her anger was justified, but there were more important things. "Brooks, wait."

"Listen, all I wanted is for you to be happy. If Curtis is the person who brings you that, if he's your person, then the past will work itself out. It's not important any longer." Those beautiful eyes were still swimming in tears. "I'll try to be done before the wedding, and maybe we can have coffee or something and talk."

"I'd like that." She'd kicked herself later for the quick response. "How about tomorrow?"

"I'm at the Piquant and I should be back by four or so. Max is better in the mornings, and I want another day in the office with no one there."

"Will you tell me?" Brooks nodded as if she didn't have to elaborate on her question.

"If you want." Brooks lifted her hand and seemed to rethink it, letting it fall back to her side. "I don't deserve to say this, but I've missed you."

She nodded and couldn't respond. Brooks being Brooks walked her to her car to make sure she was safe. That same smooth stride made her stare at Brooks's retreat. That's when it occurred to her. Brooks had been waiting for her. Whoever the pretty woman with her was, she must've not minded Brooks meeting her, or Brooks had lied. Whatever it was, Brooks had been waiting because they still knew each other that well.

"Hang tough or you're screwed." It was the only advice she could give herself.

CHAPTER EIGHT

Brooks texted Bria when she woke. She was headed for the office for a few hours to wade through the mound of financials waiting on her. Bria had plenty of friends in the city and didn't need babysitting, but she didn't want to be rude—after all, Bria had come for her.

The books surprised her—the business *should* be swimming in money. From what she could tell, they could replace the fleet as well as expand without any outside financing.

There was such a thing as too good to be true, though. This was a rosy picture that was as fictional as a romance novel. Curtis had done a good job of burying the problems so that even the boxes of records her mother had given her couldn't break through if you didn't know what you were looking at. She grabbed the folder with the year's financials and the truck keys, to go to the one place Curtis couldn't hide.

Brooks opened the door, and her momentum almost carried her into Fallon, who jumped back.

"Hey," Fallon said with her hand on her chest. "I tried calling, and your girlfriend said you were here."

"Bria's my business partner." She stood in the doorway and waited to see which direction Fallon wanted to head. "She is a girl and a good friend, but not my girlfriend in the context you're implying." Why the hell was she giving this long explanation to her brother's fiancée? Fallon couldn't care less about the relationship she had with anyone.

"I thought we could get that drink and talk." The way Fallon changed the subject and ignored her answer gave her a hint as to how this was going to go. Time to put on her cool business facade and not drop it as she sat through the anger-fueled lecture she had coming. She'd gladly do it since Fallon deserved her pound of flesh.

"How about a stop before that?" She locked the door and waited. "Sure." Fallon was hard to read, and it made her chest ache. There was a moment in her life when she could read this woman without having to ask anything. "Do you want me to drive?"

"How about if I drive, and I promise to bring you back whenever you've had enough?" She pointed to the truck and waited again.

"Let's go." Fallon beat her to the vehicle and got in like if she didn't hurry, she'd miss her chance.

The drive to Blanchard's didn't take long, and brunch was underway. She realized they'd never get a table, but she wasn't here to eat. All her answers weren't in the fake books, and Blanchard's was part of that puzzle since they were ordering plenty of seafood from them. The maître d' hugged her when he noticed her, and she remembered all the lunches she'd had with him. Miguel had been with Blanchard's for years, but he was ready to start his own place.

"Miguel." She patted him on the back, liking his genuineness. The guy could write a set of books about how to successfully run a restaurant. "Are you getting close?"

"Keegan and Della offered me the space they've been looking at downtown. With your advice and planning along with a partnership with Della, I should be open in less than a year." After so many years with the Blanchard family, she couldn't blame him for wanting to continue the relationship, and with the experience Della and her family had in the business, Miguel would be successful.

"The financing is in place, and both Bria and I will walk you through the process." She stepped back and introduced Fallon. "Is Keegan in?"

"She's gearing up for the crowds, but she should have a few minutes if you don't mind the chef's table." He stretched his arm out toward the kitchen and allowed them to go ahead.

Brooks always loved the symphony of a well-run kitchen. When she worked on a boat in the summers, her father had insisted she go along when they delivered. Their business thrived because of places like Blanchard's. Whatever her mother was worried about and was stressing her father would be found here.

"Brooks Boseman," Keegan said with her hands on her hips. "God, it's been too long."

"It has considering how fantastic it smells in here." She introduced Fallon again and waited for her and Keegan to sit before joining them.

Kenan unbuttoned her chef's coat at the neck and nodded to the staff member who served them all ice water. "They called in the big guns to change my mind, huh?"

The question was answer enough. They were in the books, but it was bogus. "I'm more of a small pistol shooting in the dark. Want to tell me what happened?" If they lost Blanchard's, the other five restaurants they owned were most likely gone as well.

She listened and watched Fallon. Maybe it hadn't been a good idea to bring her, since she'd be a pipeline of information back to Curtis. Then again, having Curtis know that she had the information he'd tried to hide would make him come clean. Missed orders, pink shrimp, and small size at jumbo shrimp prices had led the Blanchard restaurants to a different vendor.

"The small shrimp were almost forgivable, but pink shrimp aren't something I'll ever put in one of my pots, much less on a plate." Keegan stopped to taste a couple of sauces various kitchen crew brought her in small bowls, nodding each time.

Pink shrimp were a sign of age and spoilage, so she couldn't blame Keegan for her decision to stop doing business with them. "Mom asked me to take over while Max is under the weather. If I can straighten out quality control, would you give us another chance?"

"We've known each other a long time, Brooks, so I want to be honest." Keegan glanced at Fallon before going on. "With you in charge, I'll definitely give you a shot, but if you're only here temporarily, I'll have to have some guarantees. If there's another string of problems, we'll still be friends, but the change in vendors will be permanent."

"Totally acceptable, and I'm not going anywhere until I can back those guarantees." She took a few notes after asking a few more questions and stayed until Keegan was comfortable with the deal they'd made. "As a sign of good faith, how about the first few weeks of deliveries will be on us?"

"Not necessary, but I'll take it." Keegan laughed and held her hand out to Fallon. "And I apologize for not congratulating you sooner. I was working last night, so I couldn't make it to the party, but hopefully you were happy with the food. My sister and I took care of the catering. You're marrying into an awesome family."

"Thank you." Fallon smiled but Brooks could tell she wasn't happy, or maybe uncomfortable was a better word.

"We'll let you get back to it, and thanks for seeing me," Brooks said. "I'll be in touch." They were silent as they waited for the truck.

Silence didn't bother her like it did others who had the need to talk to cover awkwardness. "Do you still want to get that drink?"

"Can I ask you something?"

She could feel Fallon's eyes on her, and that didn't bother her either. "Sure. That's what I promised last night. You can ask anything."

"Are you here to sink Curtis?"

She came close to laughing at the question, but a quick glimpse of Fallon's serious expression helped to tamp that down. "That's not my goal, no. Running the business was always not only his dream but my father's."

"Do you think that's a bad idea?"

"I don't see what I'm doing as sinking someone or trying to upset the hierarchy. What's important to me is trying to find a solution after Max put everything he and my mother have to keep Boseman's afloat. Failure means losing a lot more than losing the business, their house, and everything they own. It's a loss of my father's legacy and, more important, the livelihoods of my brothers and sisters." She'd never run head-on into a brick wall repeatedly, but she was starting to get the gist of what that would feel like. "The job I agreed to is to fix what's broken."

"That's not what Curtis thinks," Fallon said, fixated on the subject.

"I've met with Charlie, Etienne, and Prudence." She headed back to the office and Fallon's car. Not only was this a waste of time, it was a reality check. Any chance of fixing what she'd done was lost in the face of Curtis's ability to bend the truth. She was the bad guy now for more than just leaving Fallon. "They understand what I'm doing and what's at stake. This isn't about ego, or a pissing contest."

They rode in silence until Fallon seemed to notice where they were going. "What are you doing?"

"There's plenty I've done wrong, Fallon, and that's weighed on me from then on. I'm accountable for all of them, and I'm smart enough to know they can't be undone." She pulled up to Fallon's car and didn't turn the engine off. "I can apologize until I'm dead, and that isn't going to change those mistakes. But I need you to understand that whatever mistakes I've made, they were done with your happiness at heart."

"Leaving without talking to me wasn't done for my happiness." Fallon sounded loud in the enclosed space. "You made us both miserable, and for what? Money? How do you think I felt when you traded me for the life you wanted? A life that didn't include me."

As low as the plane ride to England the day after the argument with

Max had been, this moment trumped sitting surrounded by strangers as her heart felt like it was dying. That bone-deep loneliness had made her ill, and only Bria's friendship and understanding had somewhat cleared the fog. But the self-inflicted wounds still festered and bled, not enough to kill her but just enough to keep her hurting. Fallon's words ripped that scar open, and she needed to get away.

"If that's what you think, get out." Her tone was the opposite of Fallon's, but it fit since she didn't have the strength to get loud. They were in different places, with different priorities.

"You haven't changed a bit. You're still selfish and an asshole who doesn't care about anything or anyone."

Brooks had never eaten at a Benihana restaurant, but Fallon wielded her words as well as their chefs did their knives. All she had to do was survive the barrage, because Fallon had the right to everything she'd said, and Brooks could heal by burying herself in work. Curtis had won Fallon's heart, but the truth and the impact on her soul would have to come later because she wouldn't show her pain now.

"If it helps you to hate me"—she tightened her grip on the steering wheel and took a deep breath to keep herself together—"go ahead and hate me. Believe whatever you want about me and be happy. I hope you and Curtis have a great life."

Fallon screamed in apparent frustration. "You're unbelievable."

"You're right." Maybe if she was agreeable, Fallon would leave. Confrontation wasn't a great talent in her wheelhouse unless it involved negotiations. She flinched when Fallon gave her what she wanted and slammed the door hard enough to rock the truck.

It was easy to see why Fallon and Curtis had ended up together. The passion that had drawn her to Fallon had turned into something dark and vengeful. "Have a good life," she said to the rearview mirror. All that was left was to get the job done and get back to her life. There was nothing left for her here.

❖

Fallon watched Brooks drive away, and it drove her temper up a notch. She was angry, but not just at Brooks. She'd failed at getting answers because she couldn't be rational. "Fuck," she yelled as the truck turned out of sight.

"Fuck indeed."

The sound of someone being so close sped her heart rate and brought her hands up in a defensive posture. She turned and relaxed at the sight of the woman from the night before. It was already warm, but the petite brunette appeared cool and unaffected in the linen suit that fit her perfectly. This was someone who was comfortable in her own skin. She was small but demanded respect, so Fallon stood and didn't say anything.

"You did a great job driving her off—literally." The woman cocked her head and stared at her like she was simple-minded. "Forgive my manners." The smart-ass offered her hand. Fallon would have to take five steps forward to take it, so manners had nothing to do with this. It was a power play, and she was way behind with no chance at catching up. "You were wrapped up in your fiancé, so I didn't get to meet you last night. Bria Giordano—Brooks's business partner."

"She mentioned you." She hated herself for being the one who moved, but today was a total loss, so what was a bit more humiliation. "Did you walk here?"

"The hotel provided a car, and I'm waiting for a friend. I was just checking on Brooks. She has a habit of getting lost in the numbers if left alone."

"I'm sure you have plenty of ways to make her forget work." Could she check off a few more things to make herself appear pathetic today? There was no reason for her to sound like a jealous shrew, but here she was.

"Is it the heat that's making you"—Bria cocked her head in the opposite direction but added a condescending smile—"*crazy* is what you're expecting, but I hate using that word. You're acting jealous, and that doesn't make sense either. One, you're engaged, and two, you didn't give her a chance to explain herself."

"You don't know anything about me, so don't try to analyze me." In a way she couldn't blame Brooks if this was her choice. Bria was everything she wasn't, and she knew all of Brooks, at least who Brooks was now. She obviously loved Brooks and was ready to stand up for her. "That she told you what she refused me says all I need to know. Brooks was a coward then and she hasn't changed."

"Honey, I've tried to get this story out of her for years. Moving forward is only possible by letting go of the past." Bria checked her phone and moved the expensive purse to the other arm. "Brooks is an extraordinary person, and at the center of her is this place. No matter how successful she gets, she can't let go of the kid who worked on a boat in the summer and loved you."

"Maybe she didn't tell you, but she left me without a word. It's like one day she was here, and then she wasn't, and I've never heard from her again until yesterday." She was tired of having her feelings challenged, especially by someone who didn't know her. "You don't do that to someone you love. I doubt she's gained any integrity in the time we've been apart."

"She blew off a huge deal because her family needed her. That's the reason people line up to work with her. Integrity isn't her problem."

"I've known Brooks for most of my life. You don't need to tell me all the things I already know." The strange thing was she'd felt more in the last couple of hours than she had in months. Coasting wasn't the best plan when it came to life, but she'd gotten good at it.

"Okay," Bria said. Texting or calling for help—it was a toss-up at this point. "I got it, and I'll mind my own business. You go and marry someone you seem to be as interested in as I am in getting herpes. The faster you get down that aisle, the faster I get the full story out of Brooks. Admitting you have a problem is the fastest way to get over it." A black SUV with dark tinted windows stopped a few feet from them, and a large man got out of the passenger side and opened the back door. "You know, the few times she's mentioned you—at least, I guess it was you—I thought you'd be smarter."

"You're very blunt." She wasn't sure who Bria was, but she was captivating. Another trait she didn't possess.

Bria laughed as she started for her ride. "Blunt is telling you all that the simplest way I could think, but I figure you already know that you're a dumbass. I thought I was being nice and gave you a shred of credit."

Fallon stood alone and had to laugh. Whoever Bria was to Brooks, she was hard to dislike. Her day was shot, so there was no reason to try to salvage it. Curtis was quick to respond to her text, and she was glad he was still down the bayou since she needed the long drive. With any luck she could find Brooks when she was done with Curtis.

The serenity of the moss-draped trees and the waterways did let her breathe and let go of all the heaviness of the morning. She loved her house uptown, but this place was as much a part of her as Bria had said about Brooks. It didn't define her in the way Bria probably meant, yet she liked the way it made her appreciate her history. The reminder that she came from a long line of people who loved the land, worked hard, and raised families who were taught all those values was brought home every time she got down here.

She found Curtis wiping his car down with a diaper, and it made her roll her eyes. He was about as complex as a brick, but he appeared chipper. That surprised her, considering what was happening to his family. "Hey," she said, and Curtis raised his hand and came closer.

He placed the diaper on the hood, and she came close to leaving. Curtis wasn't someone she recognized any longer, and his attitude made her not want to know why he'd changed from the friend she'd depended on. All the things he'd said about Brooks last night exposed a new side of him, and she wondered how she fit into whatever this was. "Hey, you're a nice surprise." His hand was soft when he took hers and walked them out back by the bayou.

She didn't see the truck Brooks was using and was glad for now. "It's nice that you stayed with your parents last night. I'm sure your mom appreciated it."

"Yeah, she told me dad has Alzheimer's. Kind of shocking but it's good for us." He sounded so matter-of-fact as he got them a bottle of water.

"Good for us? What are you talking about?" She tried to remember any conversation she'd had with Brooks about Curtis. All she remembered was this was the only sibling she wasn't close to.

"If Pop isn't capable of running the company, I'm taking over. Now I can make the changes I want, and no one can say otherwise." He drank the entire bottle without taking a breath, and it was like putting a spotlight on him as the odd man out in the Boseman family. "The problems we've been having are due to the handcuffs my parents put on me."

"I don't think Max is completely incapacitated, and you should check to see if he didn't turn control over to your mom. She's the one who helped him build a business in this generation." It didn't take much to realize what Brooks was facing when it came to Curtis.

"Mom said she's not interested, so I called my attorney this morning."

She put her hand up to stop him. Big family dramas weren't her expertise, and she didn't want to get dragged into this one. "Think about the whole picture, Curtis. Getting lawyers involved when your family is facing what's coming isn't the way to go. You should try to spend time with your dad before the disease steals what you all love about him."

"You don't understand." All the warmth left him as he glared at her. "Dear old Dad told Brooks how it was going to be, and she fucking ran. She couldn't handle me at the top."

"Do you know what happened?" This was her chance. "The Brooks I know wouldn't have cut ties to the point she has because your dad chose you."

"Ha," he barked, unrecognizable. "You think you know her, but do you really? Brooks is a petty lesbian who couldn't hack what Dad wanted. He wanted her to help me, but all she wanted was to show me up." He stood and walked to the edge of the deck.

"Curtis," she said, standing and putting her hands on his shoulders, "I don't think that's true. There has to be more to it than that."

He turned and held her. "That's all I know, and he's compared us ever since. I was an idiot to think once she was gone, he'd be happy. All he's done ever since is compare us, and hell if I don't always come up short. I'm sick of it, and not even getting engaged to you has made him happy."

That made her push against him with the need to see his face. "What?" This was so aggravating. There were answers but they were ether, impossible to grasp.

"Don't worry about it." He pulled her closer and kissed her.

The move was unexpected and like no other kiss they'd shared. It felt almost cruel if that was possible, and the car door slamming behind them made her cock her head back. It was a hell of a time for Curtis to start acting like a fiancé. They both glanced toward the driveway, and she recognized the truck. She wanted to gloat, and having Brooks see her like this with Curtis was the sight she knew would hurt more than anything else she could do, and Brooks deserved it. She *wanted* to feel that way, but that wasn't her.

"Our situation hasn't changed, but I want you to think about what you're doing. What's happening is hard, and you don't want to regret anything. There are no do-overs, and you don't have much time." She stopped him from kissing her again. "Airing everything you think is wrong with your family isn't something you should do to your parents, no matter how you feel about them."

"We aren't the Waltons." He held her until she stepped completely away from him. "The thing I like about you is that you understand me. I don't want much, but I want to continue my family's company and be married to you. This feels like it should be more than pretend."

Before she could say anything, Curtis kissed her again, and she didn't know exactly how to react until her brain kicked into gear. Thankfully it happened before his tongue made it into her mouth. "Right now, think about helping your family and how *this isn't real.* If you can't accept that, we need to end this before it gets any more complicated."

"Why?" He took her hand and kissed her palm.

She was having an out-of-body experience. It was the only explanation for the runaway train she was on. "Because we're friends. That's all. To make a relationship work it has to be way more than that, and it's never going to be."

"You have to give it a chance. That kiss and how you reacted was real. Just admit it."

She loved when people thought for her and told her how to feel. He smiled when she shook her head. It was so patronizing. There was nothing else she wanted to say, so she walked away. She had to accept there were no good answers, and the best thing was to leave the Boseman family behind. It was a history with a murky ending, but it had to be an ending.

Brooks's truck was parked on the side of the road in front of Deuce Miller's house. Deuce had been a captain for the Bosemans from the time she and Brooks were in high school, and he was smiling as he sat on his porch. Her plan was to keep going and head home. That was her plan, but she parked in front of Brooks and waited. She was pathetic, but she could work on her willpower later.

CHAPTER NINE

Brooks shook hands with Deuce, glad he answered her questions without much cajoling. The impromptu meeting was her attempt at forgetting the kiss she'd witnessed. Leopards couldn't change their spots, but it was obvious Fallon could change the core of who she was.

"It could be she was faking it with you," she said to herself. Fallon's window was down, so she stopped next to it and leaned in. "I haven't changed my unbelievable ways since this morning."

"Do you want to follow me or ride with me?" Fallon sounded vastly different than earlier.

"Deuce," she called and threw him the keys. "Call Monroe, please. Tell her to have someone drive it back to my hotel. Thanks."

They drove in silence until they reached the city. She enjoyed the landscape, letting her head fall back, curious as to where they were going but not enough to ask. It took over an hour before they stopped at the nice house uptown. The Shasta daisies planted along the front were the only clue she needed to know it belonged to Fallon. A sudden thought that she might share it with Curtis increased her stomach acid.

"I don't want to scream at you in the car." Fallon got out and didn't look back.

"That walk hasn't changed a bit." She got out and entered through the door Fallon had left open, taking the sight of those snug jeans with her.

It was the pictures that hit her like a tsunami. They were historical markers in a life full of family and adventure, and none of them included her. Fallon had lived well and stayed close her family. It was all the things she'd wanted for her. If she was honest, maybe Curtis wasn't what she'd wanted for her, but it was way too late to fight for a life with this woman. Rivals for Fallon's love was an idiot's game, and besides, Fallon had already chosen.

"I met Bria this morning." Fallon pulled a wine bottle from the cooler and took two glasses out of the cabinet behind her. She laid the opener on the counter and stared at her.

She got the hint and got to work opening it. "Should I apologize?" There was no way to guess what would come out of Bria's mouth if provoked.

"She's certainly protective."

"The same can be said of Eliza." She pulled the cork and poured. "You can report back that I'm not going to be a problem. I'm glad you're happy, and I'll never get in the way of that. The visit and the wine aren't necessary."

"You don't know a damn thing about me." Fallon was right—she wanted to scream in private. "Goddamn you. Just goddamn you."

Her instinct was to hold Fallon, but she couldn't afford any broken fingers or to be accused of being an asshole. "Today was hard." She sat and exhaled. "When I was twenty-one, I let you go." She stopped when her throat closed, and she didn't want to break down. "It was the right thing, yet it was hard...so very hard. What took me longer to accept was that you'd never forgive me. Today proved me right."

"Tell me why. I know it has to do with Max, but I don't know exactly what." The tone Fallon used was a mixture of steel and defeat. "The way you left me gutted me."

"Trust me, I was right there too. With a bit more life experience I knew I'd fucked up, but when I left, I didn't know that. I ran because I owed it to you, even if you think I'm a bastard for it."

Fallon sat next to her on the sofa facing her. "Is it why you don't come home, not really? I know you visit, but never for more than a couple of days."

There was nothing to gain in exposing Max for who he was, considering what he was facing. Bigoted asshole or not, Max was going to be Fallon's father-in-law, her family. Your own family was bad enough when it came to acceptance, so starting over with your husband's would take time. This would be one more thing she'd have to sacrifice. Throwing blame at Max's feet would be easy, but it'd be like picking a fight with a kitten.

"What I did to you was wrong. I should've asked you to come with me, but I screwed up by picking for you. I thought it either had to be me or your family, and to me that was an impossible choice. The easiest thing was to remove the least important factor."

"Least important factor?" Fallon asked, her voice much softer. "If you mean you, you were the most important person in my life, and you were gone. Just like that."

"An apology is never going to be enough, but I *am* sorry." She swallowed, feeling her pride slide down her throat. "Even with all the pain I caused you, I'm glad you moved forward. You might not think I care, but if you need me, I'm a call away."

"Why does Max deserve such loyalty?"

The question made Brooks chuckle. "Max has had his world rocked. He might or might not have time to put his affairs in order and all that, but I won't add to his problems. All I'm here to do is fix what's wrong with the company. The rest was a surprise, but in reality, not."

Fallon nodded as she closed her eyes. "I was the last thing on your mind *again*."

"Do you think I left here and never thought of you?" Saying the words was hard, but keeping them in was impossible. "You're in my thoughts every single day. I've worked hard because I had to. Money has been easy to make—a life has not. Sometimes your mistakes scar you enough that it's impossible to start over."

"Why didn't you ever call me before now?" Fallon's wineglass made a loud ping when she put it down with almost enough force to break it. "It's been years, Brooks."

"When you dig, it's hard to stop, and you end up in a deep hole." She smiled and Fallon's tears sucked the life out of her. "I'm an idiot, but I'm smart enough to know you wouldn't be alone forever. Seeing you with someone else wasn't in me, and the longer I waited, the bigger the chances were that's what would happen. Last night proved me right."

"Brooks—" Fallon said, and Brooks put her hand up to stop her.

"You don't have to explain. Curtis is a lucky man, and I need to get back to work." She put her untouched wine next to Fallon's and stood. "Thanks for the drink."

She walked out, realizing she'd gotten a ride from Fallon. There was no way in hell she was going back in, so she started walking. "Consider that your wedding gift." She glanced back, glad not to see Fallon coming after her. "Any more baring of my soul and I'll have to give up people altogether."

❖

Fallon bit her tongue when she turned around and Bea was standing in her kitchen pouring herself some wine. Since she hadn't heard the door, her sister had been somewhere in the house.

"Don't worry," Bea said as she flopped down on the corner of the sofa. "If you'd gotten her naked, I would've climbed out the window."

"You're nothing but a giver." She took the other end and tried not to think about the long walk Brooks had to reach her office.

"True, but you also have to admit she's less of an asshole than we thought." Bea glanced at her phone, then tapped something out, which meant Eliza and Frankie were on their way. "She's not great at answering direct questions, but there might be a reason for that."

"If you're like everyone else, you know but will refuse to tell me." She got up and went to her room to change. Torture was always more tolerable in yoga pants.

Pretty much everyone she was related to was in her den by the time she put on an off-the-shoulder T-shirt. She glanced at her feet and thought about Brooks. The dark red nail polish was something she'd never given up even if it brought Brooks to mind every single time she noticed her toes.

"Do you have any more wine?" Frankie asked.

"The red is at the bottom, but that's the last of the white." She slid into some sandals and grabbed her purse. "I'll go get some."

"The tall handsome bottle shouldn't have reached Canal Street yet," Bea said. "And should've also cooled by now."

Fallon pulled out and started down the street, turning off her thoughts. It was the only way to shut down the voice in her head that was chanting *mistake* rather loudly, but it was saying the same thing the day Brooks kissed her for the first time. Brooks was standing in front of the Latter Library like she was admiring the architecture. They'd spent plenty of time here too.

"Hey, are you hungry?" Of course she'd changed into what was basically her pajamas.

"Depends." Brooks smiled at her, and she held her breath.

"Get in, asshole." It'd been years since she'd heard Brooks laugh, and it did something to her. Brooks got in and waved her on.

She thought about it after considering how they were dressed and made a turn toward the river and Tchoupitoulas. It was a gamble to bring a New Yorker to a pizza place, but the NOLA Pizza Company was a winner since it was also a brewpub.

Brooks opened the door for her, and the hostess had a smile only for Brooks. That hadn't changed much either. It wasn't until they were facing each other in a booth that Fallon thought about what she'd done. She'd wanted a less complicated life, and spending time with Brooks was going to be like getting a PhD in quantum physics.

"Can I be inappropriate for a moment?" Brooks ask.

"Depends," she repeated Brooks's taunt.

"On?" Brooks glanced up at the waitress then her. She nodded and Brooks ordered for both of them, including a summer flight of light beers.

"How inappropriate, of course." She waited for the beers and tapped their glasses together.

"I was only going to mention that you're still beautiful. You haven't changed, and you're going to be my sister-in-law, so that's all I got on that subject." Brooks still had that same tell when it came to telegraphing her nervousness, and it put them on more even ground. She twirled her glass with twitchy fingers but had no problem with eye contact. "Let's talk about now."

"Sure." She took a sip, and the coldness shocked her system. "Tell me about yourself."

"I work with Bria on the BoseLilly Hedge Fund, and that's going well. Work's interesting because it's always different." Brooks shrugged, and she wanted to laugh at the very un-Brooks move. "It takes a lot of my time, so I don't have much of a social life."

"You must do something for fun." As much as she remembered about Brooks, there was plenty different. She was closed off, but the charm hid it well.

"I get to different museums on the weekends or if I get off early enough. One of my favorites is the Neue Galerie. I could stare at Adele Bloch-Bauer's portrait for hours. The world knows her as the woman in gold, but it helps me think." Brooks's hands stopped and her face relaxed.

"Think about what?" She couldn't help but gaze down Brooks's body. She was still fit and carried it with a smooth ease that made her appear powerful even when she was sitting still. She'd felt as if nothing bad would ever touch her when Brooks had held her.

"Legacy. That family lost so much to the Nazis, but they couldn't be erased. People know their story of how they beat back fear. It didn't swallow them whole and should be celebrated."

There was no way to be sure, but she instinctively knew Brooks had shared too much by the way she suddenly stopped talking. "I've never seen it."

"If you're ever in New York, I'll be happy to show it to you. It's a beautiful piece, and she was a beautiful woman." Brooks blushed, and it made Fallon chuckle.

"It's just me, Brooks," she said. "I've been mad for a long time, but I'm still the person you know. We might not be what we were, but we can be friends."

"I'd like that, and it's more than I deserve."

It was a line. She knew that, but Brooks sounded truthful, so she didn't call her on it. "Mistakes, my dad always says, aren't fatal unless you play Russian roulette with a loaded gun. You haven't been my favorite person from the day you disappeared, but I've missed you."

"I've missed you too, and you're a generous grader." Brooks lifted her glass again and waited. "To friendship—and finding it again."

"You've become poetic, Ms. Boseman." She tapped her glass to Brooks's and smiled. "I totally agree, though."

The rest of dinner went a lot smoother, and the conversation was mostly about what Brooks had been up to. She was surprised by who Bria's family was and laughed at how many times Brooks said the word *alleged*. Investing money for the mob didn't sound like a good idea, but it was impressive. It was obvious Brooks had been able to beat back the fear as well to forge a life for herself away from everything she'd known.

"You must be good at your job." The waitress put down another round, and she thought before picking up the glass and taking a drink. There was no way she could drive home. "That's quite the niche, though."

"When I left, Max cut me off. Said he'd refuse to pay another dime of tuition until I came to my senses." It had to be the beer talking, since Brooks hadn't said a word against Max. "I worked as a bartender in England, and then I met Bria, or more importantly, I met Angelo because I'd met Bria. He's been good to me, and very generous. It wasn't like selling my soul to Satan or anything, but he traded rent for me looking after his only daughter. She became a good friend, and eventually my business partner."

"I bet," she said softly, glad that Brooks chose to ignore it. "Why did Max cut you off? I can't see Scarlett going along with that."

"It was the easiest way to get me to come home and give him what he wanted. His ultimatum was clear, and he backed me into a corner with no good choices. The safest one was leaving you and your family intact."

The light bulb went off and it made her angrier. "What business did Max have with my father back then?"

"It's ancient history, Fallon, so let it go. Right now, it'll do no one any good to dredge it all up again." Brooks sighed as if she should've just kept her mouth shut.

"Tell me," she said through gritted teeth. All this time she had a clue it was about money, and it sucked that she was right. Brooks had chosen the easy way out.

"Okay…you might not remember, but there'd been a downturn in the oil and gas business at the end of our junior year. Oil was worth nothing a barrel, but your dad chose that time to expand." Brooks gave her a history lesson she knew by heart, and it was her father's gutsy call that had given them the space and capacity they had now.

"Don't drag my father into this," she said, the anger coming back. "Neither he nor anyone in my family has anything to do with what you did."

"Your dad had gotten more contracts than he really had the ability to complete, so he expanded, and that decision led him to be leveraged a bit too much for the bank to want to help. He had one option, and Max offered a loan. It was paid back years ago and the only dealing they ever had." Brooks gave her the kind of full attention others found disconcerting at times. "You marrying Curtis will be the only other time our families will intersect."

"Huh," she said, blinking slowly. Brooks gave just enough information to answer the question, but like in all this, there was more.

"Like I said, Fallon, it's ancient history. Nothing to worry about. The other thing you don't have to worry about is Max. We haven't always agreed on much, but it's time for everyone, including me, to make their peace. He might not be near death, but he's nearing an end where it might be too late to resonate if there's something that needs to be put to rest."

"You want me to talk to Curtis." It was a fact, not a question.

"Knowing you, you've already done that." Brooks smiled again. "I'm sure you know, though, that Curtis isn't easily convinced of anything." The waiter dropped off the bill and Brooks took care of it. "This time around, don't push. Just remind him he'll have to live with whatever relationship he has now if he doesn't face this."

"Is that what motivated you?"

"Max deserves to know I don't hate him more than I need to hang on to my pride. Whatever my feelings are, those are mine, but I didn't have it in me not to try. No matter what happens, what he's facing, and how I feel about it, he's my father. Relationships with parents are often complicated, and I'm not immune to that."

She nodded and pushed the half empty glass aside. "You're a good person, Brooks."

"I'm more of a capable idiot." Brooks took out her phone and typed in something. "Come on and I'll take you home. You can get your car later."

The Uber driver hummed the entire way, and she smiled at the way Brooks mashed her teeth together. For some reason the mob didn't bother her, but humming drove her up the wall. All the cars that were in her driveway when she left were still there, and she hoped they stayed inside until Brooks was gone. The hummer waited until Brooks walked her to the door.

"Thanks for the invite. It was nice spending time with you." Brooks lifted her hand and dropped it, so it was impossible to know why she'd done it. She turned to go and stopped when Fallon said her name.

"Brooks, you *are* a good person. Don't forget that." Brooks lifted her hand again in farewell before she got in the car. "Damn, why is nothing ever easy."

CHAPTER TEN

By the end of the next week, Brooks had made visits to most of their accounts in the city and cut ties with some of the independent fishermen Curtis had approved. Only one guy, a Dellow something, had a problem with it. He and his sons had screamed at her for ten solid minutes before she walked away, not having time for bullshit.

Being short on inventory was better than trying to sell bad inventory. She was planning to spend the next couple of days and the weekend on the water, inspecting boats. All in all, she had a much clearer picture of where they stood, and had an idea of how to fix it.

She and Bria were sharing her father's office that morning trying to get through some of their business as well and managed to salvage another deal they'd been working on. An invitation to New Orleans had gotten the investors back to the table when they weighed their options with other firms.

Max's assistant knocked and appeared apologetic. "Sorry, Brooks, this guy is insisting on seeing you."

"Brooks Boseman?" The high-pitched voice and oily hair made Brooks step around the desk in front of Bria since she didn't recognize him. She'd fired enough people in less than a week to make her worry. "You've been served."

The cease and desist order had been filed by Curtis, and from the first page, her parents were probably being served at the same time. When she got her hands on Curtis, she was going to kill him. "Get Dan on the phone," she said to the assistant.

"Please," Bria added, waving the woman out.

"Sorry," she muttered as she dialed the house number.

"I was served," her mother said as soon as she answered the

phone. "They'll have to kill me to get upstairs to your father. Can you come over?"

"Let me talk to Dan, and I'm on my way. Lock the door and don't open it until I get there." She took a few deep breaths to control her temper, figuring that wasn't what her mother needed.

"I skimmed all this, Brooks, and it lists your siblings along with Curtis. Did they warn you about this?" The upset was easy to hear in her mom's tone.

"Trust me, Mom. Even if that's true, I'll work through it. I promise as long as Max is alive, Boseman Seafood will exist, and once he's gone, you'll be okay. This isn't the way to fix anything, and they need to understand there's a limited window of options to have anything to fix. If they're going to fight me at every turn, we all need to prepare for a big fire sale."

"I do trust you, sweetheart, but this is so disappointing."

"I'll get to work, and Bria is on her way. She'll stay with you until I'm able to get there."

Her mom paused and exhaled. "If we have to go to court—he's not in good shape. Today hasn't been a good day."

"Please, Mom. Go sit with him and let me handle this." She tried to sound as compassionate as she could when Charlie walked in. "It's going to be okay, I promise."

"You know what's at stake, right?"

"You're never going to lose your home, or Max's care. You have my word no matter how long he's alive, you're both going to be at home. Nothing on your end will change." She put the receiver down and gave Bria the code to the gate so she could close it behind her. It was time to circle their wagons.

"What the shit is this?" Charlie held up the envelope that was a twin to hers.

"You tell me." She glanced at Bria, and she nodded as she left. Right at the moment Bria was the only person she trusted to watch out for her parents.

"I've got no fucking idea, Brooks, which is why I'm asking." Charlie held up the papers again and appeared mortified. "Wait, you think we did this? You think any of us would go after Mom and Dad after what you told us?"

"What the shit is this?" Pru came in waving an envelope like Charlie had.

"Dan on line three," the assistant interrupted.

"We have to be in court tomorrow." Dan sounded as pissed as she felt. "We're only going with the people served, so try to keep the assholes away from your father. I have all the paperwork in order, but I'm asking for a continuance until we can get the medical experts in court to testify to the validity of what your father put in place."

"Have you talked to Curtis?" The bastard was ignoring her calls and hadn't shown up for work in days.

"No, but he deserves to be horsewhipped."

She hung up when her brother joined them. "Curtis is making a move to consolidate power and lock us out, especially me. If you have anything to do with this, tell me now, and before you get pissed, I'm not accusing anyone of anything."

"We didn't," Etienne said. "You've been working for days, though, so tell us what the bottom line is."

She'd been honest with her mom—they had a small chance of turning around without a major infusion of cash that would need to be paid back, and in the shape they were in, that wouldn't be easy, but she refused to get dragged into Curtis's tantrum. Her priority was her parents, but she also had to think about her siblings. What the hell were they going to do with themselves if they lost the company?

She was blunt since sugarcoating was a luxury they didn't have. "Your sales department has been asleep for months, and you've lost most of your large corporate accounts in the city as well as the out-of-state business. I'm not sure what Curtis has been doing, but you're all at the point of no return. As someone who brokers deals for a living, I wouldn't advise any of my clients to invest in Boseman."

"So we fold?" Pru asked.

"Tomorrow, we go to court and squash Curtis like the worm he is, and then we get to work." She pointed at all three of them. "I've been digging through these numbers, but also calling on clients."

"How was he able to hide all this? Didn't anyone in accounting ask any questions?" Charlie asked.

"Curtis had some people replaced recently, and now we know why," Pru said.

"Don't dwell on that or anything else Curtis did. You don't have the luxury of time, so all three of you need to hit the road and build your customer base back up. Your sales pitch has to be giving everyone the assurance of the quality we've always been known for." She started placing files in her briefcase, needing to get to the house. "Find people you trust at the point of purchase on the docks if you can't do it personally, and the first problem order reported back to you, fire who's responsible. It might be easier to downsize, providing quality, and build back from there."

"What happens tomorrow?" Charlie asked.

"That's easy. We fight, and if we lose, trust me that I have a backup plan." She gazed at them and smiled. "I'm sure Mom would love to see all of us today, and I need to assess where we are with Max. Mom said he was having a bad day, which means Curtis will try his best to get him in front of a judge."

"If we haven't mentioned it, Brooks, thank you for not abandoning us." Charlie came closer and hugged her. "After what happened and what's come of Dad's bad decisions, we're fortunate you haven't turned your back on us. Seeing the business fail might've been a way of getting back at him, but you didn't take the chance of revenge."

"What she said," both Pru and Etienne said.

"Remember what Max has always preached. This is a family business, and I'm still part of this family. I want to give you all back something that shouldn't die because of Curtis's need to feel important."

She had Fallon on her mind as she drove out of town. Neither of them had gotten in touch after their impromptu dinner. That was on her, though. Fallon had been generous, more than she thought she deserved considering their history. It felt wrong reaching out to her brother's fiancée. Hell, for all she knew the basis for what Curtis had done was from the information Fallon had gathered without much effort.

"Wouldn't that just be a bitch," she said, once she left the city behind. Her phone rang, and Bria's name meant hopefully one less complication. "Hey, what's up?"

"I'm at your folks', and I need you to prepare yourself. Your father's really agitated, and your mom hasn't been able to calm him down." Bria paused and she could hear shouting in the background. "It's like he's forgotten where he is and everyone in the house."

"Set yourself up in the office. I'm on my way."

The smoke was visible from fifteen miles away, and she had a gut feeling it was only going to add more shit to an already shitty day. That was a given when she drove up to their office and found two more boats on fire. Deuce was being held back by local sheriff's deputies, and only relaxed when he saw her.

"What the fuck, Brooks?" Deuce was ramped up, and she couldn't blame him. Something like this not quite at the end of the workday could kill someone.

"First, is anyone hurt?" A boat could be replaced, but an employee with a family depending on them could not.

"We were done for the day and headed to the processing plant to inspect the supply we brought from our independents. I got in my truck, and a second later two big explosions rocked this place. Two at once is no coincidence." Deuce pulled the hair at the sides of his head and stared at the carnage.

"Who's in charge of the investigation?" She spoke to both the sheriff and the fire department, promising their full cooperation. If this was deliberate, she wanted whoever was responsible to be prosecuted. Both men appeared to be satisfied with her answers and agreed to spread the word of the fifty-thousand-dollar reward she was posting.

"What the hell is going on, Brooks?" Deuce hadn't calmed down any, and she was right there with him.

"Either the shrimp have organized and turned against us, or someone in the company has a unique business plan." She got him to laugh, but she had to do what she could to prevent a repeat.

"You want me to set up security? We've never had a need."

"Go ahead, make sure to let everyone know to cooperate with these guys." She pointed to the police and fire departments. "They also need to speak up if they know anything. I'll get an expert in here to figure out how these explosions are being set up. Call me if anything else comes up, but I have to get to the house."

Charlie buzzed her in, and she found Bria sitting with her mother. They were in the den, so she wondered who was with Max. Bria seemed to read her mind and pointed to the kitchen. "We were all able to sedate him, and your brother is up there. You should go and relieve him."

She would, but she wanted to reassure her mother first. "Are you okay?" she asked her mom. Scarlett gave her the rundown of her day before asking her to go up and sit with her father.

Max had his eyes closed, and Etienne had tears falling quietly down his cheeks. Brooks hugged her brother and couldn't blame him for his emotion. The problem had started when Max didn't recognize anyone, which led to his escalating anxiety.

If Curtis was given the chance to force her father into court, she'd have to talk her mother into giving up the company. Paperwork that said Max had been of sound mind when he wrote it up would face serious scrutiny when he sat in front of a judge and testified he didn't know any of them.

"Go down and be with Mom, and I'll sit with him."

She worked for an hour in the chair by the bed before she noticed Max's eyes were open. He was staring at her, and she hoped it wasn't because he didn't know who she was. The good thing was that he didn't seem agitated. He smiled at her and held up his hand, and she moved to sit on the bed to take it.

"You remind me of my daughter." He tightened his hold on her and took a deep breath. "Don't tell anyone, but she hates me, and I don't blame her. I made her leave and now she doesn't need me." He started to cry, and his despair was like a tangible thing. "Do you think she'll come back?"

The easiest way to handle this was to tell him that she was his daughter, but that wasn't the best course here. "She's coming, Max, and she doesn't hate you." When she said that, she knew it was true.

Maturity, she was finding, came when you realized your parents weren't perfect, and they didn't have to be your best friends. That truth didn't have to negate the fact that he was her father. He'd taken care of her, educated her, and given her what she needed until that fateful day. That day couldn't continue to define what she felt for him.

"Brooks doesn't hate you at all. She's trying to help you." She had to stop when she was about to choke on the emotion stuck in her throat. The thought that the short time she'd had with him since returning would be all she got made her dread the loss.

"How do you know?" He appeared to need reassurances.

"I know Brooks better than anyone. She's doing everything she can to help you and her mom." She'd hung on to her anger too long and lost the chance to fix this very broken thing. If he didn't come out of this, comforting him as a familiar stranger was the best that she could hope for.

"I was so wrong, and I was wrong to try to change her. She was my child...my gift. That girl was special to her, and I ruined that for her too. I don't like that she's with Curtis now." It was like he could remember snippets of things that weren't ancient history, but his eyes were vacant when it came to recognizing her.

"That's ancient history, Dad, and it's not worth getting upset over." She wiped her face and tried to keep her smile. She placed her hand on the center of his chest, and it seemed to calm him. "Curtis and everyone will be fine. All you need to do is rest and not worry about any of this."

"Will you come back tomorrow? I like talking to you." It took a bit, but his hand became slack in hers as he fell asleep.

"He's right," her mom said as she placed her hands on her shoulders. "You're a gift."

"I feel more like a failure at the moment." She lifted her hand off her dad's chest and took comfort in the steady cadence of his breathing. "Do you think he'll snap out of this?"

"Snapping out of it isn't how this works, my love." The smile on her mom's face was the definition of sadness. "This is how it started, and these episodes have only happened when he's overstressed. Now, though, they're happening more often, and there's no way of predicting the length or the severity. The doctor warned me that the day will come when it's permanent."

"Damn," she said as her phone buzzed. Dan had managed a continuance so they could have the court review the paperwork Max had written up. With any luck they could skip it altogether. She showed her mom the message, glad to see the relief on her face. "Bria is helping me, so the review should be done by next week. I'll be back in the morning to check on you both. Call me if you need anything."

"Do you have to go?"

"I want to move back and start commuting in, but I need to make sure we're ready for what's coming. The court might not see it our way, and if that transpires, I need you to listen to what needs to happen." Her mom rested her head on her chest and sighed. "Some battles are won by letting go, but that doesn't mean you lose." It was too early to share her suspicions with her mother and the rest of the family. If she was right, Curtis was not only a bastard, but a thief who'd hidden his tracks well.

Bria followed her to the hotel and waved when they noticed Fallon in the lobby. She had a fleeting thought she was here because Curtis needed more ammunition. That's what she needed as well, so she kept her temper controlled.

"Hey," she said, ignoring how nice Fallon looked. The spark was still there, but her engagement to Curtis was the bucket of water that put it out. It was enough to convince her that she needed to get back to her life before she did something foolish.

❖

"Hi," Fallon said. She'd waited a week, figuring Brooks wouldn't call because of her engagement. She was beginning to think she had a major flaw in her makeup—it was either that or Brooks had a talent for drawing her in. "Do you want to have dinner?"

"Sure, but how about a drink first?" They walked up to the piano bar and sat in one of the corners for a bit of privacy.

"I'd like that," Fallon said and smoothed down her linen skirt, which Brooks seemed to have a hard time ignoring. "I heard about the boats today, and I'm sorry. The first one surprised me, but these two must be disconcerting."

"I told the police I'm planning to prosecute whoever it is until I make them sorry they tried this." Brooks ordered for them, then yawned.

"What's wrong?" She moved closer and placed her hand on Brooks's knee.

"I want to tell you," Brooks said, staring at her hand.

"But I'm Curtis's fiancée." It was ludicrous since she wasn't the one with the credibility problem. "You're going to have to believe I'm your friend, Brooks, or we can't move forward."

She listened to Brooks talk about her day and wasn't at all surprised at what Curtis had done. He was obsessed with owning a company as a way of showing Brooks up or proving his manhood. It was a toss-up at this point. He wanted to portray an image of someone he wasn't, and the ring on her finger played into that. She could see that now. Brooks had left her, and Curtis had played her.

"God, Brooks, I'm sorry, and you won't believe me, but I didn't know. Your parents and your family don't deserve that kind of stress while they take care of your father. The boats I have no explanation for, but I knew the first one was suspicious." She placed her hand on the table and slid it close to Brooks.

"I believe you." Brooks's hand covered hers, and she remembered the warmth of her. The pain and all the feelings were still there, but touching Brooks, having her this close, drowned out the negative. "And I'm willing to be a good friend to you. That you might not believe, since I'm the one who broke your trust."

It was like Brooks could read her mind. "Eventually you'll tell me the story, but right now you have to feed me. I skipped lunch and I'm starved."

"Let's walk." Brooks stood and offered her hand. "Or we can cab it. Those are some great shoes but not built for long walks."

"I have you to hang on to, so let's go." She stood and placed her hand in the bend of Brooks's elbow. This close it was easy to tell Brooks still smelled the same, was just as warm, but had become more solid. "Where are we going?" She moved closer, and the need for Brooks trumped the reasons why she should push her away.

"How about Mackie Blanchard's restaurant on Bourbon. It's the closest place I can think of, and we can try the seafood tower." Brooks winked before heading to the back elevator and didn't move away from her when the doors closed. She seemed to study Fallon in the polished brass of the doors.

"What?" Curiosity forced the word out of her, and she met Brooks's gaze in the reflection.

"Sometimes...never mind," Brooks said, shaking her head.

"Tell me." The eye contact was severed when the doors opened and they had to step out. "I want you to."

"I..." Brooks opened the back door for her, then offered her arm again. "I sometimes wonder what we'd look like—together, I mean—as I get older. You're still beautiful, and I shouldn't say stuff like that, considering."

They walked and she understood Brooks like she had in high school and college. Whatever had happened, the noble heart she'd cherished hadn't changed that much. She saw that in stark clarity now. Her mistake was not searching Brooks out and demanding answers. She tried shutting off her thoughts as a hostess greeted Brooks with a too enthusiastic hug, in her opinion, but it did get them a table faster.

"I don't mind," she said after they were alone. "You saying that, I mean. I've thought the same thing and tried to stop when I realized it was holding me back."

"You've done that," Brooks said, lifting her menu as if to hide behind it. "You're engaged and have a future to look forward to. It won't be long before you start a family, and I can't think of anyone who'll be a better mom."

There was no way to be sure, but Brooks sounded jealous. "I *am* engaged, but I'm not happy Curtis did this. It isn't right."

"I'm sure he thinks it's all being taken away from him, but that's not what's happening." Brooks nodded to the waiter when he delivered their drinks. "He's the only one who hasn't visited me in New York, and I think it was his way of siding and showing his loyalty to Max. Now that it's me, it's ratcheting up those feelings." She took a sip and shrugged. "Both of you don't have to worry. I'm not going to get in the way of anything, business or otherwise."

"Brooks." She had to stop when their appetizer was brought out.

Brooks took her plate and filled it for her. This wasn't something Curtis had ever done. He seemed to be wired to take care of himself and not anyone else. "Why do you think you need to stay away from anything? I'm not asking you to do that."

The way Brooks stared at her made her heart race, and she remembered what it was like to have Brooks's full attention. "You deserve happiness, Fallon, and you deserve to start fresh without any baggage from the past."

God, she wanted to yell out that Curtis wasn't her future. Perhaps it was too late to start again with Brooks, but she didn't want Brooks to think she'd turned to her brother, of all people. Right in that moment she felt more for Brooks than she ever had for Curtis. She'd had perfection and lost it, which was why she'd been so angry.

"You aren't baggage, Brooks." She slid her hand forward until the tips of their fingers touched because she had a need to feel Brooks. "You're my friend, and I want to understand you. I want to know the why of things."

"Curtis already has problems with me, and I'd like not to make them worse. I think me attending everything you have planned for the wedding is going to be problematic." Brooks turned her hand over and held hers. "It might be wishful thinking, but he doesn't hate me yet, and I'd like that not to be the case. I can take it, but I don't want your marriage to be about how much he wants me out of the family and away from you. The both of you deserve a fresh start without me there being a reminder of your past."

"What about what I want?" Having people think for her was a pain in the ass. "Does the entire Boseman family think they know for sure what's best for me?" She was angry again, and this was a waste of time.

Her words visibly startled Brooks. "I'm sure of very few things in my life, Fallon. I know my mother loves me, as do my siblings. My father is trying to make amends for his sins, and my brother wants to crush me no matter the consequences. All that's true, but the one thing I know for sure is my feelings for you."

"What—"

Brooks put her free hand up to stop her from talking. "You meant so much to me, and that's never changed no matter how you feel about me. That sounds trite, but it's true."

"You're the only person I know that uses the word *trite*." She was mortified not to be able to stop the tears, but dammit, she'd been waiting years for this moment.

"What happened—that was never about anything you did, and I've missed you. All those big feelings I had for you never died. My heart never allowed it, as penance for what I'd done." Brooks smiled, but her eyes watered with tears. "My brother doesn't need to know that, but he's a lucky man."

"Thank you." The engagement to Curtis meant Brooks was done with her, and nothing she could say was going to change her mind. There was no white knight in her future, so she changed to safer topics. The rest of dinner was cordial, safe, and uneventful, making her the coward this time around. They walked back to the Piquant, and she refrained from touching Brooks again.

"Good night," she said after telling Brooks she didn't need to wait as the valet left to retrieve her car. Brooks nodded and walked away after pressing her fingers to her cheek. It was like the only thing she could allow herself without making Fallon uncomfortable.

"And that's that."

❖

"Are you a complete fool?" Bria asked Brooks after she gave her a rundown of her night.

"I try never to be, and Fallon doesn't deserve me telling her anything. Let's both remember she's engaged to my brother—she's moved on." Seeing Fallon cry at dinner made her chest and head hurt. She didn't think she could experience physical pain from not holding someone, but she was wrong. "I can't believe it was Curtis of all people she's moved on with, but karma is nothing if not a bitch."

"Honey," Bria said, sandwiching her face between her hands hard enough that it made her lips pucker, "I say this with love, because you know I love you, but you're an idiot. Your girlfriend is as *in love*"— Bria made air quotes—"with Curtis as I am. And trust me, even if we were the last two people on earth, he'd still have no shot. How he's related to you is a mystery. It's like you inherited all the smarts and looks, and it took a year to restock that genetic material for Etienne, skipping over Curtis altogether."

She laughed as she kicked off her shoes. "Have you started watching the Hallmark Channel when I wasn't paying attention?" The pillow Bria tossed hit her in the face, and she caught her when she pounced on her. "That sounds sappy and totally unlike you."

"I watch true crime or nothing. Think of the day I see one of my relatives in some long-drawn-out episode of *Dateline*. We'd be riveted by that old dude with the great voice while taking care of the witnesses behind the scenes." Bria sat straddling her lap and smacked her on the shoulder. "Stop trying to distract me."

"I'm not distracting you, but there's nothing there. Right now, I think she's being nice so she can get intel out of me for Curtis. If that's true, they've got to know that having knowledge or not having it ahead of time isn't going to change the outcome." She closed her eyes when Bria kissed her forehead.

"Babe, I think you've dedicated yourself to work for so long that you've forgotten what it looks like when a woman is interested in you." Bria kissed her cheek next before getting up. "Do one thing for me and I promise I'll stop bugging you about all this."

"What?" She pointed at Bria before she trapped her with a technicality. "If it involves me declaring undying love with a violin quartet outside her house, I'm out."

Bria threw another pillow at her and laughed. "It'll work out better for you if you're cooperative."

She was so tired, but there was no going to bed until she agreed to whatever Bria had in mind. When any Giordano got something in their head, it was useless to fight them on it unless you were willing to leave the country. "Go ahead and tell me, so I can get some sleep."

"You're not leaving this room until you tell me why you left."

"I've never told anyone that story, and after today the only other person who knew it has lost the significance of it." She cocked her head back and closed her eyes.

"It's only me, Brooks. Once you tell me, it'll be easier when you have to tell her. I haven't had much experience with Fallon, but she can't hide how she feels. She deserves to know."

"I've never told you because it's embarrassing, not because I don't trust you."

"I know, honey, but it's me." Bria kissed her on the cheek. "No matter what you say, it isn't going to change how much I love you."

"We started dating in high school, and we went to college together. God, I could barely concentrate on anything but her, and we started making plans for the future we wanted. When we were in our last year, Max found out about us and found a way to break us apart from what he thought was an unnatural relationship." She couldn't find the strength to add emotion to what she was saying. This had been a defining moment in her life, and the only thing she had to be proud of was that she'd survived.

"What did he do?" Bria sat next to her and moved into her arms.

"Fallon's father, Alfred, ran into some financial problems, like lose-his-company kind of problems, and Max offered him a lifeline. The loan Alfred had no choice in taking came with parameters Max insisted on." She made eye contact and hoped Bria understood what she was saying.

Bria inhaled sharply. "The main parameter for you was either you broke it off or her father lost everything. Jesus, honey, my father could've learned a few things from Max."

"Angelo is nothing like my father even if the feds think otherwise." That she believed with all her heart. In Angelo's world, his children and their happiness were paramount.

"Go on and finish."

"I left, and I couldn't tell her why. Having her come with me meant Fallon's family lost everything, so I stayed away." She pinched the bridge of her nose, tired of this chapter of her life and how terrible it made her feel about herself. "The only thing Max couldn't foresee was my desire to never come back and give in to what he expected of me. His goal was to break me, so he took away the most important person in my life, and he came close. I would've given up if it hadn't been for you."

She cried remembering the acute pain that had plagued her for months. Not picking up the phone and begging Fallon to take her back had come close to breaking her. That level of despair was hard to fathom now, but living it was like a workout regimen. It made her stronger every day until she could manage the pain, but it had also hardened her resolve to not depend on or try to need anyone.

"I remember, my friend, and it made me scared for you. Granted, I never thought you'd harm yourself, but it was hard to watch you work through that. You need to tell her and follow it up with the fact that you still love her." Bria was about to say something else when the phone rang. "Hello."

"Put her on." Curtis spoke loud enough for Brooks to hear, so Bria handed the receiver over.

"Curtis." She wasn't in the mood to talk to him even if she'd been chasing him for days.

"Come down here," he ordered.

"You can come up or leave. There's no way I'm making a scene in the bar for your entertainment." She held Bria before letting her go. "You don't have to stay."

"I'll be in the next room, so don't take any shit." Bria repeated the advice Angelo gave them both all the time.

She rolled her eyes at the way Curtis pounded on the door. Time hadn't developed an ounce of maturity in her little brother, and he acted like the kid who liked to throw his blocks to show his frustration. His arm was still up when she opened the door and walked back to the couch. Whatever this was, it wouldn't take long.

"What the fuck, Brooks?" His voice was a high-pitched screech.

"What the fuck do you mean?" If a little immaturity with something he understood, that's the way she'd go.

"You haven't given a shit about any of us, and you're just going to walk in and take over. Unless you're a dumbass, you have to know how Dad feels about you. The last thing he'd want is you in charge." He stood and flailed his arms like he was trying to take flight.

"I wouldn't be here unless Max had called. He might be facing his worst nightmare, but he's with it enough to know the company won't make it much longer."

"What the fuck does that mean?" He took a deep breath to keep on screaming.

"A luxury sports car, a big boat, and every other thing you've bought to make yourself the big man you think you are is what I'm fucking talking about." She slammed her hand on the coffee table to cut him off. "Do you honestly think I'm slow? I figured you out after two days, and I spent the last two weeks trying to shore up enough business to keep the doors open. I've also pulled the claims on those three boats because the insurance company isn't as stupid as you are." She hated that word, but it fit.

"You *bitch*. I didn't take anything I didn't deserve. If you and Dan think you won today, you didn't. The court's going to see it my way once they talk to Max. I didn't need a doctor to tell me there was something wrong—he's completely out of it, and I took over because I had to." He paced as he spoke and pointed at her a lot. "That's what he wanted. I damn well saved us from all the bad decisions he was making, and you fucking know it."

"The paperwork he put in place says otherwise." She spoke in a normal voice, hoping he'd take it down a few notches. "All you need to do is help us give Max something that's important to him. All Mom asked me was for the company to still be viable as long as Max is alive, and that's what I'm going to give them both."

"Are you being serious right now?" Curtis was doing a good impression of a windmill now as he flapped his arms. She wondered if suggesting anger management would get him to fall to the floor in a tantrum. "When have you ever given a shit about Max and what he wants?"

"What you need to accept is that I didn't ask for this, Curtis. He called me, and you know why. You want to take over for him, but you're doing everything you can to sink it. That I don't understand—well, I do, but it's going to take me a little bit to prove it." She wasn't a fan of unhinged people, but she'd sit through this melodrama if he answered that one question.

"He told me why you left." Curtis changed his demeanor, and he spoke in a normal voice, yet he sounded somehow crueler. "This must be chapping your ass."

"What's that?"

"She chose me. You couldn't handle that Dad wanted me, and you ran like a little bitch. Now you know how bad you lost because Fallon chose me, and I'm going to take back what's mine." He laughed, and she wanted to punch him. "How pathetic you are that both of them threw you away the first chance they got."

"If you make Fallon happy, I'm glad." She stood, enjoying that she was a tad taller. A little petty never killed anyone, Bria always said. "Don't pretend to know anything about me or why I did anything." He laughed harder when she opened the door. "Remember, if you're going to take the first shot, make sure it's a kill shot. Leave me breathing and I'll make you sorry."

"You're a joke, Brooks. Go back to where you belong. That's not here." He walked out, and she softly closed the door.

Bria came out as soon as she turned around. "Families, huh?" She tried laughing it off, but he'd spoken the truth of what she'd always believed. It was the reason she still lost sleep some nights. All those questions of what was wrong with her had a way of making Swiss cheese out of her brain at times. What had her father seen in her that was lacking and not worthy of love?

"Honey, from all your stories, backed up by your siblings, Curtis is an asshole. I hope you didn't mind me eavesdropping, but you knew I was going to. I know a lot about fear because I'm related to quite a few people who know how to instill it professionally. He's terrified you're about to not only take his toys away, but expose him for the loser he is." Bria hugged her, and her head fit under Brooks's chin.

"He does know all the fleshy parts to stick the knife in so it'll hurt. All that about Dad wanting him to take over are as true as the ring on Fallon's finger. Maybe the best thing is to fuck off back home and leave them all to what they deserve." She wasn't acting any more grown-up than Curtis, but she was due a small tantrum of her own.

"Your mother doesn't deserve that, and in a way, neither does your father. Not because he was parent of the year—he was never that—but because you won't be able to live with the guilt of doing nothing." Bria kissed her chest at the vee of her shirt. "I know you, and I know how you carry all those boulders from the past. Let's not add to them, okay?"

"Let me call Mom, and we'll go grab a midnight snack."

Her mom sounded disappointed at Curtis's behavior, and Brooks hated adding one more thing for her mother to worry about, considering the stress she was already under, but all of them had to be prepared. She and Bria ordered room service, and they both called it an early night.

She lay in bed and stared at the suit Bria had picked up for her, hanging on the closet door. It fit well enough, considering the short turnaround from Saks, and it was like a sign she needed to go back to the familiar. She was ready to get back to her closet, her office, and her routine, and away from all these emotional minefields. There was no way she wanted to go back to being that scared kid who wanted the pain to end but knew it wouldn't for a long time.

"Let that go, because Bria's right. I'm no more going to go than I'm going to leave my mother homeless." The coming days would give her no choice but to be ruthless. She'd have to be if she was going to save the company, but she'd already burned plenty of bridges when it came to her family—what were a few more?

CHAPTER ELEVEN

Curtis's lawyer had been talking a solid twenty minutes two days later, and the judge appeared ready to fling his gavel into his mouth to shut him up. The guy's total presentation had been about Max's health and how the paperwork he'd put in place couldn't be trusted no matter what the doctors had written. He'd been erratic at work for months, and there was no way he had the wherewithal to plan anything that could be trusted now since he was already mentally impaired.

Fallon hadn't planned on coming, but Eliza had filled her in after hearing from Monroe. The way Curtis had planned out his war against Brooks and the rest of the family had left her shaken that he'd go to these lengths to get his way. Someone like that wouldn't be great at the compromise it took to make a relationship work. Their engagement wasn't real, but had it been, she'd have walked up to the front of the courtroom and handed his ring back.

"Are you done?" the judge asked when the lawyer took a breath. "Let's go with yes for now and give the other side a chance to repeat themselves over and over again."

"Your Honor," Dan said and concisely laid out their argument. "We ask for a continuance so the medical professionals can testify. Max Boseman realized something like this could happen, so he prepared extensively. He's not denying that he has Alzheimer's, but all this was done before the progression of the disease. You can see that by the medical experts who questioned him extensively."

"Ms. Boseman?" The judge seemed to be talking to Brooks.

Fallon hadn't had a great view of Brooks from where she was sitting, so the sight of those broad shoulders made her hold her breath for a moment. Monroe glanced her way when she exhaled in a whoosh.

She was used to relaxed Brooks, but the person she knew had been polished into this businesswoman who appeared unflappable in a great suit.

"Yes, sir." Brooks didn't glance Curtis's way and stared at the judge.

"Explain to me your part in this even though I *can* read."

"The easiest way of putting it, Your Honor, is my parents ran a successful business for years. That changed with my father's stroke. He had to step back, and my mother, who was also involved in the day-to-day operations, took time off to care for him. In their absence the business lost some important clients due to negligence."

Curtis jumped to his feet and pointed at Brooks. "That's bullshit and you know it."

"Sir," the judge said after banging his gavel for a solid minute, "either control your client, or I'll have him thrown out. If he insists on staying, I'll have him gagged. If you want to test me on that, try me."

Curtis's attorney pushed him back into his seat and whispered something in his ear. "Our apologies, Your Honor. It won't happen again."

"Ms. Boseman, please continue," the judge said.

"Once our father realized the position the company was in about a couple of months after his stroke, he invested everything he and my mother own to keep them viable. He saw that as a necessary move until he was back and able to fix the numerous problems, but that's not going to be possible." Brooks was brief and the judge nodded. In Fallon's opinion she took a couple of shots at Curtis only because he'd been warned not to answer.

"I got that part," the judge said. "Where do you fit in?"

"I'm here to see them back to where the business is not only making money but positioned for growth. My place is to give my parents peace of mind when it comes to Boseman Seafood, and that's it. The business is important to them, but it's also my family's legacy, and for as long as he can hang on, my father deserves to get what he wants." Brooks finally glanced at a visibly furious Curtis and smiled. "My father is in the battle of his life, but I'd like to think he still has plenty to offer the business. Together we'll position it for the generations to come."

"And once you achieve that?" the judge asked.

"I have a business, Your Honor, but my siblings, all of them"— Brooks pointed to Etienne, Pru, and Charlie in the first row—"they will be devoted to making Boseman's successful. Of that I have no doubt, and once we work through the problems, my plan is to leave them to do the job. I have no interest in running the company long-term."

"Thank you, Ms. Boseman." The judge took his glasses off and threw them down. "The request to remove Brooks Boseman is rejected. We will reconvene in a month to see where you all are in the process. I'd like to think all the parties involved can come to a resolution everyone can live with. I agree with Ms. Boseman—Maxwell Boseman deserves respect and peace of mind when it comes to a business that as of now is *his*, lock, stock, and shrimp nets."

Curtis left before the judge made it through the doors to his chambers, and he never noticed Fallon as he yelled at his attorney. That she didn't mind, and she glanced at Brooks one more time before leaving herself. Hearing the financial position Max had gotten himself in was a surprise, and it made her think of Curtis's new car. That he could treat himself to something like that while his parents were about to lose everything made her ill.

She left and buried herself in work for the rest of the morning. Her mother came in without knocking after lunch with the bag Fallon recognized and immediately dreaded since it contained all the wedding plans. It was stupid to hate an inanimate object, but she'd come to hate that bag and her mother's demands.

"I'm not sure what you hear when I speak, but it's clearly not registering."

Her mother sighed and tried to appear exasperated, but it was hard to hide her lack of patience when it came to Fallon and her refusal to fall in line. "I don't understand you. When Curtis proposed, you looked happy. You were ready to plan, and now it's like you're a different person." No one did indignant like her mother.

She inhaled and held it for a count of fifteen in her head as she twirled her pen on the desk. "Your memory is faulty if you believe that. I was never happy about this, and even if I was, I have the right to change my mind. You're my mother, so I hope you understand that and support me."

"Does Brooks have anything to do with your about-face?" The way her mom asked meant the only correct answer was *no*. "You can't have forgotten all that happened?"

"It's Curtis, Mom. No one else influenced my decision to back out. He isn't the person I thought he was, and that's all I'm going say about it." It was like her mom was more fixated on the fantasy wedding than her.

"That's your answer for everything lately. Why don't you talk to me?"

"I don't talk to you because you don't hear me. You think laying on the guilt or bulldozing me into this is going to work, but it's not. Curtis and I are not getting married. Accept it. It's done." Her mom stood and left angry. Fallon didn't have to be an expert on body language to figure that out, but she wasn't in the mood to soothe her mother's feelings.

She worked a few more hours before heading to the Piquant. There was no good reason for her to be there, but she went to the bar to gather her courage to call up for Brooks. That wasn't going to be necessary when she spotted Brooks with a man she didn't recognize at one of the tables right outside. Twenty minutes later Brooks and the man shook hands, and he left. She waited, and Brooks joined her at the bar.

"You haven't called me," she said as she followed Brooks's gaze to her hand. The ring was still on her finger, and it was still not something she was comfortable wearing. As soon as she got a hold of Curtis, she'd remedy that.

"Being busy isn't a great excuse, but we had court this morning, and that was our New Jersey distributor. Getting his business back gives me a little breathing room." Brooks pointed to her glass when the bartender was close. "In my defense, though, I had dinner with you a couple of days ago."

"Do you need a defense?" She was flirty, and it made her glare at her ring too.

"I might if you don't accept my apology." Brooks sat next to her and took a sip of her drink. "How about I make it up to you?"

"What about Curtis and him not hating you?" She couldn't help but drag Curtis into this. Acknowledging him was the only way to shove him aside. It was a weird psychology, but it made sense to her.

"I might've gotten that one wrong," Brooks said and smiled. "He's not happy with me, but I don't want to worry about that right now."

"What do you want right now?"

"I want to take you out, and then we could go somewhere and talk some more." Brooks seemed content to wait her out.

"Do you promise to answer some more questions?" She still wanted the answers but also to spend time with Brooks. Someone had stolen the life she wanted, and she needed the explanation of why.

"We might find better ways to spend time, but we'll go with the interrogation option if the evening hits a snag."

She pushed Brooks on the shoulder, loving the laugh Brooks let out. "You should know I'm not going to give up."

Brooks offered her arm again and got them to the back elevator. "I do know that, and I promise I'll tell you, but after dinner. No sense in risking heartburn if we can help it. Any requests?" She shook her head and followed Brooks out the door. "Then GW Fins it is."

"I doubt we'll get a table." It was her turn to laugh at Brooks's smile.

"Let's gamble that I know enough people to conjure something up. We might eat in the kitchen, but we'll get something good no matter where they sit us."

They walked in silence, but it was nice. This was what she missed the most with Brooks. Holding on to her, pressed close, and having that cologne swimming through her senses brought her the kind of peace she hadn't been able to replicate. She craved this contentedness, and it was slightly aggravating that it only came when she was with Brooks.

"What's going on in that big brain?" Brooks took her hand, and their fingers fit perfectly together.

"I should be so angry at you, but all I can think about is how much I missed you." Her statement stopped Brooks's feet. "Should I have chased after you? Was that my mistake? I called and called, but you never talked to me."

They were in front of a fried chicken place that had become popular in the Quarter. "How about a picnic in my room so we don't mess up that gorgeous skirt? The walls in there look as oily as I'm sure the chicken is, but the crowd means it has to be good."

"Won't your roommate mind you bringing someone home?" She stepped in front of Brooks and took her other hand. They weren't touching except for that, but she could swear she could feel the heat Brooks exuded in abundance.

"It's a two-bedroom suite, darlin', and Bria's busy tonight. Her father has plenty of friends in the city who've lined up to entertain her." Brooks stepped closer and looked at her as if she could see every thought in her head. "If you don't mind being alone with me, let's get some chicken and relax."

"Let's," she said, her voice cracking.

Brooks ordered, paid, and didn't shrug her off when she placed her fingers in the back loops of Brooks's pants when they stood to the side to wait for their food. Another woman waiting kept checking Brooks out, but Brooks kept her attention on Fallon. Something had changed from the night before. Brooks was more open and wasn't acting like she was radioactive with Curtis cooties, as they'd called them when they were children. This was what had made her fall for Brooks when she was a teenager. She couldn't help but know that she was the center of Brooks's world when she fixated on her like this.

Time and age hadn't changed her susceptibility to Brooks or how she quickened her pulse, her body's response whenever she gazed into those beautiful eyes. She doubted that would change until she was dead.

"Thank you," Brooks told the woman who handed her the large bag. It was nice when Brooks took her hand again and they started back to the hotel.

She'd stayed at the Piquant before for weddings and events, but it felt different to enter with Brooks. The elevator was nice since they were alone, and she moved closer to Brooks for the warmth. It was hot outside, but inside was cold, and again Brooks didn't move away.

Brooks had to let her go to get the door and allowed her to go in first. She was expecting to sit at the table that was covered with files, but Brooks moved to the large windows and set the bag down. She took her shoes off and pulled the pillows off the couch. It was intimate, and it triggered a flood of memories. Being romanced was something she'd experienced often with this infuriating woman, and then it had ended abruptly. Brooks was infuriating because it was hard to stay mad at her when she was being sweet.

"Jesus," Fallon said and couldn't stop the tears. The loneliness, pain, and longing slammed into her like a truck, and the answer to all of it appeared stricken when she faced her. She wanted to push Brooks away for everything she'd done, but her body remembered Brooks and wanted her close. All she could do was hang on and enjoy Brooks's arms around her.

"I'm so sorry, honey." Brooks sounded like she was crying too, and she held her with what could only be described as desperation. "That's never going to be enough, but I'm so sorry."

"Tell me why." That was all she wanted, because her family and work weren't going to fill the hole Brooks left. That'd be as possible as filling in the Grand Canyon with a bag of sand. "The real reason."

Brooks moved them to the nest she'd made on the floor and lay back. Fallon pressed herself to Brooks and wanted to fling her engagement ring across the room. This was home, always had been.

"You were the woman I wanted to spend my life with." Brook started slowly. "Curtis is fortunate, and I told him that yesterday when he came by to see me. He's focused on the business and you, so I'll tell you what you asked, but my intent is not to get in the middle of what you found with him."

"You need to know—" She stopped when Brooks put her finger against her lips.

"I know I fucked up, but what you have with Curtis—I don't want to know about it." Brooks sighed and covered her eyes with her free hand. "You deserve to be happy, and I'm the reason you needed to find that with someone else, but I can't force myself to think about it. Please don't ask that of me."

"Tell me why Curtis was here, then." She turned to her side and pressed herself to Brooks, placing her hand on her abdomen.

"The short version is he wanted me to take a hike, and to let me know all of it is his. You, the business, his place in the family are all his. He was the same when he was three, so that didn't come as a shock. Right now, I don't have the time to placate him about the business end. The rest I'm sure he has nothing to worry about."

"Why do you say that?" She was lying with her fiancé's sister in a hotel room, so perhaps Brooks had become dense when it came to missing all the signs—he wasn't who she wanted.

"You're loyal, and once you decide, the person you're with will be safe with you."

Son of a bitch. Telling Brooks about her deal with Curtis now would make her look worse than she felt. "You had that, and you threw it away on a whim."

"I did, but not on a whim," Brooks said in a way that made her think she'd have rather run a razor over her tongue than to admit it.

"Then tell me. There has to be a reason because no matter how much it hurt, I still know you. You were never cruel, and I doubt you've changed something so fundamental to your makeup, so something had to have happened."

"Max is vulnerable right now, but back then he had some hardline ideas about how things should be. Don't think what I'm about to tell you is me laying the blame on him." Brooks stopped and took a few deep breaths. "From the beginning Max was adamant that Curtis take over for him, but he wanted me backing him up. That summer he planned to put me on a boat, but I told him I wasn't going to work for him."

"That must have gone over well," she said as she rubbed small circles on Brook's middle. "You said you were going to talk to Daddy and some of the other companies in the area to get started on your job search."

"I was, and I told him that and how all I wanted was a life with you. After graduation, I'd find a job in the oil field or somewhere else that would give us what we'd planned. I wasn't asking him for anything." Brooks stopped talking as if she couldn't find the right explanation to keep going.

"Max didn't want that, I'm thinking." If that was true, they could've worked something out. Brooks running wasn't the answer. "Am I right?"

"I wouldn't put it that mildly, but you're right. My father wasn't the most evolved guy on the bayou, and me being with you wasn't something he was going to accept." Brooks held her, and she had to move away. "In his mind that was never going to happen, and he'd never accept it."

"So you ran? Who gives a damn what Max thought? You knew Daddy would've been thrilled to have given you a job. He and Mom loved you." She sat up and couldn't help screaming.

"I'm not that much of a bastard, Fallon. I left because Max was holding the papers on your dad's business. Me staying and being with you would've cost your family way more than I was willing to let you pay," Brooks yelled back and got up. "Do you honestly think I would've left you because I was afraid of what Max thought? Give me more damn credit than that."

"That can't be right." She had access to all the records, and there was no mention of a loan, but Brooks had never been a liar. "Daddy would've told me." What Brooks was saying, though, had to be true. All of this made sense if she put it in that context.

"Then it must've never happened. You wanted to know, and I'm telling you the truth. But you know what, believe what you want," Brooks said, grabbing her wallet. "Have a great life with Curtis. I can see why you two are perfect for each other."

"Brooks, wait." The door slammed and she cringed.

She rushed after Brooks after she found her shoes and ran into Bria. The collision was hard enough that Bria landed on her ass. The only thing she could hear was the ding of the elevator. It was chiming the end of any kind of relationship she'd ever have with Brooks.

"I'm going to go on a hunch and guess you didn't graduate at the top of your class. If you did, all that intelligence has been sweated out of you in this heat." Bria stood and gathered everything that had fallen out of her bag.

"I've got to go. Sorry for knocking you over." She had to catch Brooks and finish their talk.

"Sit or I swear I'll cut you." Bria pointed to the table after staring at the pillows on the floor. "What the actual hell, Ms. Goodwin?"

"Why do you want to know?" It was physically impossible, but it was like she was shattering and wanted to leave but couldn't.

"I met Brooks right after she left here," Bria said with her purse on her arm as she combed her hair back with her other hand. She didn't appear as if she was staying. "She was in so much pain you could see it in her eyes and in the way her shoulders slumped. Brooks wore that pain like a bad suit, and it drew me to her. I was compelled to help her because I was afraid she wouldn't last another day without someone caring for her. Whatever happened left her barely able to put one foot in front of the other."

"Brooks seems to have done fine." Why the hell was she crying again?

"My God, are you incapable of learning? If you've had some traumatic brain injury I don't know about, I'll excuse you, but if this is your norm, you need to step it up." The way Bria threw her hands up telegraphed her impatience, and it was almost comical. "I've spent years trying to get Brooks to have coffee with someone, much less actually date, but she's too wrapped up in pining over you. After meeting you and seeing you in action, it makes me question her sanity, but I'll dissect that later."

"Again, are you always this blunt?" Bria had to be one of those people who found pleasure in pouring acid into an already festering wound.

"People who think I'm blunt usually have a problem with the truth."

She pressed her fist to her forehead and took a second to gather herself. "The truth as you see it is your truth. You don't know anything about me, so guessing what I'm thinking is aggravating as hell. Actually, it's fucked up."

"She left without a word, and you stayed here with your family. She's suffered every day since then, and you healed with everyone who loves you helping you through it. You all probably sat around singing kumbaya while you weren't talking and thinking shit about her." Bria spoke to her as if she couldn't stand to be in the same room with her.

"You're minimizing what she did."

"God forbid, little girl. Open your damn eyes and see the truth for what it is, not what you think happened. She's been alone, and you're engaged to her brother. The problem with that one is he doesn't make you burn like she does." Bria tapped her fingertips with each point, and she wanted to hit her. "The next thing is a guess on my part, but she finally gave you what you said you wanted, and you called her a liar. That, lovely, is the real fucked-up thing here."

"How do you know that?" She needed to find Brooks, but her feet wouldn't move. Maybe the best plan was to go away somewhere until all this was over. It was a good fantasy, but she didn't want to perpetuate the problem by running. She really needed to get to Brooks before she was out of reach.

"Because, Ms. Goodwin, Brooks is someone who doesn't do angry very often. Her temper doesn't have many triggers, which is one of the reasons my father loves her, so you must've really gone for the kill." Bria's bluntness really was the truth, and it made her want to cry from shame.

"You didn't want her?" She wiped her face and didn't have the strength to get her voice over a whisper. "You're both so close."

"It's a bad idea to fall for someone who's in love with someone else. That's not going to be a problem for you, so don't worry about it."

"What do you mean?"

Bria laughed. "You're in love with Curtis, remember? Falling for Brooks is the least of your worries because you aren't interested in her."

She briefly wondered what the penalty was for hitting a mafia princess, but Bria waggled her fingers and left. This was who Brooks had spent a majority of her time with, so there was no doubt she'd find her first. When she did, Bria would gladly take the gift she'd so neatly wrapped and put a big bow on.

"Goddamn it." Her voice sounded extra loud in the empty room, and it was stifling. She grabbed her shoes and called down for her car. "Time to stop the crazy."

❖

Brooks had walked all the way to the river before she cooled down. She stared at the bench where she'd met Fallon and kept walking. Angelo came to mind, and their conversations about losing yourself to emotions even if they were warranted. Café du Monde wasn't full, so she sat at a table in the middle and ordered a café au lait. It was hot as hell, but this was a slice of her past that was mostly happy memories.

She stayed quiet when Beatrice sat down and ordered another cup of coffee. This wasn't her show, so she waited Bea out. This was the first sister Fallon had told about them. Bea had been Fallon's test case, and Bea had accepted her without a problem.

"Do you still love her?" Bea's question made her raise her eyebrows. "It's a simple question, Brooks. I doubt you want me to waste your time."

"Is this your family's twisted version of bad and worse cop?" She bounced her leg and took a sip of her coffee. With all the fantasies she'd had about coming back and putting all this to rest, what was actually happening was never one of her scenarios. "You wouldn't need to go through the exercise if you'd all leave me alone. Do you need me to put it in writing? I can list all the stuff I did wrong and sign it after promising never to do it again."

"I'm not your enemy, Brooks, so cut the sarcasm." Bea rolled her eyes in a way that made Brooks think all the sisters must've practiced together to get it just right. "So...do you still love her?"

"I did until about"—she glanced at her watch—"twenty minutes ago. Now I see what she saw in Curtis and why she agreed to marry him." She finished her coffee and began to stand when Bea grabbed her wrist.

"When you left, Fallon didn't speak for two months. Her whole world imploded, and she was in so much pain." Bea sounded angry, but not really. There were hints of a tired kind of sadness that Brooks was so familiar with. "None of us could reach her, and we didn't understand it any better than she did."

"All that she went through, I experienced it too, only I did it alone." She pulled her wrist, but Bea didn't let go. "I left her here because I knew you all take care of her. The truth of that was the only thing that kept me going."

"But it was all so unnecessary. You didn't have to leave."

"Bea, please, you don't know anything about it. I did what was best, and the only thing I truly regret was hurting Fallon. I loved her. The only reason I survived at all was because of Bria, and because I didn't cause irreparable harm to Fallon and your family." Jesus, all these emotional conversations were getting on her nerves. "Bria was all I had, and she felt sorry enough for me to throw me a lifeline. Fallon had all of you, so get it through your head that I'm only here for my parents, nothing else. Explain that to your family, and we can skip any more of these uncomfortable talks in the future."

"Brooks, that's not why I'm asking, and you know it." Bea let her go and she sat back. "My sister is important to me, and you're important to her."

"Correction—I *was* important to her, and now Curtis is. The wedding I'm sure will be everything your mom always wanted. Once I know my mom is okay, I'll be a bad memory. You can all sit around and talk about me at holidays." She smiled since this wasn't Bea's fault. "I'm going to stick to seeing my parents, and I'll leave Fallon alone. You have my word."

"That would be like compounding your problems, but what do I know."

"You know me," she said with her hands up. "I love living on the edge."

Brooks headed into the Quarter and the apartment the family owned, a block off Bourbon. When she needed direction, she liked sitting with the best compass she knew. Right now, the only place she wanted to go was home, so she could take the chance to again make a new life for herself. Up to now she'd worked hard to be able to stand on her own with the hope that she could repair the damage of the past. That wasn't an option.

"I recognize that droopy face," Heddie Boseman said when she opened the door. Her grandmother was the best truth teller in her life, and she was embarrassed she hadn't seen her in five months. She pinched Brooks's cheeks before kissing each one. "Come in and tell me all about it."

"We sort of won in court today." She followed Heddie to the sunroom. "I'd have rather it be dismissed, but it'll give me time to work through the problems."

"Your mother called me." Her grandmother poured her an iced tea and glanced at the courtyard outside. "I stayed away from all that since I haven't been happy with your father in quite a while. The misery he's facing is daunting, and my heart bleeds for him, but I have to make peace with him before it's too late. I'm having the hardest time with that, though, considering some of his behavior that he didn't want anyone lecturing him about."

"Think of how it all turned out, Granny. I was in the same boat, but

I'm trying to concentrate on all those years before that night. If that had never happened, I would've been happy to stay here and work for the business. That means I would've missed out on all I've accomplished."

"I'm proud of you, my love, but don't gloss over your father's faults. He's my son and I love him, but it's a hard mountain to climb."

"What did happen might've been fate, so maybe everything turned out the way it was supposed to." The finality of all these conversations was depressing, and they were harbingers of the shift all their lives were going to take once her father was gone.

"I never had a doubt you were going to make your way, Brooks, and your father and my feelings for him are about more than what happened to you. As a mother I know how difficult it is at times to raise children, but your grandfather and I tried to make them all good people. We could never figure out where we went wrong with Max." Her grandmother stirred her tea with a bit more force than was necessary.

"It has plenty to do with ego and the inability he and Curtis have to share their toys." She was glad to make her grandmother laugh. "Are you going home soon? I thought I'd stay with you."

"Some of my friends are still in town, so give me a few more days, but my guest room is yours. What are you going to do with Bria? She's been by a couple of times, unlike someone I love." Her grandmother squinted, and Brooks had to laugh.

"I'm going to keep the suite and offer her the other room at your place when we have business we can't put off."

They talked about a few things before her grandmother had to get ready for dinner. There was a sense of happiness knowing she had a soft landing spot no matter how high or far she flew. Talking to her granny always gave her that sense of home.

"Spill it before you go. Why the sad face?"

She told Heddie about the conversations with Fallon and Bea, leaving out a few details to not add to her granny's feelings about the situation. "In plenty of ways it was good. It's a relief to know it's done. I apologized even though it's not enough, and she's moved on."

"Sure she has, and if you repeat that to yourself over and over, you might come to believe it." Her grandmother stood and kissed the top of her head. "Promise that you won't let the Boseman ego get in the way of what's best for you. You inherited a bit of that from your father, so don't be a Neanderthal about it. Fallon has never moved on, and yes, I realize she's engaged."

"Sometimes the knowing of how things stand is the best. Ego

doesn't have anything to do with it, and she *is* engaged." She hugged her grandmother, loving the hints of the Chanel N°5 her grandmother had always worn. "Thanks, Granny, and I'll see you soon."

"You will, and remember to keep an open mind."

"To tell the truth, I'd like not to think about it at all. She's with Curtis, and that's a big gross factor for me." Her granny laughed again and walked her to the door. The visit and the walk had cooled her off. It was the reset she needed to deal with her father.

"You're loved, Brooks," her granny said. "I love you because you're a good person."

"I love you too, and have fun." She headed back to the hotel, not anxious to run into any more of Fallon's family, including Fallon herself. Today was the big The End on any kind of story she and Fallon could've had.

CHAPTER TWELVE

Fallon pressed her forehead to her steering wheel after arriving at her parents' home uptown. She was uneasy about this meeting because asking her father meant showing no faith in Brooks. The way Brooks had talked about how she'd had to handle their breakup had come close to breaking her. If it was true, then some of her anger would bleed onto her father.

"Hey, kiddo," her father said, tapping on her window. His appearance scared her enough to make her scream. "Sorry, but you've been sitting here for like thirty minutes."

"Hi, Daddy." She opened her door and fell against her dad when he opened his arms. "May I talk to you?"

"Anytime, sweetheart. Come on so your mom doesn't get a hold of you. She's looking at lace today, and it's a serious undertaking."

That made her laugh and wipe her face. "I'm pretty sure I'm allergic to lace, so thank you." She followed her dad to his study. Her goal was to not let her mouth override her brain until he explained.

He sat close to the fireplace and poured her a little bourbon. That had been his go-to when they were upset once they were all old enough to drink. "What's wrong?"

"I went to see Brooks today." She told him the reason for the visit and what she'd asked Brooks. Her dad nodded and his expression registered something like realization.

"She told you about the loan?" He rubbed his chin. "I know what she's trying to do with the business now, but I paid all that back a million years ago. Unless Max added some other crazy thing to the ridiculous contract he had written up."

"Why'd you go to Max?" The bile rose in her throat and the nausea made her run to the bathroom down the hall. Everything Brooks said was true, and she hadn't believed her. Her father being so blasé about it didn't thrill her either.

"Do you need me to call your mom?" he asked.

"No, I'm okay. It's just been a long day." She went to the bathroom upstairs and brushed her teeth, then waved off more bourbon when she returned. "I'd like to finish."

"Sure, but what's all this about?"

"Brooks told me about your deal with Max and what he threatened if she kept seeing me. She left because she said we didn't deserve to lose everything." She started crying for all she'd lost and from her anger at Max. He'd destroyed something beautiful for no good reason.

"I'm so sorry, honey, and I should've realized." Her father held her again. "Those were some tough and stressful times, and I was so worried about the business I didn't think of much else."

"I lost her because of all this, and it didn't occur to you?" So much for not getting angry.

"Honey, I understand, but you have to realize what we were facing. Three of the companies we had contracts with went belly-up. I'd expanded to accommodate all the new business and didn't expect the sudden downswing that followed. It's one of the reasons I'm so cautious about borrowing money. Not that the bank would've lent us a nickel, so Max was my only avenue."

"He was going to ruin our business, so Brooks picked for us." She said the words, and the weight of them made her understand what Brooks had done. It hit her like a thunderbolt. Brooks hadn't acted out of some dark place or boredom, but from the love she'd always given so freely. "She went through all that and suffered alone. I allowed that to happen."

"I understand what Max is going through, but he's a piece of work. Always has been." Her dad shook his head and took her hands. "None of this is your fault, and I'm ashamed I was so self-absorbed that I didn't realize what she'd done. Brooks is an even better person than I thought. You don't have to listen to this old man, but we both were way off when it came to her. It's your life, but remember it's long and hard when you pick the wrong person to share it with."

"Thanks, Daddy. I hate to cry and go, but I've got to run."

Her mom came in with a wedding dress book, and she ran before she burned it to get her point across. "She's got someplace to be, honey, so put all that away," she heard her dad say as she headed out the door.

She drove a tad too fast to get to the Piquant, but all she found was Bria. "All I want to do is talk to her."

Bria stared at her before waving her inside. "I'd like to talk to her too, but I've got no idea where she is. This happens sometimes, and all you can do is wait her out."

"I didn't believe her." She sat where Bria pointed and was prepared to do what Bria suggested and wait. Hell, she'd waited years—what was another couple of hours? "Why didn't I just believe her?"

"I think we've established you're not too bright, but for some reason she loves you." Bria sat across from her and glanced at her phone while she was talking. "Brooks is a charmer. The way she deals with clients is what's made us so successful. That charm could've gotten her any woman she wanted."

"Including you?" It didn't take a genius, which Bria didn't think she was anyway, to realize how beautiful Bria was. She was petite, but she owned the room with her sense of self. That was something some people were born with, and considering who Bria's father was, it must've been innate, and she figured Brooks found it attractive. Falling for her would've been easy.

Bria laughed and gave Fallon her full attention. "Yes, including me, but something happened along the way. Brooks is my family. My parents adopted her when she was alone, and we all love her. They'd go to war over her, and in my family that means something," Bria said and winked.

"That sort of answers my question." She wanted to look at her watch but didn't want to be rude.

"I'm comfortable with my spot in Brooks's life, and she knows I always have her back." Bria spoke as she seemed to be texting someone. "I love her, I always will, but she'll never feel for me the same as she does for you."

"I remember the day Brooks hesitated before she kissed me. In that one moment I planned out my whole life—four kids, a house in the Garden District, and date nights." She hadn't made plans since Brooks, choosing to simply exist. That in turn got her engaged, her mother in a twist, and her love tying her in knots.

"You need to up the IQ factor if you want to fit in three kids. If you can't keep your mouth in check, it's not going to go your way," Bria said, holding up her phone. "And she's at her grandmother's if you need to talk to her."

"Thank you." She jumped up, kissed Bria, and ran for the elevator.

She drummed her fingers on the steering wheel all the way down the bayou because Brooks's grandmother thought of the cottage on the property as home. The gate was open, and she saw Brooks's truck in front of the garage. Her only roadblock was that it was Scarlett on the path down to where she wanted to be and not Brooks.

"Are you here to play games, or have you decided on a different way to punch holes in my kid?" Scarlett never really sounded disapproving even as she was being disapproving. "If it's either of those things, please leave her alone. I get why you lashed out. All those phone calls begging me to put her on the phone all those years ago, and then silence. I didn't hear from you until you came back with Curtis." It was a succinct way of summing up her entire life. In the realm of the romance genre, her story was more of a tragedy.

"She told me what happened." It didn't explain away her behavior, but she was as lost as Scarlett seemed to be. "And I'm ashamed to say I didn't believe her."

"Max told me the same thing. The answer cost him six months of our marriage. When she left, it wasn't only you she cut off contact with. I lost plenty of sleep worrying about her." Scarlett leaned against Brooks's truck and sighed. "I somewhat understand now how you ended up with Curtis. To be honest, it's been hard to look at. I love my son, but you don't fit together."

That admission made her move toward Scarlett to hug her. "Which one are you rooting for?"

Scarlett laughed. "Both of them, but not in the way you think. What I want for all my kids is to find their puzzle piece—the one person who fits with them perfectly and only them. If you try to jam someone into your life to simply have someone in your life, it's the destruction of your happiness."

"Thanks, Scarlett, and I'm sorry for all those calls. You can blame it on me being young and desperate. I'm still in that boat," she said and laughed. "Do you mind if I go down?"

Scarlett moved aside and kissed her temple. "Don't fuck it up. Think of living the rest of your life without a hope of getting it right."

"Yes, ma'am, I'll do my best." She enjoyed the walk, not wanting to appear too eager. Brooks had changed into shorts and her feet were bare. The throwback appearance tightened something inside her, and she stopped to admire the sight that had always fueled her passion.

"Did you talk to Alfred?" Brooks never turned and looked but knew it was her.

"It's hard to believe, Brooks, and I'm having a hard time wrapping my head around what happened." She wanted, no, *craved* going to Brooks and having her hold her. The want of Brooks telling her everything would be okay made her ache. Being out in the cold for this long was excruciating, and the warmth that would make it all go away wasn't moving.

"There's nothing I can do or say that's going to make it okay. All I need is for you to believe me when I tell you how sorry I am. If this had happened now," Brooks said, finally standing and facing her, "with experience I would've laughed at Max's power play, but I was twenty-one and my fear was you'd never forgive me if I'd been selfish."

"Oh, Brooks." She covered her mouth with her hands to keep from sobbing.

"What I've learned is that I was right. No matter the reason for what I did, you'd see it as me being selfish, so I did it, leaving your family in the best position I could give all of you. The other thing I learned is that you'll never really forgive me."

"This is so unfair." She wanted to take the expression of defeat off Brooks's face, but she didn't seem like she wanted to be touched. "I wanted so many things—"

She couldn't help the tears that came as easily as the sun rising in the morning. Brooks seemed to break and stepped closer so she could put her arms around her. They stood pressed together, and she did her best to breathe Brooks in and remember. All the memories had kept her going, but there was nothing to replace being in Brooks's arms.

"We both wanted different things, but what we both found instead isn't wrong." Brooks spoke softly as she rubbed her back. "I lost you, but it helps that you've built not only a successful business but a life. That, to me anyway, makes what I gave up worth it." Fallon held her breath and Brooks kissed her forehead.

"You're wrong," she said, leaning back far enough to see Brooks's face. "Everything you think I gained was not worth losing you."

"Come on, Fallon." Brooks let her go, and she wanted to take back what she'd said. "Tell me your parents and your family wouldn't have resented me for costing them everything? My father has spent most of his life being a bastard and smashing everything that wasn't to his liking. Trust me that I'm having a hard time dealing with the fact that I'm trying to save the one thing he threw me away for."

"I'm sorry you're having to go through this now."

"The funniest thing is all those lessons the clergy taught us in school. The priests always drove home that forgiveness is good for the soul, but they never mentioned how hard the process is. I don't have it in me, though, to be that cruel. My only choice is to forgive him no matter what he's done."

"You always think of yourself last." She stepped back into Brooks's space and put her hands on her chest. "It was always one of your best traits."

"My plan was only to spare you as much pain as possible." Brooks smiled, but it didn't reach her eyes. "And in a way you ended up almost where you started. You work for your dad, and you're going to spend your life with a Boseman."

That was true, and this little bit of home would disappear along with Max. There was no way Brooks would stick around to see Curtis flaunt her like a prized show dog. Once that happened, Bria would pick up the pieces and deliver them to the closest altar in a perfectly tailored tuxedo. Max had really torpedoed both their futures.

"Jesus." She lay her head against Brooks's chest and closed her eyes, "I've missed you."

"I did too, and I want you to know that I'm here if you need anything." The rumble of Brooks's voice made her hold on tighter. "You don't trust me, and I know why, but you've never been far from my thoughts. The truth is, you never will be."

Having Bria call her an idiot ran through her head, but she needed to do a couple of things before she could have the conversation she wanted to have with Brooks. "I do trust you, and I hope you still have some faith in me."

"I keep telling you, you're not to blame in any of this." Brooks lifted her hand and pressed it to her cheek. "You still are the most beautiful woman I've ever known."

"No one has ever seen me that way since you." She covered Brooks's hand to keep it in place. "Can you make me a promise?"

"If I can."

"Don't disappear on me. Not again."

"I'll be here." Brooks smiled.

"Does Heddie have food in her fridge?" She kept her arms around Brooks and held eye contact. "I ran you off before you got to eat."

"You don't have to do that. I'd offer to take you somewhere, but I doubt I remember anything that's good around here." Brooks let her pull her inside.

"Let me take care of you," Fallon said, and she meant it. That's what she'd planned to do for the rest of her life when she was in college, and those plans hadn't changed.

❖

Brooks sat at the island in the small kitchen and waited for Fallon to cut up everything in her grandmother's vegetable drawer. The shrimp Brooks had peeled were in a bowl marinating, but that had been the only thing Fallon had allowed her to do. Now it was an exercise in torture, staring at Fallon's ass in jeans that should've been illegal and trying not to get caught.

"Are you sure you don't want anything to drink?" She couldn't sound any more like a moron if she were to try. Hell, she'd made multimillion-dollar deals, so making small talk shouldn't be this hard.

"Does Heddie have wine?" Fallon turned and smiled.

With any luck, Fallon hadn't noticed where her attention was. "It's Granny we're talking about, so it's a matter of narrowing down what you want. There's definitely wine." She went to the cooler when Fallon requested white. "So, what's been going on at work?"

"Do you want to talk about the weather too?" Fallon laughed as she popped a piece of broccoli in her mouth.

"What would you like to talk about? Please don't say wedding plans." She said it as a joke, but she was totally serious. If she was forced to go and see her brother put a wedding ring on Fallon, she was pretty sure it'd kill her.

"Do you have something against weddings?" Fallon knew how to torture, and when Brooks stayed quiet, she reached over and pinched her middle. "Don't worry, you're safe. I'm not a fan of wedding planning either." Fallon started her dish and told her about the business and her plans for expansion.

"That sounds like a solid business decision, but I can see Alfred's misgivings. Loans, I'm sure, are a touchy subject, even if this time the banks would line up for the chance to do business with you."

"I wouldn't have pushed him so hard if I'd known. There would've been so many things I would've done differently if I'd known." Fallon stirred and wiped her face.

Brooks waited until she was done and the meal was plated before turning the stove off and taking Fallon's hand. They sat on the sofa, and she put her arms around Fallon, not trying to make it worse by adding words. Her memory wasn't that faulty that she didn't remember how Fallon liked to be soothed, and platitudes weren't going to cut it.

How many nights had they done this? Not the crying or the upset but enjoying the silence together. It didn't always have to do with sex, but to simply enjoy the feel of Fallon against her. Years hadn't dulled the pleasure of holding Fallon.

"I saw you in Saks right before that disastrous party." Fallon spoke into the cotton of her shirt since her mouth was pressed against her shoulder.

"Oh yeah? You didn't want to throw something at me? Shoes or maybe high-end cosmetics?" That got her another pinch.

"Stop being an asshole." Fallon moved so they could look at each other but not far enough away that they weren't still pressed together. "It's easy to see how angry I've been, but the sight of you and what it does to me is hard to explain to myself."

"What does it really matter?" She was acting like an asshole, but she was trying to keep her emotions under wraps.

"I said to stop being an asshole," Fallon said with heat. "Do you honestly believe that?"

"I've had a lot of thoughts about how it would go when I saw you again." Fallon stared at her and she kept talking. "Trust me, I've punished myself plenty. Doing the right thing, or what I knew was the right thing, doesn't mean it didn't hurt. It ripped me in ways I couldn't fathom, because I never could've imagined pain like that."

"The truth of what you did impressed my father." Fallon moved again and straddled her lap. "You were selfless, and he was clueless."

"Alfred didn't deserve to burn because of a bad deal. None of you—" She stopped talking when Fallon kissed her. This was no friendly nice-to-see-you kind of kiss, and it completely froze her brain.

She put her hands on Fallon's hips and kissed her back. There was no guilt, remorse, or regret, and there should've been a hodgepodge of all those things. All that mattered was getting back the one thing that always made sense even if it was for a moment. Fallon fit, made her happy, and brought the parts of her that had been in hibernation to life. Her sex drive lifted its head and tapped her on the shoulder. Stuffing it back in a box was going to be difficult.

"Um…" She blinked her eyes open, and Fallon was staring at her again.

"Don't ruin it by saying you're sorry," Fallon said, taking a step back. "I'm not, and I don't want to get mad at you again by making light of this."

Fallon was gone before she could say anything else, and her delayed reaction must've given Fallon enough time to run up to her car because she couldn't find her. She grabbed her phone and cursed she didn't have Fallon's cell number. Calling anyone to get it would be a Pandora's box of shit, and that she wanted to avoid.

She stood alone in the driveway and mentally ran the different scenarios of actions she could take. The end of that kiss kick-started the analytical part of her mind, and she really wanted to ignore it—needed to ignore it because this wasn't business. This was her life, the woman she loved, and that couldn't be put in a cut-and-dried set of business models or scenarios. She started to drive to Fallon's place and tried to think of the right thing to say, but the problem was there was nothing she could say.

Loving Fallon was the best thing she'd ever done. Nothing had ever been easy, but giving in to what she wanted from the moment she'd left would've created big complications. That was true now because of who Fallon was engaged to. Standing up at a wedding and declaring her love for the bride would plop down a pile of manure that wouldn't easily be shoveled away. If Curtis didn't kill her, Eleanor would for ruining her perfect day.

She turned onto Fallon's street and stopped four houses from her destination. If she needed a big sign spelling out *complication* in big pink neon, it came in the form of the shiny new sports car parked behind Fallon's vehicle. Fallon had kissed her and run home to the old ball and chain. Her only options were turning around before she became more of a joke, or ramming Curtis's car until it flipped over.

"I'm going to need therapy before this is over." She turned around and went back to the cottage. The role of joke butt was much cheaper than the Aston Martin.

❖

It was dark when Brooks got back, and she walked into the main house. Charlie was in the kitchen making a sandwich, and she offered her half. Her sister was taking a shift with her father so their mom could go out for a little while. Brooks hadn't been home very long and had already figured out how stressful the role of caregiver was. Taking care of a patient who was cooperative and understood the steps they had to take to get better was hard enough; this situation was impossible. Their mom was going to need as much care as their dad going forward, if only to keep her sanity.

"I'll go up for a little while. You enjoy your sandwich."

Charlie kissed her cheek again for the offer and stepped outside with her plate and a mystery novel.

Brooks glanced at all the pictures lining the stairwell, stopping at the one taken on LSU's campus. Fallon was lying next to her on a blanket, their heads pressed together. The picture had been in her desk drawer in her old room, so its ending up here meant her mom must've gone snooping. That it'd been framed to hang with all the other family photos was telling. Her mom's form of subtlety was unique. Why go through life with a big stick when a two-by-four to the face made a more lasting impression?

Her dad was in bed with his eyes closed, but she didn't think he was sleeping. She sat, trying not to disturb him since he was peaceful. The last couple of days had been disconcerting when it came to dealing with Max, and her mom had warned them about how to handle him when he was agitated.

He'd been disoriented, and he wasn't snapping out of it like her mom said had been the pattern up to now. The loss of memory when it came to the recognition of his family upset him to the point where his agitation got the better of him. Once it started, it took medication to calm him down so he wouldn't be a danger to himself or anyone sitting with him.

"Hey, Dad." She moved from the chair to the bed to sit next to him and rested her elbows on her knees. "You wouldn't believe the day I've had." She spoke in an almost whisper and felt the burden lift a bit by saying it all out loud.

His eyes never opened when she talked about court, Curtis, and some of the business she'd gotten back. If another thirty percent of the contracts could be re-signed, she could show significant enough growth to shut Curtis out in court for good. She wanted to reserve the nuclear option to save Curtis some dignity, but she was closing in on it if needed.

"You can stop worrying about the business. It's going to be okay."

"What about you, kid?" Max opened his eyes and turned his head to look at her. "Are you going to be okay?"

"I will be eventually, Dad, but it'll take time." She took his other hand when he offered it and tried not to think of that night that'd crushed her world like one of the walnuts he kept in a dish on his desk. He loved the damn things, and she figured he'd eaten them all this time because the exercise of breaking them open in his fist brought his stress level down. It went right back up when her mom complained about the mess.

"You know what you need to do?" He squeezed her hand and motioned for her to sit closer with a flick of his head.

"What's that?" She kept her voice light, not wanting him to lose his good mood. The vacant stare was gone, and he appeared almost happy.

"Find that girl and tell her you love her. Go ahead and blame me for what happened, since that's the truth. You might have to grovel some, but the way she loved you, that doesn't just go away." His eyes became glassy as he spoke, but they were still surprisingly clear. "Do you promise to do that?"

"I'll think about it." That kiss was still at the forefront of her thoughts. It was easy to understand the mind of an addict since she wanted to kiss Fallon again and again. "She's Curtis's girl now, so I might've lost my chance."

"Ask your mom about Curtis. It's time you know about that, and that's all my fault too." He yawned as if the talk had sapped his strength. "Can you promise me something else?"

"Sure, Dad, I'll do my best."

"Bring the girl by once you get her back. I'd like to tell her I'm sorry. It'd be easy to blame my upbringing or beliefs, but sometimes the explanation is much simpler than you think."

"Oh yeah, why's that?" This had been one of the most surreal days of her life, but this conversation was the highlight of strange.

"I'm an asshole. There's not much time to redeem myself, and this is the most important of the things I'd like to get right. I need to do that, so I need your word you'll get her here."

"I promise." His tears fell when she kissed his cheek. "Even if all that doesn't work out, remember that I love you. We haven't always gotten along, and we've spent years apart, but you're my father. Nothing in the world is going to change that, and I'm glad we get to spend time together."

"You're a generous grader."

She looked at him, confused as to what he meant. "You're disagreeing with me?"

"You and Brooks could be twins, but forgiveness isn't something she'll ever offer and mean it. I wish you were her, but she hates me for good reason. It won't matter how many times I apologize—she'll hate me forever."

The connection wasn't there, and she wasn't sure what was okay to say that wouldn't upset him. "It's me, Pop. I'm Brooks."

He stared at her with a lost expression. "Brooks?" His hand shook when he lifted it toward her cheek. "You came."

"Yes, and I'm not going anywhere." In a way he was a small child again, completely guileless. It was strange, considering the man he'd always been, who was much more calculating and ruthless. "Thank you for all the advice."

"Did you hear all that? I was talking to your friend."

She nodded and held his hand between hers. "I heard, and you're wrong—I do forgive you." He smiled as he cried some more. "Do you want to hear about work?" She thought maybe the familiar would keep his mind tethered to the present.

"No, you promised." He held on to her and pleaded. "Go talk to her and tell her—you promised."

"Don't worry. I said I would, but right now, I want to be here with you." That was the right thing to say since he had the biggest smile she'd seen in years. "How about we go fishing tomorrow, just the two of us?"

From the time she had memory, her father had kept a small boat that was a perfect size to get around the marsh. When she was in her early teens, they'd go out in the early mornings and catch redfish and drum. They talked about different things and there'd been no demands, no ultimatums, and no resentment between them.

They'd never get back to that place again, but she had a small window to make new memories that didn't center around all those bad feelings. Maybe if they spent a morning in the midst of all that beauty that existed close to the house, they could both bury all that pain and get to a place where they both could truly forgive.

"I don't know," he said with uncertainty. "I don't like going out. We might get lost. Honey told me so," he said, talking about her mother.

"Then how about a cigar right outside?" She tilted her head toward the veranda. "You and me, tomorrow, with a good cup of coffee and a Cohiba."

"Will you tell me about her then?" The disease hadn't affected his persistence. "You need to talk to her—tonight."

"I'll go in the morning." This was her life, not some soap opera where she barged in on her brother and old girlfriend like some nutjob.

"You aren't a coward, kid. You never were, so don't start now." He closed his eyes as a dismissal, and she went back down to Charlie.

"He's better, if you want to talk to him about anything." She hugged Charlie and stepped outside to the still-oppressive heat even though it'd been hours since sunset. Maybe that was what was muddling her brain, because it didn't sound like a great idea to be listening to her father. Her other option was to go back to an empty cottage, and she didn't want to do that either.

"Shit." She twirled her keys around her finger and headed for the truck. The drive was getting more and more familiar, so it seemed shorter as the city skyline came into view less than an hour later. "Don't turn back no matter what," she said as she headed uptown. She stopped at the corner and stared at Fallon's house. "I have to be crazy, but in this case, sanity has no appeal."

CHAPTER THIRTEEN

The drive home was a blur because all Fallon could feel was Brooks's lips on hers. She slammed on the brakes in her driveway after almost wiping out the large planter close to the house. "Fuck." The place was dark, and she wanted to go back. No matter what happened, there was one truth. Brooks had kissed her back. She couldn't explain that away.

The loud engine noise knocked her out of her thoughts. Damn, Curtis was the last person she had a desire to see. He was standing outside the car with a bouquet of orange roses like he was Romeo. This was probably why that story ended so tragically. Who the hell gave orange roses unless it was the recipient's favorite color? In her case, orange was the only crayon in the box she'd never used as a kid. It was not her favorite color, and Curtis always acted like she was kidding when she'd said that.

"Hey," Curtis said loudly. She guessed it was to be heard over the loud flowers. "I need to talk to you."

She didn't accept the bouquet as she unlocked her door. "I'm glad you dropped by. I need to talk to you too." He entered ahead of her when she waved him in.

"It's nice you're this excited to see me." He went to put his arms around her, and she planted her hand in the middle of his chest. "Come on, Fallon, I thought we had agreed to go forward. You're not making me feel real welcome. I brought you these, babe."

The cute nickname *babe* made him sound like a pimp, and she almost took the flowers so she could smack him repeatedly with the entire bouquet. "Let me explain a few things to you. When you get these ideas in your head, they only ever work out in *your* head. You can't magically wish this into becoming a real relationship followed by a wedding." She took the ring off, and it was like throwing off a pile of boulders from her head. "I'm done with all of this." She placed the ring against his chest again and stepped back.

"No." Curtis grabbed the ring before it fell to the floor. He yelled so loud she narrowed her eyes. "We had a deal, Fallon. I'm in the fight of my life, and I need you with me. I need someone on my side." He held the ring out to her. "Remember why you said yes in the first place. I care about you, and I'm not going anywhere. No one else in your life is going to do that."

"I was in court today, Curtis, and I did think about why I said yes. What I saw this morning was worlds away from the guy who asked me and wanted to be my friend. You're going to war with your family, and you're willing to get what you want by embarrassing your father." She pointed at him when he started toward her. "Who does that? The man might not be my favorite person, but he's sick. What you're doing isn't right."

"Your dad believes in you, and mine turned to my sister when it mattered. What kind of loyalty is that?" He kept yelling, the ring in one fist and the ridiculous flowers in the other. "I'm willing to show the court the reality of the situation. You're right, he's sick and shouldn't be trusted to make decisions for the company or me."

"You're not a victim. All you've done is make a slew of bad business decisions and try to get your way because of Brooks." Why didn't some people accept that relationships sometimes didn't last? Curtis was the kind of guy who thought if he kept talking, he could get his way. "I appreciate your friendship, but that's all it's ever going to be. And if you keep acting like this, friendship will also be off the table."

"This is because of Brooks, isn't it?" He bumped his fist against his forehead. "She left you, Fallon. Don't be a fool. Brooks didn't want you, and she didn't want any of us."

"Time to go, Curtis." She walked to the door and opened it. "Your family is going through plenty, so think about that before you go scorched earth on them. You'll reach a point where you can't take it back, and you'll end up alone."

"I'll give you a few days to think about this." Curtis stopped a foot from her. "I know you're smart enough to come to your senses."

"Thank you, but not necessary." She closed the door and turned the dead bolt. It was the sound of freedom, and she took a moment to celebrate. Her next step was to get Brooks to get her head out of the mud and notice her before she got on a plane back to New York.

She went to her bedroom and changed, wanting to be comfortable when she called Brooks—Eliza had gotten the number out of Monroe. It wasn't a good start when Brooks didn't answer. The silent treatment she was familiar with, and it bled the joy of the kiss right out of her. A few more calls went to voice mail, which helped her work on the lecture she was giving Brooks the next day.

The dinner she'd made and didn't eat was hours ago, so she ordered from the Thai place close by and parked in front of the television until it arrived. The movie she'd picked was to stop all the wild thoughts of Brooks and Bria running on a loop. It was improbable but not impossible that both Bria and Brooks hadn't disclosed everything about their relationship.

She sat up when the doorbell rang and grabbed the money she'd set aside. That fell to the floor when she opened the door and was picked up until her feet hung inches off the ground.

Brooks kissed her, and it brought her out of her shocked stupor. She put her legs around Brooks's waist and her arms around her neck. There was a momentary panic that she was actually dreaming—then Brooks's hands landed on her ass. Wanting something for so long and getting it so easily raised her superstition flag, but she wanted to enjoy how good it was to be wrapped around Brooks before she had to think about the why.

"Hey," Brooks said, pressing her forehead to hers.

"Hey." She kissed a line across Brooks's cheek. "Are you lost?"

"I have been for a long time, but this girl came over and kissed me." Brooks walked in and kicked the door closed without putting her down. "She didn't leave me any choice but to follow her home."

There were differences in how Brooks felt. She was more solid, stronger, and yet she was still everything she remembered. "This woman sounds enlightened. You should listen to her from now on."

"She is that." Brooks sat on the sofa and didn't appear as comfortable as she should be. There was no way to guess, but she wasn't going to throw her to the curb no matter the missteps. All she needed was Brooks to commit to trying. "Thanks for being so brave and kicking me in the ass."

"Brooks…" She wanted to say plenty, but she couldn't help herself. She held Brooks's face as she kissed her. It was slow, wet, and unlike anyone else who ever pressed their lips to hers. She'd never been able to explain how perfect Brooks was to her even when Brooks was being an ass.

"God, I missed that." Brooks held her when they broke apart.

"You have no idea." She ran her thumbs along the edge of Brooks's cheeks, not to put her off but to be sure of what this was. If Brooks wanted her, there'd be no more leaving, and if it was another apology, this would be it. "Now tell me why you're here."

The big breath Brooks took made her smile. She didn't want to be the only one who was nervous, uncertain, and a bit awkward. They'd been intimate, as close as two people could be, but they weren't kids any longer. They'd lived apart for years, built lives away from each other, and had a multitude of experiences that were part of those separate lives. This time she wanted to do it right. She wanted to be sure and, more importantly, have Brooks be sure.

"The thing about you is you're unforgettable." That answer left her no choice but to kiss Brooks again.

"Go on," she said when someone banged on the door. "Hold that thought—it's dinner."

"Sit." Brooks let her move off. "I'll get it."

"The money should be on the floor," she said, letting Brooks's hand go.

"We can pick it up later," Brooks said, and she put her hand in her pocket. "I want to be alone with you, so I'll get this one." She opened the door, and Fallon was confused when Brooks stumbled backward before falling and hitting her head on the floor hard enough to make a sickening noise. She tripped herself as she quickly got off the couch.

"Are you fucking kidding me right now?" Curtis raged as he stalked to a still Brooks.

"I'm calling the police. Now leave," she screamed back. Brooks still hadn't opened her eyes, but thankfully she was still breathing.

"The fuck I'm leaving, until you tell me what's going on. Why's she here?" Curtis pointed to Brooks like she was an intruder in his perfect world.

Brooks moaned, and Fallon placed her hand on her chest to keep her down. Unless Brooks had undergone a full personality transformation, walking away from a fight wasn't in her nature. That she invested money for the mob made her think she was as fearless as she'd been when they were growing up. Curtis appeared ready to kill someone, and Brooks was going to be his first target, conscious or not.

"Unless you want to spend the night in jail for assault, get the hell out of my house." Brooks moaned again and turned her head with a grimace. "Christ, this can't be happening now."

"You're with her, aren't you?" Curtis was standing over them. If he hit her next, she was calling Bria to put a hit out on him. "Are you brain-dead? I'm the one who cares for you."

"Is there a reason the cops are coming up the street?" Eliza asked, pointing outside.

"Shit," Curtis said, finally running out. They heard the roar of his engine and the squealing of tires. The guy really was out of his mind.

"Brooks, open your eyes, honey." Fallon touched Brooks's cheek and waited. The moaning was steady, so she leaned over and kissed Brooks and kept her lips pressed to hers.

"There've been developments, I see, since I was last updated, but I doubt she needs mouth-to-mouth." Eliza got a cool cloth from the kitchen and handed it to her. "I'm going to go out and wait for the paramedics. You might end up having to talk to the police even if I was punking your boyfriend. He's really dense, isn't he."

"Not now, okay?" She wiped Brooks's face and came close to falling over when Brooks opened her eyes. "Thank God." She kissed Brooks again before pulling back and checking her face. The bruise under her left eye was already swollen and deep purple. "Are you okay?"

"Did Curtis just come in here and punch me?" Brooks sounded groggy and in pain.

"Yes, but I threw him out. Eliza's outside waiting for the ambulance." She held Brooks down when she started to sit up. "You're bleeding, so be good and wait."

"I'm bleeding?"

"You hit the floor pretty hard, and you might need stitches, but I'm afraid to roll you over to look. You might also have a concussion. Please lie here so you don't make things worse."

"You know," Brooks said closing her eyes, "I've made some big deals in my career with some scary people sometimes, but this place is on a whole different level when it comes to drama."

"I didn't ask for or plan any drama for tonight." She had to move aside when the paramedics came in with her sister. Despite Brooks complaining the whole time, they loaded her up and headed to the emergency room. Brooks kept her eyes closed for the ride but didn't let go of Fallon's hand since she'd talked her way into the back.

It took a couple of hours for the doctor to declare Brooks had a slight concussion and put eight staples in the back of her head. Brooks didn't say much when Eliza drove them back to Fallon's house. The night had started so great, but the hospital, Curtis, and the punch had given Brooks enough of a cooling to change her mind. Her silence and detached demeanor were all the hints Fallon needed to know what was coming.

"Do you want me to stay?" Eliza asked.

"I'll call you in the morning." She kissed Eliza's cheek and shook her head. "Thanks for coming with us, but go home."

Brooks was sitting in the same spot they started in with her arms along the back of the couch. Her expression was unreadable. Fallon sat on the coffee table so their knees touched. The only thing Fallon could think to do to start the conversation was to hold up her left hand. Brooks seemed to zero in on her naked ring finger, and her lips lifted in a small smile.

"I'm sorry." Brooks didn't move, and Fallon's heart broke all over again.

"For what?" She was in pain, but all the miscommunication between them was getting old, and she didn't want to get it wrong.

Brooks slid forward and held her hand out to her. "I'm sorry I waited all this time to tell you that I still love you. I screwed up when I left, and I've been thinking since then how to get you to forgive me."

"That's a lot of thinking, Boseman." She pulled on Brooks's fingers and kept a straight face. "A phone call years ago would've been a better move than the brooding I'm sure you've been doing." She pulled on the collar of Brooks's shirt next, so she'd come closer. "There's one thing I know about you, though, and that's why I need you to kiss me right now."

Brooks followed her directions, and it was good enough that she wanted to strip. "What do you know about me aside from the fact that I have a splitting headache? And trust me, I hate to say that. I'm not trying to put you off."

She laughed as she stared into Brooks's eyes. Damn if they hadn't been at the center of plenty of her dreams since Brooks had left. "You have a learning curve, and you also have a concussion, so sit back." The slight grimace came again, and Fallon moved to sit next to her and leaned against her chest. "Are you ready to answer my questions? You have to stay awake for a few hours, and you can't drive, so relax."

"What else do you want to know?" Brooks put an arm around her, and she reached up and laced their fingers together.

"Where do we go from here?" There was nothing worse than sounding desperate, but she had to know.

"I promise I'll answer you, but tell me how you ended up engaged to Curtis." There was no way to guess why Brooks wanted to know, but it was a good idea to get everything out in the open. She wanted their foundation to be rock-solid.

Curtis, though, was going to be a tough one for them to get over. "I've been working to expand our business—to ensure we were the company any oil field or other business would choose first. We probably have in common that we work too much."

"You've done a good job, and from what I've read, you guys are the juggernaut in this area when it comes to ship construction. Mom's been catching me up on all things Fallon." Brooks kissed the top of her head, then rested her chin there. "I'm not asking to punish you," Brooks said softly.

"I dated, but it wasn't ever serious until I ran into Curtis at a chamber luncheon over a year ago. That'd been the first time I'd seen anyone in your family in a long time, and we had coffee afterward to catch up." She couldn't trust why Curtis had put so much effort into building up their relationship. There was no way it had anything to do with her. "After a couple of those meetings, he asked me out to dinner."

"I can understand that, and I didn't leave you much choice." Brooks squeezed her fingers and sounded so reasonable.

The last thing Fallon wanted was for Brooks to be reasonable. She was sitting practically on top of her, willing to do whatever Brooks was comfortable with, so calm and reasonable shouldn't factor into the equation. "I was lonely, and then he was always around. At least that's how it seemed, and he invited me to a lot of things. He listened, no matter what I wanted to talk about, and it was nice. You're the last person who really listened to me."

Brooks sighed. "I'm beginning to regret I asked. The more you say, the more of an asshole I am."

"Let me finish. One night we went to Blanchard's, and he dropped to a knee and shocked me into silence." She pulled Brooks's arm down so their hands were on her stomach. "I should've said no, but I didn't want to embarrass him." She pinched Brooks when she chuckled. "It's not funny and no reason to accept an offer of marriage. When my mother saw the ring, she went wild, and Curtis was always there fanning the flames."

"You don't have to say anything else."

"Come on, Brooks," she yelled and sat up. "Sorry," she said when Brooks pressed the heel of her palm down to the side of her head. "We only kissed, like, three times, and I wasn't interested in anything else. I'm not sure why he was here tonight, but it gave me the chance to give him his ring back."

"Fallon, I can't believe I'm going to say this, but if you fell in love with Curtis and are having second thoughts only because I'm here, I'll go. I don't have the right to mess up your life again, or his, even if he's not my favorite person." Brooks gazed at her as if her life would be over if she really was in love with Curtis.

"It was all a mistake, honey." She caressed Brooks's neck and kissed her again. "When he proposed, I didn't realize that it was all about you. He takes sibling rivalry to a whole new level. There's no way in hell I'm in love with Curtis."

"I'm sorry about that too. What a mess all this has been, and Max probably had no idea the tsunami that built by the little ripples he caused. He wanted to end our relationship, and it's had lasting repercussions." Brooks held her, and Fallon pressed her lips to Brooks's neck. "In his own way he does know, and he's trying to make it right."

"How so?" She heard the doorbell and wanted to ignore it. "Don't go anywhere."

"You're hilarious, and sit. I already have stitches, so let's keep you in one piece in case it's some other pissed-off sibling in search of a cage fight." Brooks walked to the door but glanced out the window before opening it. "Can I help you?"

Fallon didn't recognize the men but groaned when they showed their badges. The emergency services callout to her house had to have triggered this, but she didn't want the interruption. She joined Brooks at the door and put her arm around her waist. The two men glanced at each other before talking to Brooks who, at the moment, appeared to have been in a war.

"Ms. Boseman," the tall guy said, "can we come in?"

"It's Ms. Goodwin's house, so ask her." Brooks gazed down at her and widened her eyes. She wasn't sure what she was trying to convey, but she figured Brooks was going to keep this as brief as possible.

"Come in, but let's be brief. Brooks has been through enough today." She held Brooks's hand as they went back to the couch, and Brooks held them on her thigh. Brooks had always liked to touch her, as if having her close grounded her, and she had to fight the urge to sit in her lap.

"Can you tell us what happened?" the other cop asked.

"Excuse me," Brooks said, holding her free hand to her chest, "I'm Brooks Boseman and this is Fallon Goodwin. You are?"

"Sorry," the tall cop said. "I'm Bob Orick and this is my partner, Stan West. We're investigating what happened tonight after getting a call from your mother. From the look of you, I'd say it was a big something."

"My mother called you?" Brooks asked, sounding skeptical. "I assure you, it was only a misunderstanding, Officer. My brother received some bad news tonight," Brooks said as Fallon pressed closer. "Breakups are always hard to process."

"You're engaged to Mr. Boseman, correct?" West asked Fallon. "Is that the breakup Ms. Boseman is talking about?"

"I was and it is," she said slowly, figuring the rumor mill would start turning earlier than she thought. "I broke it off tonight, as a matter of fact."

"Are you here to inquire about Ms. Goodwin's love life or find out what happened?" Brooks sounded in charge, and the two men straightened their backs as if understanding the reprimand, and that Brooks wasn't going to let them give her shit. "My apologies if my mother got you out here for such a small thing. I'll be checking that out, but Fallon's right. It's been a long day, and I'm ready for it to be over. If you have any other questions, I'll be happy to come in."

"Sure," Orick said. "Did your brother sustain any injuries?" He seemed to study Brooks's face and the blood still on her shirt.

"I'm sure his hand is bruised from the sucker punch, but there'll be no charges, gentlemen."

Fallon stayed on the couch as Brooks walked them to the door. "The universe hates me," she said, standing and stepping into Brooks's arms.

"Unlikely, and I doubt Mom sent the police over here." Brooks placed her fingers under her chin and lifted her head. Whatever Fallon was going to say was forgotten when Brooks kissed her. This kiss was more intense than any of the others, and she fisted Brooks's shirt to hold her closer. "You want me to call one of my more stable relatives to come get me? Tomorrow we can pick up from where we were before the punch."

"You aren't going anywhere, and we aren't finished talking." She didn't want to move away, but Brooks's shirt was full of blood, and it was caked in her hair. The smell was getting nauseating. "Let me help you get cleaned up."

She carefully wiped away the dried blood in Brooks's hair as Brooks sat in the bathroom with her face pressed against Fallon's middle. There was such a sense of belonging, being this close to the one person she wanted to be close to. That'd been missing from her life, but it came easily with Brooks. Life in general was easy with Brooks.

"What do you want to talk about first?" she asked as she rubbed Brooks's back.

"I was telling you about my father." Brooks lifted her hands from the back of Fallon's legs to the small of her back. "When you left me earlier, you twisted me into knots. You stunned me long enough to miss you when I ran after you."

"It couldn't be helped. Kissing you was something I had to do as a way of proving to myself that you were still somewhat interested in me." She stopped what she was doing and kissed Brooks's temple. "You kissed me back, and it freaked me out."

"Not the response I was going for." Brooks nipped along her stomach. "What scared you?"

"I said freaked me out, not scared me. You left the ghost of yourself on me. Your hands, your mouth, and your words haunted me. It was either stay and rip your clothes off or run. I couldn't stand it any longer, so I ran." She pressed her cheek to the top of Brooks's head. "I didn't want to scare *you* into running again."

"I followed you back here because I couldn't stand it either, but I went back when I saw Curtis beat me to it." Brooks cocked her head up and looked at her with an expression she recognized. It conveyed Brooks's feelings and her desire to have her close. She hadn't thought she'd ever see it again in this lifetime.

"I didn't invite him tonight, but it was a good time to give him the ring back. There was no other choice, considering." She ran her finger along the edges of the bruise.

"Considering what?"

"That look on your face when I walked into the party made me hurt. I knew right then that being on Curtis's arm was the ultimate betrayal when it came to you."

Brooks smiled but, in a way, it made her appear sadder. "I don't think you devised this elaborate plan to get back at me, so you don't have to worry about it."

"Don't minimize it. I'm trying to apologize to you. And if it makes you feel any better, your father didn't accept me with Curtis any more than he did when we were together. There must be something about me he doesn't like." It was hard to forget Max's stoneface when Curtis had invited her to Sunday lunch with his family. It was the same face her father made whenever he looked at Curtis, but she could sense the waves of disapproval coming off Max when she'd sat close to him.

"Max is sort of like the bottom of the deepest part of the ocean." Brooks kissed her again until all the tension left her body.

"The deepest part of the ocean? What does that mean?" She mapped Brooks's face with her fingertips, not able to stop herself from touching her.

"It's a mystery, so I wouldn't worry about it. My father is a simple man who lived for a long time in a perpetual bad mood. I'm not sure why, but he didn't treat us much differently, so I don't think it had to do with you."

"I'll take your word for it, but he seemed to be in lockstep with Curtis." She took a deep breath to build up her courage. "I have to admit that when he asked, I was flattered. For that one moment I enjoyed it because I thought it'd be the only proposal I'd ever get."

Brooks shook her head, and her chin rubbed against Fallon's stomach. "You're too beautiful for that to happen. You can be honest—I want to know everything about you, and if I'm honest, I left and went home when I saw Curtis's car because I was jealous. I left in a snit and ended up going up and talking to Max."

"You did? About what?" That Brooks was being so kind to Max surprised her, but then it didn't.

Brooks laughed and her good mood seemed to reappear. "It's not funny, but he's easy to talk to now. I can spill my guts, and I doubt he'll remember, but the ritual of saying it out loud is cathartic."

She laughed too. "You can talk to me, you know."

"I know. Max has had a rough few days, but tonight he was clear enough that he talked to me about you."

"What about me?" She was having trouble concentrating on Brooks as her hand moved down her back.

"I should clarify. He wasn't talking to me specifically. He thinks

I'm someone who looks like his kid Brooks, so he told me I should come back here and tell you how I feel."

She was careful when she cradled Brooks's face in her hands. "How do you feel?"

"Like I said, you are unforgettable, and I love you. I'm going to love you no matter if you marry someone else, even Curtis, and I'll love you even if you never forgive me."

The years she'd known Brooks spanned most of her life. When they'd become lovers, she'd learned to read Brooks, which was why all she saw now was sincerity. She could also see the sacrifice Brooks had made for her, for her family. Brooks had made sure they were all okay, and she'd carried the pain of what she'd done without anyone but Bria. Fallon's mistake had been never wondering why Brooks had done it. She'd let her go and chosen anger. That rage had cost her years with the one person who was her puzzle piece, as Scarlett had said.

"My sisters gave me the same lecture." She didn't wipe away the tears that fell, but she wasn't unhappy. "None of them, unlike my mother, have been thrilled with my decision. They weren't happy because I wasn't in love with Curtis—I never was."

"I didn't tell you all that to get you to say anything back." Brooks stood and hugged her. "How about I go and give you time to think about it? I've fucked up plenty, and the last thing I expect is for you to welcome me back without a little effort on my part."

"No, there's going to be plenty of effort on your part. I'm happy you're here, but I'm not that easy." She hung on to Brooks to keep her close. "And you're not going anywhere tonight. Come on." She walked to her bedroom and looked through her T-shirts to find something that would fit Brooks. "If I go into the bathroom to change, do you promise to stay put?"

"I have a head injury, but I'm not crazy." Brooks took the shirt and nodded. "I'll be here. No worries."

Calming down and not worrying would be a long-term goal, but for now she'd do her best to enjoy that Brooks was here. It was surreal that they'd get in bed once they were dressed for it, but deep breaths would help her cope. She was getting close to having all those pleas she'd sent out into the universe answered, and she didn't want to scare Brooks off by making big sudden movements.

The thing she knew about herself was that she'd come to crave structure. She had it at work, in her family life, and in her home. There were certain ways of doing things, and in all those aspects of her life, there'd never been big changes that were meant to blow up her life. Curtis had done that in one moment when he'd dropped to one knee. All the stress that'd piled on her after that ring went on her finger knocked her off-kilter, and in a way, this was the same. Not that Brooks was chaos, but because Brooks was a huge unknown.

She went into the bathroom and stripped as fast as she could to get her pajamas on. "Let's lie down, but don't get mad when I have to wake you to ask you a bunch of questions." She turned her bed down and got in her usual side.

"Tell me what's wrong, aside from everything I already know."

She hesitated, but Brooks lay back like she wasn't leaving anytime soon. "What happens now?"

❖

The question Fallon asked was reasonable, but Brooks had no good answer. Her life was in New York. She had a home, a business, and friends, so it was only reasonable that she go back. Staying here would be a mistake. This place and the people here had rejected her before, and it'd be a matter of time before it happened again.

There was one glaring problem with that logic. The woman she'd loved forever was lying next to her in a house in New Orleans. She couldn't deny that, but a lot of time and years had gone by. Fallon could've become a completely different person—that was true too. It was obvious from the way she dressed to the way she lived.

"We take it slow and see." She wanted to cringe as soon as the words left her mouth.

Fallon stared at her as if she had a bubble over her head that flashed *I'm a total moron* in big letters, so there was no doubt about it. There were dumbass things to say to someone she was serious about, and if there was a list written up somewhere, the number one response had just come tumbling out. She reached for Fallon's hand when she moved to get up.

"That was a ridiculous thing to say." She was encouraged when Fallon nodded. "Do you want to know what I was thinking when you were getting dressed in the other room?"

"Was it the old *It's not you it's me* line?" Fallon gave her a small smile, but it was plain that she'd hurt her.

"I did suffer a blow to the head, but I'm not that incapacitated. No, I was thinking about my life away from here." Fallon started to move away again, and she didn't let go. "It's all I've worked for, but there's one thing I can't replace no matter how hard I work or how much money I make."

"What?" Fallon seemed to let all the fight out of her go but stared at her as if daring her to say another dumbass thing.

"I have plenty of things to go home to, but the woman I've loved for most of my life is here. Right here," she said, kissing Fallon's hand. "There's no way I can go home when you're here." She let go of Fallon, not wanting to delay the rejection that was coming.

"Do you mean that?" Fallon moved until she straddled her legs. "I could always come with you." There'd been a lot of hesitance in that answer.

"There's no way I'm going to ask you to move." She bit the tip of Fallon's finger when she put it against her lips. "And if you give me a job, it'll prove my willingness to stay."

"You want to work for me?" Fallon put her hands on Brooks's shoulders and inched closer.

"I'd like to work *with* you by helping you with your plans. You're the one with the expertise, and I'm the one with financial experience. If I'm here every day, you can start to trust me." She was having a hard time concentrating with Fallon this close and her nipples this hard.

"Do you honestly think this is a good time to talk about work?" The way Fallon moved her hands across her shoulders and up her neck made her want to yell *no*, but patience was the key.

"The weather's out too, I guess," she answered, and Fallon chuckled in her ear.

She could feel those hard nipples against her chest when Fallon leaned in to her, and she placed her hands on her hips to make herself behave. Fallon wanted her, that was plain, so her phone ringing came at the worst possible time.

"Do you have to answer that?" Fallon asked.

"Give me one second," she said, kissing Fallon. "Please tell me you didn't send the police to Fallon's place," Brooks said. "Mom, don't forget it's your little boy." Brooks stopped and listened before handing the phone over. "My mother wants to talk to you."

"Is she okay?" Scarlett started talking as soon as Fallon put the phone to her ear, but her mother was so loud she heard the question.

"Don't worry, I'll take care of her until she can drive." She poked Brooks when she laughed. "And even when she can drive, I'll bring her back. The doctor said a few days of rest, so don't let her tell you otherwise if I lose sight of her." She ended the call and turned the phone off. "Does your mother have radar when it comes you? Or does she randomly call to see if you're okay from an unprovoked attack?"

"Your sister called Monroe, and there you go." Brooks went back down and held Fallon so she'd come with her. "Once my head stops hurting, would you go to dinner with me?"

"Are you asking me out on a date?"

"You can call it whatever you want." Brooks closed her eyes and tried to relax her entire body to try to ease the pain she was in. "I'd like to go to dinner and talk about something other than what happened between us. A better subject would be what's going to happen going forward."

"The sensation of being in a snow globe makes perfect sense to me now. You've come along, and from the moment I saw you, you've shaken my life and changed the landscape." Fallon seemed to be talking herself into taking a chance.

"I'm more of a nerd than a rebel, so it wasn't my intent to shake up anything." She ran her hand up and down Fallon's back, but it was more to soothe her than the other way around. "And if you want me to apologize, I will."

"Are you sorry?" Fallon asked, tensing in her arms.

"No." Short and to the point was the way to stay away from the dumbass list, so she went with it.

Fallon laughed softly and came closer to her. "Bria was right about you."

"You can't hold anything that Bria said against me." She was getting ahead of herself, but she hoped Bria and Fallon could become good friends. The second chance with Fallon was something she wanted, but she wouldn't sacrifice Bria. That relationship was so much more than friendship—Bria was her family.

"She's certainly something, and she told me you were charming enough to get any woman you wanted." Fallon sounded like she'd already had an ass-full of Bria. "She followed that up by telling me how brainless I am. Actually, she's found new and inventive ways to call me an idiot every single time we talk."

"Ah," she said in lieu of anything else. There wasn't anything she could say that wasn't going to get her into trouble. "That's Bria, but if you ask other people like my mother and Curtis, I'm not all that charming."

"That was smooth, Boseman." Fallon moved up to her elbow and smiled down at her. "I don't know about you, but I'm starving. So far today I cooked and I ordered food and didn't get to eat either time."

"How about I cook this time since I'm hungry too." That it wasn't all about food was something she didn't need to advertise right off.

Fallon laughed again, and it was plain she could still read her as easily as a children's book. "You cook now?"

"I've lived alone for a long time, so I dabble." She sat up with a slight groan she couldn't help and tugged down on the T-shirt Fallon had lent her. The damn thing was a tad too small. "Lately I work so much that I order more than I cook, and there's the fact that it's hard to cook for one person and not get sick of the leftovers."

"What's your specialty?" Fallon moved to Brooks's side of the bed when she swung her legs down.

"Scrambled eggs since it's so late, but once I have a day off, I'll cook for you."

Fallon draped herself over Brooks's back. "I'd like that." Something changed with Fallon in that answer, and it wasn't for the good.

She didn't move so Fallon would stay close. "You okay? If this is too much too fast, don't be afraid to tell me."

"It's not that," Fallon said, her forehead on Brooks's shoulder. "I'm so scared. We haven't spoken in a long time, and now you're here—in your underwear, even. My heart is thrilled, but my head can't accept that this is real."

"I don't want to spend time trying to convince you." She didn't stop Fallon when she moved off her. "Sometimes it's action that's needed and not pretty words. Don't take that answer as me trying to blow you off."

"Do you understand why I am so afraid?" Fallon spoke, and Brooks could make out the pain etched in every word. It was something that didn't need to be explained to her and was the reason she'd only shared the entire story today. She hadn't been lying when she'd said she thought of Fallon every single day, but it was a subject wrapped in yellow caution tape.

It was hard for most people to understand the long-term ramifications of something like this happening to them. What she and

Fallon had shared was what was considered puppy love, that first brush with emotions so all-consuming that they were hard to fathom. You needed that person so much all the time, and in an instant they were gone. What you were left with was a type of muscle memory when it came to opening your heart again. All you remembered subconsciously was the misery you survived. It was like getting something ripped from your body, and the pain of it wouldn't ever heal or disappear.

"You're afraid because you can't trust this or me." It was that simple, and it made her sad that she couldn't do anything right this moment to change it. "That's not going to happen overnight, and all I can do is to spend every day trying to prove you can believe in me and what we can have."

She got up and headed for the kitchen. Fallon didn't say anything as she watched her get everything out of the refrigerator, and Fallon got a pan for her. Her headache was still there, but she wanted to finish. Once they ate, she'd have Pru or Etienne come and get her. The best course was not to push Fallon into something that wouldn't make her happy. It'd be hard to accept that their time had passed, but she had to consider it.

"You sound so matter-of-fact," Fallon said, sounding upset again.

"Honey, my head is killing me, and today's been a literal pummeling. If I say something wrong, it's all going to blow up on me, so I'm being honest." She had to stop and breathe or she was going to throw up from her headache. "Let me finish this, and I'll call Pru to come and get me. Let's do this on a slower track, and we'll get back there."

The eggs went into the pan, and when she plated them, she gave the bulk of it to Fallon, having lost her appetite. Neither of them ate much, and she went to get her phone when Fallon stood to clear their dishes. She sat on the bed with her pants next to her so she could get dressed once she made her call.

"No," Fallon said, taking the phone from her.

Fallon put it on the nightstand, folded Brooks's pants, and placed them on the chest at the foot of the bed. She climbed over Brooks to get to her side. They didn't speak again, but that was for the best. Silence kept Brooks from saying anything else wrong. The one thing that grounded her was Fallon as she pressed against her and held her like old times.

"You aren't going, are you?" Fallon's question came as she was going to sleep.

She rolled them over so she could spoon behind Fallon and hold her. "You'll have to ask me to go."

"I'll never do that." Fallon sounded so sure, so she kissed the back of her head and smiled.

"That makes me the luckiest guy in the city."

"You have a black eye and staples in your head." Fallon brought their hands up so she could bite her index finger.

"I'm not going to dwell on that," she said and laughed. "It's where I ended up that's important."

CHAPTER FOURTEEN

The dim blue numbers on the clock read 3:12, but Fallon was wide awake. She'd slept like a rock, which wasn't always the norm, especially with someone next to her. There hadn't been a lot of people in her life since Brooks, but she hadn't been a nun either. The only difference had been her dislike of sleepovers. That had considerably cut down her chances of a long-term relationship.

Brooks, though, slept peacefully under her like she belonged there. They'd shifted in their sleep but not away from each other, as if their unconscious minds knew better than their uncertain waking ones. She was tucked half on top of Brooks, and she took a moment to enjoy the way Brooks held her. It was protective and loving, and that was something no one else had ever given her. The perfection of it made her feel bad she'd given Brooks such a hard time.

"If this is your normal wake-up time, it'll take me a bit to adjust." Brooks sounded groggy yet alert.

"What time do you usually get up?" She pressed her lips to Brooks's shoulder even though it was covered by the T-shirt.

"Most mornings at four thirty to check the markets, but I sleep in sometimes, which means I sit in bed and read the paper and don't actually sleep." Brooks's voice sounded deeper, and Fallon shivered at the vibration in her chest.

"How's your head? That you remember what time you get up means there's no chance you scrambled anything important." She rubbed small circles on Brooks's stomach, hoping she'd go back to sleep. If she was alert and okay, she'd be pushing to go home and away from her. It was too soon to let her go.

"If we sleep some more, then you drive me by the Piquant, I'll treat you to breakfast. If I go in this shirt, I doubt they'll let me in anywhere there's tablecloths and real utensils."

"And your head?" She repeated the question since Brooks skimmed over it.

"Much better. You're an excellent nurse." Brooks rolled on her side so she could look at her. The bruise on her face was an impressive black-purple. She touched it gently, and Brooks turned her head to kiss her fingers. "That bad, huh?"

"It's impressive."

"It's not permanent, so don't worry." There wasn't any animosity in Brooks's tone, so she leaned in and kissed her. It wasn't a reward for not being a hothead, but because she was here and interested in her.

"It's like I'm dreaming." She really did have a weakness for Brooks, considering the position they were in and how fast they'd reached it.

"I've had this dream plenty of times only to wake up before I get to kiss you. It always sucks to wake up alone." Brooks smiled, and she was still the most handsome thing Fallon had ever seen even with the bruising. "This is so much better."

"Go back to sleep, and I'll be right here when you wake up."

They shared one more kiss before she fell asleep listening to Brooks's breathing. It was light outside when she opened her eyes again, and Brooks was still next to her. Her breathing was deep and even, so she didn't move, not wanting to wake her. The quiet gave her time to think, but she just couldn't force herself to go down any worry rabbit holes.

There weren't a lot of options for what happened next. She had to listen to either her heart or her head, and both choices had consequences. Not taking a chance with her heart guaranteed safety, but there'd be no Brooks, no joy, and no chance of changing her life from what it was now.

The sound of someone banging on her door made her stiffen, and she held Brooks down when she woke up with a startled twitch. "Stay here," she said when Brooks began to get up.

"I don't think so, sweetheart. If it's my asshole brother, he's got some payback coming."

"Brooks, the last thing you need is to get in a fistfight." She kept her arm over Brooks's middle, aggravated the banging hadn't stopped.

"And you don't need to get hurt. Just stay here, please, and be ready to call the police if I get to act out my murderous thoughts."

Brooks didn't bother with her pants, which—if it was Curtis—would be like waving a red flag at an angry bull. Not a great way to start the morning, at least not how she planned it, but watching an agitated Brooks in briefs walk to the door was a mood lifter.

"All right already, I'm coming," Fallon heard Brooks say. She hoped it wasn't Curtis so there wouldn't be a repeat of last night, but it also might convince him of a few things. Mainly that their relationship was over, and that included their friendship after all he'd done.

"You!" Her mother was good at summoning up her outrage in one word, so Fallon headed for the foyer before Brooks ended up with two black eyes. "What are you doing here?" The screeching was reaching break-glass levels, so she sped up.

"Mrs. Goodwin." Brooks closed the door and met her eyes when Fallon entered, and she had to laugh at the way Brooks squinted in her direction. "I'm so sorry I missed you the other night. It was a lovely party."

She had to give it to Brooks. Her smooth delivery seemed to light a fire under her mother, and not in a good way. "Mom," she said, louder than necessary. "Is there a problem? It's too early for the yelling."

"Curtis came by this morning," her mother said, holding her purse like Brooks was going to rip it out of her hands and run out the door with it. "He was upset."

Of course Curtis went to see his greatest fan to gain sympathy and an ally in his campaign for marriage. He'd been a total kiss-ass from the moment she'd reintroduced him to her parents. "I broke off the engagement last night, which makes me wonder what you and Curtis had to discuss."

"Don't say that. You had to see him," her mother said, pointing to Brooks like Brooks wouldn't notice. "We need to talk before you do anything rash. Can we have some privacy?"

"No problem." Brooks saluted and laughed, but not before winking at Fallon.

She followed Brooks to the bedroom and sighed when she saw Brooks putting her pants on. "Were you going to crawl out the window?"

"I thought I'd hide out in here to give you moral support once Eleanor finishes giving you the stern talking-to she's dying to deliver." Brooks took her hand and dropped her pants. "Am I being an asshole again?"

"What are you talking about?" She liked how Brooks put her hands on her hips when she came closer.

"This might be a guess, but I get the sense I'm the only one who's thrilled we got to this point." Brooks took a step back as if realizing that might be the case. She rubbed the edges of the bruise on her face, and Fallon could only guess the pain was back with a vengeance.

"You aren't counting me on that unhappy list, are you?" She took Brooks's hand so she'd stop touching her injuries.

"I'm going to go with no." Brooks pointed to the other room. "And if you get rid of the Duchess, I'll take you to breakfast."

"That sounds wonderful, so don't think of bailing out the window now that I've put that thought in your head." She laughed again when Brooks made some complicated scout hand movement.

She lost her smile when she saw her mother lingering outside her bedroom door. "Let's start with a reminder of our conversation the other day. It's *my* life, and when it comes to this, I need you to be on my side." Her mother sighed when Fallon bypassed her to head to the coffeepot. "You're smart enough to know Curtis isn't as sweet as he is with you. Is it the harmless flirting or the ass kissing that's giving you a hard time letting go of the fantasy?"

"There's no need for that language, Fallon, and Curtis is in love with you. He is in pain after what you did, and I don't need to remind you of the truth. That woman crushed you by leaving without a word. Try to have some self-respect." The big purse was slammed down on her island, and she was glad for the granite. "It took you less than a month to fall for her bullshit. What's she doing here in her underwear, or should I even ask?"

"I thought you said there's no need for that language." She wanted to slam something down too but wasn't ready to shatter her coffee carafe on the island. "You don't know what you're talking about." She did not want to have this argument with Brooks in the other room. "I was wrong about her. We all were."

"Good Lord, Fallon, don't be this gullible. You're throwing away your chance at a great life with Curtis."

"Mom, I need you to do me a favor. Go home and ask Dad to tell you what happened." She stared at the coffeepot, willing it to brew faster.

"If you promise to talk to Curtis, I'll be happy to do whatever you want." Her mother drummed her fingers and the noise was driving her batty. "He told me what happened last night. Even you have to find it romantic."

"This should be good." She poured two cups and left it to her mother to fix hers however she wanted. The other cup got a splash of cream and two sugars. "I'm sure you're willing to tell me, so stay put." She took the cup and found Brooks studying her face in the mirror. "It's not as bad as it looks. Does it hurt?"

"It's tolerable, and I think the last time I had a bruise this bad on my face, you gave it to me."

"I thought we were never going to talk about that." She laughed at the memory of shoving a naked Brooks in her closet at her sorority house her freshman year.

Greek life really wasn't her thing, but she was a legacy, and her mother had insisted. Getting caught having sex after curfew would've probably gotten her kitchen duty for six months, so she'd slammed the door on Brooks before letting in the group of girls banging on her door. It was a lesson in not screaming *Oh God, don't fucking stop* in the middle of coming.

"How was I supposed to know your chin was perfectly aligned with the knob?"

"Uh-huh, and as much as I love reminiscing, your mother's waiting. She's still out there, right?"

"She is, and despite her being a pain in the ass, she's my mother and I love her. Maybe not as much when she's trying to bend me to her will, but I do love her." She covered her face with her hands and groaned. Her mother wasn't a horrible person, but her make-believe wedding seemed to have unleashed a new terrible aspect of her personality. She doubted it was going back in the box until someone walked down the aisle. "Does that make me sound terrible?"

"It makes you sound like a daughter. No matter the relationship you have with your parents, it goes through normal ups and down. Being perfect all the time isn't possible." Brooks smiled and pointed to the door. "Go and talk her off the ledge, and take your time. And if she likes, I'll answer the door naked next time so she'll really have something to talk about."

"Shut up." She kissed Brooks before heading back to the inquisition. Her mother had moved to the den, so she sat across from her and tapped her foot on the floor. "Go ahead and tell me."

"Curtis said he brought you flowers and tried to tell you how much he loves you." Her mom pressed her hands to her chest, and Fallon figured she get a big *aw*...any minute. "He understands you're having second thoughts, and he's willing to wait for you. Heck, he even fought for your honor. There aren't many men who'd do that anymore. Curtis is so noble."

"Punching Brooks in the face when she opened the door is the opposite of noble, Mother. We ended up in the emergency room when she had a concussion and had to get staples in her head." She took a deep breath, not wanting to completely lose her temper. "You're right about how there aren't a lot of men like Curtis any longer."

"Finally, we agree on something." Her mom appeared way too smug.

"I'm horrified that you refuse to see the truth. Curtis is threatened by Brooks, so he handled that with his fists the first chance he got. What happens when he feels the same way about me?" That was the simplest way she could explain herself when it came to her mother's voluntary ignorance. To advocate for Curtis after seeing Brooks made her think her mom wasn't as okay with her sexuality as she claimed.

"He'd never do that, and all I want is for you to be happy." The beginning of uncertainty finally registered on her mom's face. "You can believe what you want, but I have a hard time forgetting what she did to you and how unhappy you've been ever since. When you started your friendship with Curtis, some of that faded, and he wanted to fit into our family and with you."

"He did all that because of me?" She was cut off before she could list all the things Curtis was and was not.

"Exactly," her mom yelled. "He loves you."

"No, Mom, he doesn't love me. He did all that because of Brooks. I was the fool here, but he proposed to one-up Brooks. He also wanted to show his father he was mature enough to take over the company. It was never about love, and if you can't accept that, then talk to Dad. I don't have anything else to say." Why the hell did life have to be so hard? "Brooks isn't the bad guy here."

"And Curtis is?" Eleanor Goodwin wasn't one to let go easily. "Brooks comes here and insults you, and you make him out to be the bad guy. That's ludicrous. He came to me out of concern for you. Brooks showing up at that party was something that bothered him, as is your friendship with her. I can't blame him for that, so don't punish him for it. Last night was as much for your feelings as his."

"He acted opportunistically because Brooks wasn't expecting it. In life it's called a sucker punch, and only people who are gutless do that." She stopped to give herself a chance to calm down because her volume was going up with each word. "The fact that you want to applaud him for hitting a woman—never mind a woman who most likely can pulverize him in a fair fight—makes me ill."

"Fallon," her mom said, making calm-down motions with her hands. "I'm not celebrating violence, but listen—"

"No, I'm not going to fight with you over this." She stood and crossed her arms over her chest. "Just go."

"We haven't finished talking."

"The truth is I'm not interested in talking to you. Please leave before we say something we can't take back. Get it through your head, though, that I'm not changing my mind about Curtis or his promises. It's over."

She came close to caving to her mom's despondent expression, but talking wasn't the solution right now. Her tears didn't fall until her mother was gone, and she let them fall as Brooks came up behind her and held her.

"Want me to go?" Brooks said close to her ear.

"No, she'll have to accept me for me." She turned around and put her arms around Brooks, needing the connection. They stood in peaceful silence until the doorbell rang, and she wanted to ignore it, especially if it was her mother again.

"Go take a shower and let me take care of that." Brooks kissed the back of her hand before letting her go.

She needed a few moments to herself to try to figure out what she'd done to piss off the gods. It could be her house was built on some secret ancient burial ground and she was cursed forever with guests she had no desire to have over dropping by at all hours. Brooks was talking to someone in the other room and no one was shouting, so she followed Brooks's advice to take a shower.

Twenty minutes under the hot spray let her reset and clear her head. Brooks didn't seem rushed, so she took her time drying her hair and getting dressed. When she went back out, she smiled at Franklin and Brooks having coffee together, talking as if it hadn't been years since they'd seen each other last.

"Hey, you." Franklin stood and hugged her. "Are you doing better than Brooks?"

"She got the brunt of it, but she was a good patient." She took a fresh cup of coffee from Brooks and sat close to her brother. His visit reminded her that they'd set a meeting that morning, so Eliza and Bea were probably on the way to the office.

Franklin glanced between her and Brooks, and she waited him out. He was the worst of all her siblings when it came to reading between the lines. Finesse wasn't something Frankie had mastered. "Do you want to ride with me or do you want to drive?"

Work was the last thing she wanted to do today, but then she remembered the end-of-month stuff. Brooks seemed to understand she'd have to change their plans, and part of her wanted Brooks to tell her to stay. But she couldn't, and her problem was she couldn't say the words.

"Go ahead, and we'll catch up later." Brooks looked ridiculous in the too-small shirt and her bare feet. "I'll head back to the Piquant and grab a shower and an aspirin. We can have lunch later."

In other words, Fallon thought, *I'm headed back to Bria and her never-ending fount of advice.* "This shouldn't take long."

"I'll be showering and watching some soaps, so no rush. If Alfred's going to be there, I don't want to be blamed for mistakes if you weren't paying attention." Brooks pulled her phone from her pocket and tapped something out. "You guys can go if you're late. I'll wait for my ride on the porch." The bright disposition was starting to slip.

"Don't do anything, including looking at files or emails. You need to rest."

Brooks saluted again, and Franklin laughed. He was smart enough to leave first so she could kiss Brooks good-bye. The thought of spending time with Brooks later made her happy. It was going to be a nice day.

❖

The big black truck Franklin drove disappeared in the direction of downtown, and Brooks gently placed her hand on the back of her head. She could feel the staples, and she had to remember to have Bria take a picture later. Another truck stopped on the street, and Etienne got out.

"Not fishing today?" Her little brother with his signature thick ponytail was the definition of consistency. Etienne loved to fish and was the most likely to succeed if their financial fortunes changed overnight.

"The shrimp will wait until tomorrow." He stopped at the center of the brick path from the sidewalk and scrunched up his face, she guessed in reaction to her appearance. "Damn, sis."

"This convinces me Curtis is adopted," she said, and they both laughed. "Let's go so I can take the shirt off before the loss of oxygen kills any more of my brain cells."

"Where's your shirt?" Etienne gave her a side glance. "You usually don't go in for this tight look."

"Mine is full of blood, so Fallon lent me one of hers. She's not my size."

"Really?" He started back to the truck and chuckled. "I figured she's always been the exact right size for you."

She rolled her eyes, wishing she did it as well as Fallon and her sisters. "Don't start—it's been a hell of a night." She answered his questions until they arrived at the hotel, the valet took his truck, and he followed her upstairs.

Bria didn't say anything when they entered the suite, which was a blessing. Repeating the story for Etienne was enough for a couple of days, and she loved that Bria knew that about her. It wouldn't matter anyway. By the time she got dressed, her partner would know the entire story from her brother. The police had nothing on Bria when it came to investigating things she wanted to know.

The spray of the showerheads helped alleviate her headache, and she watched the last of the blood swirl down the drain. Getting the dried blood out of her hair was the last stop in this very strange trip. Last night was nice, but in the light of day things didn't seem as clear as when Fallon brought her home.

She put on a pair of jeans and a golf shirt, planning to take the day off. It had less to do with what the doctor had said and more with the exhaustion that swamped her desire to move. It wasn't often she needed to unplug, but even her busy mind couldn't block out the memories all the time. Last night Fallon had acted as if a future with her was all she wanted, but regret rose with the sun.

"She picked work over you," Bria said from her seat on the bed, sounding angry on her behalf.

"Maybe she's due." She slipped into a pair of loafers and grabbed her wallet. "I made a choice, knowing there was no coming back from it. Who knew how right I'd be?"

Fallon did appear sorry, but there was something about her walking out with Franklin that hurt more than Curtis hitting her. The fantasy of getting everything she was missing was just that—a plot in a children's storybook about places and things that didn't exist. Reality at times had no happy endings.

"Where are you going?" Bria got a hand on the back of her jeans before she could get away. "You have a concussion, and you look like hell."

"I'm not going to fall into the river," she said, slipping her wallet in her pocket. "It's just a walk, and I love you, but I want to go alone."

"Thankfully Daddy's not here," Bria said. "Seeing you like this would've set him off."

She relaxed and hugged Bria. "The bruises will hopefully heal before we go back, though picturing Curtis having a serious conversation with your father is entertaining. If my mom gets in touch, can you let her know I'll call her later?"

"I'll do whatever you like if you promise the walk will be short and you'll be careful." Bria kissed her chin and stepped back. "If you're not back in an hour, you know I have ways of finding you. When I do, I won't be happy."

"Are you activating the locator chip in my neck?" She hugged Bria again and laughed. "No matter what, we'll be okay."

"You're damn right. And I splurged for the one that shocks your ass if you wander too far off the grid."

Brooks snorted, kissed Bria's cheek, and waved to Etienne. The walk to the streetcar was quick, and she stood with a group of tourists and a few locals, glad she didn't have to talk to anyone. She studied the houses on St. Charles Avenue once they made it to the famous street with its string of beautiful mansions. The Garden District gave way to Uptown and she kept her thoughts on work.

Her stop came and she crossed the street to the Camellia Grill and waited for a seat at the counter. She was hungry, and it didn't take much time for her waiter to deliver the best burger she'd ever encountered and a chocolate freeze. This was one of her go-to spots whenever she was in the city.

After her meal she walked to Magazine Street and headed into some of the antique stores and unique shops that'd always lined this street. The food, walking, and ignoring what was happening in her head left her exhausted. She spotted a local coffee shop in the next block and was the only person who sat outside with a hot brew. She didn't change her facial expression when Eleanor Goodwin sat down without an invitation and folded her hands on the table like a demure debutante. Her mother had told her enough stories about Eleanor for her to know better.

"Nothing to say?" Eleanor had a way about her that made Brooks want to address her as *Karen*, because she was a prime example of a privileged angry white woman.

"It's warm today, don't you think?" There was no need to curb her sarcasm. She hadn't asked for this, so headache or no, she'd have to have this conversation. Walking away was not an option. If she did, then she might as well wave a white flag and surrender.

"Why couldn't you stay gone? You broke her heart." Eleanor raised her hand to stop her rebuttal. "Alfred told me all about your good deeds, and you were honorable, but she was learning to move on. She was happy before you got here, and with time, she and Curtis can work it out and be happy again."

"I'm here because my father had a stroke and was diagnosed with Alzheimer's, Mrs. Goodwin. My mother asked for my help, and now that I'm here, it's given me the opportunity to make amends." She finished her coffee and gently put the cup down. "Last night gave me that chance with Fallon, and this morning she's back at work where she belongs. I doubt you have anything to worry about."

"She'll never have peace if you're here."

She wondered sometimes if, in the creation of people by whatever Supreme Being you believed in, they scraped the pot and used the remnants from all the batches to create another person. It helped keep down the waste, but it also put someone out in the world missing some vital bits. Things like compassion, empathy, and gratitude—those vital components that made someone decent. Eleanor had to be one of the missing ingredient people.

"Let me see if I understand," she said. The wrought iron chair wasn't the most comfortable, but with any luck this wouldn't last much longer and she could go do something fun like a root canal. "You'd like me to abandon my parents to make you feel better?"

"It would be to make Fallon happy." The way Eleanor stared at her made her want to laugh hysterically because she was serious.

"I'll make a plane reservation tonight." She tried to sound as upbeat as she could without channeling a Disney character. To add some action, she slapped her hands together and hopped in her seat.

"I doubt you'll follow through—you never do. Your brother does. He wants to marry her and do whatever he can to keep her happy." Eleanor's finger came close to puncturing her eye when she jammed it in her direction. It wasn't something Brooks usually put up with, but she considered this her daily practice of patience. The Dalai Lama would be proud. "Alfred told me what you did."

The change of subject was like the crazy train had careened off the cliff of disbelief. "I'm sure the sacrifice wasn't Curtis-level appropriate."

"He seemed appreciative, but I don't buy it."

"That's good, since I'm not selling anything." She cut Eleanor off because everyone had a limit of bad behavior and having to put up with it. "We both do have something in common, though—we both want to see Fallon happy. I'll make sure to tell her you think that's not going to be possible unless she marries Curtis."

"You do, and it'll prove everything I believe about you. The truth is you ran because Fallon wasn't good enough for you, and now you need a diversion until you go back to your life." The story was too polished for her not to believe Eleanor had repeated it a few times. Where she got the story didn't take much imagination to guess.

"Curtis can spin a good fantasy, but you should ask yourself something. Actually, it's the most important thing." She didn't want to show any weakness to this woman, but staying would make her question all that was good in the world. That was over the top, but Eleanor was like a soul-sucking succubus. "Had it been up to Curtis to make the choice I made—leave, or stay and you lose everything— would you still have the company?"

"He's a gentleman, so that's an easy question."

It was like running headlong into a brick wall until you ripped your head open. Eleanor was stubborn, closed-minded, and didn't seem to want to change. She'd had enough, so she stood and shook her head. "There's nothing else I can say." She shook her head again. "Not true, there's plenty I can say, but I'm not going to waste my time." She flinched when someone placed their hand on her bicep.

"Eleanor, it's good to hear how charitable you've gotten with age, and how important you believe Max and I are to your family. Actually, *our* family since you believe there's still going to be a wedding." Her mother's smile was the fake social one she used when she'd rather tell someone to fuck off than have to deal with them. "Have a good day."

"Scarlett, try to understand," Eleanor said, standing as well.

"Oh, I understand much more than you think."

Brooks came close to losing her balance when her mom yanked her down the street by the grip she had on her shirt. "Why didn't anyone tell me Eleanor was crowned Queen of Sheba?"

Her mom let out a loud laugh. "Her new goal in life is social status—events that'll get her into the social pages." Her mom stopped at her car and studied her face. "Good God, Brooks, you look like a street thug."

"The street thug isn't usually the bruised one, Mom. How'd you find me?" She got in when her mom opened the passenger door and stared at her like she wouldn't like the consequences of not getting in.

"I'm your mother." Her mom let out a long breath when she got in. "I will always be able to find you, and that woman aggravates the hell out of me. What the hell was all that about?"

"She wanted to remind me that Fallon and Curtis are working things out and to stay clear." Her head was pounding, and she checked the time on her phone. It was 12:46. Just late enough to know she'd been stood up. There had to come a point when you had to accept that life was long and full of disappointment. The sun still rose every morning and the earth still spun even if that list of unfairnesses was long. "Old Eleanor might be right."

"You have to give it more than a day, sweetheart. All this will work out, so don't give up." Her mom patted her shoulder. "I gave you more backbone than that."

"Uh-huh. It's been years, so remember one thing. You need to keep your mouth shut and wear beige to the wedding. I believe that's the entire chapter in the etiquette book about your job as mother of the groom." She rested her head back and closed her eyes. Once they reached the house, she was taking something for her headache even if it scrambled her brain.

"Eventually all of you will learn to listen to your mother." Her mom placed her hand on Brooks's arm after getting into traffic. "If you decide to write a romance novel about all this, you're way behind on all the sex."

"Romance novel?" She rolled her head to the side and opened her eyes to look at her mother. "This is more of a tragedy than any great romance."

CHAPTER FIFTEEN

"Did you review the contracts we have coming up?" Fallon asked Bea. They'd been working for hours, but she didn't want to stop. Stopping meant thinking, and she was tired of that.

Eliza cleared her throat, and Franklin appeared relieved, while Bea's head did a good impression of a fan at a tennis match when she looked at all of them as if trying to guess what she was missing. "Ah, what the hell's going on?" Eliza asked when she didn't seem to respond to the conversation prompt.

That seemed to be a popular question lately. "A staff meeting, in case you haven't been paying attention." The chance to have lunch with Brooks had slipped by, but Fallon couldn't shake the thought that it was for the best. "Your part is coming up, so you might want to wake up so we're not here all night."

"You've finally gone completely mental. Why are you even here?" Eliza slapped her hands on the desk and glared at her.

"Why wouldn't she be here?" Bea appeared even more confused. "We would've ordered lunch by now, but if we get through this, I can leave early."

"Our big sister broke off her engagement last night," Eliza said, and her comment made everyone stare at her. "Then all hell broke loose when Curtis lost his shit and punched Brooks."

"What does Brooks have to do with this, aside from the obvious?" Bea asked.

She looked out her window while Eliza gave everyone a blow-by-blow of their night. Franklin added to the story by telling them about the morning, including Brooks still being at her house when he arrived.

"Brooks was wearing Fallon's clothes," Franklin said, and Eliza pointed at her. "I recognized that crawfish T-shirt."

Why had everything seemed so simple the night before? Lying in Brooks's arms felt like the beginning of something wonderful, and Brooks had agreed to go slow. It convinced her that Brooks was willing to do what she needed to get it right this time. At least, she'd believed that until that morning when Brooks casually bid her a good day and told her to go to work. It was a brush-off, and it was telling.

"So, you told Curtis to take a hike, slept with Brooks, and you left her to come to work?" Bea gazed at her with what she surmised was pity. "Is that right?"

"That's exactly right, and you're completely nuts," Eliza said, pointing at her. "Why are you here?"

"We have work to do." That was weak, but she was safer from being hurt again if she stayed. "And we didn't *sleep together*-sleep together. She was hurt and couldn't be left alone."

"Uh-huh, don't give me that shit." Bea was getting upset. "You spent years crying over Brooks Boseman because of what a bastard you thought she was, and then you find out she fell on her sword for all of us. The white knight act was for you, Fallon, so get your head out of your ass before it's too late."

Franklin nodded like one of those dogs people put on their dashboards. "And I'd bet the company she still loves you." He pressed his hands together as if begging her to hear what he was saying. "It's everything you wanted and hoped for, but you blew her off today. When you decided to come with me, it gutted her. That I noticed and you didn't is kind of messed up, but it hurt that you picked this over her."

"She didn't ask me to stay," she said, not afraid to voice her fear. Her family might tease her, but they'd never turn their backs on her.

Eliza got up and crouched next to her chair. "Brooks is taking her cues from you, sweetie. She's not going to go all ape-man on you, demanding things you aren't ready to give. Get out of here, find her, and show her you're serious." They all stared at her when she didn't move. "Go!"

"Okay," she said, needing to see Brooks more than she needed anything else. Bea handed her the car keys, and Franklin got her purse. She called Brooks from the car, not surprised when it went to voice mail. Her second call to the Piquant got her Bria. "Is Brooks there?"

"Let me ask you—were you dropped on your head repeatedly as a baby?"

"You can insult my intelligence later, but I need to talk to Brooks." She hesitated. "Please."

"She's not here." Bria, she figured, was a vault when it came to disclosing information about anything, but she surprised her. "Scarlett picked her up from someplace on Magazine. Brooks left this morning to take a walk to clear her head, which is what she usually does when she's upset. When Scarlett found her, your mother was laying down the law about how things are and how they're going to go."

"Oh Jesus."

"No, nothing holy about it. I'm sure that meant Brooks going back to wherever she came from and staying the hell away from you. Scarlett saved her from that and took her home."

"Thank you." The relief that Brooks hadn't fled back to New York made her weak. "And thank you so much for caring about her all these years. You're a good friend."

"You're welcome, and try to get this right this time. I've hoped for a long time that she'll find love, but I'm beginning to have my doubts that you're the right person for the job. The heart does make dubious choices for us, though, so I'll keep quiet until I'm sure you're that person." Bria stopped talking as if she was either doing something or thinking. "It's none of my business, but your mother has very interesting ideas. I'm not saying she got to Brooks, but Scarlett said she gave Brooks plenty to think about."

"Oh my God." She could feel her face get hot.

"I haven't known Brooks as long as you, but she's fearless when it comes to business to the point she makes *me* flinch sometimes. When it comes to her personal life, though, she's less sure, and I think your mother tapped into that." Bria sounded raw and honest. "Don't make the mistake of feeding into that as some half-assed attempt at revenge for all you think she did wrong."

"That's never going to happen." She placed her hand over her heart even if Bria couldn't see her. "I can't be sure, but I think my mother is either delusional from stress over this wedding, or she's had a stroke. She doesn't speak for me." She took the interstate and gunned the engine. It was good Brooks had gone home, and not to Bria at the hotel. "And I don't care if she never accepts Brooks, because I love her. I never stopped loving her."

"I know, dum-dum, but your learning curve is epic. Think of this is your last chance because it is."

She laughed through her tears. The damn tears again at the realization she should've confessed her feelings to Brooks first. They'd wasted enough time. "I know, and I promise not to screw it up."

"We'll see, but even idiots like you deserve to be happy. Call if you need anything."

Bria was consistent, but she was starting to like her. She concentrated on the road and called her mother to get that out of the way. "Did you really talk to Brooks today?" she asked incredulously. The comment about the stroke was a joke, but now she wasn't so sure.

"She told you?" Her mother's response answered a lot of other questions she had. "That should prove to you she has no character."

"Brooks didn't tell me anything. The information came from Scarlett, and that alone is mortifying enough." Her hand stung when she hit the steering wheel. "It's obvious you didn't get my message this morning, so let me be clear. Stay away from Brooks and me, as in don't contact us until I'm ready to talk to you."

"You need to talk to Curtis." Her mother was like a warped broken record that played a tune no one but her was interested in hearing.

"You talk to him and try to convince him you want the dream wedding more than a relationship with me. I'm sure the two of you will be blissfully happy, and Daddy will just have to understand."

"That's not funny."

"No, it's sad, Mother, not to mention pathetic. Quit meddling and writing a script no one is interested in following. You were way out of line today, so until you're ready to apologize, don't contact me." She hung up and tried to keep her nervousness to a minimum.

It was a good sign the gate was open, and no one stopped her on the way down to the cottage. If she was lucky, Brooks was inside, but she was ready to beg at the house if need be. She took a breath and banged on the door. It opened to a sleepy-looking Brooks, and she couldn't help but fling herself into her arms. Brooks caught her and held her when she wrapped her legs around her waist.

Talking was overrated in some cases, and Brooks acted like she agreed when she kissed her back. She kissed Brooks in a way that erased all doubts about how she felt, and why she was there. The universe had stolen so much from her, and she was there to get it back.

"You okay?" Brooks asked between kisses.

"You're like the tenth person who's asked me that today, but I will be." She let her legs drop so she could lift Brooks's wrinkled shirt. That Brooks let her was a major win. She took hers off next and dropped it in the foyer. "Which room did you pick?"

"Last one on the right." Brooks didn't fight her when she dragged her by the belt to the messy bed.

She waited for the door to close before uncinching Brooks's belt and unzipping her jeans. The need to feel all of Brooks pressed up against her made her hands clumsy until Brooks held them while she gazed up. Any fear of stopping died when Brooks stripped her jeans off and took the underwear with them. She pressed her lips to the first spot she reached on Brooks's chest while Brooks got her naked.

The first touch of Brooks against her slowed her down to enjoy the wonder of it. Memories were all she'd had for a long time, but nothing compared to the feel of someone you loved and desired next to you wanting all the things you did. And desiring Brooks was engrained in her. She lifted her head when Brooks put her hands on her hips and kissed her. Brooks moaned into her mouth when she pulled her hair at the sides of her head to get her to come closer. She had a need to be held, loved, and claimed.

"Please, Brooks," she said, walking backwards to the bed. "I need to feel you over me. Prove to me this is real." She spread her legs and welcomed Brooks to do what she asked and raked her nails up Brooks's back when she did. The weight of Brooks made her wetter than the first kiss, so she bucked her hips up. She was done waiting, and Brooks seemed to get the message when she lifted up to put her hand between them.

"Fuck," she said when Brooks sucked her nipple. It hardened to the point of pain against Brooks's tongue, but she needed more. The anticipation quickened her breath, and she put her hands on Brooks's face to get her attention in a way that screamed *I'm here, and I'm waiting for you. Take what's yours.*

Brooks knew her, had always known her, and what she needed. "I promise slow next time," Brooks said when she put her hands between her legs. They both glanced down and watched Brooks's fingers go in and out a few times. It was sexy the way Brooks's fingers glistened in the afternoon light.

"Yes." She lifted her hips to meet Brooks's stroke and put her feet on Brooks's calves as the relentlessness of it drove her out of her mind. Her body hummed, opening to Brooks as fast as her clothes had come off. "Like that, baby," she said, letting her left knee drop to the bed. It drove Brooks's fingers in deeper and hit the spot only Brooks had ever reached.

"Uh…yes…yes," she said as she squeezed Brooks's shoulders. Brooks was overwhelming her, and it momentarily made her think of Brooks's injuries. That flew from her mind when Brooks sped her strokes, challenging her to open up more. "Please, baby, don't... don't stop." She was so wet, and the sound of skin slapping against skin triggered an intense orgasm that stilled Brooks's hand but not her thumb on her clit.

"Come for me, darlin'," Brooks said into her ear.

It swamped her, and she bit the spot on Brooks's shoulder where it bent up to her neck to keep herself from screaming in Brooks's ear. "Right there...please...make me come." She panted the words out as her orgasm peaked, and she squeezed Brooks's fingers inside her. "Jesus," she said when she could breathe again. "No." She wanted Brooks to stay inside and on top of her, keeping her grounded.

"I'm right here, darlin'." Brooks kissed her and held some of her weight off by rising up on an elbow. "I'm not going anywhere—not again."

"I missed you so much." She moved her hands to Brooks's face again and gently cupped her cheeks, needing Brooks's attention on her. "I need you so much," she admitted, loving the smile Brooks aimed her way.

"I mean it, honey. If you want me gone, you're going to have to ask me to go." Brooks kissed her slow, like she was memorizing everything about Fallon's lips and how perfectly they fit against hers.

"I'm never going to do that, so I hope you mean it, and I'm sorry about today."

Brooks smiled and moved to hold her. It was so different than last night when they were both tentative around each other. "Do you think I'm going to punish you for taking the time to be sure?" The question and how Brooks was with her made her believe Brooks would've waited a lot longer for this aspect of their relationship and been fine with it. "You have to know that for me, there's only ever been you."

"I love you, Brooks." She gazed into Brooks's eyes when she said it. If joy had an expression, this was it, and she was happy to be the one who put it on Brooks's face. "No matter how angry I was, at the center of me that was always true. If I'd stopped loving you, it would've been so much easier to move on, but I couldn't."

"It's good to know I'm not the only one who thinks that's true. I love you too." Brooks kissed her, taking her time, and seemed to savor it. "I don't know how else to exist, and I don't want to. It's like I was made to love you and only you."

"That's so cheesy, baby, and I demand you tell my mother that the next time you see her. I'm sorry about her too. Bria told me what happened." Fallon rolled to her side and put her arm over Brooks so she'd be close enough to keep kissing her. "I'm not sure how to get it through to her that I'm not interested in what she wants for me."

"Your mother is going take some getting used to, but I'm sure she thinks she's doing what's best to protect you."

She laughed and buried her face against Brooks's shoulder. "I can't believe she followed you—so stop being so nice."

"That's a scary thought." Brooks shivered but moved her hands down her back to her ass. "I'd have guessed she stopped because she'd spotted me at PJ's, and not because of some clandestine campaign to get rid of me."

Brooks lay flat when Fallon rolled on top, and her smile widened when Brooks's hands stayed on her butt. "Do you really want to talk about my mother right now?" She sat up and straddled Brooks. The way Brooks tightened her grip on her hips started the burn again. Her orgasm had been intense, but the feel of Brooks between her legs, and her sex pressed against all that skin, drove her need. She wanted Brooks to take whatever she wanted, only she'd have to wait until Fallon had her turn touching her.

"It's better not to talk at all. Silence is, after all, golden," Brooks said, sitting up. Fallon hissed when Brooks sucked in her nipple again and came close to grabbing the back of Brooks's head to keep her in place. Stopping because of injuries wasn't on her agenda. "You can't imagine how much I've missed you—missed this with you."

"You still dominate my dreams, but the reality of you is so much better." She stopped when Brooks put her hand between them and pinched her clit. "Fuck," she yelled and bucked her hips forward.

"That's the general idea." Brooks licked the other nipple and tugged her fingers back and forth as she squeezed harder.

"Not so fast." The way Brooks chuckled raised goose bumps along her skin. "I want you." Brooks leaned back against the headboard and started to move her hand. The position gave Fallon room to touch Brooks in return.

"You have me, but slow, darlin', slow," Brooks said as her eyes raked up her body. It was as intense as a caress, and Fallon bit her bottom lip to keep her concentration. She tried her best to give Brooks what she wanted, but her body had other ideas. All she could do was keep her fingers flat against Brooks's hard clit and hang on.

"I need you." Fallon bucked her hips harder as she clung to Brooks. "Please, baby."

"Tell me…fuck," Brooks said, then she let her head drop back. "Tell me what you want."

"I love you, but I need you to fuck me." The sensation of being filled again was enough to make her stop and rest her head against Brooks's shoulder. It allowed her to see how Brooks's chest was heaving, not from exhaustion but from holding herself back. She'd always been selfless in bed, giving Fallon everything she wanted until she was sated. "I want to touch you."

She rose and came down on Brooks's fingers again, and the muscles in Brooks's abdomen tensed. "I can wait," Brooks said, out of breath and staring at her chest. It was all the permission Fallon needed to move and take what Brooks was offering. She sped her hips and Brooks kept pace, seeming to love the way her breasts bounced as she did.

"I…" She shut her eyes and held her breath. "I'm coming, I'm—" She finished with a scream. The orgasm was as intense as the first, and she tried to catch her breath before Brooks did anything else to drive her over the edge.

"Where are you going?" Brooks asked when Fallon moved down her body, dragging her tongue along Brooks's skin. She tasted of salt, and Fallon loved when she put her hand on the back of her head when she pressed her tongue against her clit. "You…" Brooks said, and it was all she managed when she sucked her in. "Fuck." Brooks tightened the hold on her hair, and she loved it.

Brooks was so hard she felt a little guilty for making her wait, so she sucked harder. She wanted Brooks to let go and come for her. In that instant, it didn't matter how long they'd been apart—only that they belonged together was important, that they belonged to each other was paramount. The grunting noises Brooks was making made her smile. They were telling, so she slipped her fingers inside.

"Come for me, lover," she said before putting her mouth back on Brooks.

"Son of a bitch." Brooks's voice reverberated around the room it was so loud, and she stiffened. "Shit." She pulled Fallon's hair again, but this time it was to make her let up. "Damn," Brooks said, cycling through all the curse words.

She crawled up Brooks's body and kissed her. "Did you enjoy that?"

"I think you can do better," Brooks said and laughed. She rolled them over and tickled her. "That was spectacular."

"You know what I want now?" She put her leg between Brooks's and licked her bottom lip.

"Tell me," Brooks said as her eyelids slowly closed.

"Feed me." That made Brooks open her eyes again as if checking to see if she'd heard right. "What? I haven't eaten in hours."

"I beg to differ," Brooks joked. "There's some stuff in the fridge, or we can go out."

"We're not going anywhere." She lifted her head and kissed Brooks before pushing off her. "Wait here."

"Want me to come?"

She glanced back naked from the doorway and laughed. "You will, baby, but let me make you a sandwich first."

It was getting dark outside, and Brooks was lethargic from the great but active afternoon. She sat up and listened to Fallon humming as she went down the hall to the kitchen after a stop in the bathroom. Fallon's scream got her tangled in the sheets before she made it to her feet for a run to the kitchen. The sight of Fallon hiding very little behind a small dishcloth and her grandmother standing in the door with the knob in her hand was almost comical.

"Made yourselves at home, huh?" Heddie shut the door as Fallon hid behind Brooks.

"You told me to get it right, Gran, so I got it right." She took Fallon's hand and brought her closer. "If you give us a few minutes, we'll get dressed and take you out for a burger. The diner's still open, right?"

"Do me a favor and take a shower and then get dressed. There are certain things I shouldn't know about you." Her grandmother waggled her finger between them, and Fallon plastered herself against Brooks's back. "When you're done, meet me up at the house. Your mother cooked and is expecting you both."

"What happened to Sarah?" Brooks asked of their longtime cook.

"Bingo night." Heddie made shooing motions and smiled. "Now get out of here. There are too many naked people in my kitchen."

She backed out and scooped Fallon up when they were in the hallway. The blush on Fallon's face was adorable, and she hoped this wasn't the end of their day. Fallon didn't let her go once they were in the bathroom behind a locked door. They kissed as the water warmed up and she kept her arms around Fallon.

"Sorry about that," she said.

"Not the way I wanted to let your family know we're back together, but it beats having announcements printed up." Fallon pinched her butt before slapping it. "Let's get going—we've been invited to dinner."

"After this it'll be more of an interrogation with food. Don't say I didn't warn you."

CHAPTER SIXTEEN

Every one of Brooks's siblings except Curtis came to dinner, and Fallon couldn't help but notice a difference in the way the family interacted with each other and with her. This was how she remembered it being when she came over with Brooks. All the Boseman siblings had a great relationship with Brooks that was easy to see, and it was wonderful. It made her think about what'd happened to Curtis. He didn't fit in here or with his family, and she didn't understand it.

"It's good you've lost that pinched look you had going on for a while," Charlie said as she filled her wineglass.

Fallon glanced at Brooks before answering, but Charlie's comment made her smile. "We all lose our minds every so often."

"We're sorry for the bitchiness," Pru said, glancing at Brooks too. "There's no excuse, but it was hard to see you with the wrong person. We all hoped you'd snap out of it before it was too late."

"If it helps, Eliza, Bea, and Frankie felt the same way." She stopped when Brooks put her hand on her thigh.

"You guys don't give her a hard time." Brooks rubbed her leg. "How was work?"

"Curtis locked himself in his office down the road and didn't talk to anyone." Etienne served everyone salad as Scarlett brought out a platter of fish and Heddie followed with two other bowls. "He almost looked afraid."

"You think it has to do with all this court stuff?" Scarlett asked.

That rang true to Fallon, and it had been from the day of the first explosion. There'd been something off about the whole thing, and it crept into her thoughts whenever she had a quiet moment. Why Curtis was fighting to claim a dying business was something else she didn't understand. The smart play would be to sell for as much as they could get. Before she could fall into another wormhole of dead ends, she noticed the quiet.

Brooks had tightened her fingers on her thigh when she noticed Max walking toward them. He'd change from the last time she'd seen him. It'd be so easy to leave and not engage, but the sight of him made her understand Brooks and her actions. The man who'd stolen so much time from them was already gone. Sure, Max hadn't slipped into the oblivion of his disease yet, but that gruff bastard was dead. This was who Brooks was trying to connect with so she could move forward and be who she needed to be for her family when he was truly gone.

It was Brooks who stood and got Max to his seat at the head of the table. Max stared at Fallon, but that too was different from the time she'd come with Curtis. "Hello, Mr. Boseman," she said as Brooks sat next to her. The family dynamic had changed again, but it wasn't horrible.

"Did Brooks tell you?" He placed both his hands flat on the table and appeared concerned.

"I did," Brooks said. She raised their joined hands and smiled at him. "It's okay."

Brooks had mentioned how agitated he got when they'd left the cottage, in case he had a screaming episode. "I love Brooks, Mr. Boseman, and I always will." God, it was too early to make those kinds of declarations, but it seemed to make him happy.

"I'm...I'm sorry." Max's eyes watered, and he didn't move to wipe the tears away when they fell. "Don't blame Brooks."

"I won't, I promise." She hurt for him and the whole family. It was almost like he had a countdown clock over his head, and everyone but him understood the meaning of it.

"Will you tell her when you see her?" The question was almost childlike. "She comes and sees me sometimes, but I think she's still hates me."

"I can promise you that she doesn't. Brooks loves you and the family." She glanced at Brooks for a second, wondering if she should stop talking.

"She doesn't know the whole truth. No one does," Max said and pushed away from the table. Brooks stood as well, but Etienne waved her back down.

"I'm sorry," Brooks said.

"I'm not," Fallon said, rubbing Brooks's back. "It's good to know that Max doesn't hate *me*."

"Do you think he's getting worse?" Charlie asked. "And he mentioned you when I sat with him, Fallon. He feels bad, but he doesn't hate you."

"It wouldn't change my mind about Brooks even if he did. My worry is for Brooks." By that statement she meant Brooks was strong and capable, but no one could carry the weight of the world without having it eventually affect them. After what they'd survived, they deserved a future free of other people's guilt.

"Thanks, honey." Brooks kissed her like they were in front of her family, so it was short and respectful. It still made her feel like the center of Brooks's world. "Why does he keep talking about whatever it is we don't know?"

Scarlett didn't say anything, and Fallon laid her hand on Brooks's back. Everyone seemed riveted, and the mood changed yet again. The air around them seemed stilted and awkward because of the silence. This was what she was tired of. Secrets had a way of rotting the foundation of your life, and it was unbearable to know it was happening again. At times she felt trapped, and she'd learned that staying quiet didn't make it go away.

"It's okay, Mrs. Boseman," she said, not comfortable with first names just yet.

"Fallon, come on," Scarlett said. "You were almost family," she said with a sly smile. "It seems you found the right puzzle piece, so there's hope your joining the family is still an option." Fallon relaxed when Brooks put her arm around her. "I'm Scarlett to you."

"Thank you, and you were right." Brooks did fit with her, and no one else would ever be that perfect. That was something they both realized faster than she would've guessed.

"About what?" Scarlett pushed her plate away as if the appearance of Max sapped the joy out of their evening.

"There was only one who was my match, and it makes me realize something important." She reached across the table and touched Scarlett's hand. "All of us staying quiet and keeping secrets cost us more than I'm willing to pay again."

"I'm not saying I don't know, but can you all give me some time?" Scarlett sighed as Charlie put her arms around her. "There's only so much I can take."

"He doesn't seem to be able to make certain connections," Pru said, turning toward the stairs. "How can he get this bad this fast?"

"He's been dealing with this longer than you know. The doctor told us some people can compensate better than others." Scarlett was emotionless as she spoke. "Your father's good at compartmentalizing. The business taught him to multitask, so he's been able to keep his grasp on the now."

"He can't do that forever, can he?" Brooks asked.

"We don't know that, so you all have to spend time with him and enjoy his company." The way Brooks gazed at Fallon made her believe she was begging for her to convince her. "A lot of people don't ever get the chance."

"What do you know about family?" Curtis came in and slammed his hands on the table. The move was getting old, but Curtis seemed to have a limited range of reactions. His go-to was acting like a bully on the playground, figuring everyone would be intimidated. "You're nothing but a—"

"Think long and hard before you say anything else," Brooks said loudly. "And cut the tough-guy act. The assistants at the office might buy it, but no one here is that weak minded."

"Come on, sister. She'll move on to Etienne by next week. Fallon's got an itch no one—"

Curtis stopped talking when his head snapped back. The injury still visible on Brooks's face didn't impede her speed. It'd been a hell of a long time since anyone defended Fallon's honor, and with such enthusiasm. She didn't want to laugh, but Curtis holding his nose and gagging from all the blood was hilarious. Charlie wasn't having that problem, and Fallon smiled at her before having to jump in to keep Brooks from getting arrested.

"Honey." She took Brooks's hand and pulled her away. The afternoon had been a seismograph of emotion, and she wanted to go back to being alone. "We need to go." All she could think was Scarlett saying she'd had enough. There was only one thing that was true, and she stopped when it hit her. She was over all the hurt, and there was no going back. "Let's take a walk."

The heat outside was welcoming, and in an odd way it seemed to cool Brooks off. Everything that had happened in the last couple of days was so out of her norm that Fallon started laughing as she tugged Brooks toward the water. By the time they were on the deck, she could barely breathe, and she was glad her humor was contagious as Brooks laughed beside her. It was almost like she could read her mind.

She pressed herself to Brooks and kissed the side of her neck. It was freeing to be able to do that while she was awake. She'd done it forever in her dreams, but this was so much better than even the memory of having Brooks close before. Brooks had become everything she'd known and hoped for, so no matter where this led, she wasn't letting go. Not again. Wherever Brooks went, this time, she'd follow.

"I know your life is much more exciting than mine with the mob princess, but all this family stuff is a bit over the top. Even you have to admit that."

Brooks held her and nodded. There was a certain peace that came from being in Brooks's arms that made Fallon dream of marriage, children, and legacy. That'd never happened with anyone else because she'd never allowed herself to go there. Her heart was sure, had always been sure when it came to Brooks, and it explained why her life had become chaos. Curtis had gotten through the heart of her defenses because he'd been like getting a little bit back of what she'd craved. That familial bond and degree of separation had softened her up enough to lose focus.

"I'm actually boring, but I agree. This is no one's normal." She pressed closer, and Brooks moved her hands to her lower back. "The truth is I'd do it all over to end up here."

"You've gotten poetic with time, honey." It was wonderful to hear Brooks laugh. "And you're never boring." With all this going on, she was unsure of what came next, but she was ready to be alone with Brooks again.

"I blame you and all those romances you love so much."

She laughed and bit Brooks's chin. "I wanted to open your eyes to those happy endings."

Charlie walked up and cleared her throat. "Curtis left after threatening everyone in the house. He also promised to move up the court date and force Dad into testifying."

Fallon released Brooks and pushed her toward Charlie. All of the Bosemans seemed shell-shocked by all this, especially by their father's condition, except for Curtis. It wasn't a time to be selfish, so they'd be there for a while. Brooks seemed to be Charlie's safe harbor, and she fell against Brooks and sobbed. This was so much more than her pain, and Fallon was glad Brooks was here to make this easier for her family. Perhaps it wasn't fair to dump all that on her, considering, but those broad shoulders appeared capable.

"If he does that, it'll speed all this up in our favor." Brooks sat, keeping her arms around her sister. "Curtis seems lost, but don't let that fool you."

"I don't care at this point—all I can think about is Dad and Mom. We're adults. I should handle this better, but I can't." Charlie cried some more, so Fallon stayed on the other side of her and took her hand.

"Things are going to change, honey, but you'll always have Brooks and me." She rubbed Charlie's back and glanced at Brooks. "None of us can change the outcome of all this, but we can be there for each other."

"Thanks, Fallon. I'm happy about you guys." Charlie wiped her face as she turned toward her. "Please be careful. It's worrying me that Curtis is this out of control, and you picking Brooks over him isn't improving his outlook. God only knows what he's capable of."

"Trust me," Brooks said, swiping her thumb across Charlie's cheek to catch the last of her tears. "He touches Fallon, and I'll introduce him to a world of hurt he can't imagine exists."

"You're not in the mob, baby," Fallon said with a smile.

"No, but Bria tells me all the time it's good to have friends." Brooks sighed as Charlie stood back. "We're almost done with all this, and Curtis trying to expedite the court hearing might be the best move."

Both Fallon and Charlie stared at Brooks with disbelief.

"And if he calls your father to testify?" she asked.

"Everyone's going to have to trust me that it won't get to that." Brooks held her hand out to Fallon. "Let's go make sure everything is quiet, and I'll get you home."

She didn't let go of Brooks when she went upstairs. If they were lucky, Max would be asleep. Brooks cracked the door and tried to be quiet. Etienne was next to the bed holding Max's hand, appearing stricken. The way he gazed at them was almost a plea for comfort.

Max stopped his mumbling when he saw Brooks. He reached out for her, and she went to sit on the bed. Fallon watched as Brooks spoke to him softly and the tension left him. This was who she'd fallen in love with, and she was happy that for all the things different about Brooks, her giving heart and compassionate nature hadn't changed.

"I want her to be happy, but I need time," Max said. He held Brooks's hand between his, acting like he was out of time. "I need to fix what I did. It's just so hard to remember." Max squinted and his voice started to rise. "I promise I'll do better…I need more time."

Brooks shook her head but stayed quiet. It was probably the wrong move, but Fallon stood next to Brooks and covered his hands with hers. "Max, you need to concentrate on your family."

"What?" His breakdown snapped as he looked up at her.

"You need to see how much your family loves you. Once you do, you'll realize you have all the time you need to do whatever you need to."

He closed his eyes and let both her and Brooks go. "Will you tell Brooks and the others—I need you to tell Brooks because of all we lost. Sometimes I think she's here, but I drove her away."

She pressed Brooks's head to her chest and kissed the top of it. "She's here, Max, and she's happy. All that stuff is in the past, and she comes by every day to see you. That's something you need to keep in your heart. All your children love you."

"Even Brooks?" The way he asked made her think of an innocent child. It was like the disease had wiped away all the bad traits and left this kind soul.

"Especially Brooks. If you open up your eyes, you'll see for yourself. She's here."

"Brooks, you came." Max's smile was luminous.

She moved behind Brooks and let her finish. Max fell asleep soon after, and Brooks held her hand on the way down. The nurse had come in for the late afternoon shift so there was no reason to stay. Everyone was in the den listening to Heddie's stories, but she stopped when they entered.

"Scarlett, sit for a bit, and I'll go up," Heddie said.

"Stay, Gran," Brooks said.

Fallon wasn't sure how old Brooks's grandmother was, but Heddie was one of the coolest people she'd ever met. Clearly she knew how to read a room and realize what everyone needed. Brooks kissed her cheek, and they sat close to Scarlett. It had been a long time since Fallon had been this emotionally spent, so she didn't know how Brooks was holding up.

"All I need to know is if you have an idea of what he's talking about." Brooks showed more patience with her mother than Fallon would've, so she stayed quiet to see if Scarlett would answer.

"Yes, but—"

"It's okay, Mom, when the time comes I'm sure you'll tell us. I just don't know at times if it's only in his head."

"Thank you, my love, and not to change the subject, but I'm happy for you both." Scarlett embraced Fallon first before kissing Brooks's cheek. It made Fallon hope her mother would come to see with Scarlett did.

"I'm headed back to the city, but I'll be back tomorrow." Next

Brooks hugged Heddie, who still appeared upset, and Fallon could only guess it was because of the state of her family.

"I'm moving back in here to help Scarlett, so you'll have the cottage to yourself." Heddie held one of Fallon's hands and one of Brooks's and glanced between them. "I need you both to hang tough and lean on each other until we get through this. No more running."

"We promise, and we'll be here to help out," Fallon said, answering for them both. There was no way she'd leave all this for Brooks to do alone.

They drove back to her place without much conversation, but both of them enjoyed holding hands in the quiet. After their day, all she wanted was to go to bed and feel Brooks next to her. She couldn't help but feel selfish, but she wanted to shut the world out and celebrate that they'd found each other again.

"Will you stay with me?" She couldn't help some of the insecurity that crept in.

"The night my mother called me demanding I come home, I purposely didn't try to think about you." Brooks's words were like darts landing on a wall of balloons, only it was her good mood that deflated. "Let me finish."

"I know you're going through a lot. Don't worry about it."

Brooks pulled over and faced her. "She needed me, and because it sounded serious, I knew it wouldn't be a short trip. Before that, I could only handle a few days at most before I ran home like a scalded cat."

Those beautiful eyes always drew her in, and now was no different. Brooks's voice was like smoke that surrounded and enveloped her, and she leaned in with no fight. "Why?" she asked, managing only that word.

"Because I love you. Leaving, suffering, and all of it hasn't ever changed that fundamental truth. I love you, and when I'm here, all I can see is you. The places I kissed you, talked to you, and made love to you are real. When I'm here, it isn't my imagination or memories, and not having you made all those places torturous." Brooks cupped her cheek and caressed her face with her thumb. "You made it impossible to let go."

"Why are you telling me all this?" She was confused, but this seemed to be important to Brooks.

"Because all those memories are what we had. The years have changed us both, and I want to know who you are now. I want that and to love you so I'm not wasting any more time." Brooks leaned in and kissed her. "If you need time to process all that and want to wait until my family soap opera is under control, that's okay too. We can date until you're ready."

"Bria already thinks I'm short a few brain cells, so no. I want to be with you as much as I can. There's no more letting go. I'm not letting you out of my sight."

"Good, then we'll head to your place after a quick stop at the hotel. I need to pick up my stuff so I don't have to borrow your clothes. We can take the time to talk you up to Bria."

Fallon laughed and gently sucked on Brooks's bottom lip. "I can't wait."

Chapter Seventeen

"Y ou ready?" Brooks asked Fallon once she'd packed for a couple of days. Her quick meeting with Bria meant they were on schedule, which meant goading Curtis along.

Fallon nodded as she stared at Bria. Brooks's old friend was dressed to go out, but she was still barefoot as she faced off with Fallon. "Look at you, dum-dum. You finally got it right. Try not to backslide."

"Be nice," Brooks said as Fallon put an arm around her waist.

"I'm sure she doesn't know how," Fallon said.

Bria chuckled, and she stuck her tongue out at them. "That *was* me being nice."

"*Uh-huh*," Fallon said, dragging out the word. "Thank you for your help."

"The fact is she's been pining for you forever, so I'm glad you both got your heads out of your asses." Bria winked and waved. "Go on and get some sleep. I'm going to finish up on some work before my dinner date."

Brooks laughed and waved back. "Be careful, and call if you need anything."

They drove to Fallon's after stopping at the Mexican place they both loved and getting takeout. After the day they'd had, she was ready to have Fallon to herself for as long as she could get her. She dropped her luggage while Fallon locked the door, then turned to look at Brooks like she had something on her mind.

"Hungry?" Brooks held up the food bag, putting it down when she got no answer.

"Do you think you'll go back?" Fallon asked as if she had to run her tongue over a razor to do it.

"To New York?" she asked and Fallon nodded. "Every so often when I have to close a deal, but that's one of the things Bria and I talked about." She placed her hands on Fallon's hips. The kiss she pressed to Fallon's lips was as gentle as she could make it. "What we do can be done from anywhere, so I'm here until you tell me to get lost."

Fallon nodded again, and Brooks took a small step back so Fallon could reach the button on her pants. "You're way overdressed for the next part." She fell back on the sofa when Fallon pushed her. It didn't take much time for her to be naked from the waist down.

She got a forefinger to the forehead when she shifted to sit up and return the favor. "Let me touch you."

The way Fallon laughed made her shiver. "Honey, touching's definitely on the menu tonight, but I need you to sit and be good."

The sight of Fallon standing over her as she ran her fingers through her hair made her want to take over. Fallon stood again and put her hands on the top button of her shirt. If what Brooks thought was happening was actually happening, she sat on her hands as a way of giving Fallon what she'd asked for. When they'd been together, Fallon at times needed to take charge and rev her up. She'd never asked Fallon to explain, but she figured it was to prove to herself that Brooks really wanted her.

"Do you have any idea how much I missed you?" Fallon paused at the fourth button as if not expecting an answer. "It confused me."

"Why?" Talking solved a lot of problems, but that second to last button coming undone was making it difficult to concentrate.

"You'd hurt me, so I didn't want to waste my time missing you." The shirt was open now, and the white silk bra was visible. The memory of how it felt under her fingers forced her to look up. "I did, though. You're so ingrained in my heart that I couldn't completely forget you."

The shirt dropped to the floor, and Fallon placed her hands on the button of her pants. "I'll try my best to make up for the pain I caused you. There's no way to completely erase it, and I won't ever take it for granted—take you for granted. You're too important for that."

"Do you really love me?" The button popped open, and she wanted to see the matching panties.

"I love you." She moved her hands to her sides and spread her legs. "And I'm all yours."

The declaration was followed by the pants falling to the floor and Fallon stepping out of them. Brooks threaded her fingers in Fallon's hair when she knelt between her legs. Her hand dropped back when

Fallon put her mouth on her and she sucked her clit against her tongue. It was lovingly possessive, and she tightened her hold on the sofa cushions. The truth of Fallon owning her unchained that part of her that was terrified of hope.

"Fuck." Fallon was relentless, like she wouldn't accept anything but total surrender. "Fuck," Brooks repeated as her orgasm started. It was fast and furious to the point of being embarrassing. She tensed her legs and had to pull Fallon back. Fallon gazed up at her with her chin resting on her stomach and her mouth glistening with the evidence of what she'd done. It was a beautiful sight.

"You know what I want," Fallon said as she rose to straddle her lap.

Brooks put her hand inside the sexy underwear and put two fingers in. There was no need for explanations of what Fallon was asking. Fallon rode her when she placed her thumb on her clit, holding herself up by squeezing Brooks's shoulders. "Please, Brooks," she said as her hips lost the rhythm she'd started with.

"Oh God"—Fallon's voice came out strained—"give me what I want or I'm going to stop."

Brooks kissed Fallon before moving to her neck and sucking. "Fuck," she said when Fallon squeezed her fingers in the most intimate way possible. "God," she said loudly as she put Fallon on her back, driving up her need. She bit down gently on her nipple through her bra and sped her fingers as much as she could since Fallon's underwear was still on. "Do you belong to me?"

"Yes...yes...God, yes," Fallon said as she tensed. Brooks stayed inside when Fallon pulled her against her even as her sex squeezed her fingers. It took a moment for Fallon to catch her breath, and Brooks held her. "I do, you know—belong to you."

Brooks kissed the side of Fallon's head and ran her hands up to unhook her bra. She'd never understood Fallon's insecurities. The closest Fallon had ever come to explaining was she wanted Brooks to want her, but she knew Brooks could have anyone. And when Brooks had disappeared without a word, she had proved all her insecurities right.

"You need to trust me on one thing. I belong to you." She looked Fallon in the eye so she could see she was telling the truth. "There's never going to be anyone else."

"That's how I feel about you." Fallon combed her hair back and kissed her. "I haven't belonged anywhere since you left."

"You belong to me—with me. We've been apart for a long time, so I have plenty to make up for." She laughed and tweaked Fallon's nipple. "I also want to have fun with you, and don't take that to mean I want casual."

"I know and I agree, and I forgot your quotient for sap isn't very high." Fallon took her shirt off and glanced down her body. "You think I'm strange for asking you that, don't you? That I demand you ask me if I'm yours?"

"Whatever's important to you is important to me. I always understood why you needed that, but not why you never asked it of me." She wiped the few tears that fell from Fallon's eyes, then cupped her cheek. "This time we need to talk more and guess less."

"I never asked because I was afraid, but not anymore." Fallon smiled and stood. She grabbed the shirt Brooks had been wearing and walked to the kitchen island. "How about dinner in bed?"

The food could be a congealed mess by now and Brooks wouldn't care.

Fallon had her sit and straddled her again to feed her.

"Hold this, honey," Fallon said, handing her the container with what was left of the food. The phone was ringing, and Fallon leaned over to grab it. "Hello." Fallon rolled her eyes and listened to whoever had called. "That's not my problem any longer, Mom. If *you* want to talk to Curtis, go ahead, but leave me out of it."

The conversation lasted a few more minutes, and Fallon was aggravated by the time she hung up. She put the food aside and opened her arms to Brooks. Families, even the best of them, were interesting entities. Sometimes it was just a good old tug-of-war. The tugger here was Eleanor.

"She loves you." She held Fallon against her and spoke in a whisper.

"She loves the idea of who she thinks I can be." Fallon was never someone who let anyone knock her down.

"She loves you enough to try to guide you toward a life that'll be the easiest." It didn't take them long to bag the trash, turn off the lights, and lie back. "And you have to admit, Curtis can be charming when he needs something."

"I don't give a damn about that," Fallon snapped, then took a deep breath. "Sorry. I don't like it when people think for me even when it's for my own good."

"That hasn't changed, then," she teased. Fallon molded herself against her side, and the darkness was almost welcome. Sometimes it gave the freedom to say things that were scary in the light of day.

"She doesn't understand what will make me happy. That's been missing for so long that *I'm* not sure anymore. Even if you don't want this, I have to choose for myself."

It took courage for Fallon to voice what was in her head, and it was going to take time to put all those fears to rest. "Remember all the plans we made in college?"

Fallon nodded against her neck. "That was the last time I did that. Now business plans are the only thing I concentrate on. I think it's why all the wedding stuff freaked me out."

"It's been a long time, but the dreams we had haven't changed at all. I still want all those things, and I'm willing to wait for you to feel the same." She kissed Fallon's forehead and held her. It was enough to calm her.

"What if I don't want to wait?" Fallon sat up so she could look at her. "Tell me the business tycoon can't be a little romantic."

"This is the planning phase of the deal. The execution will be much more intimate."

Fallon laughed and abruptly stopped when Brooks's phone rang. "Can no one make a move without checking with us first?" Fallon sounded exasperated. "Sorry, it might be about your dad."

"Boseman," she said, not recognizing the number.

"Brooks," a man said with a gruff voice, and it took her a moment to place it. Deuce wouldn't call unless it was something important, and whatever it was wouldn't be good news. "Another one went up, but the guys you hired caught the bastards before they could rig the others they had planned. I did what you asked and called the sheriff."

"Good. Give me an hour and I'll meet you at the jail. Do me a favor and call Dan." She didn't want to get up, but she had no choice.

"What?" Fallon held her down after she put the phone back on the nightstand.

"Another boat blew up." In a way she was happy her father wasn't aware of the battle over his beloved empire. She had no desire to get sucked into a Cain and Abel type situation, but it was time to step up and take over. It wasn't what she wanted long-term, but this had gotten way out of hand. "No one was working, so thankfully no one was hurt, but we saved two of the boats."

"That's some good news at least," Fallon said, rubbing the side of her neck. "That *is* good news, right?"

"I asked Angelo for help through Bria," she said slowly. "His guys have been guarding the facility and have been asking questions. Tonight wasn't a total surprise."

"Did you not trust me?" She felt Fallon withdraw a bit.

"I don't trust Curtis, love. You"—she waved between them—"*us* has nothing to do with any of this. What I feel for you isn't about business. It'll be part of who we are going forward, but my love for you is mine. Money, family, and everything else come second to that."

"Get dressed, then, and tell me the rest." Fallon kissed her in a way that made her believe Fallon was happy she was there. "Thank you for saying that, and I love you too."

They showered together, and she told Fallon everything she knew. She didn't really condone Angelo's business dealings, but he was handy when it came to gathering information. Fallon didn't interrupt her as she got dressed, but she did stare at her like she was having trouble believing her. It hit her then that Fallon was getting dressed as well.

"You can stay if you want. I'm coming back when I'm finished."

Fallon finished putting her jeans on and pointed at Brooks. "Um, you look like you were mugged, and you're not supposed to be stressing yourself." She covered up the pretty bra with a long-sleeved T-shirt. "I'll wait in the car if you want me to, but I'm not letting you go alone."

And that was that, since she took it as an order. "Do you think Monroe and Eliza will end up together?"

Fallon slipped her feet into sandals. "Strange change of subject, and I don't know. They act like they're in the fifth grade sometimes." Fallon helped Brooks button her shirt. "Why do you ask?"

"We might have to rethink the partnership when it comes to more than this. You might want to ditch me during the day eventually, but I like the idea of working with you." She lowered her head when Fallon pinched her chin.

"You're hilarious if you think I'm ditching you ever, but we'll iron it out later. Let's get going."

The sheriff's office and small prison attached to it needed a makeover, but there'd been a storm down here, and Brooks thought it was in better shape than most of the other buildings they'd driven by. She hadn't kept up with the local politics, so she wasn't sure who they'd be seeing—she'd leave that up to Dan. The big black truck parked in front was massive, and she recognized the guy who got out.

"That's the sheriff," Fallon said. "Remember his dad held the job for years."

"Carl something, right?" Fallon nodded and they got out. Brooks took Fallon's hand and smiled when the guy walked toward them. "Hey, it's been a while. Congratulations on the position."

"It's been too long. Sorry you've come home to all this crap. Deuce called and said you lost another boat and caught the guys, so we'll take over if you want." They went in, and Brooks whistled at the size of the moose on the wall.

She stopped when Fallon elbowed her in the stomach. "That belonged to your dad, right?"

"I had to agree to keep it if I wanted him to campaign for me. I'm more into fishing." They all laughed and sat. "How do you want to handle this?"

"I want them held for twenty-four hours if you can. Don't break any rules," she said, knowing this was legally possible. "Then I'd like to meet with them, but that's not a deal-breaker. I'm sure you guys can find out who hired them."

"If they're responsible for all of it, the DA said he's going to add attempted murder because of all the people around when they set off the ones before tonight." He gazed at Brooks before glancing at Fallon. "You and I both know they were probably working with someone."

The rest was left unsaid, and she knew the game of chicken she was playing with Curtis's future. The two numbskulls sitting in holding weren't the only ones going to jail if she pressed charges. "All I need is the name. We'll go from there if you can get it. There might not be as much paperwork for you if everyone involved cooperates."

"Hang out in here," the sheriff said. "I'm telling them they have ten minutes before I charge them."

"You're letting Curtis get off?" Fallon asked as soon as they were alone.

"That depends on his honesty, but he's going to pay no matter what. Three boats destroyed along with what it'll cost to clear them off will eat into his share of the business. He can agree to that, or jail time and that. He's paying no matter what." What her brother had done was, in a word, disgusting, but it did make her wonder if any other heir had tried to do the same thing. She had enough experience with money to know it made some people lose their minds, but it was disheartening when it was your own family.

"You told me your plan, but I still think he should suffer for all this crap he's putting you through." Fallon ran her fingers along Brooks's palm, and it made her want to give all this a pass.

"There's jail time, honey, and there are conversations with Angelo's guys. One requires you to follow certain guidelines and the loss of your freedom, and the other is an exercise in trying not to crap your pants. Trust me," she said, smiling, "Curtis will lose his tough guy persona in less time than a cow can last in piranha tank. I say that because it's a visual those guys will give him."

Fallon stared at her before smiling. "You have an interesting array of friends, love. Let's hope they still like you when you move."

The sheriff came back in and sat under his moose. "That was easy. The surveillance you put in doesn't leave any doubt as to who done it, and they weren't going down alone. Your brother Curtis gave them five grand per boat."

"I can't tell you how to do your job, but a trip down here for questioning should be beneficial in helping him learn his lesson. Only if you're agreeable."

The sheriff chuckled. "Brooks, your mama's good people. I don't mind a bit."

They drove back to Fallon's place, both of them tired and ready for bed. The only salvageable thing about the night was there was still a chance to get some sleep. Brooks stood and watched Fallon undress her. That Fallon was naked already was an added bonus.

"You can stop right there," Fallon said even though she hadn't moved.

"I'm just standing here," she said as Fallon took her hands.

"I remember that look." Fallon pulled her to her side of the bed and sat her down. "You need some sleep. After all that earlier, I'm not worried about your head as much, but do you feel okay?"

"My headache's almost gone—Curtis's is just beginning." She lay back and opened her arms to Fallon.

❖

They were in the same position when they woke four hours later. Brooks opened her eyes when she felt Fallon's fingers circling her belly button, and she enjoyed the chunk of time they spent kissing.

Her enjoyment was cut short when her phone rang and her mother wanted answers. The police had picked Curtis up after he'd unwisely stayed in his office. According to her mother, he'd refused to talk, and they would let him go as long as he promised not to leave town. After spending time with the sheriff, Curtis had to know she knew everything he'd been up to. He was about to learn the importance of doing his homework. It also pushed him in the direction she wanted him to go.

The best position to negotiate from was desperation, but only if you weren't the one who was desperate. Aside from greed, Brooks really didn't know what motivated Curtis. All the steps he'd taken didn't make much sense to her, and in a way, that was her talent. When she knew the truth of why someone wanted something, it was the road map to getting the job done.

"What do you have on tap for today?" Fallon's voice cut through the stillness, and it knocked her out of her head. "Aside from all the Jerry Springer stuff you have going with your family."

"I asked my mother at the beginning of this for some time to get all this done, and I'm done. Because I am, today we'll have a family meeting to tear it down before putting it all back together." The way Fallon touched her brought back all the memories of being the person Fallon loved. It was the greatest accomplishment she'd ever achieved.

"Can it be fixed?" Fallon moaned when her phone rang next. "Sorry. Hello."

Brooks went to the bathroom when the call sounded involved, and she got the shower running. This would be the most peaceful part of her day, and she took her time when Fallon joined her. They dressed and moved around each other like they'd been together forever. She was not at all surprised to find all Fallon's siblings in her kitchen when they came out.

"Good morning," she said as Fallon linked their pinkies together. "I'll leave you to it."

"Sit down," Fallon ordered. "Coffee first, then breakfast. It won't take long."

Eliza and Bea gave Brooks the most grief, which had always been the norm, and she smiled through it. Fallon kissed her on the porch and held her long enough that she was anxious to finish and get back to her. She threw her jacket on the passenger seat of the truck and called Pru.

"Good morning, sunshine." She headed for the office first to pick up the paperwork she needed. Bria was already waiting for her. "We need a family meeting with everyone, including Curtis."

"We're heading to the house. The sheriff called me this morning. He'll drop Curtis off in an hour. Deuce's working on cleaning up." Pru sounded tired and disgusted. "What the actual fuck, Brooks?"

"We'll cover all that when I get there." She grabbed the box she needed, and Bria sat next to her reading the report. She did glance at

Bria before she called Fallon. "Hey, I'm headed down the bayou with Bria. We'll hopefully be done before lunch, so how about I come back and take you out?"

Fallon was quiet long enough for it to be uncomfortable. "Bria's with you?"

"Yes, the way forward will require some financing, so we put something together. Once they agree, I'll have to talk to someone about some boats we'll need built." She smiled at Bria's snort.

"What if they don't agree?" Fallon said, not quite ready to change the subject.

"Then I'll need an office and a place to live."

"Give me the phone," Bria said with a snap of her fingers. "Good morning, dum-dum."

"*Bria.*" Brooks reached for the phone, but Bria held her back.

"Do we need to discuss next steps?" Bria asked Fallon. "Our job can be done from the middle of the ocean if need be, so I'd jump at the boat offer. That and start searching for an organized gay man or old woman to be the assistant in our New Orleans office. You seem the jealous type."

"Listen, you—" Fallon sounded as if she was revving up.

"Sorry about that," Brooks said, recovering the phone. "So, are you free for lunch?" She stuck her tongue out at Bria, getting a slap to the arm.

"Yes, and I refuse for dum-dum to be my nickname. We're headed down to the yard to take care of a few problems. I'll meet you at your parents' place."

"Okay, and I love you. If you need me for anything, call."

"Love you too, honey, and remember to give them hell. By that I mean Curtis."

"Sounds like all is right in your world." Bria squeezed Brooks's hand and sighed. "I'm happy for you, but I need you to promise you won't forget me. Your friendship is one of the most precious things in my life."

"You don't have to worry, and you might have to go house shopping with me. You could split your time between New York and here."

They talked about the logistics of moving forward while Brooks thought of running Boseman Seafood on top of her regular job. She couldn't hand that off until they were back to normal and positioned for expansion since she and Bria would be providing the capital to get it done. There were plenty of vehicles in front of the house when they arrived, so hopefully everyone was there and ready to start.

Her mother let them into the dining room, and her puffy eyes drove Brooks's anger. Curtis hadn't considered her father's illness for sure, but he'd also ignored their mother's feelings. His conquest mentality had done harm to more than the company, and that drove her to fix it. She had to, not only for the promises she'd made to save the company, but to give her mother peace.

"It's going to be okay, Mom," she said as she hugged her.

"It's going to be a shit show, my love, but we'll survive."

The expression on everyone's face was one of wariness—except for Curtis. He was still angry, and he appeared disheveled. A night in interrogation had shattered his put-together facade.

"I don't think we need to go over the boat we lost last night, and the two we saved because of increased security," Brooks said.

Bria opened the box she'd carried in and handed out files to everyone.

"This is a family meeting," Curtis said, pushing the paperwork away from him. "Why's she here?"

"Curtis, sit there and be quiet," her mom said. "You're going to do that, or I'll have you tied to that chair and gagged until your sister's finished."

"The two dumbasses who got arrested last night confessed that you paid them to destroy the fleet, a few boats at a time," Brooks said, pointing at Curtis.

"That's total bullshit," Curtis screamed and slammed his hand down. "Why would I do that?"

She glanced at Bria and the next folder was passed around. "Not total bullshit." She held up a picture of Curtis paying the guys currently in custody. "These guys are brainless, in my book, but they were smart enough to keep every text message you sent. They aren't going down alone."

"Again," Curtis spoke over her, "why the fuck would I do this?"

"The system basically runs itself. You sell seafood across the country to suppliers and restaurants. It's idiotproof," she said and smiled.

"Fuck you, Brooks." He pointed at her before turning to the family. "She threw us away, and you're going to believe her?"

"When Mom called and asked me to come, it surprised me how far out of control the company had gotten. The distraction of the boats wasn't necessary. Your actions had driven you to the brink without the fireworks." She handed out the last report with the numbers. "All this boils down to the will and how it's written."

"What do you mean?" Charlie asked.

"As the oldest son, Curtis gets the company. You all, though, have to be paid your share of its worth," she said to her siblings and turned to the second page. It broke down the information. "Three years ago, each of you were due twenty million over time." She stood across from her mother because she wasn't sure about the next part. "That's when Dad started showing signs of cognitive impairment. Am I right?"

Scarlett nodded.

"So what?" Curtis said.

"It was a perfect opening for you because you could blame Max."

"Again, what do you mean?" Etienne asked.

"Turn the page, brother. Your share has dropped in value dramatically. If Curtis is successful in getting Max declared mentally unfit, he doesn't need him to die. He takes over and buys you out at a little over two million each. Once that's done, I'm sure the turnaround will be miraculous." Brooks, holding her mom's hand, glanced at Bria. Her mother had raised five children, so she was confused as to how one of them could be so different. Bria had told her it was cutthroat, and not even her father would do that to family.

"She's fucking lying," Curtis said. "She can't prove anything."

"Curtis, you have options as long as you're in this room." Her mom nodded, so Brooks went on. "You can sign over your portion of the company to Mom and walk away. That means no consequences for the boats or bad business decisions."

"Fuck that." Curtis stood up and so did Etienne. "You fly back to wherever you came from and leave us alone. All of this is about Dad giving me control of the company, and nothing else."

"Your second option is staying and going through with what you planned." She held up her hand when he gloated. "Only that choice comes with risks." She held up all the information she'd amassed on him. "All this goes to the sheriff and the fire chief. Maybe those guys are lying, and maybe they'll be convincing enough to sink you. No matter which way you go, we'll win in court and give Mom and Dad what they want."

"Fucking try it and I'll make you pay." Curtis took a step toward her, and he was a fool if he thought that would faze her.

"Not taking that first choice, then?" She raised her left eyebrow, hoping his answer was *no*. Well, a small part of her hoped that.

"Son," her mother said as her tears fell, "your father doesn't have that much time, and we all need to be here for him."

Curtis stared at Scarlett with the kind of hatred that made no more sense than any of this. "That's a joke." The words came like sharp knives, and each one visibly cut. "Don't pretend to give a shit about me. He told me."

Etienne beat Brooks to Curtis and knocked him down with one blow.

"Don't talk to her like that," Pru yelled.

All the noise must have been enough to get her father to come down because he was standing in the doorway. He appeared disoriented, and Brooks went to take his hand. She sat him in his usual seat and placed her hands on his shoulders. This was part of their history she hoped she could erase.

"I don't understand," Charlie said. That seemed to be the case for everyone.

"He told me, so don't deny it." Curtis fell back in his chair and wiped his mouth of blood. "I don't belong to you, so I guess that means you can screw me over with no problem."

That was not on her bingo card of possibilities, and her mom squeezed her hands into fists. "You do belong to me, and you can believe what you want, but I raised you. I raised you because I loved you."

"Tell the truth," Curtis yelled, and Max flinched. Curtis was crying, and it was good to see he wasn't emotionless. "I don't belong to you."

"That can't be right," Pru said.

"He's your brother in every way that counts," her mother said softly. There was also a tinge of guilt.

Brooks kept her hands on her father and tried to quickly work through this in her head. The answer she was so sure of had to be missing some pieces. That Curtis wasn't her parents' second child wasn't the missing link she'd considered. He bore a family resemblance, so they had to be related somehow.

"You adopted him," she said with certainty. Inside she was trying to keep it together. If that was true, then her father had chosen him over all of them, and that hurt. That was her first reaction, but her mother was right. If they'd taken Curtis in and adopted him, it was with love. They wouldn't have treated him any differently.

"Curtis, you're ours, but your mom was Max's sister. She died when you were three months old, and she asked us to raise you. It was our honor to keep that promise, and you were my son from that day." Her mom cried harder, and Brooks believed every word. "I called Brooks because of the downturn we've had and for no other reason."

"You called her because Brooks can do no wrong. This was something you should've told me." Curtis stopped talking, and then it was back to making accusations. "My father told me how you—"

"Max Boseman is your father," her mother said with conviction.

"Wait," Brooks said, waving her mom off. "Who's your father?" she asked Curtis.

"Dellow Hayes," Curtis said and his chest puffed up.

"He's one of the independent fisherman we use, right?" she asked, going back to the box of information.

"Yeah, so?" Curtis lowered his voice and acted like he needed to be on high alert.

"His sons DJ and Garth are the two guys in lockup, you stupid bastard." She pulled the file from the sheriff. "You threw your family away on the word of a guy who raised this kind of shit. If you'd thought it out, the fact is Dellow had to give up his parental rights for Mom and Dad to have adopted you."

"They paid him. Fucking tell them," he screamed at their mother again.

"We told him we'd help raise you. The ten thousand was his idea, and your father couldn't change his mind." Her mother raised her voice as well.

"You're lying—he told me you pushed him out of my life." Curtis was like a learning-impaired snapping turtle. A Louisiana snapping turtle bit down and wouldn't let go unless you burned its ass. They were the definition of stubborn.

"So he helped you sink the company with a promise to rebuild it. Once that happened, Dellow was going to help you run the place." All the pieces clicked in place, and she wanted to light a fire under him that would burn his world down. "Did you both come up with this bomb idea, or was that all Dellow?"

"We have insurance. What's the big deal?"

"Insurance fraud carries ten to fifteen, depending on the amount."

"You're seriously going to turn your brother in?" Curtis laughed.

"Brother?" she said in the same tone. "You just said we threw you away. We stole your chance at a life with your *real* family." She tossed the file at him. "Now you and your *family* blew up quite a few million dollars' worth of equipment. Pay us and walk away."

"I'm not paying for shit. It's mine and I got rid of it. There's nothing illegal about it."

"You're assuming the company is yours, but you should've read the will." She waited until Bria finished handing out copies of what Max had put in place. If she had one wish, it'd be to have Fallon here with her. "If you look at the section about the company, it was changed six years ago. Max didn't tell anyone, and had I read this sooner, it would've saved us a trip to court."

"What the fuck?" Curtis said after reading the highlighted portion.

For as long as Boseman Seafood Company had existed, it had one sole heir per generation. One *male* heir who ran the company until death. It was theirs no matter their mental capacity, age, or business acumen. Being dead was the only way to move to the next heir. That had been the precedent from the beginning. So even when her father was incapable of going to the office every day, he was still the sole heir running the company. And as that sole heir, he'd named the next one to take the reins. That, unfortunately for Curtis, was not him.

"It's written into the will like it has been for generations, so the boats you blew up, genius, belong to *Max*. That brings us back to my first offer. Leave quietly or we get the law involved." She sat down at her father's right and waited. The door slamming open was not what she was expecting.

"Where is he?" Fallon yelled.

"Jesus." Fallon's tone meant more drama and another pile of shit. Brooks, for one, was tired of shoveling.

CHAPTER EIGHTEEN

A re you serious?" Fallon walked up to Curtis and poked him in the chest hard enough to make him flinch.

"What the hell, babe?" Curtis grabbed Fallon's hand and really grimaced when Brooks wrapped her fingers around his wrist and squeezed.

She turned and put her arms around Brooks as a way to ground herself. The emergency call that morning was about bombs on three boats in their dry-dock bays and had required a call to the state police bomb unit. Brooks had shared what she'd found out and what she planned to do about it, so it wasn't a stretch to figure out who had planted the bombs at their place. Fallon realized the person both she and Brooks owed was Bria—and her family connections.

"What's wrong?" Brooks asked her. Etienne had come and pushed Curtis into a chair.

Fallon explained what they'd found and what they had on their security system. They'd had no choice but to evacuate their yard, and the police were still there investigating. "Had those gone off while my people were in the engine rooms, they'd be dead."

"But they didn't go off," Curtis said as if that mattered.

"One of them did go off because it was too unstable to move. This isn't something we can handle ourselves anymore, honey. The state trooper in charge is starting an investigation, and he'll begin with the guys in parish jail." She felt better when Brooks held her, and no one else aside from Curtis seemed upset by the development.

"What the hell, man?" Brooks asked Curtis, not letting her go.

"Leave me alone." Curtis sounded venomous. "You get everything—again." He pointed between them. "You leave and ignore everyone forever, then come back and get everything handed to you. You've stolen my life, and you're not getting away with it."

"You're kidding, right?" Fallon asked. "Are you the only person not to see your obsession with Brooks is making you irrational? It's the only thing that'll explain what you've done."

She'd been a fool for not seeing Curtis for who he was. His looks were close enough to Brooks to blind her, but her father had always told her that rot would eventually make its way to the surface. "How did you think you were going to get away with all this?"

"All I was doing was trying to give us a solid future. You're better off with me." Curtis stared at her as he spoke and was creepier than sweet. "We can put all this behind us and start over with my family."

"Your family all act like starting over with you is the last thing they want." She turned her attention back to Brooks and wasn't happy with what she saw.

"Curtis met *his family* recently and brought them into all our lives. They fish and blow stuff up." Brooks sounded pissed, and if Fallon understood what she was saying, she couldn't blame her.

"What should we do, Brooks?" Scarlett asked.

"That's not up to us, Mom." Brooks turned and took her hand. "Curtis, I could cover for you when it came to our property, but you went a step too far. Mom and Dad gave you a family, a home, and love, only for you to throw it away. In the coming weeks you should remember two things."

"Yeah"—Curtis laughed again—"what's that?"

"When you feel the noose Dellow tightens around your neck, think about today." Fallon put her free hand in the bend of Brooks's arm and squeezed. "The other thing is to hire a good attorney, or you'll never get out of that noose when Dellow throws you away to save his sons."

"You don't know what it's like to be compared to you all my life and always fall short."

"I sacrificed everything for the woman I love. All those years without my family while Max groomed you for the big chair. I stepped aside and left you alone. You used all that time to steal something you had coming to you anyway. Does that sound like your parents thought less of *you*?"

"Stop trying to change history. They wanted you in the end."

"Shut up, Curtis," Scarlett said. "Your father changed his mind because of what you did to the business. It had nothing to with Brooks. All of this wasn't necessary."

"I'm out of here." Curtis ran out, and they heard the door slam behind him.

Fallon let Brooks go and went to Scarlett. The way she was crying was what she imagined despair sounded like. "It's not your fault."

"She's right, Mom," Charlie said.

As the Boseman children rallied around their mother, Fallon stepped back and helped Brooks get her father back upstairs. She figured Brooks needed space to process everything, but in her gut she knew giving it to her would be a mistake. To be Brooks's partner meant showing her she'd always have someone to count on and lean on.

Brooks led Max to the bed and spoke softly to him. Downstairs he'd gazed around the room with wild eyes as if he'd somehow stumbled into a bad situation with people he didn't know. He might not recognize Brooks completely, but her presence did appear to calm him. The way Brooks held his hand made her think of children—their children. A family with Brooks wasn't a dream she'd let go of, and watching her brought it completely out of hibernation.

Max seemed to fall asleep, and Brooks sat a moment longer and stared at him. Fallon couldn't tell from Brooks's expression what she was feeling. It wasn't a stretch to think Brooks wasn't happy. The watery eyes made her rush across the room to stand between Brooks's legs and press Brooks's face against her chest.

Heddie came in and stood next to her with her hand on Brooks's shoulder. "All this, my love, is not your fault. God knows you've paid for it more than anyone. I should apologize. My daughter wasn't so worldly, I guess, and that asshole took advantage of her. When she died, your father insisted on raising Curtis."

"I'm sure he wanted a boy after my big disappointment." Brooks sounded defeated and hurt, as if her whole life had been a lie.

"Brooks, stop being so damn noble. You have a right to be angry." While Heddie spoke, Fallon combed her fingers through Brooks's hair, trying to make her feel better. "Your father took Curtis in, and your mother accepted it. We all knew he'd be better off with us, but I told Max to try to keep Dellow in Curtis's life. Dellow said he'd be happy to, for a price."

"Sounds like a charmer." She wanted to take Brooks home and away from these people who didn't appreciate her. "I'm sure Max and

Scarlett love him, but Brooks was their child too. They threw her away and handed the kingdom to Curtis simply based on gender."

"I'm sure that's what you think," Heddie said. "I agree, up to a point, but Max bent to his father's influence, and he tried to force the same on both of you. He saw you as damaged, and that was wrong."

"What does it matter now? It's all in the past and we can't change it," Brooks said. "We have enough problems without any of us dwelling."

"We do have a problem, and it started when Dellow met Curtis. I doubt he thought your father would give Curtis the business and only got involved when Curtis proved to him that was the case."

"You knew?" Brooks asked.

"Dellow's mother is a friend of a friend, and a bragger. I told your father, and that's when he changed his will and put it in writing in case something happened. He didn't want to admit he was wrong until he was staring at what's happened to him head-on." Heddie bent and kissed the top of Brooks's head. "All these years wasted—it changed how I felt about my child."

"You should let it go for your own peace of mind," Brooks said as if she didn't have the strength to speak louder. "Max was a creature of habit, but all it would've taken was a conversation from either you or Mom. The truth would've been a good thing when loving Fallon became a reason to throw me away."

"We didn't know," Scarlett said from the door. "You'll never believe us, but Max didn't tell me or Heddie. When he finally explained, he said he didn't think you'd stay gone. He did all of this, but in a way, he was proud that you made such a success of yourself."

"That supposed to make her feel better?" Fallon asked with heat. Her defense made Brooks smile.

"Brooks, you're my child," Scarlett said. "I have loved you from the first day I threw up from morning sickness. When Max finally admitted what he'd done and why you left, you were already in New York. It's why I spent a month with you. I was seriously thinking of leaving."

"We all survived, and I got a second chance with Fallon. I'm not holding a grudge and I'm not leaving, but I'm not going to interfere with what happens to Curtis." Brooks stood and threaded their fingers together. "He's on his own, but he's also your son. If you want, hire a good attorney for him. He's going to need it."

"That's where you're wrong, *sister*." Curtis said the title with a good deal of heat. "Dellow Hayes is my parent. He's the only one who's never lied to me."

"It's like a party in here." Fallon moved so that they were pressed together. "And, Curtis, wise up."

"Everyone's like a broken record telling me that." Curtis seemed to show his true self, and it wasn't flattering or charming. She wished she could remember him as a child, but she drew a blank. Maybe he'd been sweet, but that'd died under Dellow's influence. "All I want is what I have coming to me, and a relationship with my family. It's not too late for you to come with me. Brooks is sick in the head."

She held Brooks in place. "You have lost your mind."

"You don't consider us your family?" Scarlett asked.

"You stole my real family from me, but you were good to me."

"Family is a great many things. I learned that, and it helped me face plenty." Brooks did step forward, but it was to put herself between Fallon and Curtis. "Mom has loved all of us the same, and it's insulting to stand there and throw her love for you away."

"Stop playing the martyr, Brooks. It's getting old."

"I'd listen to her," Heddie said. "You're too pretty to do well in jail."

"None of you would ever prosecute me." Curtis laughed as if their grandmother had told the greatest joke. He was the only one who did. "Y'all can have the company. It's too far gone to save, and Hayes Seafood is picking up the slack."

"The family boats are in my control. Alfred and Fallon are not," Brooks said, releasing her hand.

"I don't know about that, Brooks." He chuckled again. "You're fu—"

The rest of his disgusting comment didn't come out when Brooks punched him in the stomach so hard he doubled over. She followed up by grabbing his fist and wrenching it up behind his back. "Get out, drive that ridiculous car to the nearest attorney's office, and hire him. You want to be a big man and play hardball, then let's go."

"Do it, and I'll make you sorry."

"My God, how did I fall for this bullshit?" Fallon asked and Curtis snorted. His humor died when Brooks put more pressure on his arm. "I'm also going to enjoy stoking the rumor mill around town about how I'm sleeping with Brooks." It was crude, but she figured it was the only thing that would reach his pea brain. "I'll be happy to tell them how inadequate you were."

Brooks let him go and gave her a big smile. Curtis huffed and smoothed his shirt down before taking the stairs two at a time. A few moments later the back door slammed again. That part of their daily drama was over.

"Ready?" Brooks asked, and Fallon nodded.

"Brooks, wait," Scarlett said.

Fallon noticed Charlie hovering at the bottom of the stairs and waved her up so she could sit with Max when they left. It was ridiculous to continue this in Max's bedroom. With Charlie there, Brooks gladly followed Fallon down with Scarlett and Heddie close behind. The information thrown at Brooks today was mind-boggling, and Fallon hoped they were at the end of the truth train. She also hoped her family didn't have anything to pile on.

"We should've told you." Scarlett, she could tell, was out on a very steep ledge, and it was their job to reel her back in. "There's no excuse, and I doubt there'll be complete forgiveness."

"Mom, there isn't a day, if I'm honest, that all this doesn't cross my mind. It's like a small dead thing inside me that I've tried to heal so it'll go away. I can't ever forget, but I wasn't lying when I said I forgave. There's no way I would've dropped my life to come here otherwise."

Fallon watched the two women most important to Brooks, and she saw shame. It wasn't misplaced, in her opinion.

"Please tell us there isn't more," Etienne said. Curtis and Brooks resembled each other, but not as much as Etienne and Brooks.

"Any more and I'd curse us out," Heddie said. "You were always loved, Brooks, and you always will be. That year we didn't know where you were gave Scarlett and me a lot of sleepless nights. Please don't punish us by doing that again."

"Brooks made me a promise. She isn't going anywhere," Fallon said. "I'm holding her to that, and I'd like you to let me deal with Curtis."

"Okay," Heddie said. "He's an ungrateful little shit, but I don't want him spending the rest of his life in jail, so don't try for the maximum."

"Let's see what happens, but maybe it's time he faced some consequences for his actions." Brooks put her arm around Fallon's waist and stayed quiet. "Goodwin is certainly not going to take responsibility for the boat that's a total loss. He's going to have to step up."

"I'm sorry for all this, Fallon, and you're right. Curtis is my son no matter what he says, but he's out of control. Hurting people or taking the risk of doing that needs to be dealt with."

"Good. We'll talk about it tomorrow. It's early, but we were called out in the middle of the night. Call if you need us for anything." They walked out the back, ready to be alone. She kissed Brooks for opening her door and took her hand when she got in. "Didn't see that one coming, not going to lie."

"I'm still trying to work out how they thought it'd stay a secret in a town the size of an acorn. Today's been like a pummeling." Brooks started the truck and headed back to town. They were quiet for the most part, but Brooks pulled off when they reached the street where the bayou widened with miles of marsh on the other side. Brooks got out and came to open her door for her. There wasn't much traffic down here, so they sat on the open tailgate.

Brooks put her arm around Fallon and lowered her head to kiss her. God, it felt good. It was a gift to be with the one person who could hold her bruised heart and heal it. That was something they'd do together. A shrimp boat coming in blew its horn, breaking them apart but not too far.

"You are the most gorgeous woman I've ever known." Brooks kissed her slow with plenty of heat. "Thank you for today."

"We're in it together, honey. Any more drama and we'll get our own reality show." She moved to kiss Brooks again and smiled against her lips. "You're sure, right?"

"About what exactly?" Brooks appeared happy again.

"You and me, moving back here, us." She didn't want to sound desperate, but she *was* desperate.

"I think you repeated something in there, but yes. There might be some trips back to New York for work, but I promise to try to keep them short."

"Do you have any ideas about Curtis?" Damn if she didn't want Curtis to go to jail, and she knew Brooks wouldn't interfere if she really wanted that, but this was more than destroyed boats and a shitty attitude on Curtis's part. He'd done everything he could think to punish the people who'd raised and loved him, and that deserved some misery on his part.

"I'm still thinking about that. In my business the only way to move forward is a one-word answer. Compromise."

She laughed and came close to crawling into Brooks's lap. "What's the compromise here?"

"Restitution."

"Does he have that much money?"

The smile Brooks gave her made her laugh. "We'll see."

CHAPTER NINETEEN

"That's it for today, Dan," Brooks said. "I have a date tonight."
"You're sure tomorrow is good? The judge has an opening in
three weeks." Dan put all the files they'd worked on in his briefcase,
and she decided to let him handle it. Max had trusted Dan from the
beginning, and she would too. It hadn't taken too many questions to
know he had a handle on what she wanted.

"Waiting three weeks doesn't get us anything. Unless Curtis and
his criminal family decide to blow up my car." She put her jacket on
and grabbed the flowers she'd had delivered.

The last time she'd been on a date with Fallon, they'd been in
college, yet she remembered everything about that night. Plenty had
changed, but a lot stayed consistent. It was those constants she was
drawing from tonight. They were going to go to the same restaurant,
she'd gotten the same flowers, and most important, the girl still loved
her.

"He does that, and it'll be a competition between your mother
and grandmother as to who takes him out first." Dan waved over his
shoulder and left.

Pru came in after and dropped a few contracts on her desk. "You
ready?"

"Yes, and thanks for the ride." She didn't have a vehicle in New
York, but she needed one here. The online shopping option at the local
dealership made it easy, and her new Yukon was waiting after she
turned over a check. She didn't want Fallon to have to climb into the
truck, so she'd picked something nicer before meeting with Dan.

She pulled into the driveway and got the flowers before ringing
the bell. She was staying with Fallon and had a key, but she wanted

tonight to be special. Fallon opened the door in a black dress that made her inhale and hold it. "Wow," was all she could manage when she exhaled in a whoosh.

"Did you lose your key?" Fallon appeared flattered by her reaction and held her hand out to her.

"I thought tonight should be the first of many dates, so I didn't want to barge in." She kissed Fallon, glad she hadn't put on lipstick yet. "These are for you."

"You realize there are flowers other than orange roses?" Fallon sounded teasing.

"My dumbass brother?" Fallon nodded and laughed. "Don't worry. I'm clueless about a lot, but not that clueless." Their reservation wasn't for another hour, so she reached for a bottle of wine while Fallon took care of the bouquet. "You really do look beautiful," she said as she popped the cork. "That's what the *wow* was about."

"You're hilarious, and you're the best at compliments. Pour us a glass and meet me in the bedroom."

She sat on the tub's edge as Fallon finished her makeup. It wasn't necessary, in her opinion, but Fallon never used much. Tonight her eyes were smokier, and she held up a tube of lipstick but didn't open it. She instead placed her glass down and stood between Brooks's legs. They'd been kissing for two weeks, but she still got the same thrill when Fallon pressed her lips to hers. Fallon put her hand on her cheek as if to hold her in place, but she'd never move away. She liked to think it was Fallon's way of expressing her desire to explore. Kisses like this were slow and sensual enough for her not to want to stop, but Fallon made that decision for her.

"I love that I can do that now. You being here makes me think wild thoughts." Fallon pressed one more kiss to her lips before going back to her lipstick.

"What wild thoughts?" It was interesting how Fallon didn't make eye contact. "I'm interested in all your thoughts, and you'll never know if we're on the same wavelength if you don't tell me."

"My mother's been hounding me forever about planning a wedding, and I wasn't in the right headspace for that." Fallon stopped, and Brooks thought she could guess the rest.

"Only now you might be interested?" Her mother's call to come home felt like a lifetime ago. She'd thought it would be a quick trip, then back to her life. The problem, though—well, *not* a problem—was that this was her life. She'd run from it, and now she was ready to face it. That was true because this woman loved her. Loved her enough to want all of her.

"Let's wait before I'm totally honest."

"For you, love, I have all the time in the world. Let's get going before they give away our table."

Brooks stopped at the valet stand in front of Blanchard's, and Fallon squeezed her hand in what seemed to be a bad way. The story of Curtis's sorry proposal had to be it. She leaned over and kissed Fallon gently. "This place was ours first, so it doesn't matter what came after. None of it is important."

"How do you know?" Fallon held her close and put her hand in the collar of her shirt.

"Because you're mine, and I'll always listen. There'll never be a moment, no matter what's happening, that I won't see you." She kissed her again, and Fallon didn't settle for sweet this time.

She gave the valet a good tip for waiting and headed inside. The thing about Blanchard's was the clientele. No matter the day or time, or the frequency of your visits, there was always someone you knew. This time the tables had plenty of people they both knew, and the last time they'd seen them was the engagement party. If New Orleans had an effective whisper system that reached all the way down the bayou, it would be busy tonight.

"You ready for a coming out party, baby?" Fallon glanced back as they followed one of the hosts to their table. Brooks winked, not letting go of her hand.

"We should have thought of this right off." She pulled out Fallon's chair before the waiter could and went along when Fallon tugged her down and kissed her.

The lull of conversation while their lips were together was comical. "A table in the middle of the room should make for big news tonight."

They sat, and Brooks gazed across the table. If she hadn't already fallen, it would've happened then. She listened to Fallon, glad to learn about her life while they were apart. Her siblings had stepped in, and they all enjoyed working and traveling together. Still, she could hear that Fallon had missed her. Fallon must've been pissed, but she'd missed her.

They shared a dessert, and Fallon held her hand as they went home. The house that Fallon had bought was nice, and it fit who she understood Fallon was now. Their styles were similar but not quite the same, but that didn't matter to her. Fallon was all she needed in the house. The way Fallon walked in and presented her back was a precursor to their night.

Brooks lowered the zipper and ran her hand along the smooth skin it revealed. All the things she'd wished for and desired in her life ran through her head, and nothing on the list came close to Fallon. From that first kiss, she'd made her oblivious to any other woman. This had always been her honor—touching Fallon was a privilege she'd never take for granted.

"Baby," Fallon said as she pushed the dress off her shoulders. It pooled at her feet, and she took Brooks's hands and put them on her abdomen. Brooks kissed a line down her neck to her shoulder and slid her fingertips under the elastic of the black hipsters Fallon wore. "Touch me."

She got to the top of Fallon's sex before she moved to cup her breast. "The first time you let me do this, I thought I'd have died happy."

"You didn't want to do it again?" Fallon sounded amused.

"I misspoke." She moved her hand down again and squeezed Fallon's clit between her fingers. "I want to live a thousand years if I can spend them like this." She stroked until Fallon fell back against her. "You're so beautiful."

"Please…take me to bed." Fallon held her hand in place. "I need to feel you."

She picked Fallon up and brought her to the bedroom. Fallon reached behind herself and unhooked her bra, then shimmied her underwear off. It was the best incentive to get naked. The first touch of Fallon's skin along her length was like a bolt of lightning that allowed Brooks to see heaven. She touched her lips to Fallon's as she put two fingers to the opening of Fallon's sex.

"God, yes," Fallon said. This time Brooks wanted to bring Fallon to the edge with her mouth. She slowly put her fingers inside and she sucked her clit in. Fallon pulled her hair hard enough to almost dislodge her. "It's too fast. Ah…ooh." Fallon's voice went up two octaves.

She flattened her tongue and swiped up slowly to try to make this last, but Fallon pressed her face harder against her sex. The bucking of Fallon's hips was making her hard enough to lose concentration, but she wanted to make Fallon come. She sucked in again, and Fallon arched off the bed.

"Yes, like that. I…I'm coming." Fallon sat up a little and held her in place as she moaned. Two more thrusts were all she could manage before she went slack and fell back. "Fuck." The word came out like a sigh, and Fallon pulled her hair again, only this time it was to get her to move away.

She kissed Fallon's clit one more time before kissing her way up her body, stopping at both nipples before reaching her lips. "I love you."

"You're really good at it, and I love you too." Fallon rolled on top when she lay next to her and rested her head on her shoulder. "You have a way of dismantling me."

"Hopefully all in good ways." She kissed Fallon's forehead and held her. Nights like tonight proved that love heightened this act. Sex might've been a biological release, but when you shared it with someone who knew every secret you possessed, it was a different level of intimacy.

"The best ways," Fallon said as she put her leg between hers. "And you need to feel that way too." She rose and moved her leg to make room for her hand.

"Ah," Brooks said, not wanting to embarrass herself. All the flirting, having Fallon running her foot up her pant leg, and touching her had her on a hair trigger.

"That's an interesting sound." Fallon stroked harder, and she had to concentrate on not coming. "Do you know what I want?"

"No." She sounded like a strangled chicken to her own ears.

"I want you to come for me with my mouth on you."

It seemed like a second later when she did just that. Her impression of a teenager with no idea of control was impressive, and Fallon laughed. "I promise I have more stamina than that, but I couldn't help it," Brooks said.

"I'll pat myself on the back later." Fallon moved up and kissed her before tucking herself against her using an arm and a leg to hold her in place. The only way Brooks was going anywhere was if a meteor fell on the house. "Thank you for tonight. It was a good way to relive old memories and make new ones. The best part was you didn't embarrass me by proposing in front of a crowd."

"Honey, the day I propose, I'll make it romantic, I promise. I know you better than that." Fallon was outgoing and fun, but when it came to something like a proposal, Brooks wanted to make it about Fallon and them as a couple. It would never be a public spectacle. "What I have to say to you on that day is only for you."

"Do you want to?" Fallon kept her face pressed to her shoulder.

"Life doesn't often give you second chances when it comes to getting back all the things you love, so I'm not going to squander it." She pressed her lips to Fallon's forehead and pulled her closer. "So to answer your question, I do want that. Hopefully I'll get a yes."

"Don't worry about that." Fallon relaxed against her, and she could feel the smile against her neck. "Can I go with you tomorrow?"

"Of course. With any luck it'll be smooth sailing for the last bit of putting all this together." It never hurt to put that out into the universe. "Good night, my love." The morning would be easier to face now.

❖

The courthouse was crowded with desperate-looking people, so Fallon hung on to Brooks as they made their way up the steps with Dan and the rest of the family. Their morning had been relaxed, and their siblings had promised to meet them there. With the explosions at the Goodwins' place, this was no longer just a Boseman problem.

Fallon smiled when Eliza hugged and kissed Brooks's cheek, followed by Bea, then Frankie. This had been the reaction she'd hoped for, and it only got better when her father shook hands with Brooks and hugged her as well. Brooks had always been his favorite when it came to people she'd dated, not that there'd been a lot.

"This is some crazy shit," her father said, and Brooks laughed.

"I'm sorry, sir, but someone's going to pay, one way or the other. You have my word I'll make it right if the court won't."

Her dad smiled at Fallon before putting his hand on Brooks's bicep. "That's what we have insurance for, kid. The only thing you have to worry about is keeping a smile on my daughter's face."

"That I can do." Brooks held Fallon's hand while talking to her father, and he kept glancing from Brooks to their hands.

"Brooks, we're ready," Dan said.

Brooks kissed her before moving to the front with Dan. Fallon stayed with her family and listened to Dan lay out the changes to the business, the explosions that'd happened at both their businesses, and that Scarlett was ready to testify. Max wasn't capable of running a company, but the woman who'd run it with him for years was ready to step in to assist Brooks.

The judge listened as he turned his attention to the other table. Curtis wasn't there, and his attorney seemed to be waiting his turn. Dan finished by showing the video of the two brothers, who were still in jail. The quality was surprisingly clear, and Fallon's father made grumbling noises.

"What are you asking for?" the judge asked.

"There's a criminal investigation, but if Mr. Boseman and the Hayes family make restitution, my clients won't press charges. The Boseman and Goodwin families can't stop the authorities from bringing charges, but they won't pursue anything. Curtis Boseman also has to agree to relinquish his job with Boseman Seafood Company." Dan closed the file he'd been reading from and unbuttoned his jacket.

"Anything else?" the judge asked.

"No, Your Honor."

The judge turned his attention to the lone man representing Curtis. "Where's your client, Mr. Gerard?"

"He's been called out to a job his father asked him to do. Mr. Boseman had nothing to do with any of what's happened, so asking him to make restitution is ridiculous. The one stipulation he did agree to is leaving his job with Boseman." The attorney looked at Brooks and smiled. "He recently connected with his true family, so that's where his priority is."

"Would his family extend to the two in lockup for setting bombs?" the judge asked.

"He had nothing to do with those men, Your Honor."

"I call bullshit," a man across from them yelled. Fallon had to think of who he was.

"Order." The judge slammed his gavel four times, getting everyone to quiet down. "Any more outbursts like that, and someone is going to be held in contempt. Who are you?"

"Dellow Hayes, and my boys were hired by Curtis Boseman. If anyone has to pay, it ain't gonna be me or them." Dellow sounded like an idiot, but he had no clue. Admitting to anything in open court was not a sign of genius.

"Come forward," the judge said.

Dellow was sworn in and sat. "You need to talk to Curtis," he said before anyone could ask him anything.

"Unless I ask a question, please don't talk," the judge said. "Are those your sons, Mr. Hayes?"

"Yeah, but none of it was their idea." Fallon sat and shook her head at this guy. "All of this starts and ends with Curtis. Sometimes I can't believe he's mine."

She had to cover her mouth with her hand so she wouldn't laugh out loud at the expression on the judge's face. "Mr. Hayes, can I ask, how do your children know anything about bombs?"

"The younger boy served in the Army for two years. He got thrown out, but that should count for something."

"Uh-huh." The judge turned and waved to the attorneys. "Since Mr. Hayes is cooperating, do you have any questions?"

Curtis's attorney stood first. "Mr. Hayes, isn't it true that you and Curtis Boseman went into business together? Specifically, the seafood business?"

"We were picking up the business Boseman lost. It isn't illegal." Dellow appeared like a man in control. "Things weren't going good for him, so he asked to come work for me."

"Why would Mr. Boseman do that if he was set to inherit the Boseman company? The company is worth a considerable amount, so why would he need you and your sons to blow up his property? It makes no sense."

They'd reached the part of this where all the rats turned on each other. In a way, Dellow was making Dan's argument for him. Fallon smiled, and Brooks gazed back at her and widened her eyes as if she couldn't believe what she was hearing. This might be the easiest way to finish everything Curtis had started. Once it was done, all that was left was the road forward.

"He wanted the company without having to shell out a lot for it." What Dellow laid out was every point Brooks had told her family. Curtis had come close to gutting the company and stealing it from the people who loved and depended on it.

"Do you have proof Mr. Boseman asked you or your family to do this?" The attorney didn't seem so smug the longer Dellow spoke.

"He paid us," Dellow said with heat. "Weren't you looking at the TV when they showed it?"

"No further questions."

Dan stood and looked at Brooks, who shook her head. "A moment to confer with my client, Your Honor."

"Ten minutes."

Fallon stood when Brooks did and held out her hand. "Alfred, you as well," Brooks said. The small office they crowded into was stuffy and hot. "It's up to you, Mom."

It had to have been hard for Scarlett to hear the depth of Curtis's betrayal, because that's what it was. He wanted it all so he could share it with a man who'd thrown him away. There wasn't a bit of doubt when it came to that.

"We all know he can't pay it back," Scarlett said, "but there's no way he pays for this alone. Dellow Hayes is behind this, and he needs to be held responsible. Let it play out. It's what Curtis told all of us he wanted."

Brooks kissed Scarlett's cheek and said something to her softly. "How about we do this so none of us feels guilty?"

"What do you want to do?" Dan asked.

"I'd like to talk to the judge." They didn't have to wait long before the clerk came for Brooks. All of them waited for Brooks to finish, which only took fifteen minutes, and her father held her hand tightly.

"All rise," the clerk said, and her father put his arm around her.

"My ruling is for Brooks Boseman. If it is acceptable to Mrs. Boseman, her daughter will take over for a two-year tenure." The judge stared at Dellow. "Mr. Hayes, you have a month to repay the Boseman and Goodwin families. If not, you'll forfeit your company and resources."

"The hell I will."

"Mr. Hayes, if you fight this, I'll be happy to testify at any legal action you take. Admitting to what you did wasn't smart. It makes no difference if someone hired you. The bombing of a business for personal gain is never legal."

"We'll see." Dellow left before anyone else could reprimand him.

The judge and everyone else watched him storm out. "If there's nothing further, we're adjourned."

Everyone started talking at once when the judge disappeared into his chambers. All Fallon cared about was getting to Brooks. Her lover and Curtis might've never been the best of friends, but losing the relationship had to hurt. Brooks opened her arms, and Fallon took her up on the invitation. It was nice to kiss her and have their families with them. It was like they all knew things were back to normal.

"The judge approved the lien on his property, so let's see what happens in a month," Dan said. "I filed on both your behalf."

"Thanks, Dan." Brooks shook hands with him before heading toward her mother. "Don't start rehashing this and blaming yourself. We all grew up in the same house, and you didn't treat him any different."

"He does need to face consequences, but he's still my son. I'm always going to worry."

"It's why you're a good mom," she said, taking Scarlett's hand.

"At least this is something to be happy about," Scarlett said, motioning to Brooks and Fallon. "I'm looking forward to having you be part of our family, and to planning whatever parties you want, sweetheart."

"Thank you. I'm happy about this too."

Brooks left her for a moment to talk to her siblings, so Fallon did the same—she was going to take the rest of the day off. They went home and she changed into shorts. The drive down the bayou was nice without all the stress they'd been under. She enjoyed holding Brooks's hand and just staring out the window. There was a boat waiting for them at the dock at Boseman's, and Deuce helped Brooks unload the stuff from the back of the Yukon.

Fallon stood behind Brooks as they cast off and kissed between her shoulders. They'd done this before, and she always loved these getaways. In the past they'd fished, lain on the deck, watched the sky, and made love. That only happened when Brooks was sure no one else was around. Brooks stood and placed her hand over hers where it rested on Brooks's abdomen. She lifted her head when Brooks bled off speed and noticed the camp at the cusp of the marsh.

It appeared new with solar panels on the metal roof and fresh foundation pilings that held it twenty feet over the water. The dock was new too, and it had a deck over open water, which would be perfect to fish from. "One of the local guys built it and decided it was too small."

"It's beautiful out here," she said, moving to face Brooks.

"Let's go up." Brooks tied them off and took her hand. From the large porch Fallon could see miles out, noticing they weren't on a major waterway. "I wanted to show you I was serious about staying."

"You don't want to live out here, do you?" She laughed as she asked, glad to see how relaxed Brooks was.

Brooks laughed with her and sat in one of the Adirondack chairs, so Fallon sat in her lap. "I started with this place to set down roots, and I'd like to build on the property down here like Gran did. My family is no way the Waltons, but they're mine, and I'd like to be close to my parents to help my mom with Max. My dad's going to need more help as he navigates all this."

"This is one of the reasons I love you so much." She framed Brooks's face with her hands and kissed her. "What else do you want?"

"A place in New Orleans."

"You have a place in New Orleans." She loved the way Brooks laughed when it came from the belly. "If you want a place that belongs to both of us, I'm okay with that."

"I thought a place big enough for kids and our family." Brooks gazed at her with such an open expression, she wanted to weep.

"Is this a proposal?" If it was, she'd say yes, but she'd imagined something a little bit more romantic.

"It's planning for the future, my love," Brooks said, running her hand up her back. "When it's a proposal, I promise you won't be disappointed."

"You don't think it's too fast?" That was her biggest fear. It was unfounded, probably, but she was scared that Brooks wouldn't be as interested once they really got to know each other again.

"The way I see it is we're way late. I'll wait until you're ready, but I want the world with you."

That did make her cry, but Brooks seemed to understand the sentiment. "Thank God."

"Let's go explore and find the bedroom."

She clung to Brooks as they went in, and she couldn't have cared less if they'd decorated the place in red velvet. They spent the afternoon in bed. As evening approached, she followed Brooks to the deck. The light over the water would hopefully draw dinner. Brooks baited her hook, and they sat to fish. As frantic as their day had started, it ended in the most ideal way possible.

"How many kids?" The question popped into her head as Brooks handed her a beer.

"Two or three, but I'll be happy with whatever number you have in mind." Brooks shrugged, and it made her look adorable.

"Start thinking of that proposal, then, and we can get busy." Her bobber sank, and she struggled to reel in the large redfish. Yes, this was the life she wanted, and there was so much more to come. "I love you with all I am."

Brooks glanced up from getting the fish off the hook. "I love you too, and I always will."

Fallon's eyes watered, and she almost couldn't stand how happy she was in that one moment. In her mind she could see doing this for years. The simple truth of it was Brooks made her happy. It didn't matter anymore what had driven them apart. They'd survived—their love had been strong enough to survive, and she couldn't wait for what came next.

The fish thrashed a bit when Brooks threw it in the ice chest, and it made her cry harder. Brooks washed her hands in the water and wrapped her arms around Fallon. This was her place, and nothing could touch her here. Brooks waited her out and didn't fill the silence with unnecessary words.

"Sorry," she said when her emotions cooled. "I swear it wasn't a freak-out moment."

"Have you become vegan or something? I can throw it back."

She laughed and pressed her hands over Brooks's heart. "That first day we saw each other again, my heart broke at your expression. Then I saw Bria and it broke all over again." She gazed into Brooks's eyes, and it gave her the courage to go on. "I didn't want to be there, and I didn't understand why this had gotten to that point. How had we ended up so far apart? And who were these people with us who were going to make sure we stayed apart?"

"When I thought of a rival for your love, Curtis was my last guess." Brooks wiped away the tears with her thumbs. "I understand what you mean. I did try to stay away from you, but it was like trying to hold my breath. Possible but only for so long." The sun was starting to set, and it made the spot more perfect. "Are you sure you're okay?"

"I'm wonderful, and thinking of coming here with our children and grandchildren. There was no way I ever thought I could be this happy."

Brooks let her go to toss the fish back. "We can have peanut butter sandwiches later. Right now, I'm interested in our happily ever after." Fallon laughed when Brooks picked her up and threw her over her shoulder. "Are you ready?"

She slapped Brooks on the ass and hung on. "With you, I'm ready for anything."

EPILOGUE

Garden District, New Orleans, four months later

"It's a big decision," Fallon said to Brooks. It'd taken a couple of months for Brooks to finalize her move south, so Fallon had done some house hunting on her own. This was the place that gave them both most of everything they wanted, and she wanted to do one more walk-through before they put in their offer. Her place would be fine until the repairs and the decorating changes she wanted to make were done.

"I'm not in a rush, and I want us both to be happy." Brooks had her hand on her hip as they both stared at the place.

"Did you have any questions before we go in?" the Realtor asked.

"Brooks wanted a bigger kitchen, so you're sure we can add on, right? She doesn't cook, so I'm not sure why she wants that, but she's hard to say no to."

Brooks laughed and kissed her temple. The truth was there hadn't been much Fallon had said no to from the moment Brooks promised her forever. Fallon had been shocked when her father had done the same thing when Brooks pitched him the finance package for the luxury yachts she'd wanted to do. They were starting production in a couple of months.

"The addition won't cut into the yard too much since this one has one of the largest yards in the area, so there won't be a problem. Do you want to see the dimensions to get a better idea?"

"That might help." She slapped Brooks's hand when she pinched her butt.

"Here." The woman handed over the key and opened her trunk. "Let me get my rolling tape measure."

She unlocked the front door to a small table with a beautiful bouquet of dark pink roses. The card on the table had her name on it, but she inhaled the scent of the flowers before opening it.

> *My love,*
>   *Stop overthinking and welcome home.*

There had to be three dozen flowers in the vase, different from her usual weekly delivery. At first she thought it was some kind of rote thing Brooks thought she expected. Every week, though, Brooks delivered them herself at the beginning of their date night. She saw the joy Brooks got from giving them to her, and it made her love flowers again.

"No delivery this week?" She turned to Brooks as she traced one of the roses with her finger.

"I thought a housewarming gift was in order." Brooks appeared happy. "So, what do you think? Can you see yourself here with me chasing you through the place for years to come?"

"Yes," she said because she could do just that.

"Then let's celebrate," Brooks said when the Realtor handed over the keys. No more overthinking was necessary, so she'd finalized the deal.

The horse and carriage waiting outside were a different speed than the Aston Martin, and the roses in vases on each side of the carriage weren't orange. That alone made Brooks perfect. Fallon put her arms around Brooks's neck and kissed her long and passionately. If they were going to live here, the neighbors had to get used to the sight.

"Let's go for a ride, honey." Brooks helped her up and settled in beside her, then motioned the driver to go. The driver turned until they followed the bend of the river toward downtown.

She moved closer to Brooks and rested her head on her shoulder. So far this had been the best date Brooks had planned. "Why do you want a bigger kitchen?"

Brooks laughed. "That's easy. Our parents had big families, and all of them are at your house most mornings and weekends. Once they all start having families, I'm sure they'll all want to hang out in our kitchen too." Brooks sounded like she'd thought this out. "I want to make sure we have room for all of them."

"That sounds heavenly." Just like Brooks, she could see herself there with kids and their extended family running around.

The clop of the horses lulled Fallon into closing her eyes and enjoying Brooks's warmth. "I love it, and there's a guesthouse that Bria can use until she finds a place. She mentioned she wanted enough room for *her* family. I'm not sure how often they'll visit, but there's hope she finds a new nickname for me before that happens. Dum-dum isn't my favorite."

"I think I found the best solution for all of us."

"What's that?" She liked Bria but not enough to have her in the house.

"She stays in the guesthouse until the house is done, then she buys your place. That way you don't have to list your house."

It was a good idea, and as much as she was looking forward to the new house, having made love on pretty much every surface of her house was going to make her miss it. "You think she'll be interested?"

"All she needs to know is you're okay with it—but I don't want to talk about Bria right now."

Fallon opened her eyes. They were close to the aquarium. There was another bouquet of roses on their bench, and she kissed Brooks on the cheek when she spotted them. She jumped into Brooks's arms when she got down, and she held on to her arm when they walked to their spot. Their date was probably heading home after this, because she wasn't leaving the flowers behind.

These roses were yellow, and Brooks put them at her feet. "Are you ever going to tell me which ones are your favorite color?"

"I'd tell you if I had one, but I've loved all the ones you've sent me." She pulled Brooks in by the lapels of her jacket and kissed her. "If you need a hint, though, no red. You have more imagination than that. And no orange."

"I do know that about you. My main goal is to make you happy."

"You're good at that." She stopped talking when Brooks slid off the bench to one knee. All she could concentrate on was her breathing. She'd been waiting for this.

"I've known life without you. It's survivable, but it's not living. Waking up with you these last months has been the answer to what I need to be happy. You're who I want, and I want to make your dreams come true, whatever those dreams may be." Brooks took a box from her jacket, and the creak of it opening sounded loud. "Marry me and make my dreams come true?"

"Yes." She came close to knocking Brooks to the ground when she threw herself at her. "Oh my God, yes." The spot wasn't exactly as private as she expected, but she couldn't wait to tell their children about it.

Brooks put the ring on her finger, and Fallon stared at the square-cut diamond. "Do you like it?"

"I love it, and I love you." She kissed Brooks and stopped when she heard the applause. Everyone from both their families, minus Curtis, was there.

Curtis and his new family were serving a three-year sentence for all they'd done. It was the least amount of time the district attorney was willing to accept. With that behind them, Brooks had been able to put the business back together, and they were back to their regular sales and gaining ground. Dellow Hayes and his boys were taken out of the courtroom kicking and screaming once they were found guilty, but they had plenty of time to review where they'd gone wrong.

Today wasn't the time to think about that, and Fallon wasn't surprised the first person to hug her was Bria. "It's good to see my work here is done," Bria said and winked. "Congratulations."

"Thank you," she said as the rest of their family offered their congratulations. That was followed by dinner at the Four Seasons. She didn't want the night to end but looked forward to being alone with Brooks.

They stood outside on the balcony while the party went on without them in the restaurant on the fifth floor. Their family could still be heard, and it made her laugh. "Are you ready for all of this? My mother will be in full wedding frenzy before tomorrow morning."

"We'll assign Bria to help her. All I care about is marrying you." Brooks hugged her until her hands landed on her butt. "Once that happens, I'm sure your mom will be easier to deal with."

"I love you, and I can't wait to be married to you." That she meant.

"Thank you for saying yes, love," Brooks said softly into her ear. "Want to go and start practicing the honeymoon?"

She bit Brooks's chin, getting her to lower her head. "Just a little longer, honey, and we'll go wherever you want. This party is one I want to enjoy as much as I'm going to enjoy my life with you. Are you ready for the madness that is our family?"

"For that and all that comes after, because I get to share it with you."

"That was sappy, and I want to hear more." Yes, she wanted to be there, always at Brooks's side along with their families. These were

the people who'd help Brooks and Scarlett with Max, who was holding
steady with a regular routine. His inevitable decline was the only dark
cloud in their future, but he still remembered Brooks and enjoyed
Brooks's visits. The long talks they had were healing them both.

"Only with you, so keep that to yourself. It might mess with my
ability to close deals."

Fallon laughed and caressed the side of Brooks's neck. "You and
your secrets are safe with me. Let's get started on all the happy times
we have in our future. The sooner we do that, the sooner I get you all
to myself."

"You promise?"

She kissed Brooks and smiled. "I do for as long as my heart beats."

About the Author

Ali Vali is the author of the long-running Cain Casey "Devil" series and the Genesis Clan "Forces" series, as well as numerous standalone romances including her newest, *Rivals for Love*.

Originally from Cuba, Ali has retained much of her family's traditions and language and uses them frequently in her stories. Having her father read her stories and poetry before bed every night as a child infused her with a love of reading, which she carries till today. Ali currently lives outside New Orleans, where she cuts grass, cheers on LSU in all things, and is always on the hunt for the perfect old-fashioned. The best part, she says, is writing about the people and places around the city.

Books Available From Bold Strokes Books

A Talent Ignited by Suzanne Lenoir. When Evelyne is abducted and Annika believes she has been abandoned, they must risk everything to find each other again. (978-1-63679-483-9)

All Things Beautiful by Alaina Erdell. Casey Norford only planned to learn to paint like her mentor, Leighton Vaughn, not sleep with her. (978-1-63679-479-2)

An Atlas to Forever by Krystina Rivers. Can Atlas, a difficult dog Ellie inherits after the death of her best friend, help the busy hopeless romantic find forever love with commitment-phobic animal behaviorist Hayden Brandt? (978-1-63679-451-8)

Bait and Witch by Clifford Mae Henderson. When Zeddi gets an unexpected inheritance from her client Mags, she discovers that Mags served as high priestess to a dwindling coven of old witches—who are positive that Mags was murdered. Zeddi owes it to her to uncover the truth. (978-1-63679-535-5)

Buried Secrets by Sheri Lewis Wohl. Tuesday and Addie, along with Tuesday's dog, Tripper, struggle to solve a twenty-five-year-old mystery while searching for love and redemption along the way. (978-1-63679-396-2)

Come Find Me in the Midnight Sun by Bailey Bridgewater. In Alaska, disappearing is the easy part. When two men go missing, state trooper Louisa Linebach must solve the case, and when she thinks she's coming close, she's wrong. (978-1-63679-566-9)

Death on the Water by CJ Birch. The Ocean Summit's authorities have ruled a death on board its inaugural cruise as a suicide, but Claire suspects murder, and with the help of Assistant Cruise Director Moira, Claire conducts her own investigation. (978-1-63679-497-6)

Living For You by Jenny Frame. Can Sera Debrek face real and personal demons to help save the world from darkness and open her heart to love? (978-1-63679-491-4)

Ride with Me by Jenna Jarvis. When Lucy's vacation to find herself becomes Emma's chance to remember herself, they realize that everything they're looking for might already be sitting right next to them—if they're willing to reach for it. (978-1-63679-499-0)

Rivals for Love by Ali Vali. Brooks Boseman's brother Curtis is getting married, and Brooks needs to be at the engagement party. Only she can't possibly go, not with Curtis set to marry the secret love of her youth, Fallon Goodwin. (978-1-63679-384-9)

Whiskey and Wine by Kelly and Tana Fireside. Winemaker Tessa Williams and sex toy shop owner Lace Reynolds are both used to taking risks, but will they be willing to put their friendship on the line if it gives them a shot at finding forever love? (978-1-63679-531-7)

Hands of the Morri by Heather K O'Malley. Discovering she is a Lost Sister and growing acquainted with her new body, Asche learns how to be a warrior and commune with the Goddess the Hands serve, the Morri. (978-1-63679-465-5)

I Know About You by Erin Kaste. With her stalker inching closer to the truth, Cary Smith is forced to face the past she's tried desperately to forget. (978-1-63679-513-3)

Mate of Her Own by Elena Abbott. When Heather McKenna finally confronts the family who cursed her, her werewolf is shocked to discover her one true mate, and that's only the beginning. (978-1-63679-481-5)

Pumpkin Spice by Tagan Shepard. For Nicki, new love is making this pumpkin spice season sweeter than expected. (978-1-63679-388-7)

Sweat Equity by Aurora Rey. When cheesemaker Sy Travino takes a job in rural Vermont and hires contractor Maddie Barrow to rehab a house she buys sight unseen, they both wind up with a lot more than they bargained for. (978-1-63679-487-7)

Taking the Plunge by Amanda Radley. When Regina Avery meets model Grace Holland—the most beautiful woman she's ever seen— she doesn't have a clue how to flirt, date, or hold on to a relationship. But Regina must take the plunge with Grace and hope she manages to swim. (978-1-63679-400-6)

We Met in a Bar by Claire Forsythe. Wealthy nightclub owner Erica turns undercover bartender on a mission to catch a thief where she meets no-strings, no-commitments Charlie, who couldn't be further from Erica's type. Right? (978-1-63679-521-8)

Western Blue by Suzie Clarke. Step back in time to this historic western filled with heroism, loyalty, friendship, and love. The odds are against this unlikely group—but never underestimate women who have nothing to lose. (978-1-63679-095-4)

Windswept by Patricia Evans. The windswept shores of the Scottish Highlands weave magic for two people convinced they'd never fall in love again. (978-1-63679-382-5)

A Calculated Risk by Cari Hunter. Detective Jo Shaw doesn't need complications, but the stabbing of a young woman brings plenty of those, and Jo will have to risk everything if she's going to make it through the case alive. (978-1-63679-477-8)

An Independent Woman by Kit Meredith. Alex and Rebecca's attraction won't stop smoldering, despite their reluctance to act on it and incompatible poly relationship styles. (978-1-63679-553-9)

Cherish by Kris Bryant. Josie and Olivia cherish the time spent together, but when the summer ends and their temporary romance melts into the real deal, reality gets complicated. (978-1-63679-567-6)

Cold Case Heat by Mary P. Burns. Sydney Hansen receives a threat in a very cold murder case that sends her to the police for help, where she finds more than justice with Detective Gale Sterling. (978-1-63679-374-0)

Proximity by Jordan Meadows. Joan really likes Ellie, but being alone with her could turn deadly unless she can keep her dangerous powers under control. (978-1-63679-476-1)

Sweet Spot by Kimberly Cooper Griffin. Pro surfer Shia Turning will have to take a chance if she wants to find the sweet spot. (978-1-63679-418-1)

The Haunting of Oak Springs by Crin Claxton. Ghosts and the past haunt the supernatural detective in a race to save the lesbians of Oak Springs farm. (978-1-63679-432-7)

Transitory by J.M. Redmann. The cops blow it off as a customer surprised by what was under the dress, but PI Micky Knight knows they're wrong—she either makes it her case or lets a murderer go free to kill again. (978-1-63679-251-4)

Unexpectedly Yours by Toni Logan. A private resort on a tropical island, a feisty old chief, and a kleptomaniac pet pig bring Suzanne and Allie together for unexpected love. (978-1-63679-160-9)

Crush by Ana Hartnett Reichardt. Josie Sanchez worked for years for the opportunity to create her own wine label, and nothing will stand in her way. Not even Mac, the owner's annoyingly beautiful niece Josie's forced to hire as her harvest intern. (978-1-63679-330-6)

Decadence by Ronica Black, Renee Roman & Piper Jordan. You are cordially invited to Decadence, Las Vegas's most talked about invitation-only Masquerade Ball. Come for the entertainment and stay for the erotic indulgence. We guarantee it'll be a party that lives up to its name. (978-1-63679-361-0)

Gimmicks and Glamour by Lauren Melissa Ellzey. Ashly has learned to hide her Sight, but as she speeds toward high school graduation she must protect the classmates she claims to hate from an evil that no one else sees. (978-1-63679-401-3)

Heart of Stone by Sam Ledel. Princess Keeva Glantor meets Maeve, a gorgon forced to live alone thanks to a decades-old lie, and together the two women battle forces they formerly thought to be good in the hopes of leading lives they can finally call their own. (978-1-63679-407-5)

Peaches and Cream by Georgia Beers. Adley Purcell is living her dreams owning Get the Scoop ice cream shop until national dessert chain Sweet Heaven opens less than two blocks away and Adley has to compete with the far too heavenly Sabrina James. (978-1-63679-412-9)

The Only Fish in the Sea by Angie Williams. Will love overcome years of bitter rivalry for the daughters of two crab fishing families in this queer modern-day spin on Romeo and Juliet? (978-1-63679-444-0)